THE

TRAVELERS

ALSO BY CHRIS PAVONE

The Accident

The Expats

THE
TRAVELERS

A NOVEL

CHRIS PAVONE

FABER & FABER

First published in the UK in 2016
by Faber & Faber Ltd
Bloomsbury House
74–77 Great Russell Street
London WC1B 3DA

Published in the United States by Crown Publishers,
an imprint of the Crown Publishing Group,
a division of Penguin Random House LLC, New York.

Printed and bound by CPI Group (UK) Ltd, Croydon, CR0 4YY

A CIP record for this book
is available from the British Library

ISBN 978–0–571–29887–7

FSC
www.fsc.org
MIX
Paper from
responsible sources
FSC® C101712

2 4 6 8 10 9 7 5 3 1

THE
TRAVELERS

To know that one has a secret is to know half the secret itself.

—HENRY WARD BEECHER

PROLOGUE

The door flies open. Bright light floods into the dark room, framing the silhouette of a large man who stands there, unmoving.

"What?" Will demands, raising himself onto his elbows, squinting into the harsh light. "What's going on?"

The man doesn't answer.

"What do you want?"

The man remains in the doorway, saying nothing, a mute looming hulk. He surveys the hotel room, the disheveled bed, discarded clothing, burned-down candles, wine bottle and glasses.

"*¿Qué quieres?*" Will tries.

Will had been lying in bed, staring at the ceiling, worrying. But not about this, not about an intruder. Now Will's mind is flooding with competing scenarios and their different levels of emergency: drunk hotel guest, confused night porter, hotel security, jealous boyfriend, burglar, murderer.

Will's panic is rising, and his eyes flicker toward escape, the French doors that he opened just a few minutes ago, doors facing the vineyard that falls away from the hacienda, with the snowcapped peaks of the Andes in the distance, under the big fat moon. He pulls himself to a sitting position, uncomfortably aware of his bare chest. "Who are you?" he asks assertively, trying to project confidence. "Why are you here?"

The man nods, takes a step forward, and pulls the door closed behind him.

The room falls into the semidarkness of flickering candlelight and the bright blue LED glow of the clock, 2:50 A.M. Will's eyes readjust while his heart races, his breath coming quick and shallow, fight or flight, or both. His imagination hops around the room, trying out different items as weapons, swinging the standing lamp, breaking the wine bottle. A fireplace tool—the poker—would be the best, but that's on the far side of the room, on the other side of this trespasser, this indistinct peril.

"No," the man breaks his silence. "Why are *you* here?"

The man's hand finds a switch, a soft click and a harsh transformation, Will's pupils contracting a sliver of a second too slowly. In the light, Will realizes that he has seen this man before. He can't remember where, or when exactly, but it was sometime recent. This discovery feels more like a defeat than a victory, as if he has found out that he lost something.

"Who are *you*, Will Rhodes?"

The man's English doesn't have any trace of an accent, Argentine or otherwise. This is a big beefy American who's continuing to walk toward the bed, toward Will, slowly, menacing. It takes a while; it's a large room, luxuriously decorated and extravagantly linened, with superfluous furniture and wine-country knickknacks and signifiers of the Pampas—mounted horns, a cowhide rug. It's a room designed to remind well-off guests of where they are, and why they're here, when they could be anywhere. Will has stayed in many different versions of this room, all over the world, always on someone else's tab.

"Are you robbing me?" Will inventories the valuables he might lose here, and it doesn't amount to much.

"Kidnapping?" No one except the most ill-informed amateur would take the tremendous risk of kidnapping for the paltry rewards that could be traded for Will Rhodes. This guy doesn't look like an ill-informed amateur.

The intruder finally arrives at the bedside, and reaches into his jacket. Will scoots away from whatever potential threat is being withdrawn from this man's pocket, in the middle of the night, halfway across the globe from his home, from his wife, his life.

If Will had any doubts earlier, he doesn't anymore: he's now positive he made a terrible mistake tonight. The whole thing seemed too easy, too perfect. He'd been an idiot.

"Look," the man says, extending his arm, holding something, a little flick of the wrist—here, take this—and the smartphone falls into Will's palm. He glances at the screen, a still image, an indecipherable blur of faint light amid darkness, unrecognizable forms in an unidentifiable location.

"What's this?"

"Hit Play."

Will touches the touchscreen, and video-navigation buttons appear, the recently invented language we all now know. He hits the triangle.

A video begins to play: a naked woman straddling a man, her hips pistoning up and down, like an out-of-control oil derrick, a dangerous situation. Will watches for two seconds, just enough to figure out who it is in the poor-quality video, low light, an oblique angle, garbled audio. He touches his fingertip to the square button. The image is now frozen, the woman's back arched, head thrown back, mouth open in ecstasy. Apparent ecstasy.

Of course.

Will isn't entirely surprised that something bad is happening. But this particular end seems to be an excess of bad, disproportionate bad, unfair bad. Or maybe not. Maybe this—whatever this turns out to be—is exactly the appropriate level of bad.

His mind runs through a handful of options before he makes a decision that's by necessity hasty. He considers trying to get on more clothes— "Hey, how about you let me get dressed?"—but clothed, he might look like a threat; wearing only pajama bottoms, he's a victim, sympathetic to the guard he hopes to encounter. This new hotel takes security seriously, peace of mind for their intended mega-rich clientele, with round-the-clock rent-a-cops and a close relationship with the police.

Will extends his arm to return the phone, rolling his body toward the bedside.

Here we go.

When the man reaches to collect his device, Will hurls it across the room.

The intruder spins to watch the phone's flight—*crack*—while Will springs up, heaves his body into this man, knocking him over, landing atop him, pajama'd legs astride the guy's bulky torso, a punch to the face, and another, blood pouring from his nose.

Will hops up, barely feeling the engagement of his muscles, his blood-stream flooded with survival-preservation hormones. He flies through the parted curtains. He's out on the moonlit lawn, barefoot and shirtless, sprinting through the cool dewy grass toward the glowing lights of the sprawling main house, toward the security guards and their weapons and their hotline to the *federales*, who at the very least will detain the intruder while Will has a chance to make a call or two, and now Will is feeling almost confident, halfway across—

The fist comes out of nowhere. Will stumbles backward a step before losing his feet entirely, his rear falling down and his feet flying up, and he thinks he can see a woman—*the* woman—standing over him, her arm finishing its follow-through of a right hook, just before the back of Will's head slams into the ground, and everything goes black.

PART

I

1

A man is running along the sidewalk of a quiet leafy Brooklyn street, panting, sweat beaded on his face, quarter to six in the morning. He's wearing jeans, a dirty tee shirt, dingy white sneakers. This man is not exercising; he's working. He reaches into a canvas sling, cocks his arm, and tosses a newspaper, which flies across a fence, over a yard, landing on a townhouse stoop, skittering to a stop against the front door. A perfect toss.

In the street beside him, a battered old station wagon crawls at three miles per hour, the car's tailgate held partly open by a couple of jerry-rigged bungee cords. It's his sister behind the wheel of the Chevy, which they bought from a junkyard in Willets Point owned by another guy from Campeche. There are a lot of Mexicans in New York City, but not too many from the west-coast Yucatán city. Four hundred dollars was a good deal, a favor, a chit to be returned at some indefinite point, for some unspecified price.

The sling is empty. The man jogs into the street, and hauls a pile of papers from the way-back. He returns to the sidewalk, to the house with scaffolding over the portico, and a piece of plywood covering a parlor-floor window, and a stack of lumber plus a couple of sawhorses dominating the small front yard, whose sole greenery is a rosebush that's at least half-dead.

He tosses the newspaper, but this time his aim isn't perfect—he's been throwing papers for an hour—and he knocks over a contractor's plastic bucket, from which an empty beer bottle clatters onto the stone stoop before falling to the top step, crash, into pieces.

"*Mierda.*"

The man jogs to the stoop, rights the bucket, picks up the broken glass, sharp shards, lethal weapons, like what his cousin Alonso used to warn off that *coño*, that *narcotraficante* who was grabby with Estellita at the bar under the expressway. Violence has always been a part of Alonso's life; sometimes it's been one of his job responsibilities. For some people violence is woven into their fabric, like the bright blood-red thread that his grandmother would weave into the turquoise and indigo serapes on her loom that was tied to the lime tree in the backyard, before that type of work relocated to more picturesque villages within easier reach of the *turistas*, who paid a premium to travel dusty roads into tiny hamlets to buy their ethnic handicrafts directly from the barefoot sources.

The man runs out to the car, deposits the broken glass in the trunk, then back to the sidewalk, tossing another paper, racing to make up for lost time. You waste ten seconds here, twenty there, and by the end of the route you're a half-hour behind, and customers are angry—standing out there in bathrobes, hands on hips, looking around to see if neighbors got their papers—and you don't get your ten-dollar tips at Christmas, and you can't pay the rent, and next thing you know, you're begging that *coño* for a job as a lookout, just another *ilegal* on the corner, hiding from the NYPD and the DEA and the INS, until one night you get gut-shot for sixty dollars and a couple grams of *llelo*.

He tosses another paper.

The noise of the breaking bottle wakes Will Rhodes before he wants to be awake, in the middle of a dream, a good one. He reaches in the direction of his wife, her arm bare and soft and warm and peach-fuzzy, the thin silk of her nightie smooth and cool, the strap easily pushed aside, exposing her freckled shoulder, the hollow at the base of her neck, the rise of her . . .

Her nothing. Chloe isn't there.

Will's hand is resting on the old linen sheet that bears someone else's monogram, some long-dead Dutch merchant, a soft stack that Will purchased cheaply at a sparse flea market along a stagnant canal in Delft, refitted by an eccentric seamstress in Red Hook who repurposes odd-shaped old fabrics into the standardized dimensions of contemporary mattresses and pillows and mass-production dining tables. Will wrote an article about it, just a couple hundred words, for an alternative weekly. He writes an article about everything.

Chloe's note is scrawled on a Post-it, stuck on her pillow:

Early meeting, went to office. Have good trip. —C

No *love*. No *miss you*. No-nonsense nothing.

Will had gotten out of the karaoke bar before falling into the clutches of that wine rep, back-seam stockings and hot pink bra straps, a propensity for leaning forward precipitously. She was waiting to pounce when he returned to the table after his heartfelt "Fake Plastic Trees," a restrained bow to the applause of his dozen inebriated companions, whose clapping seemed louder and more genuine than the measured clapping of the thousand pairs of hands that had congratulated Will hours earlier, in the ballroom, when he'd won an award.

"You look great in a tuxedo," she'd said, her hand suddenly on his thigh.

"Everybody looks great in a tuxedo," Will countered. "That's the point. Good night!"

But it was two in the morning when he got home, earliest. Maybe closer to three. He remembers fumbling with his keys. In the hall, he kicked off his patent-leather shoes, so he wouldn't clump loudly up the wood stairs in leather soles. He thinks he stumbled—yes, he can feel a bruise on his shin. Then he probably stood in their door-less doorway, swaying, catching a glimpse of Chloe's uncovered thigh, eggshell satin in the streetlight . . .

She hates it when Will comes home in the middle of the night wearing inebriated sexual arousal like a game-day athletic uniform, sweaty and stained and reeking of physical exertion. So he probably stripped—yes, there's his tuxedo, half on the chair, bow tie on the floor—and passed out, snoring like a freight train, stinking like a saloon.

Will shades his eyes against the sunlight pouring through the large uncurtained six-over-six windows, with bubbles and chips and scratches and whorls in the glass, original to the house, 1884. Built back when there were no telephones, no laptops or Internet, no cars or airplanes or atomic bombs or world wars. But way back then, before his great-grandparents were born, these same glass panes were here, in these windows, in Will and Chloe's new old house.

He hears noise from downstairs. Was that the front door closing?

"Chloe?" he calls out, croaky.

Then footsteps on the creaky stairs, but no answer. He clears his throat. "Chlo?"

The floorboards in the hall groan, the noise getting nearer, a bit creepy—

"Forgot my wallet," Chloe says. She looks across the room at the big battered bureau, locates the offending item, then turns to her husband. "You feeling okay?"

He understands the accusation. "Sorry I was so late. Did I wake you?"

Chloe doesn't answer.

"In fact I was getting ready to come home when . . ."

Chloe folds her arms across her chest. She doesn't want to hear this story. She simply wants him to come home earlier, having had less to drink; their time home together doesn't overlap all that much. But staying out till all hours is his job—it's not optional, it's not indulgent, it's required. And Chloe knows it. She too has done this job.

Plus Will doesn't think it's fair that once again Chloe left home before he awoke, depositing another loveless note on the pillow, on another day when he's flying.

Nevertheless, he knows he needs to defend himself, and to apologize. "I'm sorry. But you know how much I love karaoke." He pulls the sheet aside, pats the bed. "Why don't you come over here? Let me make it up to you."

"I have a meeting."

Chloe's new office is in a part of the city filled with government bureaucracies, law firms, jury duty. Will ran into her one lunchtime—he was leaving a building-department fiasco, she was picking up a sandwich. They were both surprised to see each other, both flustered, as if they'd been caught at something. But it was only the interruption of the expectation of privacy.

"Plus I'll be ovulating in, like, six days. So save it up, sailor."

"But in six days I'll still be in France."

"I thought you were back Friday."

"Malcolm extended the trip."

"What?"

"I'm sorry. I forgot to tell you."

"Well that's shitty. There goes another month, wasted."

Wasted isn't exactly what Will would call the month. "Sorry."

"So you keep saying." She shakes her head. "Look, I have to go."

Chloe walks to the bed. The mattress is on the floor, no frame, no box spring. Will has a mental image of the perfect frame, but he hasn't yet been able to find it, and he'd rather have nothing than the wrong thing. Which is why the house is filled with doorways without doors, doors without doorknobs, sinks without faucets, bare bulbs without fixtures; to Will, all of these no-measures are preferable to half-measures.

This is one of the things that drives Chloe crazy about the renovation project, about her husband in general. She doesn't care if everything is perfect; she merely wants it to be good enough. And this is exactly why Will doesn't let her handle any of it. He knows that she will settle, will make compromises that he wouldn't. Not just about the house.

She bends down, gives him a closed-mouth kiss. Will reaches for her arm.

"Really, I'm running late," she says, but with little conviction—almost none—and a blush, a suppressed smile. "I gotta go." But there's no resistance in her arm, she's not trying to pull away, and she allows herself to fall forward, into bed, onto her husband.

Will sprawls amid the sheets while Chloe rearranges her hair, and replaces earrings, reties her scarf, all these tasks executed distractedly but deftly, the small competencies of being a woman, skills unknowable to him. The only thing men learn is how to shave.

"I love watching you," he says, making an effort.

"*Mmm*," she mutters, not wondering what the hell he's talking about.

Everybody says that the second year of marriage is the hardest. But their second year was fine, they were young and they were fun, both being paid to travel the world, not worrying about much. That year was terrific.

It's their fourth year that has been a drag. The year began when they moved into this decrepit house, a so-called investment property that

Chloe's father had left in his will, three apartments occupied by below-market and often deadbeat tenants, encumbered by serious code violations, impeded by unfindable electrical and plumbing plans—every conceivable problem, plus a few inconceivable ones.

The work on the house sputtered after demolition, then stalled completely due to the unsurprising problem of running out of money: everything has been wildly more expensive than expected. That is, more than Will expected; Chloe expected exactly what transpired.

So flooring is uninstalled, plumbing not entirely working, kitchen unfinished and windows unrepaired and blow-in insulation un-blown-in. Half of the second floor and all of the third are uninhabitable. The renovation is an unmitigated disaster, and they are broke, and Chloe is amassing a stockpile of resentment about Will's refusals to make the compromises that would allow this project to be finished.

Plus, after a year of what is now called "trying" on a regular basis—a militaristically regimented schedule—Chloe is still not pregnant. Will now understands that ovulation tests and calendars are the opposite of erotic aids.

When Chloe isn't busy penciling in slots for results-oriented, missionary-position intercourse, she has become increasingly moody. And most of her moods are some variation of bad: there's hostile bad and surly bad and resentful bad and today's, distracted bad.

"What do you think this is about?" she asks. "The extended trip?"

Will shrugs, but she can't see it, because she's not looking his way. "Malcolm hasn't fully explained yet." He doesn't want to tell Chloe anything specific until he has concrete details—what exactly the new assignment will be, any additional money, more frequent travel.

"How is Malcolm, anyway?"

As part of the big shake-up at *Travelers* a year ago, Will was hired despite Chloe's objections—both of them shouldn't work at the same struggling company in the same dying industry. So she quit. She left the full-time staff and took the title of contributing editor, shared with a few dozen people, some with only tenuous connections to the magazine accompanied by token paychecks, but still conferring a legitimacy—names on masthead, business cards in wallets—that could be leveraged while hunting for other opportunities.

Hunting for Other Opportunities: good job title for magazine writers.

Chloe came to her decision rationally, plotting out a pros-and-cons list. She is the methodical pragmatist in the couple; Will is the irrational emotional idealistic one.

"I think the takeover is stressing Malcolm out," Will says. "The negotiations are ending, both sides are doing due diligence. He seems to have a lot of presentations, reports, meetings."

"Is he worried for his job?"

"Not that he'll admit—you know how Malcolm is—but he has to be, right?"

Chloe grunts an assent; she knows more about Malcolm's office persona than Will does. Those two worked together a long time, and it was a difficult transition when Malcolm eventually became her boss. They both claimed that her departure was 100 percent amicable, but Will had his doubts. The closed-door I-quit meeting seemed to last a long time.

They also both claimed they'd never had a thing—no flirtation, no fling, no late-night make-out session in Mallorca or Malaysia. Will had doubts about that too.

"Okay then," she says, leaning down for another kiss, this one more generous than their previous good-bye. "Have a good trip."

People can spend hours packing for a weeklong overseas trip. They stand in their closets, desultorily flipping through hangers. They rummage through medicine cabinets, searching for the travel-sized toothpaste. They scour every drawer, box, and shelf for electrical adapters. They might have some of the foreign currency lying around somewhere, maybe in the desk . . . ? They double- and triple-check that their passports are in their pockets.

It's been a long time since Will was one of those amateurs. He collects his bright-blue roll-aboard—easy to describe to a bellhop, or to spot in a lost-and-found. It would also be easy to ID on a baggage carousel, but that will never happen. Will doesn't check luggage.

He mechanically fills the bag with piles from dresser drawers, the same exact items he packed for his previous trip, each in its preordained position in the bag's quadrants, which are delineated by rolled-up boxer shorts and socks. It takes Will five minutes to pack, long-zip short-zip upright on the floor, the satisfying clunk of rubberized wheels on bare parquet.

He walks into his office. One bookshelf is lined with shoeboxes labeled in a meticulous hand: W. EUROPE, E. EUROPE, AFRICA & MIDEAST, ASIA & AUSTRALIA, LATIN AMERICA & CARIBBEAN, USA. From W. EUROPE Will chooses a small stack of euros from among other clipped-together clumps of paper money, and a packet of Paris Metro tickets, and a burgundy-covered street-map booklet. He grabs a plug adapter, refits his computer charger with the long cylindrical prongs, ready to be inserted into exotic European outlets.

Last but not least, his passport, thick with the extra pages from the State Department, filled with stamps and visas, exit and entry, coming and going. It's the rare immigration officer who fails to comment on the peripatetic paperwork. Will has been detained before, and no doubt will be again.

Will stands in the doorway, looking around, worried that he's forgetting something, what . . . ?

He remembers. Opens a drawer, and removes a box clad in wrapping paper and bound in silk ribbon, just small enough to fit into his jacket pocket, just large enough to be uncomfortable there.

Will clambers down the long flight of rickety stairs to the parlor floor, and out the front door. He picks up the newspaper, descends more dangerous steps, and exits their postage-stamp yard, where a surprisingly undead rose vine clings to the iron fence, a handful of perfect red blooms.

He sets off toward the subway, dragging his bag, just as he's done every few weeks for a decade.

The bag rolls over the remains of a single rose that seems to have met a violent end, petals strewn, stem broken. Will glances at the little red mess, wondering what could have happened, and when, why someone would murder one of his flowers right here in front of the house. He can't help but wonder if it was Chloe who did this.

Will has been increasingly worried that his bride is slipping away, that theirs may become another marriage that succumbs to financial pressures and work travel and the looming specter of infertility. Worried that love is not always enough, or not permanent enough. Worried that all the non-fun parts will eclipse the fun parts.

Will bends over, looks closer. This decimated flower is not a rose, not from his yard, nothing to do with him. It's someone else's dead carnation, someone else's crime of passion.

Maybe he's worried about all the wrong things.

2

The door's plaque reads simply EDITOR, no name plate, as if the human being in there is interchangeable with the ones who came before, and the ones who will come after. An office that's occupied by a job, not by a person. There have been only four of them in the magazine's seventy-year history.

"Come!"

Malcolm Somers is sitting in his big executive chair behind his big executive desk, across from Gabriella Rivera, her profile framed by the floor-to-ceiling window onto Avenue of the Americas. Nothing is visible outside except other office buildings, up and down the avenue, thousands of windows into other lives, suits and ties, computers and coat racks, ergonomic chairs and solar-screen blinds and pressed-wood L-shaped desks exuding formaldehyde, and not even the barest glimpse of sky above nor street below, which can be seen only with face pressed against the glass, something no one except a child would do. Malcolm's kids do it.

Gabriella doesn't turn to see who's entering. She remains sitting perfectly still with her perfect legs crossed, one low heel dangling from the aloft foot, a sleek elegant figure, like an ad for something, a product, Sexy Professional Woman Sitting in Stylish Chair™. An ad for the product that is herself.

"Sorry to interrupt," Will says. "I've got a flight . . ."

Will stands in the doorway of the big room, waiting for permission to enter, for Malcolm to dismiss Gabriella.

"Gabs?" Malcolm asks.

The deputy editor waits a punitive beat before she nods. She stands and smooths her skirt, a garment that straddles the line of decency, depending on point of view. Most men would say it's just the right amount of tight and short; most women would disagree.

Gabriella turns, gives Will that dazzling smile. But beneath the veneer of those white teeth, those plush pillows of lips, Will can see the resentment at her interrupted meeting, maybe more. Will senses something in the air here, between these two. And not for the first time.

"Sorry," Will reiterates, apologizing to another woman who doesn't want to hear it.

She shrugs, not his fault, something else at play. "Have a good trip. France, is it? How long?"

"A week."

Gabriella cocks her head, considering something. "We should have a drink soon," she says, though Will doesn't think that's what she'd been considering. "It's been a while." On her way past, she squeezes Will's arm, and he feels a jolt from the strong current of sexual energy that flows from this woman.

Malcolm calls after her, "The door, please?"

She shuts it from the far side, perhaps a little too firmly, but still perfectly deniable, not a slam.

Malcolm's suit jacket is hanging on a wooden valet, his sleeves are rolled at the cuff. As always, the top button of his shirt is undone, the knot of his necktie loosened, like he just finished a long hard day, having a glass of scotch, neat. He looks exhausted, bags under his eyes, a hollowness to his cheeks. He's usually an extra-healthy-looking specimen, a natural athlete who spends his weekends outdoors, on boats and grass and sand, with little children and golf clubs, with the wholesome perks of his position.

But not now. Now he looks like crap.

"How are things, Rhodes?" Malcolm asks. "Sorry I couldn't stay for the after-party last night. Who was there? Did that hot wine rep of yours come along?"

"Come on, man, stop saying things like that. You know someday somebody is going to overhear you, and get me in a whole lot of trouble."

Malcolm holds up his hands, mea culpa, a smirk that's the tell that his baiting is mostly—or partially—an act. Malcolm is playing a role, a trope, a fictional misogynist, a guy's-guy buddy. Just as he plays the role of hypercritical boss and mercurial editor-in-chief, the role of lustful middle-aged married man, one role after another that he inhabits with patent detachment. Malcolm is so consistently ironic about so much that he's even ironic about his irony, which makes it tough to know what Malcolm truly feels about anything.

"And the Luxembourg trip? You went to a formal thing at the—what was it?—palace? Castle? How was that?"

"Deadly. Though I did get to shake hands with the grand duke. The party was at his palace, a sprawling pile in the middle of the city. Diplomats and bankers and a smattering of Eurotrash nobility and, probably, no shortage of spies in black ties."

Malcolm stares at Will, one corner of his mouth curled, not quite committing to a smile. "So tell me, Rhodes"—he says, shifting gears—"are you *ever* going to turn in that sidebar on the Swiss Alps? How long does it take to write three hundred words? You think that just because you're not hideous to look at, you can get away with—"

"Not true."

"—anything, but if we have to hold the issue—"

"*Stop!* I'll finish today."

Malcolm stands, stretches, walks around his desk. His limp is always most pronounced when he's been sitting awhile. After two hours in a theater or airplane seat, he hobbles like an arthritic old man. But not on the tennis court.

"I just need to cross my i's and dot my t's. I'll hit Send before liftoff. And it's five hundred words, not three hundred, you ignorant bastard."

Malcolm plops into an armchair, next to the coffee table. "Listen, sit down, will you? I want to talk about that new column I mentioned. It is indeed for you. Congratulations, Rhodes, you're moving up in the world."

"I'm honored."

"Try to restrain your enthusiasm. It'll be called 'Americans Abroad,' and it'll be about—wait for it—Americans, who are living where?"

"I'll go out on a limb: *abroad*?"

"That's the sort of sharpness I expect from you East Coast media-elite types."

"I'm from Minnesota."

"With your Ivy League liberal-arts degrees."

"I majored in journalism at Northwestern. But didn't you go to school somewhere in the Northeast? Athletic uniforms a color called *crimson*?"

"It'll be the whole expat experience, Rhodes, the communities, the lifestyle. Why'd they move there? How'd they choose the locale? Did they integrate into the local culture, or not? We'll explore the reality behind the fantasy. But without digging too deep, without unearthing all the ugly sad lonely crap down there. You know . . ." Malcolm gestures in the vague direction of ugly sad lonely crap, which as it happens is toward Times Square.

Will is not sure that he understands. "What's the point, Malcolm? What's this about?"

"What's it ever about?" Malcolm extends his hand, opens it, explanation self-evident, voilà. "Escapist fantasy. Aspirational lifestyle. Ad sales. It's a pay bump, Rhodes, five K per annum. Plus feature bylines with big contributor-page photos guaranteed for four issues per year. That is, if you can deliver the four pieces, you lazy shiftless piece of shit."

Will turns this idea over in his mind. It's not exactly the career advancement he was hoping for, which is an elusive concept to begin with. Will doesn't have any concrete vision more rational than a movie deal for an article he hasn't written, a contract for a book he hasn't conceived.

He'd like to imagine he'll get what he deserves. He wants to believe that this is how the world—or at least his world, upper-middle-class, college-educated, white-collar white-people America—works: meritocracy. This is the promise.

But what does Will Rhodes merit? Does he have the right to be envious of what he doesn't have? Or should he be extremely grateful for what he does have?

Will is on the cusp of the collapse of his idealism, alternating hope and despair day by day, sometimes minute by minute, wondering if his life can still turn out to be perfect. Like being twelve years old, toggling back and forth between little kid and teenager, crushes on girls but also clutching a teddy bear in the middle of the night.

Malcolm is on no such cusp. A decade separates the two men, and somewhere in there is the point at which idealism gave way to pragmatism, completely and irrevocably. Will doesn't know how this is supposed to happen, or when. Is it getting married? Having kids? Is it when one parent dies, or both? Is it turning thirty, or forty, fifty? What's the thing that happens that makes people think: it's time to grow up, face reality, get my act together?

Whatever it is, it hasn't yet happened to Will. So he finds himself constantly disappointed in the world, in its failures to live up to his ideals.

"What are we looking for, Mal? Anything different?"

"We're *always* looking for something different, Rhodes, you know that. Different, in the same precise goddamned way. Plus, you know what this assignment means?"

Will shakes his head.

"Rampant opportunities. There are a lot of expat housewives out there. Bored, hot, *horny* expat housewives. A target-rich environment."

"Give me a break."

Malcolm smiles. "Start putting together notes. That's why we booked you for a few more days in southwest France. The Paris bureau has contacts for you."

"Really?"

"What? You have a problem with drinking wine in the South of France?"

"No, it's just that I've been going through the archives, and we've run dozens of full-length articles—no exaggeration, *dozens*—about southern France."

"The archives? You're shitting me. Why?"

"What can I tell you? I take my job seriously."

"And I appreciate it. But the *archives*? I don't even know where we *keep* the archives."

"Down on twenty-eight. Across from corporate accounting."

"You'll recall that I didn't ask."

"But I bet you're gratified I told you. You're welcome."

Malcolm mugs a dubious look.

"For a long time," Will continues, "there was a France piece every third issue or so. I think Jonathan overharvested that crop."

They let the ex-editor's name hang in the air. Jonathan Mongeleach was loved around here, the center of every party, women swirling around him along with lurid rumors, many of them about his extramarital love life, his acrimonious divorce, his varied vices.

Jonathan was missed. On the other hand, it was when Jonathan disappeared—truly disappeared, didn't come to work one day, no one ever saw or heard from him again—that Malcolm got promoted to the corner office, at first temporarily, then provisionally, then permanently. Which is when Malcolm hired Will. "I'll be honest," Malcolm said, "I need an ally. A wingman, aide-de-camp, consigliere, and tennis partner. The list of qualified applicants is one. You up for it, Rhodes?"

They'd both gained something by Jonathan's departure, and they couldn't pretend otherwise. Will had gotten a more senior job at a more prestigious company. But Malcolm had gained far more: it's a huge jump to become editor of a major magazine, with car and driver, clothing allowance, an expense account that for all practical purposes is unlimited. And all this on top of the gorgeous wife and the adorable children, the beautiful apartment and the summer house, the everything. Malcolm already had everything, then he got more.

During the first days of Jonathan's disappearance, the assumption was that he'd been murdered. There were plenty of people who admired Jonathan, but also a few who loathed him. As time dragged on and no body was found, suspicion shifted toward the possibility that Jonathan had chosen to disappear himself. There were allegations of gambling debts and bankruptcy, a vindictive ex-wife and a predatory IRS. There was talk of suicide, and fake suicide, of a life insurance policy that named his estranged daughter as beneficiary. But so far, nothing concrete had been proven, and not much disproven.

Everyone moved on, these two men into these two chairs.

"Maybe he decided to go to France," Will says, "and never come back."

"Yes, maybe. But wherever Jonathan is, he certainly doesn't want to be found. If he's even alive."

"You think he's not?"

"That's possible. We all knew he was a strange guy, and he was definitely a cunning guy—a brilliant guy—and it looks like he was into some strange shit, some of it maybe dangerous. So who knows?" Malcolm opens a drawer, removes a padded envelope. "Speaking of France, this is for Inez. Drop it off whenever."

Will glances down, another hand-delivery to someone in a different country, a red PERSONAL AND CONFIDENTIAL stamp.

A year ago, when Malcolm first handed him such an envelope, Will asked what it was.

"You see that stamp there?" Malcolm responded. "*Personal and confidential,* addressed to someone who's not you?"

"Yeah."

"That means it's *personal* and it's *confidential*, for someone who's *not you.*"

"Gotcha."

"You remember the Sony hack, Rhodes? The Office of Personnel Management? JPMorgan Chase? *Snowden*? Digital information—digital communications—are as insecure as ever. So around here, we do things the old-fashioned way." Malcolm tapped the envelope. "We send each other shitloads of paper."

Since then Will had received plenty of these envelopes to tote overseas, as well as more than a few for himself: personnel memos and payroll forms and health-insurance paperwork and workplace-law notices and legal waivers.

"Listen, I need to jump on a call, so go." Malcolm makes the shooing motion. "Get the fuck out."

Will stands, strides across the big office, reaches for the doorknob.

"And hey, Rhodes?"

Will turns back.

"Let's be careful out there."

FALLS CHURCH, VIRGINIA

The room is the size of a basketball court but with the ceiling height of a coat closet, low and claustrophobic, fluorescent-lit and gray-carpeted, flimsy upholstered chest-high dividers separating the cubicles, nearly a hundred workspaces in here, all with laminate desktops and gooseneck lamps and plastic-and-mesh chairs on casters that glide across the pieces of hardened rubber that sit on the floor to make it easy to roll around, but no more than a foot or two in any direction, because these are small cubicles.

Every cheap desktop has a computer with a twenty-three-inch monitor. Every low-end plastic chair has an occupant. There are no vacancies, nor is there space to hire more personnel, even though more would be welcome—this is a round-the-clock operation with three shifts every day including weekends and holidays, never a moment when it's acceptable for the lights to be out.

The demographic is primarily South Asian, male, mid-twenties to late thirties, earning from eleven to nineteen dollars per hour. On the higher end, in a cubicle identical to all the others, Raji notices an incoming alert pop up, one of a dozen that he receives daily about the travel details of any of the fifteen hundred individuals on his segment of the watch list.

Raji copies the information into the relevant windows at the prompts:

U.S. PASSPORT NUMBER: 11331968
FLIGHT: 19 JFK TO CDG
TICKET CATEGORY: B11
SEAT: 12A
ALERT CODE: 4

He hits Post, then returns his attention to his bag of barbecue potato chips.

NEW YORK CITY

"*My* man," Reggie says, wearing the same ear-to-ear grin as ever. Will has never seen the old guy in a bad mood, and Reggie has been working curbside check-in for decades.

"Where you off to this time, 007?" Reggie likes to kid that Will isn't a writer, he's a spy; that his magazine byline is just a cover. Over the years, Reggie hasn't been the only person to have made this tongue-in-cheek accusation.

"It's France this time, Reggie."

"Ooh-la-la." The two men bump fists.

Will reaches into his pocket, removes the gift-wrapped box. "For Aisha. It's a few of those chocolates she loves."

"Oh, you shouldn't have."

"Happy to. Plus, I got them for free!" He didn't. "How's she doing this week?"

"Better, thank you."

Will nods. "Please tell her happy birthday for me."

"I will, Mr. Bond." Reggie winks. "You have a good trip."

Will doesn't understand how someone with such a crappy job can enjoy it so much, or can pretend so convincingly. But then again, there's a lot about normal forty-hour-per-week jobs that Will doesn't understand. He has barely ever had one.

In the terminal, Will examines himself in a mirror, surrounded by all this corporate signage, Kimberly-Clark and American Standard, Rubbermaid and Purell, a barrage of brands. He himself is a brand too, Will Rhodes, Travel Writer, with his little suede notebook, his canvas sport jacket over oxford shirt and knit tie, twill pants, rubber-soled brogues, sturdy comfortable clothes that won't wrinkle or crease or collect lint or stains, none that'll look any worse for wear after twenty hours hanging off his lanky frame, flying across the ocean.

After takeoff he washes down his sleeping pill with a whiskey. He reclines his seat, inserts the ear plugs, and stretches the mask over his eyes, a well-rehearsed routine. Almost immediately, he falls into an innocent sleep.

NORTH ATLANTIC OCEAN

Will doesn't know how long he's been out—ten minutes? three hours?—when a loud rumble wakes him, the shuddering of the 747, the vibration traveling up his thighs and tailbone through his spine.

He pushes down his mask, unplugs his ears. Turns to the man-child next to him, a thirty-year-old wearing high-topped sneakers and a backward baseball cap who'd been preoccupied with a lollipop and a video game when Will last looked.

"What's happening?" Will asks.

The guy looks ashen, eyes wide, mouth agape. Shakes his head.

"Ladies and gentlemen, please ensure that your seatbelts are *securely* fastened, and all trays are in their upright position."

These are the same words Will has heard hundreds of times before. Sit back relax and enjoy the flight. We know you have your choice of carriers. Our first priority is your safety. We'd like to extend a special welcome . . .

A flight attendant hurries past, gripping each seatback tightly as she passes, banging her knee into the frontmost armrest, pausing to gather her balance and her wits before launching herself across the open purchaseless space to a jump seat, which she falls onto, buckles herself in, pulling the straps tight, taking a deep breath.

Oxygen masks fall from their overhead doors, and an audible wave of panic ripples down the fuselage. Will places the mask over his face, and tries as instructed to breathe normally, pinned under gathering terror to the soft leather of seat 12A.

The plane plummets.

People start to scream.

NEW YORK CITY

Malcolm walks the perimeter of the thirtieth floor, looking for any last stragglers who might interrupt him. Everyone still here is too junior, and none would have the nerve to barge in on the chief at seven-thirty, except the food editor, the guy everyone calls Veal Parmesan. Veal never seems to leave. But he also never visits Malcolm.

Malcolm closes his door, turns the knob to lock it. He takes a few steps along the wall that's decorated with framed *Travelers* covers, decades' worth of the magazine's best work, like a museum exhibit for the people who traipse through this office regularly.

He squats in the corner of the bookshelves, pushes aside a handful of old guidebooks, reaches his hand past the books, all the way to the back wall. He locates a button by touch, and presses it.

For a few decades, this was the only security mechanism. But during a wave of paranoia in the post-Nixon seventies, the new editor-in-chief Jonathan Mongeleach was convinced to add a second level of security. In the eighties this analog lock was replaced by an electronic device, then over the past two decades by ever more sophisticated digital models, with increasing frequency of upgrades, as strongly advised by the consultants and developers who never fail to push each year's advance as an exponential technological leap, last year's security laughably outdated this year. Or so claimed by the people who profit from the technology, with no practical way for any of its consumers to assess the claim, least of all Malcolm. What a racket.

So now this mechanical button is merely a secondary system. Malcolm activates the primary system via a hidden panel at chest height, behind a big thick reference book, using his thumbprint and the input of a long access code.

With a nearly silent click, the entire section of bookcase is released. The wall swivels open a couple of inches of its own accord, on sturdy brass hinges; this is a heavy section of wall, hundreds of pounds. Malcolm pulls it open wide enough to walk through. Then he closes the door behind him, and disappears into the wall.

3

PARIS

The big man's phone dings in his pocket, the sound reserved for actionable alerts. The message had been encrypted on another continent, then decoded by a complex proprietary app that gets updated regularly. He seems to spend half his life waiting for his devices to update, plugged into outlets and the Internet, *Updating . . . Please wait . . . Updating . . .*

He walks through the dimly lit shabby-swanky bar of a four-star hotel in the 2ème that's frequented by international businessmen and high-end hookers, which is why he's here, looking for a blue-eyed blonde to fulfill a recurring fantasy that he's been unable to shake while spending copious time in the professional company of a blue-eyed blonde, sometimes even talking with her about sex, God help him. He steps outside to the deserted boulevard, and places a call to that same blonde, who at the moment is lying in bed in a marginally seedy hotel in downtown Bordeaux, reading Robert Hughes's book about Australia.

"Yes?" she answers, putting down a glass of room-temperature mineral water. Her hair is in curlers, her face slathered with a mud mask. She's doing everything she can do tonight to look as good as she can look tomorrow. Except being asleep. It's very late.

"He's airborne," the man says. "You ready?"

She sighs. This is a stupid question, requiring either a stupid answer or rudeness. "As ready as I'll ever be, Roger."

"You're going to be great." He probably thinks he's being reassuring, but he doesn't have any idea how to help her. This is not something he'll ever experience or understand, not remotely. Of all the crappy things she has already done in her life, this is going to be a new one.

"Just great," he reiterates, one of those meaningless phrases of pat encouragement that pass for supportiveness.

She puts down the phone, and puts down the book, and stares at the ceiling, hoping she can fall asleep.

NORTH ATLANTIC OCEAN

As suddenly as it started, the unexpected turbulence subsides, then disappears entirely, then the plane is once again cruising smoothly thirty-six thousand feet above the ocean, hundreds of miles in any direction from the nearest land, in the dead middle of the night.

It had lasted only a few seconds, the feeling that he was about to die. Maybe a half-minute, not very long at all. But long enough for Will to discover something about himself that he wished he hadn't.

PARIS

In the misty morning, Will walks past the Louvre into the fog-shrouded Tuileries, young mothers with babies, old men with newspapers, the people who sit in parks on weekday mornings, the same everywhere. He exits at Concorde and continues up the Champs-Élysées, toward l'Arc de Triomphe, the Eiffel Tower off to the left. A greatest-hits album.

"*Excusez-moi, monsieur.*" An old man is blocking Will's path, holding out a piece of paper, a haphazardly folded map. There's a woman by his side, a stern, disappointed-looking wife. "*Je cherche le café qui s'appelle Le Fouquet's. Est-ce que vous le connaissez?*"

People are constantly asking Will for directions in places he doesn't live, and he often knows the answer. The people who are doing the asking are almost always tourists, asking about tourist destinations. People like this man, speaking French with a Russian accent.

"*Oui.*" Will points toward the famous arch. "*Là-bas.*"

"*Merci, monsieur. Vous êtes très gentil.*"

Since childhood Will has been an obsessive student of maps, memorizing streets and lakes, inventing routes to Tierra del Fuego and the North Pole, filling his wall-mounted world map with pushpins in a color-coded system to divide natural wonders from man-made attractions, the places he had already been from the ones he wanted to see.

Past the Grand Palais, Will turns off the boulevard, and the traffic and noise fall away in the quiet elegance of the 8ᵉᵐᵉ, barely any sidewalk on this street. Will is tired and distracted and not attentive enough, walking too close to the curb, and when a car approaches he needs to jump to the side, to flatten himself against the coarse stone for the Peugeot to wheeze by, the driver's arm resting on the open window, just a few inches away. Will could reach out and steal the guy's watch.

Will turns one corner and another without needing to consult the burgundy *plan* that's tucked into his back pocket. He finally stops at an elegant Belle Epoque building, TRAVELERS etched on a brass plaque, scratched and tarnished, an old piece of identification that had been affixed to this exposed expanse of limestone wall a half-century ago.

It's well known in the *Travelers* family that Paris was the very first overseas bureau, an experiment in a boutique high-end travel agency that surprised everyone with its success. At its height, in the mid-nineties, the magazine operated nearly three dozen overseas bureaus, all of them part travel agency and part magazine outpost, providing New York with local editorial talent and also attracting advertisers and promotional opportunities.

The past decade has been kind to neither type of business. But in an age when all magazines are casting about for new revenue sources—festivals and conferences, apparel lines and home-decorating services—*Travelers* is the trailblazer, the first to extend its brand recognition and consumer loyalty into a completely different business.

And some of the travel bureaus are still profitable. Even at ten on a weekday morning, the ground-floor office in Paris is open for business, albeit with only a skeleton crew. One adviser is seated at her desk, directly behind the plate-glass window, holding up *Le Monde* with perfectly manicured hands. There aren't many customers at this early hour. But extended hours is one of the services that *Travelers* offers in places like Paris.

Will isn't here to visit the travel bureau.

He pushes a plain key card—no markings, just a magnetic strip on a blank white card—flat up against a reader. The front door unlocks with a nearly inaudible click. He climbs the sweeping staircase to the *premier étage*, eighteen-foot ceilings, marble floors, an oversize brass knob set into the middle of the towering double doors.

Will has no idea what goes on in the rest of this building. He has seen a few people coming or going, but there are no other plaques on doors, no signage of any sort anywhere, no indication of any other place of work.

He depresses a button on the office door. A soft whoosh as a waist-high panel opens in the wall. He swipes his ID card through a slit, and another door clicks open.

Will walks into the Paris bureau, one very large room that's shared, in the abstract, by two people. Today it's the young French woman; at other times it's the middle-aged American man. Will has never seen both at the same time. He vastly prefers Inez, with her scarves and freckles and wide-set deer-in-the-headlights eyes.

"*Bonjour, Monsieur Rhodes. Comment ça-va?*"

"*Ça va bien, Inez. Et toi?*" He removes the envelope from his jacket, hands it over.

"*Pas mal.*" She takes the envelope. "*Et merci.*" Inez punches in the six-digit touch-tone code that unlocks a cabinet drawer, a handful of audio frequencies. The lock's notes are barely audible, but they definitely remind Will of something, a melody, maybe the theme of some song his band used to cover. It bothers him that he can't place it, feels like this might be the onset of memory decay; hearing loss and erectile dysfunction can't be far behind.

It's now Inez's turn to remove a file from this drawer, then an envelope from the file. The overseas bureaus were founded well before the advent of computers and the Internet, and their paper filing system functions perfectly. Every few years someone new proposes a digital overhaul, and the editor rejects it.

Will takes a seat, slices the envelope with a letter opener, sharper than it needs to be, dangerous. He removes a few sheets of paper, runs his eyes down one page. He looks at some six-by-nine glossy photos. Then a couple of maps, which he will study closely, memorizing the major routes, identifying the locations of his destinations, familiarizing himself with the names of streets and parks, beaches and museums, towns and villages and mountain ranges. Whenever Will arrives somewhere, he wants to already know where he's going.

"These are all new notes?"

"*Oui. Je croix que c'est vrai.*"

"Some of this looks familiar. Are you sure?"

"You know quite well, Monsieur Rhodes, that I am not."

The girl doesn't know anything; she never does. "Ah!" she says, finger up. She unlocks another drawer, and hands over a bulky nylon bag.

Will takes the packet, unzips it, peeks inside. "*Merci, mademoiselle, comme toujours.*"

"*De rien, Monsieur Rhodes.*"

He spends a long day scouting, hopping on and off the Metro, into cafés for fortifying espressos while scribbling notes. He takes a late-afternoon shower, puts on fresh clothes, exits the hotel between a pair of potted topiaries complemented by a pair of burly doormen who could be either welcoming or the opposite.

A woman is emerging from a long black Mercedes in a miasma of perfume and hair spray and shopping bags, like an ultra-*riche* Pigpen. She gives Will a once-over, then lowers her sunglasses, extends her legs from a Chanel skirt to the rue St-Honoré. She glides into the hotel, another successful afternoon of shopping accomplished, and now to a deep bubble bath with a glass of chilled Sancerre and a home-décor magazine, a nibbled dinner at L'Arpège, an eau-de-vie nightcap, and finally a deeply gratifying earthmoving fuck with her handsome jet-setting husband . . .

Maybe not. Maybe that's merely the mythical version of her life that Will is conjuring so he can try to sell it, the type of fantasy he attempts to invent every time he sits down to type, to project unto readers the striving and yearning, and hopefully the transference from the unattainable fantasy of this woman's life to a more attainable, less fictional one, relatable to a woman who lives in a big house in North Indianapolis, a woman who isn't coming to Paris on a shopping spree but nevertheless can purchase the handbag that's advertised on page 89, facing Will's byline, a handbag that any woman can find at any upscale mall in America, and perhaps pretend that she bought it here, on the rue St-Honoré, and hung in the crook of her arm as she strode to her prime-time table on the rue de Varenne.

Most of the time, it goes unsaid. But Will is always aware that at the end of the day, *Travelers* is in business to sell that handbag to that reader.

He takes a circuit of Plâce Vendôme, mostly to see if anything has changed, but nothing ever does, except the progress of the Ritz's renovations. He makes his way over to Palais-Royal, and strolls the seventeenth-century arcades, poking in boutiques, antiques and leather goods and artisan jewelry. He buys a tee shirt for Chloe, with the picture of a terrier whose name apparently is Gigi. His wife is fond of terriers. Though not quite fond enough to own one; Chloe doesn't think she'd be a good parent to a dog.

There are a handful of wine bars strewn about the northern end of Palais-Royal, and he has a glass of white with appetizers at one, an airy room with light wood and big windows. He walks around the corner to a smaller, more crowded *bar à vins*, a place he's been before. He watches the crowd through the huge mirror while he eats spicy lamb stew and drinks a barnyardy red, perched on a leather stool at the battered bar, scribbling in the suede-covered notebook he bought in Florence, pliable and worn and filled with notes he has scrawled on all seven continents. It's a perfect little thing, his notebook.

The lamb stew is nearly flawless—marginally overseasoned—as is the room, dark and intimate, walls lined with a diagonal zigzag of wooden shelving that holds hundreds of bottles, and worn leather, and bare wood tables with mismatched hotel flatware, and scratchy old jazz on a turntable that gets jostled once in a while, a screech and a skip, customers straightening their spines, but it's part of the thing, the ethos.

"*Ca était, monsieur?*" the bartender asks.

"*Formidable, Pierre. Formidable.*"

The room is filled with an appealing assortment of women wearing chic skirts and high heels, and the accompanying men in wavy hair and silk scarves, laughing and arguing and jabbing each other with the tips of their fingers and the force of their convictions. Will likes it here.

Paris is one of those places where Will can't help but imagine living. He's always doing this, weighing the possibility of living here, of living there, the pros and cons of occupying some town or another, living a different life. This is what travel is for: dipping your toes into unfamiliar waters, seeing if it suits.

He often needs to fight the urge to write that he'd love to live somewhere—the Marais or Malibu, the Dordogne or the Cotswolds. This sentiment is not what readers want; it's not experiential. But even though he never makes the case explicitly, he's pretty sure the idea emerges: this would be a fine place to inhabit an alternative universe.

Will pays his check, says good night to Pierre, and steps out to the quiet nighttime street.

There are parts of Paris where the after-dark life is dense and loud, taxi-hailing and making-out, cigarette smoky and cell-phone loud, "*J'arrive!*" But this part of the 1ère *arrondissement* isn't. Will walks a very long, very quiet half-block before he freezes—

He left his notebook on the bar.

He spins, retreats in that rushed distracted way of anyone who has left behind something important, not paying much attention to anything else. Certainly not enough to notice the big guy walking toward him, studiously not meeting Will's eye.

Will meanders through the mostly deserted streets, lost in himself, until the not-so-distant sounds of a woman's yelp and a slamming door drag him back to awareness. Sometimes he's too oblivious to the threats that lurk in the late streets of big cities. He looks over his shoulder now, quickens his pace.

Back in his hotel room, amid plush velvet and a surfeit of throw pillows, gleaming chrome fixtures and virgin white tiles, the solitary quiet of this generic cocoon, Will's regrets return. Everything that had raced through his mind while the plane plummeted is now occupying his consciousness again like political protesters, chanting loudly, refusing to be ignored, presenting the united front of this message: he should be happy, but he's not.

Will wants everything to be perfect. He wants the perfect wife, the perfect kids, the perfect old townhouse, perfectly restored, where he'll serve perfect food accompanied by perfect wines in perfect glasses. He wants his suit to be perfectly tailored, his shoes perfectly shined. He wants the hotel room to be perfect, the overnight train ride, the local tour guide. And he has made the relentless pursuit of perfection his career.

But perfection is always over the next horizon. The next job, the next meal, the next trip. Next year, or maybe the year after.

Chloe now isn't quite as perfect as the ideal of Chloe had been, before. And they're broke in a way that often looks permanent, living in a crumbling house in a dodgy neighborhood, waiting for the extra income that's always more likely next year, money to finish renovating the house, to furnish it for the baby they're trying to conceive, to start living grown-up life, still in the imprecise future, after some nonspecific milestone, floating up ahead in the indefinite unsatisfying *soon*.

Will knows that he's very lucky, that he does something uniquely enjoyable for a living. But he is jaded, and he is bored. He increasingly suspects that he chose the wrong career, and possibly the wrong wife too. He is thirty-five years old, halfway to dead, and he has already made the most important decisions of his life. Have they all been wrong?

4

===

"Thank you to everyone for coming 'ere tonight. From America. From England and Sweden and, *comment dit-on*, Africa South? From Australia, even!" The winemaker holds his hands over his head, and claps, and everyone joins. "This is our two 'undredth anniversary *au château*! We are very 'onored that you are able to join our celebration. *Merci à tous! À table!*"

The long table is out back of the château, on a broad stretch of flat grass before the terrain slopes down toward the river, rows upon rows of grapevines receding into the night. Gurgling fountains with floating candles occupy either end of the lawn, and the long table between is set with dozens of little votives in glass cubes, the perimeter flanked by torches on posts, the trees strung with lanterns. Flamelight flickers everywhere.

Will finds his place card, heavily inked calligraphy with an excess of flourishes, silver napkin rings, little vases holding tiny sprays of miniature white calla lilies. He loves this about the French, their unabashed pursuit of beauty. It makes him feel unself-conscious about his own often-mocked perfectionism.

On Will's left is a woman wearing the severe frown of someone who's prepared to be disappointed by everyone and everything, all the time. Will recognizes her name, a veteran wine journalist famous for her idiot-savant palate, troglodyte social skills, and unremitting snobbery.

And on Will's right, wow, someone he definitely hasn't met before. "Elle Hardwick," she says, holding out her hand.

"Nice to meet you. Rare to find someone who's willing to go by one letter alone. Like Bono, but even bolder."

"Ah, no." She smiles. "That's Elle spelled as in the magazine." She has a pronounced Australian accent. "Or the French pronoun."

"Or the supermodel?"

"If absolutely necessary. *Elle, qui s'appelle Elle, lit* Elle."

"I guess that makes more sense."

"Glad you agree. And what do people call you?"

"They call me Mr. Rhodes. Will Rhodes."

"Oh, Will Rhodes! I'm a fan. A pleasure to meet you. *Genuine* pleasure."

Will reluctantly turns away from Elle, to do his ten minutes' duty with the belligerent oenophile. Unsurprisingly, she has a distinct distaste for Americans, and more generally for men. There's no charm of Will's to which she is not allergic, and he feels himself sinking deeper and deeper into the quicksand of her odium.

This social nightmare on one side is tailor-made pre-penance for the alternative on his other, and Will relishes the discomfort of the woman's hostility and dismissiveness, the absurd perfection of it, the delay of gratification, the investment of pain for the promise of pleasure.

When the empty *amuses bouches* plates are whisked away, he turns to Elle.

"You're something of a legend, you know, Will Rhodes."

"Ha! That's a ridiculous thing to say, but I thank you for saying it. And you, Elle Hardwick? Who are you?"

"*Australian Adventurer* magazine. Speciality in adventure."

"Are you new?"

"New to what?"

"To this." He sweeps his hand across the table. "I've been going to these for a long time. Put on by winemakers. By hotels. By cruise lines and liquor distributors and restaurateurs. Hundreds of them, cocktail parties and luncheons and long boozy dinners. All for the benefit of the people who write about these topics. People like me. There aren't that many of us, you know. And I would think I'd've come upon everyone, sooner or later. But I've never come upon you. As it were."

Good God, did he really just say that? "If you'll forgive the phrase."

She grins at his dirty joke. Not insulted, not scandalized, not embarrassed. Amused? More? "I guess I *am* rather new. Still looking for one's big break. How'd you get yours?"

There are professions with specifically demarcated milestones—

partner, tenure, vice-presidency. But Will's isn't one. "I guess that depends on what you call a big break."

Elle regards him over the rim of her wineglass. "So tell me, Mr. Will Rhodes, what was your first job? I'm going to interview you."

"Oh I don't think so."

"Please?"

Will shifts in his chair, turns to face this woman, wearing the hyper-stylized hair and meticulously applied makeup of a good-looking woman who is making a concerted effort to be spectacular. Like a tall man wearing boots.

"It may not be easy to understand, from where you sit," she says, leaning toward him a few inches, which somehow seems a lot closer. "But you *are* at the top of our field. And I *am* near the bottom. You can't blame a girl for wanting to climb up a bit."

It's true: he's a big fish in a small pond. And here is this attractive angler, casting her lure his direction. "After college I moved to New York, which is one of the things that people do in America when they want to write."

"Is that so? I'd never have imagined."

"I had a series of miscellaneous jobs while looking for freelance work: pitching stories and submitting spec articles, contributing short pieces to trade magazines. Getting poorer and poorer with each passing month. You know how it is, I imagine?"

"I do."

"I finally landed an editorial job at a glossy magazine, with health insurance and a regular paycheck. A few months later, a writing position opened up, on the food desk."

"Did you always want to write?"

"I did." It was way back in third grade when Will decided to become a writer. He took his book reports seriously, he edited his high-school paper, he got a journalism degree at what may have been the last moment when ambitious young people still aspired to be establishment print journalists. Not only to write for a living, but to write about other things, other people, not about themselves; reporting, not memoirs and blogs and tweets and status updates, not a permanent state of navel-gazing.

"Did you always want to write about *food*?"

"I'd never given it any thought. The grade-schooler me could never have imagined that his adult self would write the equivalent of book reports about Italian blue cheese."

She laughs, covers her mouth a split second too late for decorum.

"I eventually got a better job at a food magazine, where I worked for a few years. Then *Travelers.*"

On the face of it, he has achieved what he set out to achieve. He is a full-time professional writer. He has been on three safaris, visited Machu Picchu and the Galápagos and Antarctica, seen the northern lights and the midnight sun, ridden the Orient Express and the *Queen Elizabeth,* seen the Red Sea and the Dead Sea and Death Valley and the Valley of the Gods. Take that, Johnny Cash.

Now what?

"And there you have it, Elle Hardwick: my résumé." He takes a sip of water. This is going to be a long night, and he doesn't want to get too drunk, too early. No, he wants to get just the right amount of drunk, at the proper time.

"What has been your secret of success, Mr. Rhodes?"

"No secret. Not that much success."

"Come on."

"Oh I don't know. I guess I work hard."

"Meaning?"

"I read a lot. I eat and drink a lot. I *learn* a lot."

"And the writing bit?"

"I revise a lot. Writing *is* revising." Enough. This is as long as he should talk about himself, which was already too long. "And you? What did you do before . . . um . . ."

"*Australian Adventurer.* I'm freelance for them, actually. Not on staff."

"Right."

"Before this, I . . . I guess you could say I got around. For example: I got around to that panel discussion you were on, in Austin."

For a second Will draws a blank, then remembers. "Oh good God. You didn't."

"I certainly did. I thought you were brilliant, Will Rhodes. Absolutely brilliant. But I didn't recognize you without the beard. You look better this way."

He appraises her in the candlelight, the dimples and the half-smile, the arched eyebrow, the long elegant neck and the tan toned forearms, the ring finger that doesn't bear a ring. A beautiful sexy stranger who lives very, very far away.

"So, any advice for me? What should I absolutely make sure to do?"

Will knows how he wants to answer, but suddenly he's afraid of the double entendres, the direct glances, afraid of flirting too much. Flirting usually seems innocuous, nothing will come of it, no harm, no foul, just fun. But here, now, her? Will is not so sure. This doesn't seem all that innocent.

"You should say yes to everything."

"*Oui*, Monsieur Rhodes?" She raises that eyebrow again. "*Every*thing?"

Will's night rushes by in the distracting haze of this woman's alluring gaze, course after course—soup and fish and meat and salad and cheese and dessert—with wines to match from the famous cellar, and the wax cascading down the sides of the candles in windblown patterns, spreading leeward onto linens splattered with ruby drops from the pheasant's berry sauce and golden drips from the fish's saffron sauce, littered with bread crumbs and flakes of white-dusted cheese crusts, and spent wooden matches and ashtrays filled with lipstick-stained cigarette butts, and purses and eyeglasses and corks and a knocked-over vase whose single lily lies on the table, as if reclining, having had too much to drink, deciding to just go to sleep here in the midst of the party, good night.

"So let's get back to our interview, Mr. Rhodes. Tell me," Elle says, leaning forward, elbows on table, "about your childhood."

"Well, Ms. Hardwick, I was born a poor black child."

A burst of surprised laughter escapes her. "We don't hear a lot of references to *The Jerk* in Australia."

"I'm surprised you hear any."

"Well, I do get out, every so often."

"And we're all grateful for it."

"Are you, Will Rhodes?" She arches that eyebrow.

"Yes. I think I am."

They stare at each other, holding gazes for a time-stopped eternity, before she breaks the spell. "So where are you from? How far has your life traveled to arrive here at this table, with me?"

Will takes a sip of wine, swirls it on his palate, pretending to do a bit of his job before returning his attention to something that's not.

"Nondescript upbringing in St. Paul, Minnesota. Do you know where that is?"

"Hmm. Do I fly over it on my way to New York?"

"You fly over everything on your way to New York."

"Well then, I know *exactly* where it is."

"I graduated from a Midwestern university with negligible employment-related skills and a fortune's worth of student debt. Does this go on in Australia? Borrowing for university?"

"Of course. Are you still broke then? Uni couldn't have been that long ago."

"You flatter me."

"I suppose I do, Mr. Rhodes." That sly grin again, something more than a little playful. This is a dangerous woman here.

"Well, to be honest, Ms. Hardwick, I never did dig out from that financial hole. I've moved sideways in my debt structure. Excavating new subterranean passages, like a whole ant colony of interconnected financial obligations that bears a passing semblance to solvency around a fundamental core of what is, in essence, bankruptcy."

Will never believed that writing would make him rich, but his extreme level of unrich has come as a shock, and it's possible that in a few years his job may no longer even exist. Not even Chloe is aware of the full extent of Will's—of their—financial woes. When they first started dating, Will was so ashamed of the sorry state of his affairs that he refused to acknowledge to himself that there was any problem at all; he just surged forward. Matters improved when they started living together, sharing expenses. But Will is still carrying an embarrassing load of consumer debt, and he has found himself unable to come clean to his wife.

"That's a truly sad story, Will Rhodes. *Très triste.*"

"This is what keeps me up in the middle of the night. Spirals of self-doubt and fear, and this recurring nightmare that I'll end up living in a trailer park in north Jersey, alone and destitute on my deathbed, frothing-at-the-mouth resentful that no one ever suggested I learn Mandarin, or code-writing, or, I don't know, trusts-and-estates law."

He's not sure why he's unburdening himself on this stranger. Actually, he is sure, but he doesn't want to admit it to himself, so instead he keeps talking. "On the plus side, these fears are what impel me out of a sleepless bed to my computer, where I churn out three hundred words here, a thousand there, sometimes an overblown modifier-laden three thousand, which I deliver triumphantly with an envelope packed with expense receipts. I'm at my most productive when seized by financial panic in the middle of the night."

She bites her lip, perhaps biting back a flirtatious response, substituting instead a flirtatious look. "So tell me, Will Rhodes, what is it that your wife does for a living?"

Ouch. Will wonders if Elle is purposefully shifting the mood, dragging reality to intrude on this fantasy. Or is she trying to accomplish something else, something more subtle? Yes, Will, I know you have a wife, but I don't care.

Again, she arches that eyebrow. God damn, he loves that arched eyebrow.

This Elle Hardwick, she certainly looks like a woman who's going to wreck his marriage.

The guy from *Saveur* has moved down to sit across from Elle, next to Bethany the publicist whom Will has met at a half-dozen things, and now next to Will is a jovial lecherous Scottish chef named Callum, and everyone roars at the winemaker Bertrand's joke, and it's all fun in the way that these things can be fun, plus tonight there's been a sexy stranger at Will's side, a woman who either wants him badly or has spent the evening pretending to.

"So you're married?" Callum asks.

"*Mmm*," Will says. "I am indeed."

At the end of the table, a megalomaniacal chef is making a big show of opening a jeroboam, a big bottle of a big wine, cackling and feral, like a drunk French hyena.

"There's a lot of temptation." Callum inclines his head at Elle. "Isn't there, mate?"

Will doesn't answer.

"How do you resist?"

"With great difficulty," Will says, rising. "*Excusez-moi.*" He pats the guy on the shoulder, walks away, a bit unsteady on liquored-up legs on squishy grass.

Inside, it's too bright. Will's pupils, accustomed to the candlelit night, are slow to close up here in the house. The drapes are too purple, the tiles in the bathroom too blue. His face in the mirror is splotchy and stubbly, his eyes shot with red lines. He has been drinking now for—what?—seven hours. It's surprising how much of his job is about staying up very late, drinking alcohol, with strangers. Maybe that's all jobs.

He splashes his cheeks with cool water, trickling into his eyes, onto his lips. It feels good. He dries his face, pushes back his hair, adjusts his tie. He stares at himself in the mirror, searching his eyes for his resolve, alone at a party, far from home, without his wife.

His wife. If only she were here, taking his hand under the table, as she does, just their secret for a few seconds, I'm here, I'll be here later, I'll be here tomorrow, that's what a wife is. But she's not here, not now.

Will never knew what exactly ruined his parents' marriage, but they ended up loathing each other, hostilities were open, they referred to each other in the third person—"Please tell your father to come inside"—in the other's presence, occasionally screaming. Then when Will was eleven, Dad died. Rumors eventually reached Will—Mom driven to alcoholism, Dad to serial philandering. But these were the symptoms, not the illness.

He'd been too young to have ever had any conversation with his father about this. And when he was mature enough, he could never bring himself to ask his mom. So Will's imagination festered, conjuring dozens of scenarios, of reasons why a couple could be driven to hate each other so much. He told himself cautionary tales. Promised himself that whatever it was, he wouldn't do it. That he himself would grow old with his own wife, would die at her side, and along the way he'd avoid all the pitfalls, overcome all the obstacles. And that if he somehow failed, he'd admit it, and he'd end it. He'd rather be divorced, rather live with a failed marriage in the past tense than with a shitty marriage in the present.

And yet here he is.

Will takes a deep breath. He opens the door, and there Elle is, just like he knew she'd be, waiting for him, leaning against the wall, face turned down but big blue eyes turned up, appraising him from the cool remove of her enviable genetics.

This is the situation that he has both desired and dreaded. What's he going to do?

One of Will's main fortifications against adultery has been that men always have to make the first physical move. Women may drop innuendo all night, but none has been willing to initiate the physical encounter.

Until now. Elle takes the step that separates them, and raises her hand, and places her thumb on his cheek, fingers on his neck, and as she begins to pull his face to hers, there's a brief period when Will can still halt it, he can avert his face or pull back, keep his mouth closed or put his hand up, but he doesn't do any of these things, he allows it to happen, at first half-way reluctant but then unrestrained, and for a minute or two—how can you measure?—they stand in the short hall next to the washroom in an ancient château in southwest France, very late at night and very far from home, melting into each other.

Then voices—it sounds like Bertrand, with that sommelier—and Elle pulls back, stares at him hard for a second, wordlessly extending a promise. She blinks, and he reads in that blink her reiteration: yes, I'm yours, take me.

At the end, only a handful of people remain; that's what makes it the end. They stagger along the pebbled path toward the taxis, drivers leaning on hoods, eyeing passengers with the superiority of sober people accommodating inebriated ones.

"You're staying at the *auberge*, aren't you?" Elle asks, slowing her pace, creating distance between the two of them and the others, public privacy.

"I am."

"What's your room number?" she asks. Quietly, without looking at him. Their heels are crunching on the stones. The plastered Scot stumbles, rights himself, none too steadily.

Will can barely stand it, how much he wants this woman. And who would ever know? *Who?*

He would. He already feels crappy about that kiss, crappier with each passing second. He's not a guy who does this, who succumbs to this cliché. Oh, Will Rhodes? *Of course* he had an affair with a beautiful Australian on assignment in France. How could he *not?*

"Listen, Elle."

She stops walking. "You're *kidding.*" Elle is staring at him, mouth open in shock, affronted. Will wonders if this woman has ever before been rejected.

"I'm married."

"Marriage has nothing to do with this, Will. Nothing." The appalled look slides from her face, replaced with bemused resignation. "Though I guess I'm not the married one, am I?"

Will is pretty sure this question is rhetorical, and he doesn't want to make a fool of himself by answering.

"Have it your way," she says. She resumes walking, and he lets her take a couple of steps before he joins. "Or, rather, *don't* have it."

If this is the end of it, if this is all, everything will be just fine. Beautiful stranger, foreign country, one late-night drunken kiss. Who cares? He'll get over it. No one will know.

5

"I'm sorry," Elle says. "I was out of line."

Will looks up from his plate, silky ham and soft bread with salted butter, fresh berries, the spoils of a European breakfast buffet, similar everywhere but for the regional additions, the herring in Scandinavia, the baked beans in England.

"No, I'm the one who's sorry." Is he apologizing for rejecting her? For missing out on an experience? Both? "Join me?"

She's less put-together in the morning, as everyone is. No makeup, hair tied back, baggy tee shirt, jeans. She looks more real, here in the breakfast room in bright daylight, a real person with real feelings, not an impossibly sexy stranger at a glamorous party, where she was more of an idea, an ideal, than a reality. This is no goddess. Just a mortal woman who if she really tries can look fantastic, especially in candlelight.

"Look, I—no, let me finish—I'm sorry, Will." She takes a seat. "I'm not like that. It was just that I felt such a . . . connection, last night. Didn't you?"

He nods.

"And the truth is, I'm in a relationship too. I'm not married, or even engaged, but we might . . ." She trails off, staring at a spot in the distance, the rough plaster wall. "I just didn't want last night to end. And that's what happens next, isn't it? Kissing?"

Yes, he thinks, that certainly is what happens next.

"But I know better, this morning. And thank God you knew better, last night."

"I'm not sure *better* is the right word."

She smiles, maybe blushes. She leans toward him. "It *was* fun, wasn't it?"

So they spend the morning together, the odd familiarity of two people who met and kissed last night, uneasy glances, a long walk on the paths among old roses, a drive into town for a predictably unsuccessful attempt to find a replacement charger for Elle's phone.

And then, suddenly, heartbreakingly: "I've a plane to catch."

Will wonders if it makes any sense to drive her to the airport. Is that the type of relationship they now have? He doesn't want to overstep the boundary, to ruin something good with something not. But he has never been here, isn't sure where this boundary is.

He kisses her on the cheek. There: that's the boundary.

But then right away he crosses it, leaving his lips on her skin for one second, and two, and ten, for far too long. But she never pulls away. She continues to make it clear that she isn't going to be the one who stops.

When he finally leans away, she sighs, looks him the eye, "Bye-bye" in a melodic voice, which is one of the many things he adores about this woman he didn't know yesterday, and will probably never see again.

ST-JEAN-DE-LUZ

Will pokes around the old town's whitewashed rusticity, the crescent beach, the striped deck chairs and faded umbrellas, the distinct sense that this place used to be chic, but that was a world war ago, maybe two. There's always charm to faded glory, but also the melancholy of a moment past, a perfection irretrievably lost.

He occasionally realizes that he's grinning, that he looks silly, smiling to himself like a simpleton. But he can't help it, his mind keeps darting back to that arched eyebrow, those smiling dimples, that delicious kiss. How did this happen? So quickly?

The last time Will felt this way was after his first evening with Chloe, whom he'd known for years but only vaguely until their proper first date, a magical night. The next day he was walking back from a tedious lunch with someone who was frustratingly non-Chloe, beaming there on West Forty-third Street, when through his self-involved fog he heard, "What the hell are you so giddy about?" It was his old friend Dean, blocking the sidewalk.

"A girl," Will had said, unnecessarily. There's only one reason that men walk around looking like that. This was a half-decade ago.

Will returns to his hotel room overlooking the pool that hangs over the cliff. He lies in bed with the laptop in his lap, and works up his notes from yesterday and last night. His narrative arrives, inevitably, at the detail he's been saving for last, another delayed pleasure.

He Googles Elle Hardwick, first for images, a handful of smiling-for-the-camera snapshots, all local to Australia, including a blood-rushing bikini pose on a beach, sunglasses, cleavage, a tanned tight tummy, hip cocked. Oh good God.

He takes a bracing dip in the cool pool, then tries to call his wife.

After a nearly perfect dinner—oysters, sea bass, Meursault, galette—in a nearly perfect dining room with a view of the sun sinking into the Atlantic, Will returns to his nearly perfect room. He hammers out the remainder of his notes, then starts turning slapdash sketches into grammatically complete sentences, into complete paragraphs, into a full story about food and wine and springtime in southern France.

But his mind keeps returning to Elle. He fights the urge to search for her again, to text her, to call her, to get on a goddamned plane and find her. Because in that impossible universe where he can live other realities, he'd like the other one to be here, in this other place, with this other woman.

PYRÉNÉES-ATLANTIQUES

The little Fiat whines on the steep ascent, climbing away from the coastline into the sere ragged mountains, sun-bleached and forbidding. He spends an hour visiting with a retired French pilot at his farm, being introduced to each goat by name. He has lunch with a Basque nationalist in a lively partisan bar, a loud game of pelota on the wall outside, soccer on the television. Conversation isn't easy through an ad hoc interpreter from the Basque into Spanish, a language in which Will is far from fluent. He's not sure how much he has understood.

Will continues driving into the mountains, the signs of civilization increasingly sparse, quiet little villages where everyone is somewhere else except the dogs and old people. He listens to the reassuring progress reports from the GPS that he'd unpacked from Inez's nylon case, a labelmaker's strip glued to the backside, PROPERTY OF TRAVELERS. RETURN TO LOCAL BUREAU.

He turns off the main road, bumps along a narrow rutted lane that follows the banks of a stream, curving and climbing, potholes filled with puddles from an earlier downpour, weather he missed down at sea level. The going is slow.

"Arriving at. Destination."

The hamlet is tiny, a dozen structures, none commercial, clustered near an oxbow in the stream.

He walks to a pump on the side of the street, pistons the handle, eliciting a gush of water. He cups his hand and takes a sip, cold and clear and perfect. He snaps a picture of the pump, painted an incongruous shade of pink, recently.

Will walks to the stream, wide and shallow and filled with rocks. A footpath runs along the banks, and Will follows it upstream, toward the tall mountains, blue against the low late-afternoon light, the sinking sun on the far side. He can't hear any sounds other than natural ones, the rushing water and the birds, a goat in the distance, a braying horse.

His mind drifts back to Elle, to that overpowering sense of infatuation, of mutual attraction, of an uncontrollable force that one day isn't there and the next day suddenly appears, undeniable, irresistible. What is it that makes one person love another? Is it the shape of her face, the elegant curve of her long neck, the purely physical? Is it the arch of her eyebrow, the way she leans forward to listen, the dimples when she smiles? Is it the dimples themselves? Why the hell would anyone love face indentations?

Is it what she says, or how she says it? Is it the things she believes, or the things she knows, or how she reconciles the difference? Is it her jokes? The music and books she likes, how she dances? Who she thinks she is, who she wants to become? Is it any of those things? What *is* a person, and why does one fall in love with another?

Will stumbles, distracted, the path narrow and uneven and difficult to manage, especially when it veers along the rocky banks of the meandering river. He's afraid of falling in. He picks up a waist-high branch, strips it of twigs and leaves, and starts using it as a walking stick. The light is nearing the golden hour, and the sky is coming alive with the birth of bugs in clouds, and the murmurations of starlings, and the call-and-response of bird conversations. He stops to snap pictures, to jot notes, to focus on being here.

The stream tumbles down a modest rapids. At the bottom is a wide pool where a white-haired man is standing in waders, fly-casting. Will watches the guy cast, a long graceful arc of filament, the man-made midge landing on the water with an inaudible plink, pulled across the surface in hops, attracting ripples from trout underneath, but not a nibble. The man casts again, an exact replica of the previous, with exactly the same result. And again.

"¡Buenas dias!" Will calls out. "Yo soy Will Rhodes. Yo—"

"You're American?"

"Yes," Will says. "I am. Are you?"

The man nods. He begins to wade toward the bank, through water that Will can now see is moving faster than he would've thought. The man takes a tentative step in unpredictable footing, then another, then holds out his hand.

"Taylor Lindhurst. Nice to meet you, Will. You're a tourist?"

Will shakes his head. "Journalist, sort of. I'm a travel writer."

"You don't say."

"I do. Are the trout biting?"

"Well, not in the past couple minutes, since you showed up and started making a fuss. But yeah, in general. I catch my dinner here most nights."

"Not a bad diet. You live here?"

"Yes sir. Retired out here." Despite the white hair, this guy doesn't appear to be retirement age. Or if he is, he's very well preserved. Lean, strong-looking, forearm muscles rippling, straining the collar of his tee shirt and fishing vest. He removes a pack of cigarettes from one of the pockets of his vest, then a shiny gold lighter, out of character with the rest of the getup.

"And you?" the guy asks. He exhales a long plume of dense smoke. "This is off the beaten path, ain't it?"

"I hope so. Otherwise someone's written about it before. Know what I mean?"

"Yes I do. Have you been to town?"

"Had a sit-down with old Rinaldo, holding court in the café. And went out to see Monsieur Larozze's goats. Interesting combination of Spanish and French and Basque up here, isn't it?"

"That's one of the things that appealed to me. The border is right over yonder a couple klicks." The guy indicates with his rod, fold after fold of scrub-covered hills leading to the rocky peaks of the high mountains.

"It's awfully remote."

"That also appealed. Listen, Mr. Rhodes, is it?"

"Yes."

"It's nice to meet you. But I'm runnin' outta time to catch my dinner. So unless there's somethin' special I can help you with?"

"Nothing in particular. Just trying to get a feel for the place. I'll let you get back to it. But do you mind if I take your photo? Write down your name?"

The man freezes, tensed, but then answers, "That would be fine. That's Taylor spelled as you'd expect, Lindhurst too, unless you're a very creative speller. I imagine you want to take my picture while I'm in the water?"

"Yes." Will smiles. "That would be great."

So Will snaps a photo of the guy standing in the trout stream somewhere along the French-Spanish border, casting a long perfect arc into the soft late-afternoon light. It's a pretty good shot, a gold star on a fine day.

"Nice to meet you, Mr. Lindhurst. Thanks for your time."

This is Will's life—in countries not his own, with people he doesn't know.

When Will is out of sight, Taylor Lindhurst casts again, but he has lost his concentration, and is no longer really fishing. What he is doing is killing time until the interloper is decidedly gone.

Then Taylor wades to shore. He glances after the journalist, doesn't see any sign of the guy. He packs his tackle quickly, growing more rushed with every item. He hustles down the path, stubbing his toe on a moss-covered rock. Comes up limping but continues to hurry, practically running when he hits the turnoff to the landscaped portion of his property.

He owns the entire side of this hill, a few hundred savage acres and a pristine stream, a sturdy old house surrounded by a wildflower field, a swimming pool to one side, and a very long driveway, the keys sitting in the ignition of a beat-up Renault truck. He wants to live well, but he doesn't want to look that way when he's in town, buying groceries.

Taylor stuffs items into his overnight bag, wondering if he should take the truck or hike into the mountains, over the border, disappearing into the wilds of northwestern Spain.

He never expected it to happen like this. If indeed this is really happening; he's not sure. It's possible that this guy is exactly what he claims, a harmless travel writer.

Taylor climbs into the faded yellow truck he bought from the same grizzled old farmer who sold the house to him. Taylor turns the ignition, a sputter, a cough, a stall.

Damn.

He primes the engine, turns the key again. Another sputter, another cough . . .

This time it turns over, thank God. He hopes he can reach the main road before the young American can return to his car, which probably sits a kilometer downstream.

The truck bumps down the narrow dirt drive, hemmed in on either side by tight dense shrubs and towering vine-choked trees, a spine-rattling thud through a deep pothole, the glove box popping open, ejecting insurance papers and his driver's license and a tattered Faulkner paperback he keeps in there for unanticipated reading opportunities.

He ignores the new mess, and twists his torso to retrieve his mobile from his pants pocket, but bangs his knee. Even in the privacy of his own truck, he refuses to cry out.

Taylor scrolls through his contacts, one distracted eye on the treacherous road, doing a poor job of both tasks, and the front right side of the vehicle suddenly falls away, a loud thud and a violent jarring that he feels in his entire body, with an emphasis on the rib cage and the top of his head, which hits the ceiling.

The truck is no longer moving.

"Damn." He pushes open the door, a creak and a hitch halfway through, a loud screech at the end, the panels hanging even less plumb now. But the upside is that with the truck stopped, Taylor can pay full attention to his phone. He finds the contact, hits Call.

Call failed.

"Oh you've got to be joking."

The single bar of reception blinks, disappears, reappears, disappears again. He shakes the phone, to no avail, to no surprise.

Taylor glances around, looking for altitude. He sets off away from the river, trudging through the low scrub and small trees, scrambling over dusty rocks. He looks at his screen, a solid single bar, a second bar flitting in and out, a flirty little tease.

He tries the call again, waits fifteen seconds for the ringing to commence, a multicarrier call to a different country.

Finally: "Yes?"

"It's Panther," he says. "I'm blown."

6

Will holds up his racquet, applauds into the strings, game-set-match to Malcolm, again. Will heads for the net, his water bottle.

"Good match," Malcolm says untruthfully, holding out his hand for the customary shake. Both men grab their phones, scroll through emails, searching screens for things they hope not to find: problems, urgency.

"So France was good?" Malcolm puts down his device, picks up his water, watches an errant ball bouncing away from another court. Malcolm follows the ball's path to the woman chasing it. Today is that first spring day when every woman in New York seems to be wearing something short.

"I *love* tennis skirts," Malcolm says, picking up the eternal thread. Malcolm's lust is equal-opportunity, everywhere, all the time, there are women he wants, and he tells Will about it. Will usually indulges the train of thought, but not today.

"France was terrific," Will says. "The wine-bar piece will be good. But I don't think there's anything to say about the château dinner. It didn't feel special." This is not true, not remotely, but the dinner's specialness isn't something Will can write about.

"Okay. Did you forward your notes to the Paris bureau?"

"Yes sir."

"You talk to anyone particularly interesting?"

Malcolm's new mandate is to try to make every single story personality-driven. Whether those personalities are international celebrities or local nobodies, people are supposed to be the hook of every story, a face in every photo, a quote in every column.

"Not really, no."

"Anything else?"

"Such as?"

"Don't give me that bullshit. You know such as what. I'm sure there was someone. There always is."

Will shakes his head.

"Come *on*." Malcolm punches him in the arm, not all that lightly. "Do you know when the last time I was on a date was?"

"These aren't *dating* trips, Mal. I'm not going on dates."

"Eleven years ago. Eleven goddamned years, you lucky bastard." Malcolm pulls his sweat-wet tee over his head, and Will can see the thick ugly scars across his shoulder, the wartime injury that changed his life. There's also the leg scar from a previous life-changing injury, a quarter-century ago. Malcolm is a constellation of scars.

"And you're gallivanting around the world in your cuff links, with women heaving themselves at you in five-star hotels. Let a guy live vicariously, will you? I'm dying here."

"Really? It looks to me like you have the perfect everything. What is it you're complaining about, exactly?"

"It's all just different shades of green, Rhodes." He pulls on a fresh shirt. "So are you telling me you didn't stumble across one single interesting attractive woman?"

There's a certain amount of confessing—or would it be bragging?—that Will would like to do; discussing it would make it more real. But does he want that? Or would it be better if he forgot about it, turned it into a fantasy instead of a memory? Maybe if he doesn't mention the kiss, if he keeps the truth of his small indiscretion—and it *was* small, he keeps telling himself—a secret, then maybe it doesn't really matter, maybe he didn't do anything terribly wrong. Just one kiss with an irresistible woman who threw herself at him. *And he resisted.*

He should get a goddamned medal, is what should happen. Or a citation, calligraphy, parchment, a wax seal. Albeit presented at a very low-key, extremely private ceremony.

"Well . . ."

"*Tell* me."

"There was this woman. Australian."

"*Ooh.* I *love* Australian women. They live on the *other side of the world.* The only thing better would be Japanese."

"We were leaving the dinner—we were all staying at the same inn, this was very late—and she asked me—get this—she asked me what *room* I was staying in."

"No way. No *fucking* way. So what did you do?"

"I'll tell you, it was hard."

"I bet it was."

Will wonders if Malcolm will ever behave like a grown-up. A married man in his mid-forties with two schoolchildren, the editor of a famous magazine, dozens of people working for him. Shouldn't this guy be an adult? Or is there no such thing? Maybe all men are permanently trapped in psychological adolescence. Some just do a better job than others of hiding it.

"I can't tell you, Mal, how attractive—how appealing in every single way—this woman was."

"Show me a picture."

"It's not just that she was great-looking." Will opens his phone to the web browser, a few pages already loaded, among them a search of Elle Hardwick images. "And smart and funny and entertaining, and that accent—"

"I *love* that accent."

"—but it was clear that she wanted me."

Taps his screen, a picture of a browned blond bikini'd babe.

"And her desire was just . . . irresistible. Or, rather, extremely difficult to resist."

Behind them, a train rumbles by on the Williamsburg Bridge, a loud angry growl in the bright blue sky, one of those crisp cloudless days that Will has long thought of as September 11th weather, even if it's on the other side of the summer solstice.

Will hands over his phone. Malcolm looks down at the screen, then closes his eyes, and nods, as if finally comprehending a nugget of sage advice.

"You," Malcolm says, handing back the phone, "are a jackass. You know that?" Malcolm sighs. "We get only one life, Rhodes. It could end at any given moment—poof, over, dead. Don't you want more?"

"You know I do."

"Wouldn't it be better—fairer—if there could be *more* before we die? *More* experiences. *More* women. *More* everything. If you could just go bed a beautiful Australian woman in France? What would be the harm?"

They've covered this topic before.

"So, Rhodes, are you telling me that you did?"

"Did what?"

"Resist?"

Will takes a swig of water. "I always do."

Malcolm shakes his head.

"But I'll tell you," Will says, "*not* having sex with that woman? That was the hardest thing I've ever done."

Chloe pulls open the iron-and-glass door of Ebbets Field. She glances around the standard-issue industrial chic—bare brick walls, Edison bulbs hanging from cloth-covered wires, brass-bladed fans, recycled floorboards and matte metalwork and dark gray paint. It's the sort of studied place that she knows is going to feature small-batch bourbon and home-made bitters, with those really big ice cubes that stack one atop the other in a highball glass. Half the barstools are taken by dining-alone guys parsing the menu.

"Hello there." It's a good-looking stubbled man, with a great big smile for her.

"Oh my God, if it's isn't Dean Fowler. What in God's name are you doing here?"

"Will didn't tell you?"

"No."

"I'll have you know that I own this place."

"Really? Since when do writers own restaurants?"

"Well, co-own. Which is to say that I dumped a shitload of money into the build-out, and since opening night I haven't seen anything except more outstretched hands. It turns out that a pretentious gastropub isn't quite the fail-safe investment vehicle I'd been led to believe." He gives Chloe a once-over. "You're looking pretty damn good, Chloe Palmer. You know that?"

"I'm married, Dean." She gives the smallest grin she can manage, which isn't that small. "I go by Rhodes now."

"Of course you do. Can I get you something?" He beckons the bartender with no more than raised eyebrows. "This is Marlon, our resident professor of mixology."

Marlon nods.

"I'll have a Negroni, rocks." She knows she's supposed to specify the brand of gin, probably the vermouth too, but she refuses. Marlon, to her relief, doesn't ask, despite the seriousness of his tie-barred skinny necktie and his sleeve garters and his porny little mustache.

"Were you always this hot, Chloe Palmer?" Dean meets Chloe's eye firmly, direct and unambiguous.

Marlon grins down into his mixing glass, with the look of a man who's heard something similar before, and not just once or twice.

"Or is it that marriage to Will has treated you surprisingly well?"

Chloe doesn't dignify any of this banter with a response; she knows that Dean doesn't expect one. He's just tossing these lines out there, information to be filed away, a port in a storm. But it's a good compliment to get. As part of her post-*Travelers* lifestyle, she has been exercising like a madwoman, and it's nice for someone to notice, and to say so. Will hasn't.

Dean and Will have been friends for a long time, but recently they'd been drifting apart. Chloe didn't kid herself that it was because Dean had a thing for her—he wasn't the type. In fact she suspected it was the opposite: Dean resented Chloe for domesticating Will, for absenting him from singles bars and ski weekends and all the other fun that Dean manufactured. As a married couple, they hadn't socialized with Dean once.

"So you finally succumbed," Dean says, "to the inevitability of Brooklyn." He has the sense to push past his own ridiculous come-ons. "Your parents' house, is it?"

"My dad bought it as an investment. But he filled it with a variety of problems that are nearly impossible to get rid of." The house, like so many other of Chloe's parents' pursuits, was not in itself a terrible idea. But they had an uncanny knack for half-assed execution, poor timing, and bad luck. Then her dad died, and Chloe inherited the problems.

Will was the one who'd been convinced they should fix it up. "We can do this," he'd said. "We're good at doing things!"

"Are we?" Chloe hadn't been so sure. They were by no means a broadly competent couple. Will was good at a small handful of things, and Chloe was good at most of the same plus a few other skills, none of which had anything whatsoever to do with fixing up a house.

"We could be!" he'd said. "It'll be fun."

"Are you sure? That's not what people tend to say."

"But"—he pulled her close, kissed her on the lips—"that's what we'll say."

Will had been confident that they were special, that they'd be immune to the problems that beset other couples, rip them apart. His irrational optimism, his unwavering belief in the possibility of perfection, was one of the things Chloe had loved most about Will, a foil for her own dispassionate pragmatism. Now it has become one of the things that makes her crazy. And although their old apartment on the Lower East Side had been tiny, cockroach-infested, and even dangerous, at least the infrastructure problems had not been their responsibility.

"The house doesn't look quite, ah . . ."

"Finished? No, it certainly isn't." She tries to project that this isn't the most welcome topic. "Anyway, congratulations! I saw you were at the Oscars. That must've been amazing."

"I've never felt so insignificant in my life. I couldn't get out of L.A. fast enough. I think I was still plastered when I got off the plane here, and bought this joint to make myself feel better."

"And did it?"

"Tell you the truth, yeah. I feel pretty good, Chloe Palmer. Do you?"

"In general."

"I heard you left *Travelers*. Mind if I ask why?" Dean is skimming a lot of topics whose depths Chloe doesn't want to explore. "Did you have enough of working for that tiresome douchebag Malcolm Somers?"

She forces herself to hold Dean's gaze. "Malcolm's not so bad. But when Will joined the staff, we thought that two travel writers for one magazine in one marriage would be one too many low-paid absentee spouses. We'd never see each other. *Ever.* Plus, you know, print journalism is not what's referred to these days as a growth industry. So it seemed prudent for one of us to, um, divest from our single revenue source."

"Why you?"

"Will was brand-new, and he was excited about the magazine. Me, I'd been there a decade. That's a long time with one employer, doing the same thing. Life isn't that long, and it's getting shorter every day, and it seemed like maybe I should see if I could do something else with my life."

"So what is that something else?"

She knew this question was coming, and she knew she wouldn't have a great answer for the eminently enviable Dean Fowler, who has three careers flourishing at once. "Right now, I'm still trying to figure it out. In the meantime I'm doing a little of this, a little of that. I'm part-time at an advertising agency, writing advertorials."

"Ooh. Sexy."

"Plus articles for wherever, traveling now and then." She shrugs. "You know, freelance life. Just like you, albeit without the bestsellers and the literary prizes and the Academy Award nominations and the question-able investment choices and the long line of pretty young things waiting to unfurl their panties for you."

"You know you could always jump to the head of that line, don't you?"

Now that Chloe has wandered down this alley, she doesn't quite know how to exit. "So this place is draining your bank account, huh?"

Dean accepts her non sequitur with equanimity. "You know, I've never in my life made a single decision based on money."

"And yet here you are, rich."

"And yet here I am. Just so."

Chloe takes a sip of her drink, and watches Dean's eyes watching her mouth, and she lets that moment play out. It doesn't take much effort to make men useful. She runs her tongue across her lips.

"Ah!" Dean says, his attention shifted over her shoulder. "There he is!"

Chloe spins around to see her husband, popped up out of nowhere. But that's not true, not at all: it's her husband, appearing exactly where and when he's supposed to appear. She'd allowed herself to forget that, to forget Will, momentarily blinded in the flattering attention of another, more engrossed, less familiar man.

She halfway regrets never having been to bed with Dean, finding out what the big deal is. Another experience she has never had, never will. For a long time she thought of life as an accumulation of experiences, but recently she's realized that it's also the opposite: a narrowing. Living the same day, over and over.

This is one of the reasons she left *Travelers,* looking for new ways to fill her days, to crawl out onto a different, more exposed branch of her career's tree. She hasn't yet found any fruit out there.

FALLS CHURCH

Raji is packing up, contemplating dinner, when Brock struts by, his shirt-sleeves rolled up, carrying a squeeze ball, distorting the SEMPER FI tattoo on his hypertrophied forearm. "Whassup, Raj-man?"

Raji nods at his supervisor while the tiny tinny speakers of his monitor bling at him, a supposedly pleasant trill that drives Raji berserk. This new alert is an advance check-in to a flight that departs tomorrow evening, a long-haul overnight trip to another hemisphere.

U.S. PASSPORT NUMBER: 11331968
FLIGHT: 8 JFK TO EZE
TICKET CATEGORY: B2
SEAT: 19D
ALERT CODE: 4

This guy sure does get around. Raji himself hasn't been out of the northern Virginia suburbs in a half-year, hasn't even been into D.C. proper since last fall. He has never left the United States in his entire life. And here is this guy, just back from France, headed to Argentina. Who the hell knows why.

But why is not Raji's concern. Raji's concern is that he's hungry, and it's 6:08. The Chinese place last night was, no question about it, horrible. To-night he should beat a safe retreat to the greasy, salty, fast, cheap dependability of Applebee's. Tomorrow night, maybe, he'll try something new.

"Listen, Raj-man, I just received new marching orders for you, from our mystery client."

As far as Raji is concerned, all the clients are mysteries. There are hundreds of them, all identified solely by codes, which he assumes represent operations within the CIA, or possibly in other governmental agencies. Raji sends his alerts and his reports via a closed network to numerical accounts that aren't associated with any names, any locations, any clue who's on the other end of his communications.

One client is even more mysterious than others, outside the standard protocols. All the resulting intel is eyes-only, with no VDA management in the loop. Even in the context of VDA's hush-hush standards, this is notably secretive. And yet more mysterious is that Raji himself was specifically requested by the client, a circumstance that prompted Brock to ask, "Who did you have to blow?" When this client put in the request six months ago, Raji had no idea why. He still has no idea.

"Your watch list has been narrowed down to a dozen, Raj-man. Much smaller list, obviously, but intensely expanded coverage."

Raji clicks his keyboard and reexamines the screen. Most of the people on this shortened list work for a magazine in New York City; some of the others are their spouses. A couple are foreign citizens, living abroad. This is a strange combination of people to monitor.

"The client wants absolutely everything on these subjects—every card swipe, ATM withdrawal, phone call, text message, E-ZPass scan, online order. Anything whatsoever, anytime, anywhere."

NEW YORK CITY

Will kisses his wife, long and lithe and impeccable, high heels and a hip-hugging skirt and a scoop neck with a pendant necklace that makes it impossible to ignore her breasts. There's something cold in Chloe's response, perfunctory. Is this a fresh fight they're in? Or just the remnants of an old one? It's sometimes hard to tell where one ends and another begins, and Chloe has a tendency to hold on to them tenaciously, all of them.

Will knows that of course he *should* be in the doghouse. But how can Chloe know? She can't. Maybe she senses something coming off him, some aura of wrongdoing. He certainly feels it.

For a few days after Elle, Will had been elated, traveling in beautiful places, with a fresh wonderful memory, and the immense sense of well-being from knowing that he was desired by the one person in the world he most desired. What's better?

But the thrill wore off, and his eventual flight back to New York was a tortured exercise in sappy self-loathing. He opened his computer and worked badly, then he opened a book and read distractedly, then he watched a mediocre movie halfheartedly. The flight seemed to go on for-ever.

He arrived home tired and sad, and not at all sure what the point had been, in the end, of saying no to Elle. He had lost something there in France: he'd lost his rightness, and his certainty. And he can't see what he'd gained.

And now here he is, standing beside his wife, listening to Dean asking, "So, Will, how's life on the road?"

Will puts his arm around Chloe's waist. "Not bad; you know they make it easy for me. Safe places, like Argentina tomorrow. But *you*! Everything good?"

The spy accusation leveled against Will is a popular idea of a joke, or at least Will thinks it is. But against Dean, it's not. Dean has spent large chunks of his career as an international journalist in dangerous places, always accompanied by the conjecture that he's chummier than necessary with Langley's operatives.

"Never better."

"Dean doesn't think our house project looks quite finished," Chloe interjects. "Surprised that we're willing to live in such a dump, I think is what he was communicating to me."

"Houses are never-ending works in progress," Dean says. Will can see Chloe roll her eyes, annoyed that another man appears to be taking Will's side, though Will doesn't like to think of them as on opposing sides.

Their dining companions arrive, another brownstony-Brooklyn couple, with bro-hugs and cheek-kisses and introductions to Dean. The foursome head to their table in the dimly lit dining room, with the hand-written chalkboard menu replete with the inescapables—the kale salad and heritage pork and house-cured charcuterie, organic everything, lo-cally sourced and painstakingly provenanced, of a piece with ride-share bicycles and recycled denim and vintage vinyl. Suddenly Will feels like a cliché, like he's living in one of his own articles, eating meals in res-taurants that have been written about dozens of times before, by him, in the company of people he may have invented out of his imagination. The waitress reading specials from her pad, reciting the catchphrases he hears in his sleep—the "line-caught" that follows "tonight our fish is a," the "medium-rare" that comes after "the chef recommends."

Will can anticipate all two hours of couple-y conversation, the preordained debate about the second bottle of wine, the halfhearted tussle for the check, always 20 percent more than anyone expects it to be, everywhere, all the time.

He can imagine the slow walk home, the streetlight streaming in the window, flickering through the swaying branches of the oak, as his wife lies back in bed, spreading her legs, guiding him in and shutting her eyes, licking her lips and bucking her hips, and he can't help but wonder if Chloe will be pretending that someone else is atop her, while he pictures himself thrusting between the long tan Australian legs of Elle Hardwick.

"Hey," Will says, rubbing his eyes. "What's happening?"

"Can't sleep. Going for a run." Chloe kisses her husband on the top of his explosion of bed-heady hair. "Go back to sleep. Love you."

Out on the sidewalk, she looks both ways before setting off. This neighborhood is gentrifying, in the present tense; housing projects loom at the end of the block, known drug dealers occupy a nearby corner with the disciplined rigor of a military platoon. Chloe doesn't wear headphones when she jogs these streets; she doesn't want to lose track of herself, of her surroundings, their dangers.

It takes twenty minutes of running west to arrive at land's end, at the riverfront amid the bridges that connect Brooklyn to Manhattan, all of them huge structures, astounding feats of engineering and construction. She can't imagine bridges like these getting built today. That's no longer how public-sector America works.

Not a soul is visible to the end of the street, which dead-ends at an unoccupied park, a buffer between the refurbished industrial buildings and the shimmering quilt of river, reflecting the lights from the bridges and skyscrapers beyond. She can't help but think of Woody Allen, I don't care what anyone says, this city is a knockout.

She turns her back to the knockout view, faces up the street.

A man turns the corner. He too is a jogger, running toward her, quickly but unrushed, long legs and an athletic stride, a slight limp. As he approaches she can see his ratty tee shirt, HARVARD FOOTBALL, an ill-considered choice, an adamant invitation: mug me!

Chloe scans the cobblestoned street, the darkened windows of loft buildings, the eerie black voids behind the windshields of a dozen cars. Her eye is drawn to a rat scurrying into a drainage grate, down into the invisible world beneath the street.

The man is slowing. Then he's walking. He comes to a stop a few feet from her.

"Hi Malcolm," she says.

"Chloe." He kisses her on the cheek. "You look fantastic."

"Thanks."

"I guess this change has been good for you?"

She looks away from his accusatory gaze. "It was time, Mal."

He nods. "Do you want to hear that I miss you?"

She doesn't answer.

"Well I do."

"Mal—"

He holds up his hand. "But that's not why I needed to see you tonight."

He takes a taxi back across the river. A half-mile from home, he gets out of the cab, and jogs the rest of the way. Malcolm doesn't particularly want the additional ten minutes of exercise, and his knee is really sore. His goal is visual in a more short-term sense: he needs to work up a credible sweat. Because what he doesn't want is to be caught by his wife returning from a supposed midnight jog sweat-free. Allison would think he'd been with someone, and Chloe might be whom she'd suspect. Allie is an irrational mess these days. But she'd be halfway correct.

Malcolm is running against traffic, headlights in his face, horns blaring, lights blinking on bicycles.

He's worried about Will. Malcolm had assumed he'd be able to trust Will with no reservations, without needing to worry about Will snooping, or being compromised, or being any type of pain in the ass. That's why Malcolm hired Will to begin with: to be reliable. But suddenly he's looking a bit un-.

Malcolm is also concerned about this new life of Chloe's. And about Gabriella too—she has had a truly terrible year.

Plus Malcolm is always concerned about *Travelers*—the day-to-day challenges of putting out a magazine, of managing existing staff and hiring new, of precarious finances. And of course he's worried about the secrets.

It's all so tenuous, always so close to falling apart.

Around the next corner is the front entrance to his building, but he keeps jogging past it.

When he and Allison were apartment-hunting last year, one of Malcolm's few requirements—unspoken—was that their new home offer two different exits, on two different streets. He had a hard time investigating this while touring apartments with the broker. "Is there a garage? I'd like to see it," he'd said. "The laundry room is in the basement? Can we check that out?" Allie had looked at him like he'd lost his marbles.

Small buildings were out of the question, unless they were on a corner lot. Eventually Malcolm had to claim to Allie that he wanted to live in a big building, a starchitect skyscraper with twenty-four-hour doormen and a live-in super and a garage and, you know, *amenities.* In truth the only amenity he wanted was a back entrance on the next street.

He needed a way to sneak out, and a way to sneak back in, which is exactly what he does now, drenched with sweat to mask his secrets.

7

Will suffers through a deeply disturbing tango show, a nightmare interlude in a David Lynch movie. As an antidote he heads to a karaoke bar, which is one of the things he does to amuse himself at eleven at night, in other countries, alone.

He sings "What a Good Boy." His college band once warmed up for Barenaked Ladies in a little club in Wicker Park, a lucky gig to have landed, back when Will vaguely imagined that music was what he'd do. The band imploded due to a love triangle, nothing to do with talent or ambition, just the predictable entanglements of youth. Six months later Will had a new girlfriend, and a busier position on the school newspaper.

He steps off the small stage, and notices a text message from someone he doesn't know, an unfamiliar local number, giving an address. *Who's this?* Will replies.

Luis! Esteban's cousin!

Esteban is the hotel concierge. Will gets the distinct feeling that Esteban is an avid procurer of whatever it is that his guests could want. Will wonders what exactly Esteban has anticipated Will wants. But the club is nearby, and as a rule Will really does say yes to everything. It's not a come-on line he uses on beautiful Australians.

Will picks his way around the uncollected dog-shit and trash on the sidewalks under the palm trees, he pays the cover and tips the doorman, he jumps around on a foreign dance floor until he's soaking with sweat, his pores purging the Malbec and the lingering chill of the tango, those middle-aged men with their Brilliantined hair, those women with too much rouge and too high heels, their gazes lingering too long, too close, too needy for too much.

"Here!" Luis pushes a shot glass across the bar to Will. Then another pair in the other direction, toward two young women. "*¡Salud!*"

All four of them throw back their little glasses of potent liquor, grimace.

"I miss America!" Luis screams, apropos of nothing. "I attended college in North Carolina! Two years! This is our other cousin Magdalena! And her friend Tatiana!"

"*¡Mucho gusto!*"

"*¡Hola!*"

Will looks at the women, two barely distinguishable versions of the same type of Argentinean sexiness, long dark everything.

"*Oyé*, Will!" Luis leans closer, exuding a potpourri of liquor and cigarettes and sweat. "We leave to go to after-hours party! Stay until dawn!" Luis taps his nose. "It is Friday night!" Explanation enough. "You come?"

The dance club is in the basement of a mid-fifties apartment building on a boulevard lined with similar structures, Travertine marble and potted palms, doormen behind wide desks in glass-walled lobbies. With the disco and the blow, the whole thing seems like Miami in the eighties, Don Johnson about to show up, flash that fictional smile. But instead these real girls flash their own real smiles.

It's as if the whole world is conspiring to turn Will into an adulterer. It's comical, flirting with tragic.

"*Muchas gracias,*" Will says, backing away once again from the tragicomedy. "But I'm sorry to say"—hand on Luis's shoulder, sincere regrets—"I cannot join you."

CAPRI

The American woman glances at her buzzing phone, an incoming text message from her husband, a photo of a pretty place. *Wish you were here. How's Istanbul?*

She looks around this cliffside terrace, a picture-postcard view of the sea, the cliffs of Capri, the Sorrento Peninsula in the distance, the Amalfi coast, Positano, storied places. She arrived here just a couple hours ago after two planes, a ferry, and a taxi.

She checks the weather app on her phone, the forecast for Istanbul.

Humid, rainy, gross, she types. *Wish I was there.*

She puts down her phone. Lights a cigarette, suppresses a cough. Jesus, how do people smoke these things? But cigarettes present a lot of opportunities. For example: to stand, to saunter across the terrace, where she collects an ashtray from a different table, all of this activity affording her the excuse to scout her surroundings.

She carries the ashtray to the low wall that separates the *terrazzo* from the hundreds of feet of nearly vertical cliff down to the boulders of the shoreline. It's not a serviceable beach down there, offering no access to any outpost of humanity, no road or path. Just wild seacoast, severe and beautiful and perfect.

"*Un'altra limonata, Signora Delgado?*" the waitress asks. Marina Delgado is the name she's using here in Italy; that's even what she's calling herself in her head. Marina Delgado.

"*Sì, grazie.*" She had a friend in middle school named Marina, which makes it easier.

There are eleven hotel guests lounging on the floral-print canvas cushions that match the umbrellas, surrounded by ceramic planters of cactus and lavender, and wrought-iron table frames topped with pebbled glass holding beaded drinks and glossy magazines and folded eyeglasses. Marina herself is wearing giant sunglasses, frames that cover half her face. She's not recognizable, not unless someone is looking for her, and no one would be.

There are more luxurious hotels on the island. Better restaurants. Bigger suites and grander lobbies and more resourceful concierges. What this hotel offers is this landscaped platform hundreds of feet above the Tyrrhenian, facing the craggy cliffs that rise dramatically from the azure sea dotted with sailboats and speedboats, the mainland on the horizon. It doesn't get any prettier. If you stay in this hotel, you lie on this terrace. That's the point.

Right now there's a German couple out here, both tall and pink and muscled.

A fat mustached man who looks possibly Spanish.

A pair of teenage girls, both staring at their devices, the view and surroundings lost to them, inhabiting social-media worlds, the locale nothing in its own right, just another selfie backdrop, here I am, please look at me, tell me you like me.

Another pair of middle-aged women—the girls' mothers?—are sitting far away, giving the girls privacy, talking in hushed tones, exchanging bits of gossip, mortifying anecdotes about other teenage girls, their bad choices and predictable outcomes.

A trio of pensioners, perhaps a married couple with a spinster sister.

Marina is the eleventh person, just another scantily clad woman reading fashion magazines and smoking cigarettes on a chaise longue at a fancy hotel. Noticeable, but also ordinary. There are always people like her in places like this.

Now a twelfth person arrives, wearing one of the hotel's sea-green terry-cloth robes, ostentatious gold crest embroidered on the breast.

Marina feels her pulse accelerating while she delays looking directly at the newcomer, until she can't help herself anymore, and then from the safety of her sunglasses she redirects her eyes to examine his face—

But no.

ARGENTINA

Will rides horses at an estancia, learns to rustle livestock, to milk cows at sunrise. He looks the lamb in the eye before the farmer slits its throat and hangs the carcass from the rafters, draining blood into a dented tin bucket.

The next night they grill the lamb on an iron spit over a wood fire in an open pit, and eat big chunks, hewn by a machete, accompanied by an unlabeled bottle of young Malbec from the neighboring finca.

Will can now go an entire day without thinking about Elle, who's fading into his past, dragging his guilt out with her receding tide. He'll be fine.

CAPRI

The ice in her drink melts. The late-afternoon wind picks up, flapping the umbrellas, blowing around the cellophane wrapping of a cigarette packet. The magazine slips from her lap and tumbles to the terra-cotta tiles.

Marina wakes with a start, momentarily unaware of where she is, of who she is, with the dry pucker of a jet-lagged mouth. She takes a swig of her watery warm *limonata*, and runs her tongue around the inside of her mouth, rubs the sleep out of her eyes.

She looks around the patio, whose contents have shifted somewhat during her unintentional nap. There's a new person out here. A man, white hair, late-middle-aged but very fit, virile looking, confident.

She gathers her wits, focuses her mind. She carefully examines the other guests, a somewhat different crowd from before she fell asleep, and the waitress, and the pool boy. She checks the time, checks her messages. Thinks through her plan, yet again, step one and step two, steps three and four and five, up through eighteen, all the things she's going to do, and when, and what alternatives she'll pursue if something goes wrong, her mind buzzing, her body coming alive—

And then: stop.

Deep breath, exhale. Deep breath, exhale. Just like yoga. Except sort of the opposite.

She taps a cigarette out of the packet. Tries the lighter once, twice, failing to ignite. She shakes the thing, and flicks her thumb across the wheel again, again, again, growing visibly frustrated. "Fuck," she mutters.

Marina glances around the terrace, as if she's searching for evidence of other smokers, but that's just pretend, she already knows what she's going to find, and where. She stands and adjusts her bikini, a garment that no one, anywhere, would consider modest. She can feel the man's eyes turn her way, an instinctive reaction.

She takes a step, pauses, as if reconsidering. She bends over—again, confident that she's drawing attention—and plucks up a towel, wraps it around her waist. She wants to be seen to be a woman who doesn't want to seem titillating on an outrageous level.

She walks across the tiles, one foot and then another, repeat, repeat, and remember to breathe evenly, in, out, in, out.

"*Scusi?*" She smiles down at this man, but not too warmly. A perfunctory smile is what she's going for, the type of smile a pretty young woman gives a man because she wants something, and thinks she has to be nice to get it. "*Parla inglese?*"

"Yes," he says, "I do." He's better-looking than she expected.

"Might I use your lighter? Mine seems to be, um, dead."

"Of course." The heavy gold lighter has a smooth action, a steady blue flame, a pleasant click when the cover closes. This lighter is not to her taste, but she'd like to keep it anyway. Maybe she will, a souvenir. Though that's obviously a mistake.

"*Grazie*," she says, then returns to her chaise, walking slowly.

Step three: complete.

ARGENTINA

"This certainly seems like quite a life," Will says, looking over the wide-open expanse of the plains, seemingly limitless, boundless, anything possible. The two nearest big cities, Buenos Aires and Santiago, are both five hundred miles away. "What the American West used to be, before it became shopping malls and call centers."

Fernando doesn't understand this, but doesn't bother asking for clarification. It's not part of his job description.

"Are there any Americans living out here? Retirees? Old people?"

"*Sí.*"

"Do you think we could find any? I'd like to talk to some."

So they go see the middle-aged couple from Nevada who bought a working cattle ranch, turned it into a bed-and-breakfast, but almost no one comes. A few towns away is a woman who left Palm Beach when she fell in love with a polo player, followed him to B.A. and got pregnant and then jilted, and moved out here to a new friend's guesthouse to raise her child, a horrifically thought-out parenting decision after what was clearly a long series of other ill-considered lifestyle choices.

"Want a glass of something?" she asks. Will is afraid of her, and her poor decision-making rubric. "The kid is asleep."

Will begs off, returns to the quiet ranch, an arthritic little terrier named Chico at his side while he writes, trying to stick to his regimen. Then he goes to sleep alone, in the middle of nowhere, far from home, again.

MENDOZA

The representative from the hotel chain is, as usual, a good-looking young woman, efficient and informative, an adequate guide and a companionable companion. She shows Will around the city, then drives out to their new flagship property in the nearby countryside, a sprawling lodge nestled in vineyards, with polo fields and a stocked lake and eighteen holes of golf, the Andes in the distance below a deep cerulean sky.

Will grabs a nap and a jog, a shower and a shave, a fresh shirt and tie, shoes shined.

"*Bienvenidos,* Señor Rhodes." The restaurant hostess smiles warmly, big white teeth and jet-black hair. "Please, this way." She leads Will across the fussy room, around a corner, down a few tiled steps, and through a wide wood-framed entryway into the large private dining room, already populated by people with glasses in their hands. Directly in front of Will is a blonde in a snug dress, facing away. A waiter hands Will a glass.

"*Gracias,*" Will says, and at the sound of his voice the blonde slowly turns, and looks over her shoulder—

8

I t's dark when she returns to the hotel, a harrowing taxi ride up the narrow winding road from the lively town where she had dinner.

"*Buona sera,*" she says to the girl at the front desk, dark hair and green eyes and the look of someone who'd much rather be doing anything else.

"*Buona sera Signora Delgado.*"

She continues through the dining room. Earlier, when she was reserving a table that she ultimately canceled, she'd glanced at the reservation book. So she knows that the white-haired man had an eight o'clock, so he should be finishing soon. She's confident that he'll be facing the door, which means that at this very moment he's watching her walk by.

What does he see? He sees her stumble, like a woman who's had too much to drink. He sees her reach down to remove one heel, then the other. He watches her exit the dining room on the far side, no doubt heading to the terrace, a young woman traveling alone in a romantic hotel, maybe suffering from a recent heartbreak, tipsy and vulnerable . . .

The breakfast room is empty, dimly lit. She drops her shoes into her voluminous handbag, and removes a simple-looking little box, six sides of stainless steel, one facet of which features a single switch, On-Off. She turns the switch to On. As she walks past the long buffet table, she sets this cube behind a tall vase of flowers, ten feet from where the wireless camera is mounted on the wall. The range of the device is supposedly fifty feet, but with these things it's always preferable to be closer, safer.

She uses her shoulder to push through the terrace door, and rushes around to the side gate, where she places a second small cube. Then she finds a seat, orders a bottle of house red from a waitress.

When the wine arrives she immediately dumps some of it into a potted plant, then a splash into her glass. She swirls the liquid, coating the glass, its rim. She takes a tiny sip, just enough to get the wine's color on her lips, on the rim. She's not drinking alcohol tonight.

She double-checks the view from the retaining wall. There's nothing she can see down there now, pitch-black. She searches for lights, for signs of habitation that were invisible in daylight, hidden among the dense vegetation. There appears to be a house off to the west, but not close enough to be an issue.

Okay, she thinks. There's nothing left to check, nothing left to plan. Nothing left to do but execute. She takes a deep, deep breath, and she waits.

MENDOZA

Will's mouth is hanging open.

"Fancy," she says, "meeting you here."

"My God" is all he can manage.

"Well, God*dess,* if you want to be precise. And I know you do."

They're still standing in the dining room's doorway. She leans toward him and he reciprocates, purses his lips into the air near her ear, as he would to thousands of other women. But he can feel her actual lips settle on his cheek, and rest on his skin for a second longer than they should.

"But who'm I to split hairs?" Looking him in the eye, clear and confident, holding him with a firmish fist encircling his arm, something of a caress with the side of her thumb.

He'd been working hard to pull his wife back into the forefront of his sexual consciousness. And he'd been succeeding, almost.

"In any case," she says, "it *is* lovely to see you, Will Rhodes. I wasn't sure I'd ever again have this particular pleasure. But why are you here?"

"Should I not be?"

"I thought you were European correspondent?"

"Well, Argentina is sort of European, isn't it?"

She squints at him.

"Our Americas man isn't terribly expert in wine, and that's putting it diplomatically. And we're looking for a wine story. So they sent me."

"You're a wine expert? You speak Spanish?"

"*Pfft*. This is Argentina. I'm getting by."

"Yes," Elle says, a mischievous grin sliding across her lips. "I'm quite sure you are."

This night, in this hemisphere, it's a much smaller table, just eight people. There's a lot of Spanish being spoken, too much for Will and Elle to fully engage in the conversational flow, so they turn to each other by necessity as well as preference.

It becomes another of those nights, hard to keep track of the food courses, the talk progressively looser and looser, with more and more laughter, with touching on the forearm and the wrist, two hands brushing. Elle glances down at the incidental contact, which was maybe not so incidental. "You have nice hands," she says, staring down at them. "Like a pianist. Or a pickpocket."

The already-thin ice, Will knows, is cracking.

Dinner is breaking up. People are exchanging business cards, shaking hands, promising to follow up about something or other, that lodge in Chile's Lake District, the winemaker who's doing interesting things in Extremadura.

Elle arches her eyebrow at Will. Damn that sexy eyebrow. "Won't you join me for the superfluous drink you know you want?"

Will can pretend to himself whatever the hell he wants to pretend, but he knows what she's asking. And he knows what his answer should be. But instead "Yes" is what he says.

They perch on plush seats in the lobby bar, consume I-don't-want-this-night-to-end drinks, accompanied by an unburdening of her past romances and disappointments, a conversation that's an unabashed invitation to intimacy, a second-date conversation and all that accompanies it—the flush, the butterflies, just like when he was fifteen years old, or twenty-five, but now at thirty-five he hasn't been on a second date in a long time, and he'd forgotten this part of it. Maybe he'll still feel this way at eighty-five? Or is this the last time he'll ever feel this way? Last times are obvious only in hindsight.

One A.M. sneaks up. The lobby is deserted now except for the night manager at the desk, who's looking down at something, probably his phone. The front doors are still open, the armed security guard leaning against a pillar out there.

"So," Elle says, but there's suddenly nothing left to say, now that they've shed the bartender's distant company, his implicit chaperoning. The talking portion of the night is finished. What remains to be seen is if there will be another portion of the night.

"Well," he says. "I guess this is good night." He can't bring himself to meet her eye.

"I'm down this corridor," she says. "You?"

Will reaches into his pocket, removes the big leather fob. Number 32. "I don't know." The number doesn't explain enough, and he can't remember, and he's confused.

"You are too," she says.

Has he ever done anything this hard? What has been more difficult than standing in this empty secluded corridor, late at night, alone with this beautiful woman who wants him—who has already invited him to bed—and not kissing her?

I am not a cheater, he thinks. I'm *not*.

But Will can feel the pull of her, gravitational, and the pre-kiss buzz in his head is deafening. He tries but fails to think of something that's not her, and the more he tries, the more insistent the images become, rapidly escalating from romantic to pornographic, the shape of her breasts, the scent of her, the feel as he slides—

Will turns halfway to Elle as she's already turning to him, both of them having made the same decision at the same moment, and neither needs to move feet to lean in, mouth on mouth, but bodies not touching.

Elle disengages her lips. She walks away, down the carpeted hall, without saying anything, leaving him standing there alone, arguing with himself . . .

CAPRI

The man is approaching slowly, cupping his postprandial cigarette at an upward angle, sheltering it from the wind, maybe a bit overprotective, or self-conscious. "It's a beautiful night, isn't it?" The trace of a Midwestern accent, but hard to place.

"Oh," she says, "I guess so." She's a dejected woman, not contemplating beauty. She's out here wallowing, is what she's doing.

"Do you mind if I join you?"

She opens her mouth but hesitates visibly before saying, "Sure."

He extends his hand, says, "My name is Sean." She knows this is not true. Sean Cullen is one of his many aliases. In the Spanish Pyrénées, he was apparently calling himself Taylor Lindhurst.

"I'm Marina," she says, giving her own false name. But he doesn't know that she's lying. At least she hopes not.

She's sitting on the low wall that separates the horizontal plane from the vertical, terrace from cliff, sea from sky. She puts down her glass, unsteady on the rough surface, tendrils of vegetation springing from the cracks and air bubbles of the volcanic rock. She shakes his hand, wonders if he can feel that her palm is moist, sweaty. He holds her hand a second too long, the unmistakable come-on, just as expected.

She has never done this before. She has come close—everyone like her has come close, she supposes. But she's never followed through, never gone all the way. She knew she'd be nervous at this point, but not this much, and it's probably not going to get easier if it takes longer.

It's time.

She picks up her glass to take the final sip, step number fifteen, and to initiate the most crucial sequence, the point of no return. But just as she's raising the glass she senses movement, and she glances over her shoulder.

It's the waitress again, being solicitous.

Marina supposes that the expected thing would be to ask the waitress for a glass, so this man can share her wine. She wants this man to stay with her, but she can't invite him. That would seem too forward, unnatural. Suspicious.

She cuts her eyes to her bottle, then away.

He notices. "Would you mind if I had a glass with you?"

"Um." She cocks her head: a drunk woman realizing she's a drunk woman who's maybe about to make a mistake. "Sure?"

"*Signorina*," he says to the waitress, "*un bicchiere, per favore?*"

So now she needs to wait. Waiting is most painful when you don't expect to do it.

MENDOZA

There is of course a bottle of wine in his room, and candles to help Will explore every inch of Elle's body, shoulders and breasts and neck and ears, the exquisite torture of extended foreplay, the lengths of her legs and the darkness between, straining and aching and finally exploding with spine-shuddering release.

And then, spent, a reassuring glow from within that lasts just seconds before regret initiates its counterattack, marching into Will's consciousness and establishing a forward position, accusatory and unforgiving, even as he's still short of breath, lying there on the soft sheets in the large bed, with this naked nubility straddling him, slicked with a sheen of sweat, the scent of sex. Will can feel the burning of scratches on his back, the soreness of his overteased cock, which he knows will soon be aroused again, sucked again, fucked again, because they will stay awake till sunrise, engaging every conceivable position, indulging every fantasy and scenario, extracting every possible memory from one night, because this won't—this can't—ever happen again.

He has imagined this moment before, the fantasy of a hotel bed on the other side of the world, with a beautiful woman who's not his wife. The reality is far better than he imagined, while at the same time much worse.

Elle climbs off him, and out of the bed, her body golden in the flattering flickering light. She pops a bottle top and pours herself a glass of water, drinks.

Will spins off his side of the bed, unlocks the French doors, pushes them open, a refreshing breeze fluttering the curtains, cooling his over-heated, over-aroused body. He looks out at the full moon, then falls back onto the bed.

But she doesn't. Instead, she's rooting around on the floor. She finds her panties, pulls them on. Her bra too.

"What are you doing?"

She locates the tiny pile of her dress.

"Why are you getting dressed?"

She pulls the little black dress over her head, shimmies into it. "Well," she says. "Thank you, Will Rhodes. I didn't expect to enjoy that."

He doesn't understand what she can possibly mean. He suddenly fears that he has fallen into the clutches of a psychopath. This possibility hasn't been Will's primary disincentive to adultery, but it has certainly ranked high on the list of compelling reasons to not cheat: the impossibility of knowing what another human being is capable of, motivated by, desperate for. Sex is putting your life in someone else's hands. And unless you really know that person, you can't know what will end up happening.

Something odd is happening right now, that's for sure, and Will doesn't understand it, doesn't know how to respond. Maybe this near stranger is playing some game, making Will's heart race for the sheer entertainment of it, another type of tease.

She sits on the edge of the bed and straps herself into her high heels, bright red fuck-me shoes of the highest order. She wipes a finger across her cheek. Is that a tear she just wiped away? Then she stands, and without glancing at Will or saying another word, she opens the door to the blindingly bright hall, and walks out.

What? Did that really just happen?

"Elle?" he calls out. "Hey! Elle?"

Then Will lies there, half-expecting her to walk back in. Did she go get ice?

A minute goes by. Two.

Will climbs out of the bed, vibrating with nervous energy. He pours himself a glass of water, downs it in one go, refills the glass with shaky hands. He pulls on pajama bottoms, ties an awkward knot. He returns to the bed and glances at the digital clock, 2:48 A.M.

He tries to lie still, confused, disturbed, staring at the ceiling. He pushes his hand through his hair, takes a deep breath. Did he just ruin his life?

That's when the door flies open.

CAPRI

The man is trying to impress her with anecdotes about a billionaire friend in Abu Dhabi, a gazillion-star resort in the Seychelles, et cetera, ad infinitum, ad nauseam. I'm rich, I'm important; my dick is big, let me put it in you.

Marina is not really listening. They're sitting side by side on the low wall, just a couple feet high, not tall enough to stop someone determined to vault over it, but enough to prevent stumbling mistakes.

She looks around the deserted terrace, and runs through her list again, the action steps, back to the beginning of their relationship, her initiation of that first encounter, a day and a half ago. A lot can develop during what looks like mostly nonevents:

1. Pull out cigarette, try to light it, fail
2. Look around for another smoker, go to him, get a light
3. Depart without being friendly
4. Reserve dinner table in person, for opportunity to check reservation book
5. Cancel table
6. Go to town for dinner, return via taxi
7. Walk through dining room, stumble as if tipsy
8. Pause, remove shoes, walk barefoot; all to draw attention
9. Place first wireless scrambler on table, second wireless scrambler on gate
10. When waitress arrives, order bottle of wine to terrace
11. Dispose of portion of bottle into potted plant
12. Pour two sips of wine into glass to dirty bowl and rim, take one sip
13. Sit on wall and wait
14. When man arrives, take final sip
15. Walk to table to refill glass
16. While walking, pull on glove in pocket
17. Return to wall
18. Stab man in neck with switchblade and push him off cliff

PART

II

9

Will returns to consciousness in layers. The first, outer layer is thin and vague, the sense that he's being dragged across the grass, his heel catching on something, twisting his leg, ouch, then some time later dumped, plunk, ouch again.

The second layer is thick, full of conjecture and fear and pain. There's the pain in his nose and cheek and lip from the punch; in the back of his head where it collided with the earth. But that's all nothing compared to the psychic pain of knowing that he's in trouble, probably deep, and that the trouble is his own fault.

Maybe some people know it when they're about to make the mistake of their lives. Pulling the ski mask over your face and walking into the bank. Turning the ignition while seeing triple from all that tequila. Not Will; Will hadn't known it. Maybe he should have. Now he does.

Will becomes aware that Elle is next to him, applying ice to his face, cubes in a washcloth. Will is reclined on the chaise in a corner. The man—the intruder—is across the room, upright in a chair, holding ice to his own face.

Did Will really imagine that he could simply have sex with this woman, this beautiful stranger, and there wouldn't be any consequences?

"Don't worry," Elle says, "this isn't as bad as you're probably thinking."

"What the hell is going on?" Will demands, painful through his swollen lip, too terrified to wait for these people's pace of explanation.

The man puts down his ice pack, picks up his phone, says, "One of your wife's email addresses"—huh?—"is Chloe dot M dot Palmer at Travelers dot com. Isn't that right? She still uses her maiden name professionally?"

What the fuck kind of question is this? "Are you trying to extort me?" Will asks.

Elle rises from the bed, walks to the bathroom, leaves the door open.

She runs the tap and rinses the washcloth, wrings it out, rewraps it with fresh ice.

"But I don't have any money. You know that."

"No." She reapplies the icepack to his cheek. "Extortion is not what's going on. Not exactly."

Her voice sounds different now, though Will can't place how.

"I could send Chloe an email this instant," the man says. He holds up his phone, look, I'll prove it to you. The same device with the incontrovertible evidence. This phone is Will's enemy. "Or I could send it tomorrow. Or next week."

Will feels like he missed something important. Maybe they were explaining while he was still emerging from the unconscious? And he missed crucial information?

"Or I could send Chloe an email never. *Instead*, I could transfer ten thousand dollars into your bank account, which I believe is exactly what you need to clear the building-department violations, and resume construction."

Will has definitely seen this man before. Short-cropped gray hair and a firm, square jaw, very closely shaved; thin eyebrows that hover like beach umbrellas over dark beady eyes, with a long scar looking like its handle, on an angle, in a stiff wind; deep crevasses of lines across the forehead, a permanent indentation between the eyes, a sneer on his lips. This looks like a mean, angry person. His posture is rigid, shoulders back, everything tight and coiled. A cop, maybe, or military. A man who's comfortable with violence.

Will glances at Elle. Is this really the same person he was in bed with just minutes ago? Also the person who punched him in the face while he was sprinting across the lawn?

"Then I could transfer another ten thousand dollars into your account next month. And I could repeat this transfer every month. Indefinitely."

Will looks around, trying to figure out the vantage of the hidden camera. His gaze settles on the desk, the bright turquoise numbers of the digital clock.

"Bingo," Elle says, confirming his suspicion.

Will realizes what's different about her: she no longer has an accent. "You're not Australian," he says. "You're American?"

"And then some."

"What the hell does that mean?"

The man reaches into his pocket, and removes his wallet. He slides a stiff laminated card out of a slot, and tosses it toward Will with a spin, as if dealing blackjack on felt.

Will realizes where he's seen this man before: a month ago, on a dark quiet street after a wine-bar dinner. "You were following me? In Paris?"

Will looks down at the ID, turns the thing over, then again to the front. "How do I know what this is?"

"I guess you don't," the man says. "But if it's fake, you have to admit it's pretty good. Right? Look at that hologram, the paper pattern, the biometric photo. That's a professional-looking ID. Didn't come out of some video-arcade vending machine."

Will doesn't have any way of assessing any of this.

"Do arcades exist anymore?" the man continues, pursuing this irrelevancy. "Or does everyone now play video games at home, sitting around rec rooms in their underwear?"

"We can provide methods of verification," Elle interrupts. "There are people you could call. We could arrange for you to visit headquarters, though honestly that would be complicated, and sort of inadvisable. But possible."

Will feels bile churning. God, he *really* doesn't want to throw up, heaping humiliation onto an already tall pile of unpleasant emotions. On the other hand, maybe vomiting would complete the set, a full complement of all the ways in which he could feel crappy at once. Maybe there'd be a satisfaction in that, the accomplishment of perfect debasement.

He swallows his peristalsis.

"What the fuck," he says, through gritted teeth, "do you want from me?"

"Not much," Elle answers.

"That can't be true."

"Well," Elle says, "the reality is that it wouldn't be much for *you* to do, and it wouldn't be dangerous. But the results would be meaningful to *us*."

"Just a little information," the man interjects. He seems intent on proving his value, despite the evidence that it's the woman who has done everything.

"Fuck you."

Elle prickles, and Will is briefly worried that she's going to smack him; he hadn't even considered the possibility of that bonus humiliation. Then her face softens into a wry smile. "But Will Rhodes, you already did that."

Will wants to throttle this horrible person.

"Listen," she says, softening her tone to comradely, reasonable. "This is not a negotiation. But you don't have to make your decision right now. You have till breakfast."

She stands, and so does her burly companion.

"You'll become an asset of the CIA, Will Rhodes. Or we'll ruin your life."

CAPRI

She leans over the wall and stares into the black void, trying to adjust her eyes to the total darkness, to see something down there. But no, nothing.

She can't believe she just did what she just did, can't believe how quickly it happened. It took only a second to kill a person, to end a human being's life. A quick jab to the trachea, completely unexpected; he never even began to defend himself.

She'd been hoping that she wouldn't have to use the knife, that she'd be able to simply push him over. But his body position had been wrong; he'd looked balanced, steady, like he might be able to withstand even her most violent shove, and then where would she be? Screwed. She'd be in hand-to-hand combat with someone bigger and stronger and, probably, a better fighter.

She'd purchased the knife from an obviously disreputable shop near the Naples train station, a well-known locus of disreputability, an open market for petty criminal enterprises, nonpetty ones too. She never touched the knife with her bare skin, never left a fingerprint on it. So she could leave the weapon where it was, lodged deeply and securely in the man's neck; removing it would've risked spraying everything—including herself—with his blood. Then she shoved him into the void. He disappeared without a sound; she didn't hear him hit bottom.

She had prepared plans for other scenarios, of course; she hadn't been absolutely confident that she'd be able to seduce him. And she'd been halfway afraid that he'd catch on, try to kill her. But he was thinking with his penis, exactly what she'd counted on, the high-percentage play.

Her entire body seems to be vibrating, as if the blood in her veins has been replaced with high-voltage electricity, everything tingling. She needs to be careful now. It's easy to kill someone; what's hard is not getting caught.

With trembling hands she removes the packet of disinfecting wipes from her pocket, uses one to clean the wineglasses—his and her own—and the bottle. She flings all three objects in a direction that she knows is something like a seventy-degree pitch, too steep for investigators to canvass, not to mention terrain that's covered with vegetation that'll capture this evidence, prevent it from tumbling down to shore, where it would be more easily retrieved. That's where they'll eventually find the corpse.

She removes the latex glove, rolls it inside out, capturing any blood inside. She shrugs off her linen jacket, which is possibly spattered; it's hard to see in this light. She rolls the jacket into a tight cylinder, which she also puts into her bag.

She strides quickly across the terrace to the pool. She kneels, and washes her hands and forearms and face in the cool water. She puts on a thin silk sweater, and running shoes, and a red-and-gold Roma cap, and a pair of clunky-framed eyeglasses with clear lenses.

That's when she hears the faint click of the door handle engaging.

Shit.

Of all the people this could be, please let it not be the waitress. *Please.*

She's facing away from the hotel's door. It would be unnatural if she didn't turn to look at whoever was interrupting her privacy, so she does, a glance over her shoulder, with her heart in her stomach.

It's no one, an older couple, the man wearing a pale jacket and woven loafers, the woman multiple strands of pearls and no deficiency of hairspray.

The man notices her, says, "*Buona sera.*"

"*Buona sera,*" she answers. All she needs to do is retrieve her wireless scramblers, and get the hell out of here. She won't return to her room, where she didn't touch anything except when wearing latex gloves. She left plenty of DNA around, but that's very different from fingerprints.

The old couple are now at the wall. The woman looks down, leans forward, cranes her neck. What is she looking for? Her husband also leans over the precipice, and they both talk quietly, in Italian.

The man looks at Marina, then down again. Could he possibly see anything?

There's suddenly a boat out there, a decent-sized yacht with a lot of lights, pulling into the cove.

She puts her bag on her shoulder, strides toward the door, reaches for the handle, stops herself just in time. She turns, looks around, plucks a towel from a neat stack, uses it to grab the handle. Inside, she retrieves the scrambler from the buffet table, and walks back out to the terrace. She refolds the towel and leaves it at the top of the stack.

The couple are still leaning against the wall. Marina hustles alongside the building to the gate, from which she removes the second scrambler. Both devices continue transmitting their jamming signals. Better safe than sorry. Always.

She scampers down the narrow path, hugging the shadows, and suddenly hears someone say, *"Ciao."* It's a kitchen worker, smoking a cigarette.

Fuck. Fuck fuck fuck.

Floodlights at the front of the hotel are seeping around to this path; she can make out every pockmarked pore on this guy's face. But can he see her? She's wearing a cap with a bill; her face should be in deep shadow. He can't see her face.

But what if he can? She has just a second to decide.

No. She can't kill this guy. She doesn't even have a weapon, though that's probably a surmountable obstacle. But his death would get noticed immediately, even if she did manage to hide his body. He's working, he'll be missed, searched for—"Where's Giancarlo? Snorting meth again?"—and his body will be discovered, the police summoned, a manhunt initiated . . .

So, no.

She notices his drug-ravaged face, his tattoos, his furtive stance. This guy won't volunteer this encounter. Certainly not unsolicited. Maybe when the body is discovered, but probably not even then. This isn't the type of guy who willingly interacts with police.

"*Scusi,*" she says. "*Una sigaretta, per favore?*" Cigarettes to the rescue, again. Ironic.

He inhales while examining her, a hotel guest probably, might be sneaking out, but who knows why, who knows who she is, could be rich or powerful, not a woman to refuse casually, not for the price of a cigarette. He pats his pockets, finds the packet.

"*Grazie,*" she says, leaning forward, retrieving the cigarette with her lips. He flips open a Zippo and flicks its wheel, a whiff of the sparked flint followed by a strong hit of butane, then tobacco smoke pouring into her lungs. It takes all her power to not cough.

"*Prego.*"

She continues to the front, and lifts the gate latch with the cuff of her sweater, allows it to reengage quietly. Her footsteps are nearly silent in rubber soles. She hustles to the dark embrace of the unlit street.

A car comes speeding up the road, which seems even narrower on foot than it did when she was a passenger. She'll need to be careful to not get killed here.

At the bottom of the hill, it's an abrupt transition from quiet night to noisy civilization, clusters of houses, landscaped yards, parallel-parked cars and streetlamps and—*shit*—the unmistakable strobe of police lights.

What should she look like? Who should she be?

She ditches the cap, the fake eyeglasses. Fluffs her hair, makes a quick pass of lipstick, swaps out sneakers for heels again, places her handbag into the crook of her arm. There.

It's late, but the town is very much alive, clusters of people in piazzas, in the cafés and restaurants, drinking and smoking and eating. The police car's lights are flashing while the cop mediates between two men who are obviously intoxicated. Only a handful of police on the planet will ever in their lives chase a serial killer, but in most countries every single cop will break up a fight between drunks again and again.

The policeman, bored with his tedious task, glances her way. Her heart sinks and she almost stumbles, meeting this cop's eye from fifty feet away.

She offers a tiny smile, trying to quell her panic. She really doesn't want to talk to police. This might be the very cop who ends up investigating the disappearance, the homicide. The Capri police force can't be huge.

She's careful not to speed up, but maintains a steady pace. She feels eyes on her back, watching her ass, watching this single girl walk up the street, late at night, the ever present specter of sexual assault mingling with the unique risk of being arrested on suspicion of murder, opposite ends of the danger spectrum, both risks real.

Maybe she didn't think this through clearly enough.

She turns onto a narrow lane, climbs the stone steps of the two-star *pensione.*

"*Buona sera,*" she says to another clerk at another hotel. "*Otto.*"

She checked into this hotel this morning, deposited her carry-on in room 8, paid a surcharge for early occupation, along with the night's fee, in cash.

She stares at herself in the mirror that hangs over the cheap bureau in the tiny room. A single bed? She hasn't slept in a single bed in years. It looks like college.

Will she be able to sleep tonight? Should she even bother trying?

Did she really just murder a man in cold blood?

She looks in the mirror for signs that she's different, that she has become a different person. She searches her irises, the same eyes she's been meeting in mirrors for three decades, except—what's this?—a little fleck of something on her skin, at the corner of her eye, and she reaches up tentatively, dabs the tip of her forefinger onto her flesh, and she wipes it away, the dead man's blood.

She's still who she is. Isn't she?

MENDOZA

"Why me?" Will asks. They're sitting at a secluded outdoor table on the tiled patio. It's chilly; all the other hotel guests are inside. "Why go to all this expense and, um, *trouble* to recruit me?"

"You recently took a weeklong trip to Belgium and Luxembourg, where you spent three hours at a party in the residence of the grand duke, whose guests were some of the most prominent businessmen and diplomats in the Low Countries."

"How do you know about that?"

"After the party you went up the block to an expat bar, where you drank with a crowd that included at least one MI6 agent, and an arms dealer who flirts with breaking the law—he's careful—and the Romanian mistress of an Eastern European ambassador. Do you remember her? Long legs, long eyelashes, no bra?"

"Uh . . ."

"You travel around the world, in and out of embassies and palaces and exclusive events, with press credentials. With the impunity that comes from an ironclad legend. How many people in the world have similar access and cover, do you think? A couple dozen?"

"How the hell would I know? How would *you* know?"

"We are the largest, most thorough intelligence-gathering service in the history of civilization. Because of technology, it's now possible for the CIA to identify many of the best possible assets in the world without leaving Virginia. And you, Will Rhodes, are one of them. We've been watching you for a long time."

"Why the whole convoluted extortion? Why not just ask?"

"Because you'd say no."

"How are you so sure?"

"Because the college classes you took in government and history were *all* taught by left-wing—many of them radical—professors. You took a class in Marxian philosophy. For a course about American foreign policy, you wrote a paper about the Agency's misadventures in Latin America, claiming that the CIA has no right to do nearly everything the CIA does."

Will barely remembered. Did he really write such a paper? "That was long ago."

"Have you changed your mind? You're a longtime subscriber to *The Nation* and *The New Republic*, *The New Yorker* and *The New York Times*. The web pages you click through to—exclusive of the porn—"

"Hey, c'mon—"

"—of both the sexual sort and the culinary and architectural sorts—

are consistent with a far-left ideology. You've signed petitions that oppose the NYPD's stop-and-search policy, and the federal government's domestic surveillance program, plus those that support gay rights, Planned Parenthood, and an increase in taxes on the ultra-wealthy. You participated, in a passive way, in Occupy Wall Street. Do you want me to go on?"

Will is shell-shocked.

"You would've said no, Will Rhodes. My job was to get you to say yes."

NAPLES

Police are everywhere. She feels herself wilting in their gazes, eyes darting, sweating, fidgeting, fingering her eyeglasses, clutching her boarding pass and Colombian passport, a document she acquired for this trip, the ID of a person who can't be found, doesn't exist.

She realizes that she looks like a version of precisely what she doesn't want to look like. She needs to get her shit together.

But the TV on the far side of the departures lounge is deeply alarming. On-screen, *polizia* are milling around an indistinguishable location, clumps of uniforms and clusters of suits, holding walkie-talkies, looking like they're gossiping, talking about football, women, whatever. The headline says something about murder, but the screen is too far away for her to read, and she doesn't want to leave the queue.

A blue-uniformed policeman is walking in her direction. Her eye is drawn reflexively to the cop; she can barely bring herself to glance at anything else.

She's really falling apart.

The boarding queue is moving slowly for this short flight to Rome, a ticket bought last night, changed today to an earlier departure once she'd arrived at the airport, after the sunrise walk down to the jetty, the ferry across the bay, the bumpy taxi to the airport.

Assuming the worst. What's the worst? That the cops have already discovered the body. Maybe someone on that yacht noticed something, *Aaah! Call the police!* And they came immediately, though it's the weekend? And the police connected the dead body to her hotel? And they located last night's staff, the waitress and maître d' and desk clerk, who identified their dead guest? And the dishwasher did, after all, admit to their cigarette encounter? And they retrieved the register's photocopy of the Colombian passport she's holding? And they located the flight reservation and its change? All within a few hours? And they dispatched officers . . . ?

Assuming all that: there'd be a whole team swarming around her at the gate. Not this one cop, looking hungover and bored. No. This guy is not looking for her.

No one is looking for her. Not now, not yet, probably not ever.

It's unlikely that the hotel staff will notice their missing guests until tonight. And even when—if—they notice, will they care? They have credit cards to charge for both the Colombian woman and the American man. Or wherever his passport claims.

Finally, the gate agent takes the boarding pass, whew.

By the time anyone really looks for her, the woman carrying the passport that identifies her as Marina Delgado will have cleared customs in Turkey, walked out of the terminal, and disappeared into Istanbul.

Then the woman will walk back into the airport and board a flight home to her real life, her real husband, who thinks that she's somewhere else entirely, doing something completely different.

10

===

This is the ultimate walk of shame, coming home from the stupidest mistake of his life. Will feels as if he went out into the world, and acquired a gun, and filled it with bullets, and handed this loaded weapon over to a naked woman he didn't know, here, I'm giving you the unencumbered option to inflict immense pain on me, on my wife, look I even flipped off the safety, go ahead, fire at will, it's completely up to you.

Now he can't do anything about it. Once done it's done, no take-backs, no renegotiation or second-guessing, nothing to choose except how to live with it, how to try to fall asleep knowing that there's this loaded gun out there, in this stranger's hand, and anytime she wants she could just shoot. Shoot him. Bang.

Will can't believe he did this to himself, to Chloe, to his whole life.

He unfolds himself from the taxi, stares at his ramshackle house, rusted fence. The rosebush, despite Will's benign neglect, has continued to refuse to die.

Just inside the front door, he calls out, "Chloe?"

No answer.

Will leaves his bag in the foyer and walks through the parlor floor, across the damaged elaborate parquet to the barely functional kitchen with the secondhand French stove sitting proudly but ineffectively in the corner.

He'd be surprised if his wife were home, midmorning on a weekday. Even though her new job is neither permanent nor full-time, Chloe still leaves first thing every morning, maintaining a working person's schedule, to help her avoid becoming a nonworking person.

Will doesn't want to see her here, now, nervous about their reunion, about the first time he'll greet his wife as an adulterer. As a liar. As an asset of the CIA. What a combination of attributes that he didn't possess when he left for Argentina, a very long week ago.

How did he allow himself to believe that a woman like Elle would throw herself at him, at a married man, or for that matter at any man? He refused to see what he didn't want to see.

He'd been made an utter fool—he'd been genuine with Elle, while she'd not. It's fine to be a fool in love, everyone hears that again and again, in books and movies and poems and songs, it's even okay to be a fool in love with the wrong person, to be in impossible love, in unrequited love, there's a certain type of martyrdom to it, like a war wound. But this? This was just humiliating.

She took so much from him, so easily.

"Chloe?" He wonders if his wife will be able to tell, from his kiss, from the look on his face. "You here?"

There's no sign that anything in his house has changed. Will was vaguely, irrationally expecting to find something different. But the only thing that has changed is him.

He finds Chloe lying in bed, pushing a sleep mask up onto the top of her head.

"You okay?" he asks, standing in the doorway, reluctant to enter.

"Just tired." She'd taken on a last-minute freelance gig that required a couple of long flights. For as long as they'd been together, they'd both been this way, midday naps, midnight meals, perpetually trying to conquer jet lag. "And you? How was Argentina?"

Will has this one chance to tell the truth, before he starts lying; this is the fork in his road. Another fork. Once he utters the first lie, omits the first truth, he knows that this lie will engender an avalanche of others, and he won't be able to untell any of them, they will instantly become part of his permanent record, of his marriage, his life. He will be a cheat and a liar, and that's what he'll be forever.

Or he can just come out with it: I got seduced, Chloe, and I cheated, I got blackmailed, it's the CIA, they want me to inform for them, they'll pay me, I can do it or not, completely up to you, I was wrong, I'm sorry, you tell me what to do, and did I say I'm sorry? I'm really very extremely sorry.

He could tell the truth. It would be painful, no doubt about it. It would be horrible. But they would survive it, wouldn't they? Should they?

Yes, he could tell the truth. But he doesn't.

◆ ◆ ◆

"Jesus," Malcolm says, "what happened to you?"

Will jumps in his chair. This is the first time anyone has come to find him here in the small room that houses the archives.

"Oh?"—reaching up to touch his swollen cheek, as if he'd forgotten about it—"I got into a scuffle, in a dance club."

"What? Where? What happened?"

"B.A. Not a big deal, this looks a lot worse than it is. It was late, there was pushing and shoving, fists flying, one landed on my face. I don't even know what the fight was about, or who hit me. I was just an unlucky bystander."

"My God. Did you go to a hospital?"

"For this? Come on, Malcolm." Will feels his foot tapping under the table, nerves from this lying he's doing, one lie after another.

"Okay, macho man." Malcolm stands in the doorway, in his rolled-up sleeves and his loosened necktie and his smooth, easy smile. Not a care in the world, the lucky bastard. "So what are you searching for today, Rhodes?" Malcolm looks around disapprovingly at the windowless, charmless utilitarian space. "More overexposed locations?"

Will hasn't been searching for anything, not in the old magazine pages. But he has to answer Malcolm somehow. "We've published a lot of jingoist propaganda over the years."

· "Oh yeah? When was that?"

"All the way through the eighties. Ugly, sometimes racist stuff."

Malcolm doesn't look entirely comfortable with this conversation. He's the guy in charge, the one who'd need to take responsibility, to make apologies, for the missteps and mistakes of his predecessors. This is how institutions work.

"Tell me about the rest of Argentina, Rhodes. The contemporary, non-violent parts."

"It was good." Will practiced, at home, in the mirror. "Very photogenic, very easy to understand from images. I think I've had enough Malbec to last a lifetime"—he tries to chortle, though it comes out more of a cough—"but there was a wide variety of it, and compelling personality-driven wine-ish anecdotes. It'll be a fine piece, done quickly."

"Well, I guess you're not completely worthless."

Will has actually spent the past hours completely worthlessly, not saying or doing much of anything, not talking to anyone. He was worried that people could see it on him, smell it. So he'd come here to hide.

"You sure you're okay, Rhodes?"

"Me? No. I mean, my face hurts . . ."

Malcolm is still staring at him, assessing. Will struggles to maintain eye contact, to not flinch, not blink, not look away. He feels his heartbeat accelerating, the seconds ticking by.

"You finally did it, didn't you?"

"Did what?"

Malcolm breaks into a smile. "You gave in to temptation. You *bastard*. Who was it?"

Will shakes his head.

"Not going to tell me? After all these years, Rhodes? You're going to keep this a secret? From *me*?"

"There is no secret."

"Is *that* what got you punched in the face?"

Will doesn't say anything.

"You lying to me, Rhodes?"

"Asked and answered." Will tries to smile wider, increasingly panicked that he's saying wrong thing after wrong thing, digging into a hole while Malcolm shovels soil onto his head.

"I'll get it out of you sooner or later, Rhodes. You know that, right?"

Malcolm buttons his jacket, pushes back his hair, checks his plain ordinary manila folder. He's dubious of people who bring accessories like padded-leather presentation folders to meetings, résumés on extra-heavy textured paper, ballplayers with matched sets of superfluous gear, overcompensation, distracting from a dearth of convincing content with an excess of compelling package. Malcolm plays tennis in tee shirts; he comes to meetings with manila folders.

The executive conference room is large and airy, floor-to-ceiling windows onto the avenue. The long high-gloss table is surrounded by occupied chairs, people he mostly doesn't recognize, though at the head is a well-known man in a well-tailored suit.

"Hi, my name is Malcolm Somers. I'm the editor of *Travelers*."

A few heads nod at him, in hello and agreement, okay guy, let's get started.

"I may be biased—I am, obviously, biased—but I think our founding was one of the greatest product launches ever. In today's era in which consultants are paid to craft so-called authentic brand narratives, our origin story doesn't need any embellishments."

Malcolm punches a button on the laptop, and the preloaded Power-Point launches behind him. PowerPoint, like leather presentation folders, is something that Malcolm suspects is used more for obfuscation than for clarification. But a decade in conference rooms has beaten out his recalcitrance, and he finally gave in, and asked his tech guru, Stonely Rodriguez, for a tutorial.

"It's 1945, the waning months of the war. Benjamin Donaldson has been recuperating in Walter Reed from life-threatening injuries sustained in France, the Nazis' last gasp." A black-and-white photo, a man with a circumspect smile under blackened eyes. "Benji had been stabbed in Marseille, massive hemorrhaging, almost died in that alley near the old port."

Malcolm wrote a script for this, printed it out, rehearsed in a mirror, then discarded the pages. He never reads aloud, except bedtime stories. And at this point he has dozens of the kids' books memorized, so even his read-alouds aren't, technically, reading aloud.

"But before his encounter with the switchblade, Benji had seen a lot of France, and had been awestruck by the beauty." Click, black-and-white shots of the beach at St-Tropez, the Provençal massifs, medieval villages, intercut with color reproductions of Van Gogh's wheat fields, Monet's cathedrals.

"So Benji is bored to death there in the hospital, trying to figure out what to do with his life. Before the war, he'd gone to Dartmouth, then New York, a job in pulp magazines. He figures that's the business to which he'll return. But he can't get his mind off Europe. And he thinks there are a lot of guys like him, millions of them, servicemen who'd gotten a glimpse of Europe and the South Pacific and North Africa, guys who'd seen some of the world."

Click, click, click: the azure waters of the Blue Grotto in Capri, sand dunes in the Sahara, a tropical lagoon in the South Pacific.

"Benji has a vision for a new breed of American tourist. He foresees falling costs for air travel, and rapid expansion of routes; he expects a strong dollar. In fact, Benji anticipates all the factors that contribute to an unprecedented postwar tourist boom. And because he's from a magazine background, he envisages a new glossy to cater to this heretofore nonexistent demo: the middle-class international traveler.

"Benji raises money. He hires accomplished journalists and photographers, all suffering combat fatigue, PTSD before it had a name. All looking for a less gruesome version of their occupation."

Malcolm pauses, glances around, signaling that another type of comment is coming. He does this whenever he tells this story. "Their experience is something I can relate to. After years of covering Afghanistan and Iraq, and sustaining injuries—IED shrapnel in the shoulder and torso—I still wanted to write, but I no longer wanted to fear for my life."

One of the reasons Malcolm went abroad was to see what war was like. To be around mortal danger, to feel scared, all the time. He can't believe, now, his recklessness then. This is probably what it means to be middle-aged: to be horrified by the irresponsibility of your own youth.

Maybe it was for the best. If he hadn't gotten injured, he wouldn't have come home, he wouldn't have this wife, these kids, this job, his life. He might instead be dead, blown up in a hotel, or kidnapped and murdered, like their African correspondent, just last year.

"Benji's overseas personnel are joined in New York by cutting-edge designers and visionary editors. This energetic staff creates nothing short of a cultural sensation."

Click: the cover of volume 1, issue 1.

"From the debut, *Travelers'* pages are packed with stunning photographs—think *Life*, without the depressing stuff—that accompany long, evocative, in-depth articles—nearly novella-length, *New Yorker*-esque. *Travelers* is providing a total immersion, catering not only to the moneyed and/or adventurous who actually buy PanAm and TWA tickets, but also to the bigger, more rapidly expanding audience of armchair travelers. A demo practically invented by *Travelers*. This audience is irresistible to advertisers in the golden age of print, and *Travelers* is turning a profit within five years."

Click: a chart of gross revenues, ad pages, net profits. A few heads nod appreciatively at this turn toward the more concrete, measurable subject of finances. One guy even writes something down.

"*Travelers* receives a steady stream of mail, which Benji reads compulsively. He learns that many of these passionate reader-travelers have something in common: they want *more*. More advice, more specific. So he experiments with methods of delivering more to these readers: destination-specific newsletters, special issues, seminars."

Click, click: covers of special issues on Tuscany and Portugal.

"But what the audience really wants is not something that can be *delivered* to them en masse, because it's something unique, something tailored to them personally. Something that would be impossible to supply by a bunch of American writers who visit France a few times a year and while there spend most of their time plastered, chasing women."

A couple of chuckles, but the man at the head of the table remains impassive. Malcolm can't tell if he's enjoying this story or hating it or has heard it before.

"Benji decides to try a gambit that has absolutely nothing to do with magazines."

Click: a modest storefront on the rue de Rivoli.

"The first bureau of the Travelers International Booking Service is Paris, *naturellement*. A one-year lease across the street from the Louvre and down the block from the Meurice, around the corner from Place Vendôme, the Ritz. The mission is explicitly to service American tourists who want more than just guidebook Paris. They want *access*."

Click: the opulent dining room of Le Grand Véfour.

"They want impossible dinner reservations. They want private invitations, insider information, exclusive experiences. They're willing to pay handsomely for an enhanced version of travel. The brand they trust to provide this service? *Travelers*."

Click: a black-and-white photo of a dapper man, leaning on a cane.

"Benji hires an outgoing Parisian named Jean-Pierre Fourier, who quickly proves himself adept at helping well-off Americans have a superlative time in Paris. Jean-Pierre arranges Notre Dame tours and off-hours Louvre visits; he reserves tables at the best restaurants and most exclusive cafés; procures invitations to fashionable parties and books cars to Versailles, tee times at Morfontaine, sold-out tickets to the opera and ballet and the lovely concerts in La Sainte-Chapelle. He can also be counted on to arrange girls, discreetly."

Malcolm sees one of the women glance down; a man crosses his legs. Some people are uncomfortable with this reference. The man at the head of the table isn't one of them.

"It turns out that there is no luxury, no exclusive experience, that American tourists cannot be convinced they want, maybe even need. That first cramped storefront leads the following year to a bigger storefront, and then a whole building, in a quieter, more polished part of town, equally convenient to a certain type of tourist, less so to others.

"The Paris bureau is successful not only as a travel agency, but just as important as a brand extension, with the magazine fueling the agency and vice versa, both entities enhancing the other."

Click: an elegant storefront near the Via del Corso in Rome. "We open bureaus in Rome, in Florence, in Madrid and Barcelona, in Athens and London. The investments are reasonable, the exposure minimal, the audience established, the margins impressive."

Click, click, click: magazine covers from the fifties, sixties, seventies.

"The same factors that led to the magazine's initial success help the bureaus thrive. After Western Europe, expansion follows into North Africa, Asia, the Mideast and Latin America, and eventually Eastern Europe after the fall of the Wall.

"Meanwhile, the magazine continues to break new ground, to hire the best talent, to win awards, to dominate the market. The *Travelers* brand steadily expands its influence and profitability, the category leader according to every measure. By the nineties there are three dozen bureaus on six continents, ten special issues every year, as well as the most ad pages and largest circulation in the category."

Click, click: eighties, nineties.

"Then what happens?"

Click: black screen. Malcolm looks around the room. Everyone knows the answer, but like a roomful of middle-schoolers, no one wants to answer when everyone knows.

"I did," says the man at the far end of the table.

Malcolm meets the man's gaze across twenty feet of richly oiled teak, a Midcentury Danish table that was acquired to decorate this office when both were brand-new.

"I happened."

The two men stare at each other from opposite sides of the divide, the new-media baron who intends to buy the old-media bastion. They both appear to be the same age, with probably the same schooling, with overlapping social circles that further overlap their business circles, Venn diagrams with vast intersections. Malcolm is surprised they'd never met until a month ago, never shook hands on the Hamptons sands, never shared a fund-raiser ten-top at the Cipriani Ballroom, both wearing tuxedos custom-tailored at Sam's on the Kowloon side of Hong Kong.

"That's right. The content world shifted on its axis. The old delivery mechanism—paper, printed and bound and shipped to newsstands and drugstores around the country, and directly to customers' mailboxes— was in large part replaced by the web. The old fee structure—consumers paying to consume content, supplementing the revenue generated by the ads targeted at those consumers—has also been replaced by a new model."

Click: home page of travelers.com.

"I don't want to make light of this revolution—not your role in it, sir, nor the immense changes in brand identities and consumer loyalties that it has engendered. But to many consumers—to many readers—these changes are irrelevant. What hasn't changed for them is the content they love, nor the brands they trust to deliver it."

Click: the *Travelers* logo.

Malcolm glances around the room again, looking for overt skepticism. He doesn't notice any, but that doesn't mean it isn't there. His eyes again find the emotionless gaze of the person who'll probably be his new boss.

"So. The print magazine has seen a drastic decrease in circulation. I'm sure this is a surprise to exactly no one anywhere. On the other hand, the website, and the electronic editions, are robust, and steadily growing in unique users. Overall, our audience is *growing*."

Click: another chart, big numbers, getting bigger.

"Also not surprisingly, the travel services took a hit. We've shuttered quite a few overseas bureaus."

Click: map of the world, 1998, with stars at bureaus. Then half fade away, to today.

"On the other hand, we've discovered that there's a not insignificant population who aren't looking for more information, more discounts, more options. They're not looking for *more*, period. They're looking for *better*. Better recommendations, better choices. They're looking for this word that's being bandied about relentlessly these days: *curated* experiences.

"And what's the essence of a curated experience? It's *trust*. It's trust in the expertise, the experience, the *brand*. If you're asking a chef to curate your meal, you're putting your dinner in his hands, every bite. You're trusting him to provide the experience you want, without you needing to micromanage the choices. Same is true when you ask a bookseller's recommendation, a fishing guide's best holes in a trout stream, a sommelier's favorite bottle of Margaux in a Michelin-starred restaurant."

Click, click, click: streams and mountains and bottles of wine.

"This is what *Travelers* has been providing discerning tourists since its inception: curated travel experiences. Yes, the delivery mechanisms have changed. But the content has not changed. The brand has not changed. The *trust*, it hasn't changed."

Click: the current issue's cover.

"We are *Travelers*, ladies and gentlemen. The most trusted brand in international travel."

11

STOCKHOLM

The American who calls himself Joe wakes up early, as always, an unbreakable lifetime habit. He brushes his teeth, washes his face, dries off with a thin, worn hand towel, its edges frayed. The dingy old towels came with the apartment, along with a few pieces of cheap furniture—not enough for forever, but a start—and a mop. The bathrooms are constant reminders that he's abroad, the oddly shaped fixtures and inevitably cramped quarters and accordion shower doors, the smell of the grooming products, the hand-soaps and shaving creams and shampoos, they all smell like not-America.

He ambles down the far side of the hill to Folkungagatan, the neighborhood's main drag, with its hardware stores and photo labs, kebabs and pizza, supermarket and sushi bar and the cheerful little place with the surprisingly good curry.

Joe buys a newspaper and steps into the bakery. Orders his pastry and coffee, looks around the small room, a normal-looking assortment of people, responding to his presence normally. His preferred seat, in the far corner, is free.

He reads the newspaper in detail, eats carefully, drinks slowly. He has nothing to do today. He never has anything to do. For a half-century he worked all the time, even when it looked like he was on vacation. Then he needed to retire.

First he went to Iceland, established a quiet life in the countryside. Then for variety he came here, to a familiar, comfortable Western European city. He likes Stockholm.

Whenever the door opens, he glances up, but never lets his gaze linger. He ignores the television that's playing twenty-four-hour international news, nearly all of it businessy, programming tailored to whatever breed of human wants to know the share price of Intel at any given moment. Certainly not him.

A woman walks in who's so tall and so beautiful that she's impossible to ignore. She orders a cappuccino, then makes her way down the pastry display, considering her choices.

His eyes flicker to the screen over her shoulder, a bit of nonfinancial news for a change, a breaking story: a murder victim has been discovered in Capri. The case has captured the attention of the international media—a luxury hotel in a famous place, a dead man stabbed in the neck and thrown off a cliff, a mystery woman wanted for questioning.

The American tries to focus on the low-volume audio, catches only flickers. His hearing has been deteriorating, along with everything else. He's getting old, and it's coming on quickly. For a long time he felt invincible, impressed by his own resilience and stamina. Not anymore.

He stands, walks toward the TV, no longer paying any attention to the blonde.

"The victim is apparently a citizen of the United States but not a resident," the reporter says from her stand-up spot, the sea shimmering behind her. Then the screen splits to include a new image, a headshot.

"Holy crap," Joe mutters, frozen there in the middle of the bakery, blocking the path of the Amazonian Swede.

"Taylor Lindhurst's last known address was in a remote region of southwest France."

Although it's remotely possible that Lindhurst—a new name for an old acquaintance—was murdered by any number of rational people, for a variety of justifiable reasons, the most simple explanation is the likeliest.

Perhaps Joe should get out of here today. Pack a bag, walk across the Slussen cloverleaf across Gamla Stan and over to the station for a train to the airport, a flight back to Iceland. Or maybe instead he should get to the Värtahamnen terminal right now, to hell with luggage, board one of those overnight vomitoria boats across the Baltic, hide out in Latvia or Estonia, places no one would think to look for him, and no one who tried would succeed.

He made the choice to believe that he'd be safe here in Iceland and Sweden until the end of his life, either because he'd die a natural death or because they'd find him, and he'd never even hear the bullet. Which he manages to convince himself, even in the small hours, would be preferable.

NEW YORK CITY

Will steps out onto Sixth Avenue, in the middle of Midtown, the middle of the media world, Time Life and McGraw-Hill, Sirius and Fox, CBS and S&S, conglomerates strewn around the skyscrapers, the homogeneous anonymity of midcentury institutional architecture, flapping flags and sputtering fountains, massive modernist sculptures dwarfing the hot dog carts and honey-roasted nuts and all the tiny little people, scurrying around like ants, Will himself just another one, another little ant crossing the stone-paved plaza, glancing at the hundreds of faces that surround him, five-thirty on a weekday afternoon.

He stops at the corner, the traffic rumbling by, taxis and limos, SUVs and Minis, trucks and buses, honking and sputtering and belching black clouds of noxious exhaust. He stands at the very edge of the curb, toes over the precipice, dangerously exposed out there. Will can feel the crowd amassing behind him, who knows how many people, but he shouldn't turn around to look.

The light changes. He jogs across the avenue, elbows his way through the throng on the far side, up the crowded side street to Fifth Avenue, which is even busier than Sixth, with Rockefeller Center and St. Patrick's Cathedral and Saks, an immense swarm of humanity.

Will turns around, scans the crowd, looking for anyone who might be watching him.

He retreats to Sixth. Descends to the plaza under Rockefeller Center, the subway station and the shopping arcade, pizza parlors and shoeshine shops, six-dollar umbrellas. He hustles through the busy space, then up the stairs on the far side of the avenue, now walking uptown. He pauses at a magazine stand, examines a few covers, turns downtown. Onto a side street, a long block to the avenue, around another corner, onto a different side street.

Will does this for thirty minutes, scanning sidewalks, past gift shops and jewelry stores, Indian restaurants and newsstands, a grimy Irish pub where he pauses at the door, seems to consider going in, then changes his mind, backtracks to a two-story glass wall of a mega-deli with seating on a mezzanine, a pair of knee-high leather boots visible up there.

In the bright fluorescent light inside, Will is hyperaware of the physiological effects of his first ever surveillance detection route, his racing heartbeat, sweaty palms, his whole body vibrating.

Will orders a coffee, even though a stimulant is really not what he needs now. Should've gotten a cold beer. It's evening, after all. Who the hell stops at a deli like this for a hot coffee, on a warm day, at dinnertime?

He tosses the coffee into the garbage, pays for a beer, absorbs the quizzical look of the cashier. Walks past the sneeze-guarded steam tables, suffused with the ineffable sadness of dinners plucked from a cheap deli's salad bar.

Will walks upstairs, to the far corner of the mezzanine, an empty table surrounded by a buffer of other empty tables. He takes a seat that faces the rear.

He can't help but glance over at the woman, dredging a teabag in a paper cup.

Will forces his eyes to move across lines of newspaper type, but this isn't reading he's doing. He turns a page, repeats the sham on A3. Something perhaps about Pakistan, or West Africa. He takes a sip of beer, doesn't particularly taste it. He takes a gulp.

He remembers his phone, removes the battery, just as she'd instructed, down in the Southern Hemisphere, two days ago. He puts the pieces in his pocket, takes another sip of—

"Will Somers?"

She's standing at his table, smiling down at him.

"Is that you?"

He gets up from the plastic chair, manages a smile, forces a cheek kiss.

"Aren't you going to ask me to join you?"

Will gestures at the chair. "Please."

She's carrying a handbag and a magazine and a banana and a napkin and a cup of tea, and she dumps all these items on the table, instant mess. Her hair is pulled back again, her face almost entirely makeup-free. She's wearing a shapeless sweater over a staid skirt, no longer a meticulous construction of a sexpot fantasy.

He still can't believe any of this is happening. *Has* happened.

"I don't think I can do this," he says.

"Of course you can. The first time is the hardest, as with everything. And good news, Will: I already know everything about your Argentinean trip. I don't need any report."

"Then what's this meeting for?"

She begins to unpeel the banana. "Test run."

"Testing what, exactly?"

She removes another strip of peel, and another. "Our process."

"You mean my willingness to follow your orders? To come when beckoned?"

"Yes." She takes a bite of the banana, chews, swallows. "Also testing your first attempt at a surveillance-detection route."

Elle and Roger had spent hours explaining it to him at the hotel, then practicing on the streets of Mendoza.

"And how'd I do?"

"Not so great."

"Okay, glad to hear it, another shortcoming of Will Rhodes. Can I go now?"

"Really? Are you *really* going to act like that?"

Will glares at her. He finds it hard to remember how much he adored this woman, just a few days ago, back when he believed she adored him. Now he loathes her.

"Does anyone suspect anything?" she asks. "Chloe?"

He doesn't answer.

"What about your boss? Malcolm, right? Malcolm Somers?"

Will doesn't answer.

"What'd you tell him about your trip? Did you tell him about us?"

He still doesn't say anything.

"Show him any pictures? Me on the beach in that bikini, maybe?" She leans away, takes another big bite of banana. "I've never actually *been* to Australia. That was Photoshopped."

"What are we, friends now?"

"Why not? Do you think your life will somehow be improved if you make a grand show of hating me? How exactly would that make your life easier? Listen." She leans forward, lowers her voice. "We had a good time together. France, Argentina. Putting everything else aside, those nights were genuinely enjoyable for me. Even though it was my job, the fun was real."

He snorts. She ignores it.

"Anyway, nice to see you again," she says, somewhat loudly, now performing for a wider and probably nonexistent audience. "I've got to run." She stands, gathers her things, but leaves the banana peel on a napkin on the table. "I'll see you in a week."

"You will?"

She taps something—what's this? an envelope?—which she seems to have deposited along with her trash. Then she leaves.

Will waits a couple of minutes, as he's supposed to. He tucks the envelope into his jacket, then steps out of the bright surgical-room silence of the nearly empty deli into the loud dirty rush hour, all these people with their headphones and backpacks, their secrets and lies.

And look at this, across the street: Elle's partner, the man who calls himself Roger, leaning against a doorway, one ankle crossed in front of another, a phone in his hand, looking like any other guy who's standing on the sidewalk, killing time. How much has this guy watched here, today? Has Roger been following Will all day? And Will didn't notice?

Will sees the wire running from Roger's phone to his ear. Roger listened to the whole conversation, of course he did. And he probably wasn't the only one.

Will glances at his watch. Plenty of time to meet his wife for dinner. If he's not mistaken, Chloe is ovulating.

MENDOZA

"Your job," she said, "is to ID targets for recruitment."

"Targets?"

"Foreign journalists," she said. "Politicians. Policemen. Businessmen. Whoever, wherever, whenever. If they're important people, or if they have access to important people, then they're of potential interest to us. You already spend half your life with these people. You're a verifiable international journalist, but you're *lightweight*—"

He sat up straighter, insulted. But he couldn't deny it.

"—and no one would worry about you, no one would suspect that you're not exactly who you say you are. You're *perfect.* And it will be easy. And lucrative. And who knows? Maybe it'll even be fun. Exciting."

Will examined his breakfast plate, heaped high with food he hadn't touched, his second breakfast with this woman. Last time, he'd been ravenous.

"We don't expect you—we don't want you—to decide who's important. It's my job to assess the value of targets; my boss's job. Not yours. Your job is to report. To scout."

"But what am I scouting?"

"Weaknesses."

"Is that what you call what you do?"

"That's what we all do, Will. It's just that only some of us admit it."

"Here." She handed Will a small sheet of paper.

He looked down at the neat handwriting, *Arthur's Alehouse* and *Bridget's Saloon, Café Fifty* and *Drinkwaters,* an alphabetized list, one item for every letter of the alphabet, each business name accompanied by a general location, *49th St off 10th, Lex near 37th.*

"This is a list of the places we'll meet. You'll memorize this, then destroy it."

Will continued to scan the page, looking for something familiar, some anchor to his old reality, but there was none. "These are all in New York? I haven't heard of any."

"That's the point. These are dive bars, convenience delis. Subsistence eating, subsistence drinking. You're unlikely to run into anyone you know. Unlikely, but not impossible. So if you happen to notice someone you *do* know, we signal to abort. You'll sneeze, to draw my attention, then wipe your nose with the back of your hand, to confirm."

"Okay."

"Show me."

"What am I, a moron?"

"God, I certainly hope not. So show me."

He fake-sneezed, then wiped his nose with the back of his hand.

"Good. Wherever we are, whenever, that's abort. If we're already in the same room, I probably won't leave immediately. I'll just sit there doing whatever I'm doing, reading my newspaper, scrolling through Twitter, eating my hot dog."

"You eat hot dogs?"

"If we've aborted, but I'm still there, *leave me alone*. Don't come near me, don't try to make eye contact. Likewise, if I sneeze and then wipe my nose, you stay away."

"What if I just have to sneeze for normal reasons?"

"Don't."

They were walking on a dirt path, out past the working-ranch part of the finca, the horses and cows, barns and chutes and long feeding troughs, a half-mile from the guest rooms, far enough to get a hint of barnyard aroma, when the wind was right, but not too much. The constant smell of cow shit would definitely deduct a star from the luxury rating, maybe two.

"To set up our meetings, I'll text you on this."

She handed him a flimsy little flip phone.

"What's this?"

Elle looked at him like he was a dimwit. "It's indistinguishable from your basic burner. But this is a very precise GPS tracking device, which will allow us to pinpoint your location to within a couple of meters."

"Well that's comforting."

"The point is not to locate you, but rather to capture the other mobile-phone signals around you, whose numbers will be transmitted by an app on your device to headquarters, where the numbers' accounts will be traced and then monitored in the hours immediately following contact with you."

"Why?"

"To see who you spook. And to see who those people choose to call, when they're spooked. That's one of the ways we'll assess the potential targets' value."

He examined the thing, which did in fact look like a convenience-store disposable.

"It's also an actual phone, for you to communicate with me, and only with me. If you need to contact me, text or call anytime." She opened the back, removed the battery. "But when you're in America, keep the battery out. Once a day, midday, pop it in, power up, and check messages. When I want to meet, I'll send you a text with a code word—*evasive*, or *ignominious*, or anything."

"Ignominious?"

"Focus on the first letter. We'll meet at the establishment whose first letter immediately follows the first letter of the code word. So if I text you, say, Deuteronomy."

"What the hell kind of words are these?" He glances down at the list in his hand. "Our meet will be at Edgecombe's in, um, Murray Hill. What if I don't show?"

"Then I'll be pissed off."

"Uh-huh. Okay, when?"

She looks perplexed. "I'll be pissed off immediately."

"I mean, when will these meetings be?"

"You'll respond to my text with the hour you can make it, cleanly, allowing plenty of time to run a proper surveillance-detection route."

"I don't know what that means."

"You'll learn. So when you send me the reply text, you'll choose the time, which in actuality will be two hours *past* whatever time you send me. So if you text me four-thirty?"

"We meet at six-thirty."

"See? You're a natural."

He looked at her sidelong, confused, unsure what sort of relationship they were supposed to have. She's going to tease him? "Okay. This happens after every trip?"

"Correct."

"How will you know when I've come back from a trip?"

She laughed at this, at him, his cluelessness. Then she continued without answering. "When you arrive to the bar or deli or whatever, don't make eye contact; I won't either. Order something, and find a place to sit. *By yourself.* Not near me. You're just a guy getting a drink, at the beginning or end of a workday, sitting alone, at a table that offers privacy, and always facing *away* from the door, the window, the street. You understand?"

"Yes. I don't want anyone who's passing to be able to notice me."

"When I'm confident no one is following, I'll join you. Or I'll beckon you to me."

"How?"

"I'll make eye contact. But this is important: if I don't definitely—beyond any shadow of a doubt—make eye contact with you, and hold it for a couple of seconds, *do not come to me.* There may be times when I *never* make contact. Instead, after five minutes I may sneeze, wipe my nose, and leave, without ever having any interaction with you. *Do not follow me.* That meeting is not going to happen. Understand?"

He nodded.

"You understand why?"

"Sort of."

"What *don't* you understand about it?"

"Why anybody would be following me."

"Maybe they'd be following *me.*"

They walked in silence, the reality of these future activities sinking in. Overhead, a hawk was circling, floating on air currents, looking for prey. Will hoped he wouldn't be mistaken for prey. Hoped it hadn't already happened.

Was this a commonplace experience for her? Did she do this same thing last month? Would she do it again next?

"Your name's not really Elle Hardwick, is it?"

"Of course not."

"But there's a real Elle Hardwick? Someone who's actually a journalist in Australia? I've read some of her articles. I *stalked* her, online."

"The real one lives in Sydney with a lot of cats. And I mean *a lot.* Not just real-live pet cats. Also cat photos, cat paintings, cats crocheted on sweaters, cat-shaped ashtrays."

"What should I call you?"

"If we're being formal, I guess C/O Hardwick. Case Officer Hardwick. But I think Elle will suffice. We're journalists, Will. We met in France? Surely you remember."

She was his CIA case officer? But she was still an Australian freelance writer? She was someone he went to bed with last night? Or not? "You're saying we pretend to know each other?"

"Pretend? We *do* know each other, Will. Obviously. *Empirically.* There are witnesses on two continents, people you're likely to see again. So pretending we haven't met, that might get us into completely unnecessary trouble. Our story is simple, Will, because it's true. We know each other exactly how we know each other. We met in St-Émilion, and again—surprise!—here in Mendoza. Last night, we had a drink together, alone."

"And?"

"And what? You're a happily married man, right?"

Did she really expect an answer?

"You made an understandable—a predictable—mistake." She continued to explain it away, a natural story, one she'd heard before, maybe one she'd told before. "If I were you, I'd not mention it to anyone. Unless you start seeing a therapist, which frankly I'd recommend."

"I don't understand. Is this part of the cover?"

"Do you want it to be?"

He was unsure what they were talking about. His real life? Or the fictional legend they were constructing? Or was there any meaningful difference? He felt frustration welling up within him, anger.

"I *never* cheated before. Not once, not even so much as a kiss."

She turned to face him, ready to hear him out, to let him vent.

"How could you *do* this to me?" He felt so wronged. "What type of a person does this to someone else?"

"It wasn't personal." An explanation, not an apology.

"Of course it was fucking personal!"

She put her hands up. "Hey, no one forced you to do anything. You were corruptible, Will, and I corrupted you, because that's my job. And let's remember that it wasn't that difficult."

"That's horrible. *You're* horrible."

"You may not be one hundred percent guilty, Will, but neither are you anywhere near one hundred percent innocent."

He knew this was true. He was just as angry at himself as he was at her. More. He'd screwed up, and he'd done it because he was weak, because he was vain.

"And you know what, Will? Everyone is corruptible. So don't beat yourself up."

He turned from her, off toward the facsimile of a farm, a sanitized, idealized version of what's really a messy, difficult life. They'd spent the whole day together, just as they'd done in Bordeaux a few weeks earlier, back when Will thought they were two people who were unexpectedly falling in love, as falling in love always is. But they weren't. And today they'd been talking about his new job, his new life, his new relationship to telling the truth to the people around him, to his colleagues, his friends, his wife.

"Speaking of beating up, Will: I'm sorry about punching you in the face."

NORFOLK, VIRGINIA

Peaceful countryside Argentina was just a couple of weeks ago, but a world away. Here, evidence is everywhere that this is the largest naval base in the world, one of NATO's strategic command centers: aircraft carriers and submarines, destroyers and cruisers, eighty thousand personnel, big thick necks and wraparound sunglasses and the rigid, upright bearing that you just don't find in magazine offices in Manhattan.

Will is met at the airport by an unremarkable, unmarked gray SUV, civilian Virginia plates, rear windows tinted an impenetrable black. The driver takes Will's bag, says hello, doesn't offer a name.

They leave the airport, and a few minutes later pull to a stop in the middle of a very long block dominated by a shuttered factory, completely deserted, except for a lone man waiting by the curb.

"What's going on?" Will asks.

The driver doesn't answer, but instead unlocks the doors, which Will didn't realize were locked. The new man climbs into the backseat. "Hi," the guy says. He's holding something, a piece of black cloth. "I have to ask you to wear this hood. Security."

Will looks down at the cloth, then back up at this guy, buzz-cut and humorless. Will pulls the mask over his face.

Within minutes they're speeding along at a clip that feels like forty-five or fifty miles per hour, with occasional gusts of wind that shake the car, and air-pressure changes that must be a tunnel. They're traveling over the Chesapeake Bay Bridge-Tunnel, twenty-three miles over water from mainland urban to the peninsula's rural.

Back on land, they speed along the Eastern Shore, slowing and stopping at red lights, along what Will assumes is Route 13. He spent an hour studying maps, suspecting that this was exactly what was going to happen, trying to make practical use of his lifelong geography obsession.

The car takes a turn onto a bumpy road, dirt and not exactly straight. After a couple of minutes the car stops, and Will can hear an electronic hum, a mechanical grinding, as they pass through what must be a security gate.

"You can take off the mask."

Will removes the big hood and looks around, a tall chain-link fence to one side, a single-lane dirt road stretching ahead. They stop at a modest farmhouse, white shingles with green shutters, to which have been added two rear wings, low and long and windowless, big HVAC compressors sitting alongside.

"Intake is in the front hall," the man in the backseat says. He holds out his hand, and for a second Will thinks the guy wants to shake, but he just wants his mask back. "And I'll need your phone."

Up a few stairs and across a porch and through the door. There's a desk at the foot of the center-hall stairs, an unsmiling man who glances up at Will. "You'll be in room six, upstairs. But right now they're waiting for you at the outdoor gym."

EASTERN SHORE, VIRGINIA

"I understand you practiced karate as a kid?" The man is wearing a skin-tight tee shirt and camouflage cargo pants and combat boots. His name is apparently Jim.

Will had cycled through a variety of martial arts in elementary and intermediate school.

"That's a good start," Jim says. "We can work with that."

Without any warning Jim lunges at Will, who shunts him aside with a decent semblance of a knife-hand block.

"What the fuck?" Will yells.

"Welcome to hand-to-hand training."

Jim takes another pass at Will, this time more aggressively, and hammers him in the chest. Will stumbles backward, finds his footing, takes a deep breath.

Jim sets his feet again, with something that might be a little smile on his lips.

Okay, Will thinks again, confronted with another man: here we go.

"Do you think you've memorized our codes?"

Will nods.

"Good," she says. "Let's go through them again."

He recites the keypad sequences he memorized, tested, and retested over the past day. Meeting times and places. Emergencies.

"What types of emergencies?" he'd asked, when she introduced this idea.

"If you think you've been discovered by your wife, that's star-1. By your boss, star-2. By someone else, star-3."

"Is that really an emergency? If Chloe finds out?"

"Maybe, maybe not. If you think some type of law enforcement is onto you, hashtag-1. Intelligence operatives, hashtag-2. Someone else, hashtag-3."

"Law enforcement? Am I going to be breaking any laws?"

No answer.

He regurgitates the codes, yet again: home, office, subway platforms near either. And then foreign codes: hotel lobby, the closest bar to the west, the information booth of the central train station, the first-class ticket counter of the national airline, ever higher numbers for the increasing physical distance from the emergency.

"What about the American embassy?"

"You won't be going to any American embassy."

"What if I'm in trouble?"

"Follow the protocol. We'll help you."

"What if I'm in danger? Immediate danger?"

"Try to get out of it."

He looks at her, worry etched across his forehead.

"Let's get this straight, Will: there's a difference between you and me. I was recruited, interviewed, hired, trained. I get health insurance, a pension, security clearance. You don't. That's why we're at this satellite training facility, instead of the Farm. You're not an employee of the CIA. You don't work for Langley. Who you work for is *me*."

"Any identifying details," she said. "Hometown, age, physical attributes, occupations. Also where you meet, what time of day, anything notable about the physical encounter itself."

"About *everyone* I meet?"

"No. We don't care about chefs, winemakers, farmers, any of that lifestyle bullshit."

"Gotcha. You don't care about my actual job."

"What we're looking for are people of importance, people who might become assets. Anyone in any embassy or any level of any government, obviously. Also high-ranking businesspeople. Media figures. Any criminals, definitely, but you probably don't come across any self-identifying criminals, do you? And also any Americans."

"Americans? Why?"

"Let's get something clear: *why* is not part of the equation. Not now, not ever, not your business. Why isn't even *my* business. Who, what, when, where: those are our concerns. Not why."

He didn't understand why Elle always seemed to be so strident, as if she was angry at him. If one of them should be angry at the other, that was not the rational flow.

"This is how intelligence works, Will: you don't know the why, almost ever. You know what you're supposed to do, and hopefully how to do it. But even if someone *did* tell you a why, you'd be a fool to believe it."

He opened his mouth to ask why, but shut it quickly.

"Never *ask* why. If you want to guess, by all means go ahead, knock yourself out. But asking? That only makes you look naïve."

"I *am* naïve."

"I don't think that's quite true, Will. Not anymore."

"How's Virginia?"

"Hot," Will says. "Humid." He doesn't want to say too much; he doesn't want to lie to his wife more than necessary. He's supposedly on the other side of the Chesapeake Bay. This landline has been temporarily programmed to appear to be Will's mobile number, to anyone in the outside world. To Chloe.

Elle's room is a few doors down the hall; she said she's showering before dinner. Will imagines getting up off this lumpy mattress, walking down the hall, knock-knock, a pause, then wrapped only in a towel, wet, "Oh, hi, come on in . . ."

"And you?" he asks his wife. "What's been keeping you busy?"

The display shows two views of Will's bedroom, from two different hidden cameras.

"That's his wife he's talking to?" Roger asks.

"Yeah."

The audio is surprisingly crisp, the matrimonial chitchat unsurprisingly empty. Elle and Roger are sitting in the security room downstairs, in front of a bank of screens that monitor whatever anyone wants to monitor on this two-hundred-acre, forty-bed facility.

"But what I don't understand," Roger says, "is why we're giving him the hand-to-hand training."

Elle sighs. She'd been hoping that Roger's relative paucity of intelligence wouldn't be a problem; his responsibilities required more physical than intellectual skills. But now she was beginning to worry that he was a mistake, a liability.

"We're not really training him; Will isn't *learning* anything out there in the gym. We're assessing him." She inclines her head at the monitor. "And we're observing him."

12

"Business or pleasure?"

"Business."

"Your business is what, Mr. Rhodes?"

"I'm a writer."

The immigration officer peers up from Will's documents. "You don't say?"

Will doesn't say again. He nods.

"And how long will you be staying in the United Kingdom, Mr. Rhodes?"

"Um . . . I'm going to Scotland day after tomorrow. And then to Ireland." He can't remember when. "In five days, I think?"

Will considers taking a deep breath, but he doesn't want to look like a man who needs to take a deep breath in front of a border agent. "Sorry," he says. "I'm very tired."

The agent continues to stare at Will, no doubt wondering what needs to be done here, what level of crackpot he's dealing with.

But then without further incident, *stamp*, and, "Welcome to the United Kingdom."

A few minutes later Will collapses onto the train seat, trying to calm down, hurtling into Paddington, followed by a quick black-cab ride to his hotel in Mayfair, whose streets are being treated by Saudi princes like a Formula 1 course, yellow Lamborghinis and red Ferraris, screaming their immense wealth at the top of their lungs.

"Hi," he says to his wife's voice-mail box. Chloe had never been a very good call-answerer, though she was for a long time a reliable call-returner. Recently she's been neither, always in meetings, or at yoga, or on the subway, or on another call. "It's me, arrived in London. Love you."

The OPEN sign is still hanging from a hook on the glass door to the London bureau. An aged American couple occupy the leather club chairs at the first desk, across from a competent-looking woman who smiles fleetingly at Will. His contact is the slightly older man at the rear desk, shuffling papers and talking on the phone, looking disagreeable. His name is Cecil Wilmore, but everyone in New York refers to him as Mumblemore.

While Will waits, he reads a front-page newspaper article about the dead American who'd been discovered in Capri. Police are searching for anyone who might have any information about another hotel guest: a grainy image taken from a surveillance camera at a high angle, a woman in giant sunglasses, dark hair pulled back. Could be anyone.

"Ah," Mumblemore finally says, "there you are, mumble-mumble-mumble." An accusatory tone, as if Will is late. He's not.

"So you're off to Edinburgh? Right, mumble-mumble."

"Any advice for me?"

"There's a big castle? Go to it."

Will doesn't know what he ever did to Mumblemore, but the guy certainly seems to hate Will's guts.

"What else? Mmm. *Do* try the haggis." He turns back to his computer.

"That's very helpful." This is the stupidest travel advice Will has ever received. "Thanks."

"Mmm."

Will removes an envelope from his jacket, trades it for Mumblemore's, another list of new restaurants and renovated hotels, people to see places to go, just as he's done dozens of times. But this time is different. This time he's a covert asset of the CIA, gathering intelligence on foreign soil. This time he's breaking the law.

It's not what you do that defines you. It's why you do it.

FALLS CHURCH

Raji initiates another alert about U.S. passport number 11331968, a credit card run through a hotel. He opens the map app to find the hotel's location, enters those details into his alert, thorough as ever, no shortcuts, never relying on just one source of information, always cross-checking, aiming for 100 percent accuracy on addresses and intersections and time zones and flight delays, anything that anyone could want to know about the peregrinations of the subjects on Raji's newly narrowed segment of the watch list.

It looks like a very nice hotel that this guy checked into. Raji has never stayed in a very nice hotel, and is fairly certain he never will.

"Whassup Raj-man?" It's his boss, Brock, leaning on the flimsy wall that separates Raji's cubicle from Zander's. "You goin' to Scotland?"

"Yeah right."

"Who is it?" Brock leans forward, getting a closer look at the screen, the small window with the subject's details.

Raji knows the protocol, Brock knows the protocol, everyone knows the protocol: no discussing the subjects. Especially for this new assignment for the mystery client. But no one follows the protocol. This job would be too boring if they couldn't share irrelevant intel about meaningless strangers. "Some travel-writer dude."

Brock is disappointed. His interest is limited to female subjects. "All right then, Raj-man, keep on keepin' on."

The boss walks away, continuing on his predictable rounds of checking in with his team, "my guys," he calls them. Raji suspects that Brock adheres to a set of business-management tips that runs to a half-page, a listicle, maybe an off-topic feature in *Guns & Ammo*.

Brock had been the middle of Raji's job-interview sandwich, two years ago, after a human-resources specialist who'd asked for signatures on an assortment of waivers that Raji didn't attempt to comprehend, including the release of his fingerprints and a urine-sample screening. A week later Raji returned to meet Brock, then waited in the very quiet reception area until the white-bread department head was available for a pro forma ten-minute vetting.

Raji signed more waivers. Filled out more forms. Accepted the degradation of a physical exam from a supposed doctor who didn't seem to know how to operate the blood-pressure cuff. Thank God the guy didn't attempt to draw a blood sample.

Then Raji was hired. He was issued an ID card with a magnetic strip that links to the database with his identifying statistics and physical report, his educational background and history of addresses, his parents'

Social Security numbers and the contact information for his previous employers.

Raji doesn't know if he has a security clearance, or if he does, at what level. And the truth is he doesn't really know whom he works for, or what his office does, for which entity. He does care about these questions—he'd prefer to know, rather than not know—but this preference isn't overwhelming. Raji cares much more about having a secure job with a biweekly check and airtight health benefits. The physical exam wasn't very in-depth, not enough to identify what's wrong with Raji.

NEW YORK CITY

"You're not leaving," Gabriella says.

"You're mistaken." Malcolm snaps shut his briefcase, and drags it off his desk by the handle. "I am."

Gabriella is standing in Malcolm's door, arms crossed, projecting hostility and disappointment. Even though Malcolm is her boss, Gabriella seems determined to try to undermine the hierarchy of that relationship, every day, in every way. In turn, Malcolm unwaveringly makes sure to thwart her subversion. It's an uneasy professional dance, but not an unfriendly personal relationship.

"I don't know what to tell you, boss," says Stonely Rodriguez, who's sitting in Malcolm's chair, staring intently at the computer screen, right hand on mouse, left hand supporting chin. "You got some crazy shit on your hard drive."

"Yeah, I know that. But what I don't know is: can you clean it up?"

"I can *try*. Yeah."

Stonely tugs on the bill of his Cincinnati Reds cap, the one that's all red with a white C. He has a half-dozen Cincinnati caps through which he rotates. "I wear the Reds caps 'cause of the C," he'll say, to anyone who asks. "My real name is César. Stonely's just a nickname I got, because I once went a week without realizing that I'd broken a finger." Almost none of that story is true.

"Thanks Stonely. Do what you can." Malcolm turns back to Gabriella. "You can come with me, if you want. Take a ride downtown."

"Really? You've become that type of asshole?"

"Oh *shit*." Stonely snickers, then covers his mouth. "Sorry, boss."

"What type is that, Gabs?"

"The type who makes people ride in cars to have meetings?"

"Darling, I became that type of asshole years ago. Isn't that right, Stonely?"

"Don't know nothing 'bout that, boss."

"Anyway, are you coming with me or not? Because I'm leaving now. There's a zero-tolerance policy for school-pickup lateness." Although this is a new routine for him—a concession to Allison, once-a-week pickup—he has already gleaned the important conventions.

Malcolm sees Gabriella do an emotional hiccup—just an involuntary wince—but she quickly regains her composure. "Let me grab my bag."

They ride the elevator in silence. There's no one else in the big mirrored cabin, but Gabriella knows that Malcolm doesn't talk in elevators. He uses the downtime to send a tweet. A few months ago, he'd been ordered by his CEO to start tweeting. Another social-media solution to a nonexistent problem. Malcolm had been about to ask, "Tweet about what? Why?" But he realized that if he didn't ask, then he wouldn't end up disobeying explicit instructions.

His thumbs fly across his phone, tapping out: *So proud of my wonderful team! You guys are the best!! #humbled.* Many of Malcolm's tweets consist of empty pandering, usually with no connection to any event in the real world. What amazes him is that people retweet this drivel.

The car is waiting in front of the building. "School please, Hector," Malcolm says. Then adds, "Thanks." The type of asshole he doesn't want to become is the one who doesn't say thanks to his driver. But sometimes it's difficult to remember. He's still working through the adjustment of having become a guy with a driver, which itself is a de facto level of assholery with which he's not entirely comfortable. There are plenty of guys like Malcolm who unabashedly embrace their douchebaggery—they *own* it, managing to convince themselves of something that Malcolm cannot.

"Fucking traffic." Malcolm scowls at the snarl, the inevitable midafternoon mess. Glances at his watch. "We should be on the subway."

"Then why aren't we?"

"You know I can't take the subway."

"What? I don't know that. Why?"

"Unacceptable optics. Can't have the editor of the world's most re-spected travel brand slumming it on public transportation. Standing there among the unwashed, arm hanging from a strap."

"There aren't any straps, Mal. You know that, right?"

It's indeed against company policy to have any of the chief editors rid-ing public transportation to and from the office. As well as eating in a fast-food restaurant, ever. Or flying certain airlines, the uncooperative ones.

There's also a surprisingly involved set of wardrobe strictures, mostly related to size and prominence of logos; schedule D on Malcolm's employ-ment contract enumerates the accepted logos, and schedule E the forbid-den ones. Both schedules are updated annually, along with some other clauses. Malcolm pays a couple of thousand dollars per year for a lawyer to review the updated addenda. And then Malcolm himself needs to re-view these schedules against his goddamned closet. Or, rather, he needs to ask his wife to do this for him, and then he needs to suffer through Allie's scorn, her passive-aggressive delays.

A lot of new rules came with the new job. Some don't look especially burdensome; not many people would complain about the chauffeur. But sometimes he wishes he could eat a crappy hamburger, on the subway.

They're stalled in traffic next to a car with a BABY ON BOARD decal. Malcolm pulls out his phone, sends another tweet, *Baby on Board? Thx for info! Otherwise I was planning on crashing into your car, but now won't. #self-obsessed.*

At Forty-second Street the congestion vanishes, poof, and the black car is zooming through the Garment District.

"So, Gabriella, what is it we're discussing?"

The traffic lights are synchronized to the southbound flow, just shy of thirty miles per hour. For all the torture of the congested hours' stop-and-go, Manhattan can also be fast to navigate, in the right conditions.

"Why'd you give the new assignment to Will?"

"Please, don't beat around the bush. We don't have a lot of time, Gabs, so tell me straight: what is it that's on your mind?"

"I could do a *great* job with it, Malcolm. You know I could."

Malcolm sighs, exaggerated, just as he does with his children when he's trying to project his exasperation with their bickering, or poor table manners, or questionable hygiene, or all the other dispiriting behaviors of eight- and four-year-olds. "Yes, Gabs, I have no doubt that you could. But you're the one who made the decision, you came to me and said—"

"Things were different, and you know that."

"—'Malcolm, I need to come home.' And I made a *lot* of changes to accommodate you. *Difficult* changes. I invented a new position for you. A new role."

"And I've been good at it."

"Yes you have. You have made yourself indispensable. *Doing what you do.* Not doing your old job. Not doing Will's job."

She doesn't respond for a few seconds, doesn't want to argue herself out of the compliment, but she also doesn't want to accept it. "This is not me, Malcolm. This is not what I'm supposed to be doing with my life."

"What can I tell you, sweetheart? That's what it means to be a grown-up."

"And what about Will?"

"First of all, what business is that of yours? Second: Will can do the overseas job, I'm confident of that. But he can't do the one here. Your job."

"Why not?"

Malcolm dips the angle of his head, levels a look at her, doesn't say a word.

"Does he know?" she asks.

"Of course not."

"You've never mentioned anything? All these years?"

"Come on, Gabs."

"When are you going to tell him? *Are* you going to tell him?"

Malcolm doesn't answer. "Are you saying you want to still be out there?"

"Honestly, I don't know. But I don't want to be passed over because I'm a woman."

"That's bullshit, Gabs. Not what happened, not even a tiny bit, and you damn well know it." Malcolm can be accused of many things that women might find offensive. But he's not this type of sexist. "I'm a misanthrope, not a misogynist. There's a difference."

"Why is it you who has your job, Malcolm? And not me?"

Malcolm has wondered the same thing. Gabriella has been at *Travelers* longer, she has more management experience, more New York person-about-town experience, she looks and sounds better on TV and in front of a big crowd. What she doesn't have is real foreign-journalism experience, but that shouldn't matter. And she doesn't have a Y chromosome.

"I don't know, Gabs." Malcolm is pretty sure it was indeed sexism. It just wasn't Malcolm's.

They ride in silence, both knowing that Malcolm is lying, neither seeing any benefit in pursuing it any further.

"Have you heard from him?" she asks.

Malcolm shakes his head. "You?"

She too shakes her head. This time, neither knows if the other is lying.

The car pulls to a stop in front of the Village Academy. The curb is lined with a phalanx of imported SUVs, nearly all black, with hazards blinking and bourgeois-bohemian people behind the wheels, Hot Moms in workout gear and aviators, Cool Dads in trucker caps and facial hair, MONTAUK stickers in the windshields and/or surfboards on the roof racks of the Range Rovers and AMGs.

"I don't want to wait in the car," he says. "I feel like too much of a jackass. You want to get out with me? Or Hector can take you back to the office? Or somewhere else?"

"I'll get out. Survey the local fauna."

"Thanks Hector," Malcolm says. "See you tomorrow."

Malcolm climbs out of the backseat. He wishes he could pretend that this liveried car is just a onetime thing, because it's raining—it's not—or the subways are all fucked up—they're not, as far as he knows—or because he has some physical problem—he doesn't. He briefly considers exaggerating his limp, proving to all these witnesses that the reason he's getting out of a chauffeured car is that he's injured—there are plenty of injuries he can imagine fabricating—but of course Gabriella would notice, and ask, what the fuck are you doing?

Maybe he'll tell Hector to keep a cane in the trunk, for future hoaxes. Or a pair of crutches. Malcolm has an increasingly deep fascination with elaborate hoaxes.

He looks around the busy sidewalk while a few heads turn, some eyes glance up from devices. He's one of the full-time-working dads, wearing a business suit—the suit-wearing population doesn't as a rule make it to three o'clock pickup—and getting out of a black car with a stunning woman to whom he's not married. That'll get people talking.

"I see that some men are allowed to gather their young. That's progressive."

The few handfuls of guys are mostly wearing jeans and some version of sneakers. These are guys who call their sons "buddy," which Malcolm loathes, for reasons he finds himself unable to articulate.

"So, Mal, are the rumors true?"

"Sorry, what are we talking about now?"

"Are the terms of the sale final? Are we about to be swallowed up by an evil international conglomerate?" The acquisition was begun under Jonathan's tenure, and then the deal stalled, until it was renewed with heightened vigor and urgency a few months ago.

He cocks his head, rolls his eyes, *well* . . . "I don't know about *evil*."

"Good God."

"We don't really have a choice. The bottom line has been the wrong color for years."

"How is a merger going to solve that problem?"

"Efficiencies."

"You mean layoffs."

"Layoffs. And write-offs," he says. "Plus depreciation."

"You don't know what you're talking about, do you?"

"Of course not. I'm an editor, not a suit."

She looks his suit up and down.

"What can I tell you, Gabs? The sale is not my call, obviously. But we're going to have to be extra-careful now."

The merger itself isn't the threat; it's the increased scrutiny that Malcolm is worried about. The possibility that some new boss will arrive with a new curiosity about what Malcolm does in the secret room behind his office wall.

"This is a very dangerous time for us. We could both end up unemployed. *Very* soon."

This is not news to Gabs, but she nods, agreeing.

"Why the hell do we do this, Malcolm?"

He gestures at the melee unfolding, a hundred kids streaming out of the school, into the arms of a hundred loved ones. "Why does anyone do anything?"

Even as it's coming out of his mouth, he realizes this comment is a mistake. In fact, he shouldn't even have invited Gabriella to come along to school; that was insensitive. Malcolm finds it hard to remember where Gabriella is in the world, that she doesn't have absolutely everything, because she usually looks so much like she does.

"Gabs, you know I need you, right?"

"Do you?"

Malcolm sees his eldest, Sylvie, emerge from the heavy steel doors, blah-blah-blahing to her little companion, who's blah-blah-blahing right back at her, both little girls talking at cross-purposes, full volume, ignoring the other.

"Please, Gabs, I have to ask you to trust me on this."

She looks him in the eye, searching for something, then nods, walks away. The men nearby all pretend they're not watching her, but most don't do a very convincing job of it.

Malcolm wonders if Gabriella is going to be a problem, on top of all the other problems. A whole smorgasbord of problems, a rich and varied feast of things Malcolm does not want to eat. How did life get so complicated?

STOCKHOLM

The American climbs out of the taxi in front of the warehouse in the farthest reaches of Södermalm. He manages to survive the doorman's dubious scrutiny, and pays his cover charge, and walks through the thumping entry hall into the cavernous dance club, a thousand people in here, maybe more, everyone younger than he, nearly all of them by four decades, even five.

He beckons a bartender with a large-denomination bill. "I'll have a beer!" he yells. "And I'm looking for Lars!"

The cap pops off and foam bubbles over as the bottle hits the bar. "Over there"—inclining his head. The American turns to the shadowy corner, where a man by himself leans against a wall, surveying the scene, bopping his head to the beat.

"Thanks!" He leaves a big tip, a memorable tip. The American who leaves the big tips is how he wants bartenders and waitresses and bellhops and taxi drivers to remember him, a favor banked in the endless circle of transactions that is life, deposits and withdrawals, credit and insolvency. And it makes him look like someone who's not hiding; people who are hiding don't leave memorable tips.

"Hello Lars."

A reluctant nod. "Wel-wel-welcome back to The Warehouse, Joe. Do you like it tonight, is there something I can g-g-get you, I see you al-al-already have a b-b-beer, is there some-some-something else you would, ah, like?"

"What do you have to offer?"

Lars glances over, a quick assessment. "I can offer ev-ev-everything. I be-believe you know that. A young bl-bl-blond girl, perhaps? Or would it be a b-b-boy for you?"

"I'm looking for something unusual. Can we go somewhere quiet?"

Lars turns to face him fully, the disco strobe cutting a rapid bright swath across both their faces. "Pl-pl-please. F-f-follow me."

The stuttering Swedish clubber leads the way, skirting the black-painted brick wall, picking his way through the heaving humanity of dancers, under a high arch and into a wide low-ceilinged hall where kids on Ecstasy and crystal meth and coke are making out and groping at crotches and tits and asses, a bare shoulder here and an exposed breast there, a cock clutched in a fist whose every finger is adorned with at least one ring, a cluster of people looking on in expectation, unsure what's going to happen next, to whom, but it sure will be something.

At the end of the hall a red light illuminates a fire door that Lars pushes through, its alarm disabled, as these things often are, into the open air. They climb a set of exposed metal stairs to a catwalk that connects the warehouse to another structure.

It's quiet out here, the music a distant hum. The American is disoriented, in the middle of this industrial campus, unsure where's the street and where's the water, trying to figure it out from the light level on the dusky horizon, but who the hell cares.

"T-t-tell me, what is it you are loo-loo-looking for?"

"Travel documents." The American has an alternate passport—of course he does, at least one, always—but it's best to get a fresh one if possible. Fake passports have invisible expiration dates.

"This is n-n-not inexpensive."

"I understand that."

Lars lights a cigarette, exhales a cloud of smoke over the rail of the narrow bridge hanging over the truck track forty feet below, a long drop. "L-l-let me see what I can do."

13

Will stands at the top of the Royal Mile and takes in his surroundings along with a deep breath of the clean air, a whiff of salt coming from the Firth of Forth. He looks around, his vision sharply focused, hyper-aware of his surroundings, the people.

He began to notice this new excess of clarity yesterday, on the trip from London, looking up from his e-book, a CIA memoir. This was the fourth book in that genre he'd read in as many weeks, all loaded onto the tablet, so no one could see what he was reading. Now Will understands why so many people had recently become so willing to read porn.

His secret reading these days is homework, trying to educate himself about his new line of work, just like his research in the *Travelers* archives. Will has been a dedicated practitioner of homework his whole life, as much in adulthood as in childhood. He studies maps and old articles, guidebooks and language primers, essays and memoirs and cookbooks and, now, books about being a spy.

The train was passing through all those grand Victorian sheds, red brick walls and arched roofs supported by fluted columns and iron trestles, massive clocks precise to the second. The countryside was uneventful, suburban housing in turns squat stony-mossy or self-consciously modern in futuristic shapes—cylindrical structures, triangular roofs—fabricated from matte metal in primary colors. Black-faced sheep grazed fields atop dark stark bluffs beside the rocky North Sea beaches, the angry Turner sea under a brooding Wyeth sky, all the expected grays.

A teenage boy was sitting in front of Will, nervously fondling his ticket, a small overnight bag perched beside him, wearing only one ear bud, so he could hear the world. Nervous, maybe traveling alone for the first time, wearing new shoes, a pressed shirt.

Will was aware of absorbing everything, ruling out possibilities, speculating about this over-groomed boy, about everyone, the surly conductor with the incomprehensible accent, the giddy young women who boarded in Leeds, the lecherous guy who sauntered through the musty coach, giving every woman the eye.

Will felt as if he'd previously been wandering through life in a haze, all his experiences dulled in a miasma of low stakes. Not anymore.

The sights of Edinburgh are recognizable, the layout of the city familiar—you can see it all before you.

Will waits in the gathering midmorning heat amid the babel of a tourist-attraction ticket queue. Behind Will a toddler is in apparent crisis, desperately wanting something that's impossible to provide. This crowd is heavy on professional-looking tourists in their task-specific lightweight water-wicking manmade-fiber gear, with profuse zippers and pockets and mesh vents for breathability. There are hobbled undefeated old people, and panic-stricken Chinese, and towering magenta-haired German women and skinny smoky Frenchmen, everyone all pressed together, waiting to take the glossy brochure and hang the audio player around their necks, like digital cowbells.

Will always—100 percent of the time—takes the audio tour.

He eats haggis. He does the thing that's done, dumplings in Hong Kong and *mole* in Oaxaca and pizza in Naples, searching for the ideal expression of the commonplace.

And now, he's also searching for something else.

DUBLIN

The rain comes down in sheets, a steeply sideways rain, an aggressively drenching rain that no umbrella can thwart, soaking Will's pants and shoes and socks. Will totes the *Travelers*-issued camera through Georgian Dublin, snapshots of the unornamented bricks, severe façades, orderly windows and black wrought-iron gates, the understated properness of it all, Merrion Square, St. Stephen's Green, the regimented quads of Trinity College. Everything that's not gray is green.

Will takes a public tour of another ancient castle, this time with a handful of avid Irish-Americans. He takes a private tour of Leinster House, shakes hands with a couple of distracted members of parliament, on their way to and from everything more important than chitchat with a marginal American journo. It's on these rare occasions when he's face-to-face with real newsmakers, or real news reporters, that he most intensely feels the gap between what he once wanted to become and what he actually is. Carrying around his little notebook as if he's writing a real story, though it's just a couple hundred words about fish pie, or stout.

At night he meanders through the banal raucousness of Temple Bar, like the Latin Quarter in Paris, Bourbon Street in New Orleans, any other well-known party district, nominal cover charges and halfhearted ID checks, debilitating shots and saccharine chasers, the music too loud and the crowds too dense, the panicked crush of last call, stumbling in the streets, the dangerous mess of mass intoxication.

Will flees this place, nothing new here, nothing good. He heads to a working-class pub in North Dublin, a place recommended by his airport taxi driver. Away from the college kids and semesters-abroad, in a roughish-looking neighborhood, he drinks pints of Guinness, warm and flat and bitter.

He stays late, then steps out into the deserted street, a foreboding chill. A block or two away, tires screech. From another direction, a loud laugh, the threatening sort. Will hears a man shout and a dog bark, the same sounds of dangerous dark anywhere. He's more aware of them than he used to be.

He's a couple of miles from his hotel, and he suspects he's not going to find a taxi. Maybe he should return inside, ask the barkeep for a number. Maybe use his phone, try to solve the problem in the contemporary fashion.

Will hitches up his pants, takes stock. Although he wouldn't call himself drunk, he's definitely not sober.

A trio of young men round the corner, turn onto his street, and seem to notice him.

Will is ready for this, he thinks. He's been training, he's in good shape. Maybe he's even looking for it.

NEW YORK CITY

After the two days at the camp in Virginia, Will had come home with the very beginnings of fresh skill sets, both of which needed a lot of additional work. So the plan was to continue to run Will through his paces, practicing surveillance and countersurveillance on the streets of the city, early mornings and lunchtimes and the occasional fallow stretch of afternoon, following random passersby, rabbit moves and leapfrogging and route recon, observed closely by Elle and Roger, then debriefed in the secluded booths of greasy spoons and shot-and-a-beer bars.

"What about firearms?" he asked Elle.

"What about them?" She dipped a French fry into a gravy boat. Will had never witnessed anyone order fries with gravy on the side, a bowl of brown gloop with a ladle.

"When will I get a gun?"

"Are you out of your fucking mind? I certainly hope you never get a gun. There are already far too many guns in the hands of people who shouldn't have them. Almost all guns, in fact."

Will didn't have a rational rebuttal at the ready. He didn't disagree.

"You don't know how to use a pistol, do you? And you can't take one abroad. So the only thing any type of firearm is going to get you is in trouble, or shot. If you really feel the need to accomplish either of those things, just let me know, I'll take care of it for you."

Will let it drop.

At lunchtime the next day, he practiced a surveillance-detection route, unsupervised, unmonitored, on his own. He headed west, in fits and starts and double-backs, through lobbies and tunnels and big crowds and empty stretches, out past the tall modernist office buildings, out past the theaters, out past the tenements, all the way to one of the last forlorn plots of Manhattan real estate, where a dilapidated warehouse loomed next to a chaotic taxi garage.

A uniformed security guard sat in front of a tiny fan, dozing. Will walked past him, climbed two very long sets of steep steps. He pushed open a heavy steel door.

A man was waiting in the big open space. The floors were covered in mats, the walls padded.

"Hi, I'm Will."

The man extended his hand for a bone-crushing shake. "Frank." He took Will's measure without any pretense of hiding it. "So you wanna be trained in mixed martial arts, huh?"

"That's right." Will had called earlier, from the communal phone in the archive room.

"Okay." Nodding, but not really in agreement. "Why?"

"I want to be a little less bad at defending myself."

DUBLIN

The pub is behind Will, fifty yards; the menacing trio is in front, seventy-five. Will still has the option of turning around, fleeing back into the safety of the crowd, tail between legs. But maybe the pub is where the young men are going. Or even if not, maybe they'll follow him in, smelling his fear, tasting his blood.

No. He won't back down, not from this.

He walks toward them, muscles tensing, senses sharpened. He smells their cigarette smoke wafting on the wind, hears a cough. He looks at the cougher, just a kid really, skinny and pimply, and he realizes they're all kids, teenagers or even tweens, nervous, maybe they snuck out with stolen cigarettes, trying it out, coughing, giggling, worried about getting caught.

"Good evening, sir," one says when they pass, giving Will ample berth, a grown man emerging from a pub, late at night on a dark street.

Will had misunderstood. They're afraid of him.

NEW YORK CITY

Gabriella sets off on a reverse immigration from the Upper East Side, like *The Jeffersons* going back in time, leaving the de luxe apartment in the sky, an apartment that Terrance found by the happenstance of family connections, a short-term deal turned into a long-term steal, surrounded by all these upright citizens, their well-dressed kids and well-groomed dogs, not a choke-collared pit bull among them. The only other non-Caucasian in the building is a beautiful and always put-together dark-skinned African-American woman whom Gabriella thinks of as Black Barbie. It appears that Gabriella and Black Barbie have tacitly agreed to not be friends, not wanting to give the appearance of forming any sort of minority alliance.

Over on the Lexington Avenue local, the crowd is mostly blacks and Hispanics coming down from Harlem and the Bronx. At Union Square Gabriella transfers to the L train in a swarm of the North Brooklyn crowd, the college-degreed kids, who all get off within a few stops, most of them immediately in Williamsburg but the younger, more tattooed ones in Bushwick.

Then out past all the gentrification and pioneering, the subway rumbles through one slum after another, graffiti on the station walls, the stench of urine when the doors open, busted overhead lights, the ever present possibility of malevolence amid all this malignant neglect, where the real-estate stock is unredeemed and unredeemable—housing projects and six-story apartment buildings with trash-strewn concrete courtyards, abandoned buildings alongside empty lots filled with junk and junkies, police-cruiser lights flashing and engines revving as the sedans race between disaster and tragedy, cops getting out warily, hands on holsters.

The voyage can last as long as ninety minutes door-to-door, longer to ride the subway to Canarsie than to fly to D.C. She brings a sheaf of reading material with her, usually the unmanageable pile of the Sunday *Times*, and she settles in.

Her mother's apartment—the apartment Gabriella and her sister grew up in—is the second floor of an aluminum-sided house with a brick stoop, one bathroom and two small bedrooms, the four of them living in nine hundred square feet for her entire childhood. Dinner is rice and beans, curried oxtail stew, a visit from her Grandmother Teresa with her diabetes and arthritis, also the onset of dementia, referring to Gabriella with a name to which she hasn't answered in fifteen years.

"Please Abuela," she says, in her most patient voice, "call me Gabriella."

"But your name is *Crystal*." A confused look on Teresa's face, trying to understand.

"Not anymore, Abuela." She ditched that stripper name when she went to college, started using her middle name, her paternal grandmother's. Gabriella shed her original skin layer by layer, first her name and then her clothes, her accent and her music, her attitude and her outlook, trying to stand out less dramatically from the other New York girls on campus.

She boards the return subway at nine o'clock, the train car almost empty, not many people headed from the farthest reaches of Brooklyn into Manhattan on a Sunday night, just dark-skinned commuters on their way to shitty late-shift jobs wearing cheap denim and white sneakers, playing video games on phones, or staring into space.

At Sutter Avenue, in the heart of East New York, trouble gets on the subway, wearing all the signifiers of a guy who thinks he's tough, the undisguised stare, grabbing at his crotch, a predator.

"'S'up."

In response Gabriella produces the smallest possible smile, not encouraging but not entirely dismissive. You can't completely ignore guys like this, it only makes it worse.

He takes a seat next to her, far too close. She can tell that a few other people notice this intrusion, but they're all middle-aged or older, or women. No one here is going to help her.

"Where you goin'?"

She doesn't answer.

"You fine, you know that?" He strokes her cheek with the backside of his hand.

She slides across the bench. "Please don't touch me."

"You too fine for me?" He reaches to her thigh, a stroke. Right there, she thinks, sexual assault.

At the far end of the car, a woman stands, opens the door, and leaves, retreating to the relative safety of another car, a witness to nothing.

Gabriella looks at this guy: yellow eyes, hooded lids, scar across the chin, tattoo of a Chinese character on the neck. She wonders if he's armed. Anybody can get a gun these days, sometimes for as little as fifty bucks, less than half a pair of sneakers.

"Did I invite you to touch me?" she asks. "I don't think I did, Papi." She has found that semi-thugs are often intimidated by the perceived thugness of other ethnicities. So with African-Americans she'll accentuate her

Hispanic heritage; with Latins she'll pretend she's black. "So please remove your hand from my leg."

He glowers at her, his hand still resting on her thigh.

"You a big man, Papi?" She turns to face him head-on. "Sexually harassing women? On the subway? Tough guy?"

He sucks his teeth.

"Okay, tough guy. I'll give you till the count of three."

"Yeah?" He sucks his teeth again. "Then what?"

She doesn't have any intention of counting to three. She shoots her right elbow up into the bottom of his jaw, can hear the teeth knocking together as she brings her left arm across her body, a wide hook that lands dead on his mouth, busting his lip, blood spattering across the window.

"Crazy bitch!" He jumps up, and so does she, razor-focused on his body language, the position of his hands. If he has a weapon, she needs to see him reach for it before he even knows she's noticing.

But he doesn't reach for anything except his bleeding face, staring at her in disbelief, completely unprepared for this, no idea how to respond.

The train is slowing, coming into a station. Big drops of blood spatter onto the filthy floor.

The doors opens.

Gabriella can see him thinking about attacking her, charging her. He's much taller. He's pretty sure he can take her. But then again, she just fucked up his face very quickly, and if there's one humiliation he doesn't want, it's to get beaten up on the subway by a woman.

He stares at her, testing her resolve, perhaps his own. She doesn't look away; after a couple of seconds, he does. He turns, walks out, onto the dimly lit empty platform.

The doors close. The punk turns back to stare at her, sucks his teeth yet again, even in defeat unwilling to back down completely, too much pride for his own goddamned good. Lucky to still be alive. She'd considered killing him.

The train starts to move.

An old woman at the end of the car puts her hands together, clap, clap, clap, nodding at Gabriella. A couple of other people join as the train leaves the station, screeching around a curve, picking up speed.

14

DUBLIN

Will sits in his hotel lobby, highly polished Regency tables and gleaming brass lamps, taut silk upholstery with tasseled fringes. An American couple slouch on a camelback sofa, both turning the pages of competing guidebooks. Will notices these couples all the time, two people who don't seem to have had a civil conversation in a decade, yet somehow manage to tough it out. Will can't decide if it's admirable or pathetic or both.

He checks the time, does the math. Chloe is probably at work. He sends her a friendly anodyne text message, receives a quick response, nothing specific being communicated here, just the abstract desire—the commitment—to communicate.

For a while they'd tried to talk daily when one or both were traveling. But it was usually more frustrating and inconvenient than anything, with time-zone differences and dead zones and spotty reception, not to mention the work they were doing abroad. So they agreed to text instead, each absolving the other of the responsibility of stepping away from working to take an errant call from an elusive spouse.

Will looks up as a man struts into the sitting room, broad-shouldered and clean-shaven, wearing a capitalist-in-repose getup, suede loafers, pressed shirt with monogrammed cuffs, jeans with a woven belt. This must be Will's contact, consulting his wristwatch, making sure everyone notices his jewelry, his impatience, his importance.

"Excuse me," Will says, "are you Shane Nicholson?"

"Yes sir. You're Will Rhodes?" Handshaking. "Pleasure to meet you." Backslapping.

They leave the hotel, Shane showering Will with bonhomie, two American men abroad, us against them, of course Shane has never much cared for New York, in fact distrusts big cities generally, no offense intended, and here they live in a palace in the suburbs, bought for next to nothing, you know what I mean, half-tempted to sell just to turn the profit, before prices collapse again which they're bound to do within two years, tops, but then I'd have to find another place to live, and, well, I'm telling you, this house is *big*.

Yes, Will thinks: my car, my life, my everything, all big, bigger than yours.

They walk a few blocks, then down a few steps, through a door decorated with a tiny American flag on a tiny flagpole.

Inside, televisions are on. It's a cold rainy Sunday night in Dublin, but it's a bright sunny midafternoon in the U.S.A., baseball season on satellite TV. Will is introduced around to the guys, a baker's dozen of men in their late twenties to early fifties, middle and upper management, interchangeable widgety men who do abstract widgety things.

"But these guys over here? The Irish?" Shane is asking with a sneer. "You talk to them about EBITA, about quality control? They look at you like you're out of your friggin' mind." Shane takes a thoughtful sip of lager. "No one here knows how to run a business."

"*No* one?"

"Well, not *no* one." Retreating from the overwhelming ignorance of his slur, slightly. "But you know what I'm saying." You're saying you're a jingoist ass, Will thinks, but keeps quiet. He's not here to make enemies with guys who run outsourced data-processing centers.

Will turns to Bryson from Atlanta, pink-faced and white-haired and blue-blazered, a hypertensive American flag. Bryson is an avid reader of presidential biographies; he enjoys sharing pithy anecdotes in boardrooms and bathrooms and barrooms like this one. "You know, when Rough and Ready was in the White House . . ."

Bryson is another expert on everything, a man who sees life as a series of trades in expertise, that you are what you know—or can plausibly assert to know—about anything, shipping routes, the Dodgers' pitching rotation, health-care premiums, grilling meat.

Will listens to Bryson bloviate, rewards him with on-cue smiles and guffaws. Bryson is exactly the type of guy who'll say something he shouldn't.

"So tell me," Will says, letting his laugh die down from a notably un-funny joke about Danish women. "Which one of you expats here has the dirtiest secret?"

Bryson recoils, taken aback, but not really, just making a show of it.

"Anyone hiding anything ugly? Extramarital affair? Embezzlement? C'mon." Will beckons the waiter. "I'll buy another." Cash on the bar, two simultaneous transactions.

"Well, there's this one gentleman"—everyone is a lady or a gentleman to Bryson, except his wife, who's "the wife"—"comes here to watch foot-ball." Bryson looks around conspiratorially, making sure they're unob-served, while in fact drawing observation. "Doesn't really talk to anyone, doesn't say much about anything."

"Wow. What a scandal! Thanks for sharing, Bryson."

The guy chuckles into his beer, the condescending laugh of a man who knows that his companion is missing the point. He turns to face Will. "This guy?" Drawing out the moment for maximum impact. "We all think he's in the witness-protection program."

STOCKHOLM

The American cinches the straps of his backpack, and sets off on foot in the bright light of midafternoon, early summer, into the alleys and cob-blestones and ocher-tinted buildings of Gamla Stan, narrow streets ris-ing and falling, hills and stairs, restaurants and cafés. He walks past the opera house and the royal palace and into downtown, which is any other downtown, public-transportation hubs and brutalist department stores and chewing-gum-blackened paving stones, H&Ms—the originals!—and kebab shops, pickpockets and bureaucrats and a hollow-eyed panhandler slumped on the sidewalk, shaking a paper cup. He wades through this close humanity, bodies and sweat, perfume and cigarettes, the stench of a derelict as she passes, at once pleading and predatory, a young woman who's her parents' worst nightmare.

Joe removes himself from the scrum, walks past the hotels that line the promenade fronting the waterway, small ferries and water taxis and pleasure craft, broad avenues filled with joggers and strollers, café tables under giant umbrellas, awnings over windows, and always a constant sense of sky—of vistas opening out, hills and bluffs and green spaces, a view of water around every corner, and a view on every patch of grass of a young woman in a bikini, sunbathing and smoking a cigarette and drinking beer, all the things you're not supposed to do, all at once, but that seems ludicrous to these girls, alarmist, when you're young and beautiful, and life will go on forever.

He buys a newspaper and takes an outdoor seat at a café. Blue-and-white streetcars are gliding by, Porsches and Volvos, bicycles and mopeds. Gucci and Vuitton are across the street, with their merchandise scattered about this terrace too, draped on the good-looking lunchtime crowd who are dressed as if for work but look more like actors who've just departed the stage set of an office, and this café is maybe the commissary. Or the continuation of the set.

The American watches a man arrive who fits the description, says hello to another man, joins his table, beckons the waitress. She kisses him on the cheek, we're all friends, but she's the one carrying the tray of drinks, and he's the one checking out her ass.

Another man walks up the block; this must be Anders, a steroids-y guy, disproportionate upper body straining at his tee shirt. There are an awful lot of this type in the world, and these guys all wear their hair the same, short and wet and a little angry.

The man nods at the American, takes a seat. There's an empty chair between the two men, and Anders places a small shopping bag beside it, a shirt store, tissue paper visible inside.

"Tell me about this."

Anders glares at him for a second, then rolls his eyes. Shrugs, exaggerated, engaging every superfluous bulge and ripple. This guy makes a lot of movements whose primary goal is to accentuate his muscles.

Anders sighs. "It is of the *highest* quality."

The American smiles. "I'm going to the bathroom."

Anders makes a quick nasal snort, then holds out both hands, resigned, if-you-must.

The American places the shopping bag in the sink. He unfolds the tissue paper, pulls out the passport. The photo looks enough like him, with the long beard he has been wearing since he moved to Scandinavia. The age is a reasonable approximation. The pages include a not-unusual collection of stamps for a British tourist, a dirty sticker on back from a luggage tag. It looks perfect. But the most important elements can't be seen.

"Your turn," Anders says, back at the table.

The American folds back his newspaper just enough to reveal a corner of a padded envelope. Anders picks this up, disappears to the men's room, to count his money. Neither party in this transaction is the trusting type.

When Anders returns, the American is gone, around the corner, where he shrugs out of his navy oxford shirt, revealing a white tee shirt. He retrieves a cap and sunglasses from his bag, puts them on. He follows the surly thug from a safe distance, two blocks, three. No need to get too close. There's a slender electronic tracking device slipped into the padding of the envelope.

IRELAND

"I'm writing an article about expat Americans."

The man is blocking his doorway, not looking like he's going to change his mind about his unwelcoming attitude. The wind is blowing strong and salty off the Irish Sea, a churning gray at the end of the quiet street. Will pushes his fluttering hair out of his eyes.

"And what did you say was the name of the magazine?"

"*Travelers*. Have you heard of it?"

The man nods.

"So would you have a few minutes? I can keep this short."

"I'm sorry, how'd you find me?"

This is not encouraging. "Some Americans down at the sports bar."

"Why do you want to talk to me?"

"I'm trying to get a sense of what life is like here, as an American expat. Someone mentioned you watch a lot of football. Is that one of the main things you miss?"

"Who, exactly, down at the pub?"

Will stares at this man, this so-called Tom Evans, forgettable name, forgettable face.

"I'm sorry to have bothered you, Mr. Evans. I guess this was a mistake."

PARIS

Omar shares the office on the *deuxième étage* with Pyotr from St. Petersburg, Yang from Beijing, and Parviz from Tehran. Omar's desk is the best, pushed up against a window that faces the simple garden in the rear of the Belle Epoque house near the Trocadéro. The array of monitors in front of him makes it nearly impossible to see out the window, plus the shades are almost always drawn. So it's more the idea of a window than an actual view of the top of the Grand Palais a few blocks away, and the presence of natural light, that Omar finds pleasing, reassuring. His apartment in La Goutte d'Or is dark.

He'd already hacked into the rental company's antitheft tracking system, and launched his own map application to sync with the car's GPS signal. He followed the rental's progress, fits and starts out of the city, southerly, along the coast.

It's easy work to identify the landline of the house in front of which the car parked, as well as the IP addresses of the computers inside and the wi-fi network, which has a higher level of encryption than most civilians would use. It takes Omar another minute of scanning to ID the mobile-phone account that's inside the house, the mobile that's not his subject's. Within three minutes Omar is confident that he's monitoring all the communication channels that are operational at this house in county Wicklow. He pulls up the map, jumps around some photo links, a pleasant-looking street, cliffs at the end of the block. Yes, he thinks, Ireland looks nice. Couldn't be more different from Libya, but maybe not terribly dissimilar to France, not in the overall scheme of global topographical differentiation.

A half-dozen windows are now open on Omar's screen, streaming a tremendous volume of information. But Omar is always looking for more.

This time, it doesn't take long: after just a couple of minutes, his subject's phone starts moving away from the house, returns to the GPS signal of the car.

As soon as the car starts moving, another mobile account suddenly appears in the house, a phone that must have been powered off until now. It's a local Irish number, a disposable prepaid, and Omar has to hustle to locate the connection, clicking and typing frantically before the call ends—this is likely to be a short call—

The line goes dead.

Omar wasn't able to ascertain the connecting number. But he did manage to identify the general location of the landline that was called by this Irish burner: Langley, Virginia.

NEW YORK CITY

It's 4:00 A.M. when Gabriella's alarm sounds. She immediately drinks an espresso, then does thirty minutes on the stationary bike, watching portions of yesterday's late-night shows. This workout is mostly to get her blood flowing, to pump herself full of endorphins to deal with this new aspect of her job. Before she leaves, she takes a full-body selfie in the mirror, recording her outfit.

The apartment's walls are lined with prints, numbered and signed in thick pencil, *Terrance Sanders*, black-and-white photojournalism from Africa, the Mideast, Asia, agrarian life and poverty, the occasional scenic shot but always marred in some way—a dead tree, a piece of trash, a makeshift shack. There are no pristine compositions. The perfect images may have ended up on the magazine's cover, because that's what magazines want, but not here.

It's still dark outside. The Town Car is waiting in a cone of streetlight at the end of the kelly-green awning, a block-printed sign in its window, RIVERA. They speed downtown.

She shows her ID to one heavy-lidded security guard, and another appears, escorts her the two dozen strides to the greenroom, convenient to the unmarked door on the side street, where liveried cars can wait unobtrusively, unnoticed by the hordes of fans of generalized fame who congregate at the studio windows, having traveled hundreds or thousands of miles and waited hours in the dark and sometimes rain to catch a close-up real-life glimpse of the actresses and chefs and singers they've seen thousands of times before, smiling out from every form of media, here in person, on the other side of a cordon, the line that separates the civilians who watch TV from the celebrities who appear on it.

Gabriella sits on the sofa, reviewing her notes, mouthing her memorized sound bites. She fingers the ring that hangs from the thin gold chain around her neck. She digital-files this morning's selfie in the folder for TV appearances. Gabriella never wants to wear the same thing on camera twice, so she keeps records. She doesn't have a stylist, nor a wardrobe budget. She's just a normal woman who fills a normal closet using a normal paycheck, who one day was told to go to a TV studio and talk. Then it happened again and again, again and again.

"We're ready for you in makeup."

Gabriella takes a seat in a cramped, excessively lit room, mirrored and cluttered and suffused with the aromas of a staggering array of beauty products—powders and glosses and aerosol sprays—arranged on tiered glass shelves, like the tools in a mechanic's garage.

"How you doing today, baby?"

"I'm not bad, Charlene. You?"

"Can't complain, can I? Not with your beautiful skin sitting in my chair. Making me look like a genius." Charlene starts dabbing powder. "Ms. Rivera, you mind me asking where you're from?"

"From? I'm from Brooklyn."

"Oh yeah? Me too. Where at?"

"Canarsie. You?"

"*No!* I'm from East Flatbush. But you know what I'm asking, don't you?"

"My grandparents were born in Puerto Rico and Guyana and the D.R. and Rhode Island. *Their* parents were from Norway and India and West Africa and Italy, plus God only knows what combination of bloods native to the Caribbean and Central America."

"That sure is a big mix." Charlene is working on the eyes.

"I have no clue how to answer the White-Black-Hispanic-Other question. I am postracial, like the ethnically indeterminate Jessicas Alba and Biel, or Vin Diesel, or the Rock."

"I think he's going by Dwayne Johnson now."

"I could be a tremendous international box-office draw, you know that, Charlene? If only I could act."

"Oh I seen you on camera. You good!"

"Thanks. It's true I can manage a few lines without falling from my chair, but what I do here isn't the same thing as acting. I tried it, in high school."

"Where'd you go?"

"Murrow. You?"

"Tilden."

"Tough school."

"You telling me."

"I even went on some auditions, in the city. But I knew I wasn't a natural, and I didn't last long. Acting is nearly impossible even if you're great, and I obviously wasn't."

"But you're *beautiful.*"

"Thank you." Gabriella smiles. "But that's not an actual skill."

Charlene stands back to examine her handiwork, which Gabriella will have to remember to remove before she exits into the real world today. She forgot last time, and out on the street she felt like a clown.

"Okay baby, I'm finished. You're now *extra*-perfect." Charlene unclips Gabriella's protective bib, tosses it aside. "Have a good segment."

DUBLIN

"Will Rhodes?"

Will turns, surprised and alarmed to hear his name spoken here. The guy is wearing a loose-fitting shirt that does nothing to hide his massive arms, a string of tattoos up the forearms.

He now feels a firm hand in the small of his back, from the other direction, belonging to another man who's cut from the same general die.

"Can you come with us, please?" An American accent, hand extended, indicating a sedan waiting at the curb, back door open.

"Do I have a choice?"

Muscles doesn't say anything.

"Can I see some ID?" Will's heart is racing; he's thinking about his options for fleeing.

"That's an interesting idea," Muscles says. "*Or*: how 'bout I beat the shit out of you?"

The hand on Will's back exerts more pressure. Will folds himself into the backseat while Muscles walks around the car and slides into the passenger seat. The other man joins Will in back. A third is at the wheel.

Will's mind races in dozens of directions, trying to figure out what could be going on here, what level of fear he should be experiencing, what he should be preparing himself to do. The car slows, nearing a red light, and Will glances at the door handle, the lock mechanism. Did he hear the lock engage after his door closed? He can't remember. He looks out the window at the unpopulated corner, a row of houses, not an alley or open door in sight, nowhere to run, nowhere to hide.

They pull to a stop in front of a modernist building in an office park, a modest campus, brick-paved lanes that connect low-slung buildings surrounded by verdant trees and shrubs and grass, unremarkable and unimposing yet utterly terrifying.

Will walks through a lobby, past a security guard who nods while Muscles swipes a keycard to open glass doors. They walk down a carpeted hall and into a conference room, an oval table, a half-dozen chairs.

"Will Rhodes?" Another American walks in, this one wearing a suit and tie and highly shined shoes, salt-and-pepper hair, the brisk movements of a man who gets things done, and wants other people to know it. "Thanks for coming in." He shuts the door behind him.

"Did I have a choice?"

This time, Will hears the lock. "No," the man says. "No, I guess you didn't."

NEW YORK CITY

"And we're live," Gabriella hears in her earpiece.

"We're joined by Gabriella Rivera, deputy editor of *Travelers*."

The morning-show correspondent who's introducing her is in another city, on some irrelevant mission to try to boost ratings, a never-ending, unwinnable struggle for a share of a market that's irreversibly dwindling as Americans increasingly choose to do other things with their electronic attention at 7:00 A.M. on weekdays.

"Gabriella joins us every month to share hot tips, money-saving deals, and fantastic ideas for your next vacation."

This has gotten easier over the past year, but Gabriella still wouldn't say she's comfortable on live national television. She wonders if she'll ever be; if anyone ever is. Or maybe this is just one of those things that can never be totally comfortable, like dental work.

"Good morning, Gabriella!"

"Thanks Ted. It's *great* to be here!"

She beams her high-watt smile at the camera. The executive producer has told Gabriella that the camera loves her, that this is the rarest thing, rarer than a .300 hitter or a perfect high C. Lucinda was ambushing her with a job offer, at Michael's amid all the media bigwigs, glad-handing and name-dropping and consuming exorbitantly priced foliage.

"Well now with the heat waves in the forecast, Ted, we're of course starting to look forward to *winter* getaways. And this month, *Travelers* is previewing ski resorts . . ."

Then she's on autopilot, cruising through her scripted spiel, punching syllables, tittering at Ted's prattle. The more times she appears on camera, the more she understands how difficult it is to not appear and sound shifty, stupid, mean, ugly. It's harder than it looks.

Lucinda said the job offer was open-ended, if you ever change your mind. Then Gabriella walked in a daze across West Fifty-fifth Street, trying to conceive of a way she could wash her hands of the whole *Travelers* experience, go be a goddamned *television personality*—wouldn't that be something?—and finally emerge from beneath her suffocating secrets.

"Next time, Ted, *Travelers* will be focusing on Europe. Americans usually think of Europe for *summer* vacation, but fall and *winter* both offer excellent opportunities, Ted. Especially in the beautiful warm south, places like the Mediterranean coast of Spain . . ."

It's sentences like these, broadcast on network TV, live-streamed on the web, archived and recallable from any computer on the planet, seen by millions every day, available to billions, that are the real reason why Gabriella appears on television every week.

STOCKHOLM

The American is sitting across the street, up the block, at a small café. He has an outdoor table, an unobstructed view to the front door of the apartment building where Anders lives.

He is not disguised in any way. He is himself, an old American man living in Stockholm, reading the newspaper, nursing an evening drink, watching the blondes go by.

During the Cold War, this is what would happen to disgraced double agents, to the Americans who sold secrets, or to the Soviets who tried to defect and failed: they were repatriated to the Eastern Bloc, dark and gray, gruel-nourished and shabby-attired, and one day a sudden but not unexpected bullet to the back of the head on a busy city street, in broad daylight, an unmistakable warning to the living. This still happens, less frequently, today. This still might happen to him.

But it won't happen in Stockholm, and he won't be living under the Jamaican passport he has been using for the past months. He'd rather be alive somewhere else than dead here.

He has once again considered that maybe it's time to try to trade his secrets for his safety. He has thought about doing this before—almost every week, actually. Whenever he gets lonely, or scared, or starts to feel the onset of some physical malady, each new ailment possibly the thing that's going to kill him. In the middle of the endless dark of the Scandinavian winter, it was basically every night when he weighed the possibility of picking up the phone, calling the DCI, "Hey, I need to come in . . ."

But who knew what level of disavowed he has become? Who knew what he was suspected of? Or guilty of? There was no way to know who had alleged what to whom. No way to know what they were thinking of him, what they'd do to him.

Maybe running away hadn't been the best idea. Is it ever? But it's the sort of decision that you have to live with forever.

He looks up as the door to the apartment building opens, but it's not Anders, it's a young mother with two kids.

But then Anders does come out, a few seconds behind the family.

This is no good.

DUBLIN

"Who are you?" Will asks.

The man pulls out a chair, sits in it. He places a pad on the table, a pen on the pad, adjusts the angle of the pen. "I'm sorry, I guess I was unclear. *I* have a few questions for *you* to answer. Not the other way around. You're here in Dublin why, Mr. Rhodes?"

"Because I'm a travel writer, working for a travel magazine, writing a travel story."

"You getting smart with me?"

"I like to think I'm always smart."

"Not at the moment. Why Dublin?"

"Dublin is an appealing place, isn't it? *You're* here, after all."

The man stares at Will, taps his pen on the pad.

"How'd you end up in the Yankee Doodle the other night?"

"Not sure, exactly. A friend of a friend of a contact of a colleague. I'd have to consult my notes, which I don't have with me. I'm sure your colleagues will find them when they rifle through my hotel room. So in the meantime why don't you tell me who the fuck you are, and what the fuck you want from me."

The man stares at Will across the conference table, his pen still sitting atop the pad, no notes taken. Will hasn't said anything noteworthy.

"I work for your government, Mr. Rhodes, keeping our country safe from enemies."

"You work for the CIA?"

"I work for the Department of State."

"You mean to say, the CIA."

Will is scared out of his wits, using every iota of his willpower to not show it, though he's not sure why. Maybe he should just come out with it, admit that he's an asset, that they're on the same team. But he doesn't have any proof, does he? Will doesn't know the real names of his handlers. Doesn't know their bosses' names, which division they work in, based where. He doesn't have any concrete information, doesn't have any way to prove anything.

"May I see some ID?"

"Really?"

Will doesn't answer.

"Listen, Mr. Rhodes, you've shown up in a foreign country, interrogating members of our expat community, including people who work in sensitive sectors. The security of those U.S. citizens is my concern. This isn't surprising, is it? Or unreasonable?"

"No."

"I understand that you spend a lot of your life abroad. Surely you can imagine a scenario in which you yourself would be glad to call on the assistance of an American official, yes? If for example you find yourself detained in a foreign prison. In that situation, would you care if the official who showed up carried a State Department ID or a CIA one? No, I don't think you'd care."

"But I'm not in a foreign prison. And I haven't done anything wrong."

The man folds his hands on the table, leans forward. "Are you absolutely sure about that, Mr. Rhodes?"

STOCKHOLM

He wills himself to stay in his seat.

The young woman is dawdling out front, saying hello to someone who's passing. The kids are running around a pole, singing a song, playing a game.

Joe beckons the waiter, puts money on the table, nervous, wanting to get the hell out of here.

Anders walks to his motorcycle. The woman turns, says something to Anders, who laughs. Fuck, this is no good, no good at all, they're too close to each other, way too close.

Then suddenly one of her kids dashes up the block, and the other kid chases. Their mom yells but they don't listen, so she smiles at Anders, shrugs, and runs away, all three family members with blond hair flowing, getting farther and farther from Anders, who watches her run, sitting on his motorcycle, she's now sixty yards away, seventy, the kids are nearing this corner across from the café right here, it's okay now, thank God, so the American stands, and takes a step away from his table, then another, and that's when Anders turns his ignition key, and his motorcycle explodes.

PART

III

15

I t always takes much longer to come home than to leave, flying back from Europe to New York, westbound into the headwinds.

Will de-airplane-modes his phone, scans the screen for signs of crisis. He is now seeing his job—all jobs—from a new perspective on their fake urgency, their ersatz importance, their crucial bottom lines and make-or-break year-to-dates, their hairline-thin schedules and painstakingly reforecast budgets, their politics and infighting and competition, their charts and graphs and reports and memos, their hustle and bustle, their Kool-Aid passed around all the offices of all the world, this mass hallucination that what we do is important, that *we're* important, no free time, not enough bandwidth, ask my assistant to check the schedule, let's get on the calendar, I've just been so busy, you know how it is, absolutely, yes, do I ever.

He marches through the empty Global Entry lane at Immigration, bumps along the urban-blighty expanses between JFK and home, pulls to a stop in front of his house. While he was abroad the plywood had been removed from the windows, the new glass installed. His house no longer looks condemned.

Lights are on; Chloe is home.

Will trudges up the stoop, weary, none too keen to interact with his wife, to resume the barrage of lies he's forced to tell whenever he comes home. He had spent so much of his life being truthful; it had stood him in good stead, as a writer, as a person. He's having a hard time getting used to lying all the time, and he's doing an awful lot of it, elaborate fabrications in nearly every substantive conversation with his wife, his boss. It's debilitating.

He finds Chloe at the kitchen island, busy with paperwork. She accepts a honey-I'm-home kiss without getting up.

"The windows look good," she says.

"Don't they? I'm glad."

"But I have to admit I was surprised when Viktor showed up. I guess you paid him?"

Damn, is she really going to pursue this now? "I did."

"Where'd we get the money?"

It looks like she is. Will has practiced this story, but now that the moment is here, curtain rising, he's nervous, and it's about this lie in particular, demonstrably untrue. He's being careful about keeping the CIA's money out of banks, out of records. But he still needs to spend it.

"My expense backlog," he says, walking away, pouring himself a glass of water. "From last year."

He can't see Chloe's face, but he can imagine the quizzical look, head cocked, trying to remember what he'd told her about last year's expenses backlog. Which in truth was not a damned thing.

"I thought I told you about it."

"I don't remember."

"It was from when we were closing on the mortgage refi. Because your account and mine weren't on the same exact monthly schedule, in order to avoid having wildly conflicting statements that we'd have to explain, I put off submitting expenses for a couple weeks. Then I just forgot about this batch."

He feels horrible, trying to make her feel forgetful for forgetting something that never happened. This story was a bad idea. He wishes he could go back to the beginning, try something else, but that's not how it works, lying.

"I found these receipts a couple months ago. The incoming publisher—Stephanie Bloom, did I tell you about her?"

Chloe shakes her head.

"Anyway, she's apparently a stickler for accounting, so everybody's on best behavior, looking to clear expenses and invoices quickly before she starts digging into any messes. I got the check a couple weeks ago, and paid Viktor immediately."

He's a lying sack of shit, an unacceptable sort of human being.

"There's still a couple bucks left over. Want to go get drunk? I bet Dean will give us a discount."

Chloe turns her eyes up at him. She looks tired, defeated, sitting there with a stack of old bills, late notices, estimated-tax forms, the endless tedium of life.

"Sure," she says, "that's a good idea."

"Okay. Just give me a minute to get sorted." Will often comes home with leftover language from his destination, the occasional trace of an accent. It takes him a couple of days to sound completely like himself.

"Hey Will?"

He turns back. "Yeah?"

"I love you."

Will feels like a heel. He dumps his laundry into the washing machine, his dry-cleaning into a bag. He refits his phone and computer chargers with their sharp little American prongs. He doesn't unpack his toilet kit. It's always ready. Will is always prepared to leave.

He deposits the foreign currency where it belongs, the maps, the business cards, all into their shoeboxes. He steps out of the office, into the hall, his ears attentive to the sounds of Chloe below. He hears the flutter of paper being turned.

He hustles back to the office, to the radiator housing, perforated steel to let heat escape, a solid wood frame with a hinged door on top. He opens this door. Takes the CIA phone out of his pocket, reaches down into the cavity, and lays the phone on the floor.

Another secret, in another hiding spot. This spot is good enough for now. But he'll need somewhere different by autumn, when the heat will turn back on.

"Nice to see you again, Stephanie," Malcolm says, without even trying to sound like he means it. "Please"—he motions to a chair—"make yourself comfortable."

The new publisher takes a seat, crosses her legs. But Malcolm makes her wait at his desk, alone, while he grabs a red Sharpie and crosses the room to what everyone calls the Wall, a massive schematic arrangement of every two-page spread of the next issue—ad pages and content pages, full-page photos and one-column ads, the beginning of this story and the end of that, word counts and due dates, the names of writers and editors and photographers and designers, handwritten one-liners like "Malcolm's letter TK" and "Full-page food photo," fully executed final typeset text with art, approved "OK by MS" with a date scrawled in the lower-right margin. Reinventing the wheel every month.

He draws giant X's across the dummies of the eight and a half pages whose scheduled article is apparently not going to be delivered on time, or possibly ever. The print version of dead air.

"So," he says, coming back around his desk, "welcome. Glad to have you aboard."

Stephanie smiles, but none too warmly. "Listen, I know this is awkward."

"Awkward? Nooo."

"I want you to know that I have tremendous respect for *Travelers* as a brand, and for you as the steward of that brand."

"Well, that's certainly reassuring to hear."

She smiles. "It's just that, uh . . . well, I'm sure you know."

"Do I?" Malcolm stares at her from across his desk. He'd made Stephanie wait for five minutes out in the anteroom, under the gaze of his inscrutable secretary. "Why don't you spell it out for me? For, you know, an abundance of clarity?"

"It's just that the thirty-third floor wants more objective oversight of the finances. Of *every* title. It's not just *Travelers*, Malcolm. The goal is to try to keep all seven magazines solvent, and to make sure that every conceivable effort is being made, that waste is at a minimum, that every ship is tip-top tight."

"Tip-top tight? Sorry, that phrase is unfam—"

"*Efficient,* I guess would be a more traditional word choice."

"Sounds like the thirty-third floor doesn't trust us to run our businesses anymore. Doesn't trust *me* to run *my* business. Sounds like receivership, Stephanie, is what it sounds like. Like I'm Detroit. Am I Detroit?"

"Not at all, Malcolm, and I'm sorry if you've gotten that impression. I can't reiterate it enough: editorial is your domain entirely. Church and state, Malcolm. As ever."

The magazine world has a long proud history of keeping editorial matters separate from business ones. But *Travelers* had—until this moment—an unusual history of vesting the titles of both editor and publisher in one person, a single human being who supervised the content of the magazine as well as the business. Apparently that was an unattractive management structure for M&A analysts. So in preparation for selling its magazines, the board of the American Periodical Group insisted on hiring a dedicated publisher, someone who at a minimum would project the appearance of a traditional business.

APG is another independent family-owned company that's about to be taken over by some faceless international conglomerate, its fate in the ruthless impersonal hands of shareholders and quarterly reports, stock prices and dividends, with no regard to history or tradition or people, to the hundred families who are supported by the magazine. Capitalism doesn't give a damn. That's the definition of capitalism.

The someone who the board installed is now sitting across from Malcolm, trying not to be intimidated on her first day on the job. Malcolm isn't planning on cutting her a break, not today, maybe not ever. One of them is going to be dominant and the other is going to get fired, and Malcolm knows that it has to be him who wins, or the whole goddamned thing will fall apart.

"O-*kay* then, thanks for clearing that up, Stephanie. Is there anything else at the moment? Because, you know, I've got a magazine to put out. Badly, apparently."

Malcolm can't help but notice, again, the little knit cap she wears on the forefinger of her left hand. It's a bizarre accessory, and he feels an almost physical compulsion to ask about it, but he doesn't want to give her the satisfaction.

"I do, Malcolm, need the password."

He pretends he doesn't know what she's talking about. "Come again?"

"The master password."

Malcolm stares at Stephanie, this officious MBA automaton, all scrubbed clean for her first day, fresh haircut and new suit and shoes, not a scratch on the leather, probably bought just yesterday, a what-the-fuck splurge on Madison, maybe felt buyer's remorse, excitedly sleepless late at night, to have spent six hundred dollars on shoes when it's possible she'll hate the new job and quit within months—or get fired—and have to slink back to the headhunter, six hundred dollars shy of this year's financial goals, which she probably plotted on an app designed by some HBS class-mate of hers. Just the initials HBS make him shiver.

But now that he thinks about it, he's pretty sure the business degree she got a decade ago was from Wharton. He's the one who went to Harvard.

"The password that opens *all* the files on the server, Malcolm."

He continues to stare at her for a few beats, but he knows this isn't a battle he can win; he can't hide the financial records from the publisher. He writes the long alphanumeric string on a scratch sheet, holds it out. Stephanie reaches to take the piece of paper, but Malcolm snatches his hand back, a more assholy move than he intended. "Please be careful with this," he says.

"I understand."

"Do you?"

She sighs, running out of patience with the excessive, unprofessional hostility. "Thanks for your cooperation, Malcolm." Perhaps there's some class, in B-school? Up-Managing Obstreperous Colleagues 201. "I hope we can find a way to work together. We have the same interests, you know."

Do we? Malcolm wonders. I doubt that.

How is Will supposed to write about Ireland when he can't discuss his abduction? Argentina without his recruitment? France without that kiss? He has a backlog of notes, a surfeit of experiences, but so many are secret.

He's sitting in the archive room, scanning through old Ireland stories. There haven't been very many, just a handful, one of them by Jonathan Mongeleach, written back when Jonathan was merely a staff writer, like Will now, his contributions signed *JM* while he traveled the world, looking for his own manifestations of perfection. Jonathan had apparently found it in the west of Ireland, in a Gothic castle that had been converted to an inn, with lush grounds in a countryside dotted by links-style golf courses. The article concluded, "Is this the ideal place for a golfer to retire? Maybe."

That's the same sentiment that Will finds himself expressing over and over, in early drafts, before he highlights these sentences, hits Delete.

Jonathan himself didn't want to retire to the links courses of Ireland;

golf was not his passion. But maybe he did want to retire somewhere specific, somewhere he'd visited during his long career of traveling to the most beautiful places in the world. Somewhere he'd written about. Somewhere he already knew he loved.

Maybe that's where he is now.

Once again, Malcolm finds Will hiding down in the archives.

"Hey Rhodes."

Will jumps in his seat, hunched over a back issue.

"How was the United Kingdom of Great Britain and Northern Ireland?"

"Um, I was in the other Ireland."

"Fair point. So how was everything?"

"Pretty good."

Malcolm waits for Will to continue, but he doesn't. "*Pretty good?* Two words? You know that your job is to generate words about travel, right?"

Will smiles, weakly.

"What's wrong, Rhodes? You don't seem like you."

"Sorry, Mal. Just tired."

Malcolm tries to pinpoint when exactly he first noticed the shift in Will's demeanor, his withdrawal. Malcolm should've made a note of it. That was an oversight, a blind spot, caused by long-standing friendship, as so many blind spots are. Moving forward, he'll have to be much more vigilant.

In the meantime, he can't help but wonder if Will has discovered something, and from whom.

"It's like you're stalking me. Are you stalking me, Chloe Palmer?"

"*Rhodes*," she says. "My name is Chloe *Rhodes*."

Dean beckons to Marlon. "Negroni rocks?" Dean asks her. "With the shitty gin?"

"If you don't mind, Marlon, I'll take something nonshitty this time. Your choice."

Marlon retreats, leaving his boss alone with this woman, again.

Chloe takes the empty stool next to Dean. In front of him are haphazard-looking piles of paper, which Chloe assumes are related to the business. But no, it's a manuscript.

"What are you working on, Dean? A new book?"

"Oh this?" He holds his finger up to his lips, leans in close, whispers. "*Spy novel. Top secret.*" He leans away. "You here to steal my intellectual property? That's unexpectedly underhanded of you, Chloe Palmer. But also sort of sexy."

She takes delivery of her drink.

"Or is there something else I can help you with?"

"Have you noticed anything, um, *strange* about Will recently?"

Since Will and Dean had reconnected here a few weeks ago, they'd gotten together a couple of times. Without Chloe.

"Are you kidding? Will is the least strange guy in the world."

Dean is right: Will is nothing if not unstrange. But he has definitely been acting strange around Chloe recently. Everything had always been easy between them, until suddenly it wasn't. At first Chloe thought it was her own fault: her new job was distracting her with a new set of concerns, new moral quandaries, and she was aware that she herself had been withdrawn. But just because she was withdrawn didn't mean he wasn't too.

So she started paying closer attention to her husband, who was definitely unresponsive to her proddings, and unforthcoming about his whereabouts, quiet and evasive, all the things that Will Rhodes had not been. Little by little, her suspicion migrated: it wasn't her own supply of secrets that was creating the distance between them, it was Will's.

Chloe didn't expect Dean to have noticed anything, or to know anything. But now she does expect him to try to find out. Dean has been on a mission to seduce Chloe for more than a decade, and to him this will seem like an opportunity to succeed.

The space hidden inside Malcolm's office wall isn't much wider than a closet, but it's long. One large wall is dominated by a map of the world, with large violent red swaths for the U.S.S.R. and China, and the names of countries—Czechoslovakia, Yugoslavia, East Germany, Upper Volta— that no longer exist. There are big six-pointed stars for national capitals, and flat faded colors—sickly amber, anemic taupe, washed-out blue—and time-zone longitudes. A few distinct handwritings in mixed pencils and ink annotate the whole thing with large numbers, long-forgotten names, unbreakable codes, and straightforward dates at places like Bulgaria and Chile, Vietnam and Angola, Nicaragua and Cuba, all the Cold War proxies. This map is a working document, not decor.

Industrial steel shelves hold a few olive-drab lockboxes. A wood-seated stool on casters is under a small steel desk, on which sit a clunky black telephone with an accordion cord, and an empty gunmetal-gray tray, no longer used. No one had gotten rid of the in-box. No one had gotten rid of anything. The room is a time capsule.

There's one contemporary-looking item: a sleek logo-less laptop with a hard connection to a jack in a sturdy-looking metal box, exposed wires that disappear into a rough-cut hole in the floor.

The stool is not a comfortable piece of furniture, but that's okay, because Malcolm never sits here for more than a couple of minutes. This secret office has existed for more than a half-century, and he suspects no one has ever spent more than the bare minimum of time in here.

Malcolm opens the computer, whose communications go to only one destination in the world, one person. He types the note quickly, just a one-liner. It looks like an email, but it won't be traveling over the Internet.

We have a Will Rhodes problem.

16

"I was *kidnapped*."

Elle takes the digital recorder out of her bag, places it on the table, hits the red square. Will suspects that she does this to remind him, at every single meeting, of the other recordings she possesses.

"Let's not be melodramatic, Will."

"I was abducted, and forcibly detained, and interrogated, in a foreign country."

"By an American. You're sure?"

"I'm positive."

"Like you were positive that I was some Australian chick who lives on the other side of the world? Exotic little side action?"

Touché. "He was American," Will says. "He was *CIA*."

She leans away from the Formica table, keeps her gaze locked with his. She seems to be debating something. "Okay, I'll look into it."

"That's all?" He was hoping that Elle had some magical answer.

"Keep your voice down. What do you want from me?"

"An explanation."

"Thousands of people work for the Agency, Will. Maybe tens of thousands. Half of us are working at cross-purposes. So yes: it's possible that you were questioned by someone who's CIA."

He looks down at his bland lager, takes a sip, wishes he'd ordered a Guinness. Even if he didn't particularly like Guinness, at least it tasted like something.

"You don't look so hot," Elle says. "You okay?"

"I'm not sleeping."

Will had never been a particularly sound sleeper before—there has always been plenty to worry about, in the middle of the night—but things had gotten exponentially worse recently, after France and then Argentina, the subterfuge of the training in Virginia, this tense trip to the U.K., the terrifying episode in Dublin. Plus the lying to Chloe, the lying to Malcolm, the lying to everyone. He never sleeps through the night anymore.

Elle doesn't ask Will to clarify why he's not sleeping; she knows why. "Has anyone noticed?"

"My wife."

"Is Chloe the suspicious type?"

"Not really."

"What about your boss? Is Malcolm suspicious? Worried?"

"Maybe worried. I think he might be suspicious, but not of what's going on."

"About what, then? Did you tell him about me?"

Will doesn't really want to admit this, but he probably has to. "I told him about France. Told him *something* about France. Everything except the kiss. I told him I was greatly tempted by an attractive woman, but I resisted."

"You're a hero, aren't you? In your own imagination?"

"Oh go to hell."

"GEC has been our most reliable advertiser for a long time now," Malcolm says.

Stephanie flips pages, looking for information that isn't readily apparent. "So what exactly *is* it?"

"Global Enterprises Corporation is an international communications and logistics company."

Stephanie looks up from the file. "What does that mean?"

"Telecom, shipping, outsourcing, et cetera."

"Do you have any idea what you're talking about?" She turns to Gabriella. "Do *you*?"

"Last I learned was they'd landed new cell-service contracts across, um, Eastern Europe."

"Southern Europe, I think," Malcolm clarifies. Gabriella shrugs.

"And they're based in Geneva?"

"I don't think they're really *based* there. But that's where they have their nominative headquarters. I think most of their work happens in North America and Eastern and Southern Europe. They're based in Switzerland so they can pay corporate taxes there. It's called inversion. Shifting headquarters geographically to avoid U.S. taxes."

"I know what inversion is. I'm the one who went to business school, remember?"

"How could I forget?"

In front of Stephanie is a tall stack of thick files, one for each of the major advertisers: their buy histories, important correspondence and legal agreements, handwritten notes and scrawled Post-its, anything that explains what it is the advertisers want, and what it is they get, out of their relationship with the magazine.

"And why is GEC's contact editorial?"

"That's how they want it."

"Yes, but why?"

"Tradition. They've had a relationship with *Travelers* since before any of us was born, and that's how it has always been. Or so I've been told."

"And what does maintaining this relationship entail?"

"Not much. A couple times a year, one of us"—Malcolm points to Gabriella, then back to himself—"makes a presentation about our vital statistics, answers a few questions. I once went to dinner with some execs. You too, right?"

Gabriella nods. "One of those EVP types got a little, uh, grabby. That sucked."

Stephanie looks from Gabriella to Malcolm, waiting for more. "And?"

"And so I was annoyed."

"I mean, and that's it? They don't want anything else? They simply buy Cover 3 every month, with no discount or other consideration, no negotiation? Just this big transfer, fifteenth of the month? And besides inflation increases, this has not changed in—is this really true?—*fifty-two* years?" Stephanie looks down at GEC's full glossy page, a globe, interconnecting lines, vague text, an ad that communicates practically nothing. "*Why?*"

"Come again?"

"I mean, our readers aren't . . . our demographic is . . . Honestly, Malcolm, I don't even know where to begin."

"It sounds like you're complaining about this, Stephanie. Now, I understand that you haven't had as much time on the job as other publishers. So perhaps you don't understand, *exactly,* how it works, our business. I'll tell you: we sell space—our magazine pages—to adver—"

"Give me a fucking break." It doesn't come out angry, just matter-of-fact, with an emotionless stare. She simply wants an answer, which isn't unreasonable.

Stephanie had scheduled this meeting to take place in her office, but at the last minute Malcolm told his assistant to ask Stephanie's if they could relocate, no explanation. He intends to never attend any meeting in her office. He'll keep repeating this relocation farce until Stephanie gives up. Power is nothing more than the perception of it.

"What can I tell you, Stephanie? Almost all the time, things are much harder and more complicated than they should be. *Very* rarely, they're easier and simpler. This is not a broken situation; we don't need to fix it. I honestly don't understand what your problem is."

"My *problem*? My problem is that if GEC's transfer doesn't arrive for a few months, and we don't immediately find a replacement with an equal level of—how can I put it?—*largesse,* then we're essentially insolvent. This bizarrely nonrelevant company has been our most reliable advertiser for a half-century, yet we don't know why they're spending their money with us. To me, that looks like a problem."

"To me, that looks like a solution."

Stephanie taps her fancy pen—a Montblanc, probably a graduation gift, slid across the white tablecloth, *Congratulations, Sweetheart,* along with an envelope containing a check for the down payment on a co-op.

"I want to come to the next presentation."

He laughs. "I really don't think you do. But whatever."

Stephanie doesn't rise to his bait. She does an admirable job of taking shit from Malcolm without blowing her lid. Maybe it's time for Malcolm to back off. She's not actually an enemy, at least not yet. If they're both still employed after the dust settles, he can slowly let out some line. She'll get more and more invested, she'll take ownership, and she'll hold on to it all the more fiercely because of her initial struggle to overcome Malcolm's hostility and the staff's reluctance, to learn the culture, to solve problems. She'll look at *Travelers* as her own, as the husband and children she doesn't have. She'll do anything to keep it safe. Even after she learns the truth.

"Show me."

"Why?"

"What did I tell you about *why*, Will? Because I want to know. That's why."

Will takes the pen and napkin from Elle.

"Here's Malcolm's office," he says, drawing a line, another. "Here's Gabriella. Then me. This is the editorial corridor. Down this wing is art, around here publishing. This far corner is the publisher's office, Stephanie Bloom, she's new. Here's ad sales, marketing."

"Is that everyone?"

"There are corporate offices down on twenty-eight, for things like IT and legal and accounting. Up on thirty-three are C-level suites, corporate dining, I don't know what else."

"And the floors in between? Those are occupied by the other magazines?"

"Yes. There's men's, young women's, fashion, fitness, food." Will is counting them off on his fingers. "And, um . . ." He can't remember the other one. All the magazines are in the process of being sold, one party to the transaction receiving stocks in a bewildering vesting schedule, the other assets of indeterminate value. Will can't begin to understand how anyone structures such a deal, composed of practically nothing of tangible value.

"Business! That's the other one. I always forget about business."

"Of course you do." She turns a notebook page. "So tell me about Malcolm Somers."

"What do you want to know?"

"What's the most important thing?"

"Malcolm is a married man. His wife is wonderful—everybody loves Allison—and he's a very devoted husband, and a decently involved father to their two kids. But Malcolm has never been able to accept the permanent-monogamy aspect of marriage."

"Are you saying he's a cheater?"

"There's *something* between him and Gabriella—there's also something between *me* and Gabs—but maybe nothing ever came of it with Malcolm, just like with me."

Elle raises an eyebrow at this turn of the story. Did he really once find that eyebrow sexy? Why?

"Does he travel a lot?" she asks.

"Hardly ever, anymore. He doesn't write stories. If he travels, it's only for events—parties with advertisers, cross-promotional things—and then it's just in and out, one- or two-day trips. His job is in the office."

"And what about Gabriella Rivera? What should I know about her?"

Will is surprised that Elle knows who Gabs is, but then realizes that of course she knows. Maybe the CIA tried to recruit Gabriella too. Maybe they succeeded. Is it possible that Gabriella—or someone else at *Travelers*—is engaged in the same clandestine op?

"What do you care?" Will asks, testing these waters. "Why are we talking about these people?"

But "Indulge me" is all he gets, another response that divulges nothing. Will opens his mouth to press the issue, but it's pointless. Elle asks whatever she wants, without explanation. And Will answers. That's the arrangement.

"I guess the most important thing about Gabs is that she wants to be taken seriously. She's a genius—I mean, IQ-wise, an actual genius. She's fluent in a half-dozen languages, and she has tremendous recall of facts, and a huge volume of competencies. She even types faster than anyone I've ever met, which in our line of work is extremely useful."

"But?"

"But she's also incredibly good-looking. You've seen her?"

Elle nods.

"And very flirty. I think people—women as well as men—are quick to dismiss her because of it, 'Oh, that's the hot girl from *Travelers*.' Plus she's Latin-American, or Afro-Caribbean—I don't know what her ethnic makeup is, she explained it once but it's too complex to remember. In any case she's not Caucasian, or not mostly Caucasian, and she works in a field that's very white. I think she's worried about how the world looks at her."

"Who isn't?"

◆ ◆ ◆

"Why do you say shit like that?"

Gabriella squints at Malcolm. "Like what?"

"'Tap water would be fabulous.' *Fabulous?* Really?"

"Just trying to be nice."

"*Nice?* Are you sure that's what you're being?"

"Fuck off, Malcolm."

He scans the menu, though at this point he pretty much has it memorized. But he despises the presumption of people who don't even look at menus.

"Is she going to be a problem?" Gabriella asks. "Stephanie?"

"I don't think so." Malcolm can't remember which fishes he's supposed to not eat anymore. Tuna is definitely out. Mercury? Lead? Kills dolphins? What about swordfish?

On the far side of the room is that holier-than-thou busybody Ashford Warren, who would not hesitate to lecture Malcolm on his ethical-consumption violations. Ash once berated Malcolm, at length, for having purchased a bag of apples in early summer, a half-year out of season, at a moment when the market was overflowing with ripe stone fruit, grown locally. "But I want an apple, not a peach, you sanctimonious son of a bitch." The two of them almost came to blows on Seventeenth Street. Fucking prick.

Ash catches his eye, and Malcolm nods at him across the room.

The restaurant is crowded, the staff obsequious, the crowd table-hopping, proud of themselves for being here, among one another, clubby-smug in the way that every club is at least a little smug, even when it's not a club.

"Gabs, do you know if I'm supposed to be chewing or eschewing swordfish?"

She ignores this. "Are you really going to take her to the next GEC meeting?"

"I doubt it."

"Ooh. You gonna get in trouble." Singsong, a little girl in a schoolyard. "Do you know who else was up for that job?"

"Stephanie's?"

"They must've looked at a lot of candidates."

As part of his middle-aged maturation, Malcolm has struggled to reconcile himself that he should often appear less important—less informed, less respected, less strong—than he is. This charade is particularly challenging with good-looking women. Great-looking women. Great-looking women about whom he's had sexual fantasies for a decade. There's only one of those.

"Fuck if I know," he says. "I'm not consulted on things like that."

This is not true. Malcolm was consulted, and he conducted his own independent research on all the candidates. That's how he discovered that Stephanie Bloom, daughter of the famously dickish mega-millionaire Seth Bloom, suffered from a certain weakness—a few of them—that Malcolm could envisage someday exploiting. So Malcolm had lobbied strongly for Stephanie, which confused the shit out of the corporate execs, because she was maybe the last candidate they thought Malcolm would endorse, if he was even willing to endorse any, which didn't seem terribly likely. It was another of Malcolm's enigmatic moves.

"Listen, Gabs, what's up with Will recently? He's been a little distant. You know what's going on?"

"Something with Chloe, maybe?"

"Anything specific?"

"Not that I know of. How's he handling the new assignment?"

"Seems fine. He's doing what he should."

"Have you gotten reports from the overseas bureaus?"

Malcolm nods.

"So what is it you're worried about?"

"Honestly, I don't know, but something's up. Can you keep an eye on him?"

"Passively, or actively?"

"Actively."

"Beginning immediately?"

"If you don't mind."

Malcolm feels his phone buzz in his pocket. He plucks it out, glances at the screen, the alarm telling him that it's 1300. He'd gotten used to 24-hour military time during his years abroad, and kept using it. "Sorry," he says. "I've gotta tweet."

"Are you telling me you schedule your tweets?"

"Otherwise I can't remember."

His thumbs fly, *Kinda sorta lovin' lunch at café rouge!* Malcolm knows that this 100 percent insincerity is despicable, and he justifies it by his resentment about tweeting specifically, and the stupid things he has to do in general, which he realizes doesn't actually justify anything to anyone other than himself.

And the alarm wasn't really to tweet. "Excuse me," he says, and gets up. Malcolm would much rather that Gabriella think he needs an alarm for tweeting than for what he really needs to do.

Allison Rabinowitz-Somers holds one little hand of both her kids, soft and warm, a chick under each wing. She knows it's silly, this feeling of nostalgia for today even as it's still happening, mourning the loss of something she still possesses. She good-bye-kisses the silken tops of their heads, then wades through the parental hive, hellos and how-are-yous, proffered cheeks and one "call-me" gesture, pinkie and thumb extended. Allison doesn't want to call anyone who uses that gesture.

She sits on the bench of a long lunch table in the sparkling cafeteria, empty at this hour, freshly waxed floors, the pungent aroma of disinfectant. She unties the ribbon from the bakery box, unfolds the cardboard while keeping the label visible, one of those recent European imports, fawning reviews in the *Times* and blogs, the fooderati. The sticker itself is half the point.

The other moms on the committee—which committee? for a second Allison forgets—trickle in, oh-my-Godding about the pains au chocolat and croissants, even though this isn't much of a butter-and-flour crowd. Allison is no exception. Meatless Mondays evolved into no-food Mondays, and meatless weeks, and no-weekday-flour, and vegan daylight, monthly juice cleanses, one abstemious rule after another in pursuit of elusive goals, another five pounds, a half-marathon. By the time she's fifty, she'll probably be consuming nothing but wheatgrass, through a feeding tube.

"You guys?" Carrie is fake tearing-up. Carrie's hands are often pressed to heart, tears never more than a couple of blinks away. Carrie is always thrusting her altruism at everyone, tweeting and gramming her various philanthropic efforts, her rescue dog and hybrid car, her eco-friendly this and fair-trade that.

"You guys. Are. *So. Awesome.*"

Carrie is being handed a gift certificate accompanied by proclamations that "You *deserve* it!" as thanks for some selfless work. Carrie absorbed one of the responsibilities, she did something unrequired amid the litany of the marginally required, intercut with the coffee-grabbing and chitchatting—did you hear? where will you ski? those boots?—and the mandatory volunteering, to decorate for the dance or to collect gently used coats or canned food, one not entirely optional thing after another, plus the manicures and pedicures and haircuts and waxes and the occasional pseudo-therapeutic massage, not to mention the kids' medical, psychological, and educational assessments and appointments and coaching for advancements, and obviously the pediatrician and gynecologist and dentist and oral hygienist, the skin-cancer screenings and mammograms, and of course the exercise—oh God, all the exercise, just thinking about it is exhausting, yoga and tennis and Pilates and SoulCycle—and the grocery store and cleaner's and tailor's, and before you know it you're back at school pickup, then there's projects—Native American studies projects, interpretative-dance projects—that necessitate the crafts store or Lincoln Center, and the toy store—with two children and sixteen other kids per class, that's a birthday every other week, none uncelebrated—and you always, always, *always* need to buy milk and orange juice and toilet paper, and it can all easily—*so* easily—turn into a full day if you let it; if you want it. A month can go by, a year, or two, or ten.

Malcolm makes his way past the tables, all these fishes and foliages, unsweetened iced teas and sparkling waters, another urban spa. The men's room is empty. Malcolm enters the nearest stall, removes his jacket, hangs it on a brass hook. He pushes down his pants. Takes a seat.

He leans to the side, and opens the door of the toilet-paper dispenser, exposing the large spare roll resting above the half-used one. He reaches down into his pants. Removes a matte black thumb drive in a magnetic sleeve, and affixes this sleeve inside the dispenser. He shuts the little door.

Malcolm flushes the toilet, pulls up his pants, rearranges himself. Even though the bathroom is empty, he washes his hands, completing the charade. There are rules to follow, every single time.

If the drive is inserted into the port of a computer that isn't already equipped with the proprietary de-encryption program, the drive will wipe itself, leaving not a trace of any data, not even of the self-destruction script. So even if an over-industrious, bizarrely well-connected janitor—or, more likely, some operative who has been shadowing Malcolm—shows up in this men's room *and* finds the device *and* knows how to get it to an interested party, there's still no way for the information to fall into the wrong hands.

Though maybe *wrong* isn't the operating concept; *unintended* would be more accurate. Because there isn't necessarily a right and a wrong. That type of clear dichotomy is a luxury Malcolm can't afford to consider; it's his professional equivalent of owning a jet. Yes, a private plane would be nice. But its absence isn't something anyone can complain about.

Malcolm doesn't know who's going to collect this dead drop, this blind handoff of sensitive classified information. He never has. He never will. He just does what he's paid to do.

17

Will squints into his brand-new phone in the harsh glare of the summer sun beating down on the pier. He doesn't expect Chloe to answer these days, but he continues to try anyway, every day. Just because the calls go unanswered doesn't mean they're futile; it's the act of calling, the effort of trying—and to be seen trying—that's the point. A minor accomplishment, a small attempt to reach his wife, to reach out to her, to hold on to her.

Which is an increasingly dubious proposition. Chloe has been retreating further and further into her private self. Again and again, she denies that anything is wrong—that is, anything new: it's merely the recent infertility and the long-term insolvency, the ongoing renovation of the dilapidated house and the attempted reorientation of a faltering career. The same monumental issues that were concerning her before.

Before.

Before what? Before Will went to Argentina, and came home different. Chloe isn't the one who'll put her finger on that juncture, but Will sure is. That's the before.

Nearly all the recently dialed numbers on this new phone are his wife's. He hits Call, waits while the connection jumps from one European cell tower to another, then across the towerless expanse of the Atlantic, somehow picked up by American towers and eventually by his wife's device, thousands of miles from where Will is standing on a pier in the Mediterranean.

As expected, it's Chloe's voice mail that picks up.

There's something almost liberating in this predicament, being the only one who's trying. It's as if his marriage is already lost, and now he can possibly salvage it or fail, but either way he has nothing additional to lose except the dishonor of not trying. So he's trying. And he's telling himself, over and over, that it's not going to be me who walks out. Whatever else I've done, if this marriage is going to end, it'll have to be her. It's not going to be me.

Since Argentina Will has been to England and Scotland and Ireland, to the beaches of Croatia and the cafés of Salzburg and now this hot pier in Spain. He has taken a thousand photographs and written ten thousand words, had his texts edited and criticized, fact-checked and laid out and proofread and printed, distributed to newsstands and mailboxes and bookstores and libraries, hundreds of thousands of thick copies of glossy paper, with a big photo of him on the contributors' page, smiling for the camera in a burgundy banquette at a brasserie in Montparnasse.

Chloe was the one who took that photo, on their honeymoon. But in the past couple of months, it has been Elle with whom Will sits in banquettes and booths, on park benches and café chairs, while he painstakingly provides descriptions of the people he meets, the nefarious rumors he hears, every bit of scandal whose whiff wafts by. He has explained to Elle the corporate structure of *Travelers*, who does what, where, when, why, how. After an ill-advised third glass of Barolo, he even shared with Elle his concern about Chloe's growing detachment.

He has had more truthful, more personal, and more frequent conversations with his case officer than with his wife.

Between his *Travelers* trips and his CIA responsibilities and his secret martial-arts training and his actual writing, Will barely has time to sleep. He no longer has any social life, nor much of a matrimonial one. What he does have is an extra thirty thousand dollars, collected in cash from Elle in ten-grand chunks. He has been using some of this to pay his more ethically flexible subcontractors who are happy for the transaction to be excluded from traditional financial institutions. And some of this undocumented cash is what he's been using for day-to-day expenses, bolstering the solvency of his checking account. He has also managed to squirrel away a few grand, stored in a remote location, for the rainy day that he knows is inevitable.

And he now knows how to fight.

◆ ◆ ◆

The yacht is massive beyond any reasonable expectation of a pleasure boat, with a swimming pool and a helicopter pad and a submersible launch, a mind-boggling display of incomprehensible wealth. The host of this party has a net worth that's said to be 20 billion dollars, an amount that can also be expressed as 20,000 individual millions. What's 1 million dollars, when you have 19,999 other million dollars?

Will would like to think that he has a basic understanding of normal routes to wealth, routes taken by the rich people he encounters. Big salaries with bigger bonuses and stock options, bought-out start-ups and compound interest, real-estate appreciation and inherited estates. Avoid taxes. Invest early, get out at the top. Buy low, sell high.

But this? Will doesn't understand how an individual can amass such a fortune, can't comprehend a system in which any activity can be rewarded in such vast disproportion to all others. What can a person have done to deserve this? This cannot be earned money. This is either stolen money or invented money.

"Will Rhodes," he announces himself to the young woman with the clipboard, intimidatingly attractive in the way of most young women with clipboards. A black-suited guard waves a metal-detector wand across the short dress of a long woman in front of him.

Will knew there'd be a metal detector, this is not a surprise. But still he's starting to get nervous, his perspiration increasing. It's hot.

"*Bienvenido*, Señor Rhodes," the clipboard woman says. "Please." She indicates the gangway with a tan arm decorated with a profusion of silver bangles, a musical jangle. "We sail in thirty minutes."

The metal-detector guard gives Will a look that says, stop, wait, I'm in charge. He waves his wand over Will, an insignificant click at Will's tie bar, which the guard ignores, another at his belt buckle, also ignored. The noise grows more insistent at his hip, so Will reaches into his pants pocket, removes the phone, extends it in his palm.

The guard considers the phone, then dismisses it, just another benign i-device. He continues to move the wand down Will's right leg, up the left, without further incident. The guard nods, we're finished, and waves Will up. Walking the plank.

At least a hundred guests are gathered on decks. Will is overdressed, as he often is. There are very few other neckties, except for the highly visible security crew in their hired-help black and white. He can already see a half-dozen of these guys; there must be an army strewn around this ship.

The wardrobe convention is unmistakable: the older you are, the more clothes you wear, and vice versa, from itsy-bitsy bikinis and banana hammocks up to summer dresses and linen jackets and even a few ascots, worn with the sated smugness of unattractive middle-aged men who habitually have sex with staggeringly attractive young women. There are no middle-aged women on this yacht, which is the right word for it. If ever there was a yacht, this is it.

"*Buenas tardes. Me llamo Lucia-Elena.*"

"Will Rhodes." He holds out his hand to this woman, who's wearing a thin shimmery dress in a loud pattern of swirling greens and purples and oranges. "*Mucho gusto.*"

"You are American?"

"How can you tell?"

"Your name, of course."

"Not my dreadful accent?"

"Perhaps that too. *Un poco.*"

"I know, it's appalling. *Lo siento.* I shouldn't even be allowed to enter Spain."

"Oh, do not be so hard on yourself. There are many guests tonight who do not speak a word of Spanish. How have you made the acquaintance of Señor Miloshevsky?"

"I haven't, not yet. I'm a journalist."

"Oh?"

"Well, I write about food, and travel, and wine. You know, *important* subjects. I never go near anything trivial like politics or business. I'm not that type of writer."

"Would you enjoy a glass of *cava*?" She beckons to a passing waiter, a tray, a flute of bubbly for Will, *muchas gracias*. "Are you here in an official capacity, Señor Rhodes?"

"Please call me Will. And yes, I am." He reaches into his pocket, removes his notebook, exhibits this proof of his industriousness. "I'm writing a story about a glamorous party on a mega-yacht."

She smiles. "I see." She assesses him over the lip of her own glass, a clear liquid, ice cubes, a slice of lemon. "Well then, Señor—"

"Will, *por favor.*"

"Señor Will. Allow me to introduce you to some other guests."

This is when it dawns on Will that Lucia-Elena is an employee here, paid to facilitate introductions, to smooth over the rough patches where different worlds intersect, Russian energy barons and German industrialists and Spanish nobility, Swiss bankers and American investors, young women and old men.

There's a new hotel in New York that pays beautiful women to hang around the lobby, their mere presence an implicit promise of something. Lucia-Elena is a more sophisticated version, occupying a different position on the long continuum of people who get paid to help others have a good time, hostesses and bartenders, private chefs and dating consultants, exotic dancers and call girls.

In the midst of benign chitchat with a British couple—a sexy young Lord and his sexier Lady—Lucia-Elena inclines her head. "There is Señor Miloshevsky." He's a dour-looking man trying unsuccessfully to look undour, flanked by a pair of similarly forbidding men. Over their shoulders, the coastline of Spain is receding from view.

"Who are his jolly-looking companions?"

"Business associates."

This answer is not as specific as Will wants. "The one on the right looks familiar. What's his name again?"

"That is Señor Borchov."

"And the other one?"

"I do not know. I expect Señor Miloshevsky is wanting to meet you? He is very friendly with journalists. Would now be a good time for introductions?"

Will turns his body to face the host, pink-shirted and pink-faced and absolutely terrifying looking. "Of course."

Will's left hand, in his pants pocket, finds his phone. His index finger locates the button on top, which Will presses. He shifts his torso a few degrees and presses the button again, and again, a half-dozen times in a few seconds, a half-dozen photos from a half-dozen angles taken through the lens that's disguised as a diamond in the middle of his tie bar.

"Now would be perfect."

NEW YORK CITY

"Another new phone?" he asked, a few days ago. "You shouldn't have."

"It's higher tech." Elle placed a second item on the table, a little velvet pouch. "Use it with this." She pushed the pouch across the table, a battered slab of oak, carved with a hundred years' of initials and profanities and jokes, drunken proclamations and defamations, crudely drawn arrow-pierced hearts and erect penises and the types of breasts drawn by people who are unfamiliar with the shape of breasts.

Will opened the pouch, removed a silver stick. "A tie bar?" Art Deco horizontal etchings, a small diamond in the middle, a flashier piece of jewelry than Will would choose. It also seemed heavier than it should. Will turned it over, saw that it was a thick piece of silver. Tie bars aren't supposed to be thick, or heavy.

"It's a camera," Elle said. "The lens is the thing in the middle that looks like a diamond. The angle of the lens is tilted twenty degrees upward, which is this way"—she reached across the table, showed him the little triangle etched on back—"so it can capture faces when you're close. The ideal range is five to ten feet, but anything up to thirty works."

"Did I miss something?"

"The shutter—I guess it's not really a shutter, is it, on a digital camera?—is remote-controlled with the phone. When you put this switch in this position, and you hit this button, it takes a photo."

"No, that's not what I mean. I mean: did I miss some prior conversation wherein I agreed to take surreptitious pictures of thugs in international waters?"

"Let's not be histrionic."

"*Histrionic?* That's a big word. I'm not histrionic. I am rationally, calmly, terrified. And I'm asking again, when the hell did I agree to do anything remotely like this?"

"There's no danger to you."

"Oh no?"

"As far as anyone can tell, this is a phone like any other. And this? Man bling."

"Man bling?"

"Look." She turns the tie bar over, back again. "Nothing there to see. No way for anyone to know anything."

Will fingered both pieces.

"This isn't amateur hour, Will. This is next-generation technology. And this is what we're paying you for."

"Nobody ever said anything about doing something like this."

"Well, now I am."

He wondered, for the hundredth time, what would happen if he refused. Was there a level of retaliation before the nuclear option? Was now the time to find out?

"Okay," he said. "What am I supposed to do?"

"You're going to a party that's being thrown by one of the richest men on the planet, who's also among the most corrupt. He's in the process of showing off his newly immense wealth, buying yachts, buying *islands*. But it's not really showing off if there's no one there to see it, right? So he will undoubtedly invite his most important associates. Both the legal ones and the, uh, sublegal ones. We want to know who these people are. You're going to help by taking pictures of them. Every single one of them, even those who don't want to be photographed. *Especially* those."

"Oh, sure, that sounds easy. Anything else?"

"Yes."

"I was kidding."

"I know. I'm not. We also need you to attach names to those faces."

IBERIAN SEA

"You are journalist?"

"I am."

The big Russian's big hand is encircling Will's, a handshake that seems to be achieving an unusual level of threatening permanence. Miloshevsky's companions beat a hasty retreat, circling around themselves a few yards away, wanting nothing to do with any American journalist.

"It's a pleasure to meet you, Señor Miloshevsky. This is certainly a beautiful boat."

"Sure, *Catherine* is biggest yacht in Mediterranean. Not bad for poor boy from Smolensk, no?"

"No sir, not bad at all."

"Is newspaper story about party, yes?"

"Magazine. *Travelers* is a magazine."

"Am unfamiliar. Is magazine about travelers?"

"Traveling, I guess. Tourism. Hotels and restaurants, cruises and safaris."

"I love safari."

"Yes, it's a very special experience. Do you entertain often on the *Catherine*?"

"Sure. Everyone loves party on yacht."

One of the black-suited guards has edged closer, and Will is self-conscious about his hand in his pocket, fondling his phone. He doesn't want to be dragged down to the engine room, beaten to a pulp. He takes his hand out of his pocket.

"You want I should give you tour?"

"Yes sir, I'd love that. If you have the time."

"Sure. Always time for journalist."

Miloshevsky beckons to someone over Will's shoulder, a hand signal and a nod. They start walking together, trailed by a guard, not making any attempt to be discreet. That's not how security works in this sort of crowd. It's there to be seen.

The proud owner rattles off his yacht's vitals, horsepower and water displacement, top speeds and refueling range, numbers that would no doubt be impressive if Will had context, but he doesn't, so they're abstract, like pi, Planck's constant.

"You have phone? You take selfie with helicopter?"

Will glances at the helicopter. "Oh, that's all right."

"No? Everyone take selfie with helicopter. I take for you."

"Oh, no, that's very generous of you."

"For article," Miloshevsky says. "Give phone to me." The Russian holds out his hand. "I insist."

18

There's a kid crying when Malcolm walks through the door. It seems as if there's always a kid crying when he walks through the door, the tantrums and tears perhaps stage-directed by Allison—"Cue crying!"—performance art created both to shame him—do you see how difficult my life is?—and to annoy the living shit out of him. Killing two birds with one egg, as Sylvie likes to say, getting the metaphor so deliciously incorrect, like her half-correct facts about Greek myths, Krakatoa, the Lenape, bears.

Malcolm doesn't need Allie's passive-aggressive help; he already feels plenty guilty about all the things he misses, all the things he doesn't do.

Allison is in the alarmingly messy kitchen, a space designed as one of those hypermodern affairs that look serene in magazines like *Travelers*. But once a stray crumb lands on the counter, the illusion shatters.

"Hi," he says.

Allison turns to him just as a sizzling pop from the sauté pan pelts her with a globule of scalding oil. "Fuck!" She glares at Malcolm—his fault, apparently, the spatter—and turns back to the stove. "Can you deal with her, please?"

"Sylvie? Sure. What's her problem?"

Allison doesn't say anything, accentuating her focus on her martyrdom cooking. Dinner party for eight. Not his idea, not his friends, not his goddamned fault.

Malcolm walks to the living room, floor-to-ceiling windows with views of the Brooklyn and Manhattan Bridges, the Midtown skyscrapers, the twinkling blanket beyond, all the way to the horizon, all those anonymous people living in their anonymous houses in the Bronx and Queens, while he's up here, in a glass box in the sky, with a livid wife and a bawling kid.

His other, more emotionally stable child comes flying out of nowhere.

"Daddy, can I have a lollipop?" Peter is already holding the lollipop in question, its wrapper halfway open.

"Why do you think it's candy time?"

"Because yes." Malcolm has to hand it to the kid, he makes a powerful argument. No extraneous information, no wasted time.

"Sure."

"Thank you Daddy!" He flees before his father has a chance to change his mind.

Malcolm pours a scotch, takes a slug, deposits the tumbler on the coffee table. Then he reconsiders, finds a coaster, even though the liquid is room-temperature and the table is glass, and there's no possibility of condensation damage. But Allison is a coaster fanatic, and he doesn't need to go out of his way to drive his wife nuts; she's more than capable of piloting herself to that destination all on her own.

Down the long hall. "Hey kiddo," he says to Sylvie, facedown on her bed, sobbing.

She turns to her father, red eyes and splotchy cheeks and a big bubble of snot in one nostril, a balloon being inflated. "Daddy, I hate her!"

"You hate Mommy? That seems like maybe an overreaction. *Hate* is a very strong word. Why do you say that, pumpkin?"

"She's mean. She yelled at me. She said I was in the way."

"Were you?"

"She *always* says I'm in the way." The crying has already stopped. "Even when I'm not."

Malcolm kisses her on the head. "She doesn't mean it, pumpkin. She just gets angry sometimes."

"At *me*? That's not fair."

"Not at you. She just gets angry, in general."

"Why?"

The answer is too long, too complicated, too sad, for an eight-year-old.

"It's hard to explain, pumpkin. But I promise, it's not you she's angry at. You're just there sometimes when she notices she's angry. I'm sorry. And so is she, I'm sure."

IBERIAN SEA

"Is new phone?" Miloshevsky turns the device over in his palm. "Looks new."

"Um, yes." Will feels the onset of the physiological symptoms of panic, which can be visible to someone who knows what to look for. He suspects that Miloshevsky is the type who'd know.

"Camera app is where?"

Miloshevsky is handling someone else's possession with the blithe assuredness of a man who makes a habit of seizing the things he wants, surging past protestations and defenses, challenging anyone—everyone—to defy him. "Ah," he says, "is here."

In the rational part of his brain, Will knows there's no way for someone to casually stumble upon the surreptitious photo stream, the one Will captured using the secondary camera app. Or even to *find* the app. Both the app and its image library are sitting on his fourth screen, one program disguised as the New York City bus map and the other as the Long Island Rail Road schedule, neither of which anyone would consider consulting, least of all a Russian multibillionaire standing on his mega-yacht ten miles off the Barcelona shore.

There's no way.

Miloshevsky swipes the screen, swipes again the other way, brow furrowed. "Is lot of apps."

There's also the remote possibility that Miloshevsky will find the hidden audio recorder, the app that's activated by the camera, sixty seconds of sound triggered after every image, enabling Will to capture names that he'd otherwise have no way of remembering.

Finally Miloshevsky finds the default camera. He raises the phone and adopts the now ubiquitous pose, body language that hadn't been coined a decade ago.

Will can see a guard, prison tattoos on his knuckles, a slightly misshapen ear, with a chunk of flesh missing from the top.

"Done." Miloshevsky admires the screen. "Is good photo." He lowers the phone, then rocks his arm back, and forward, and tosses the device the ten feet that separates him from Will, who responds an instant too slowly, manages only to deflect the thing's flight path instead of catching the phone, which clatters to the deck and skitters across the smooth sur-face of the helicopter pad, very little in the way of friction to slow it down, metal on metal, spinning, approaching the edge of the deck—

Will lunges awkwardly, bending, stumbling, the phone slowing, three feet from the edge, two, and Will's knee hits the deck while his hand reaches out, just inches remain, the thing approaching the edge and still just beyond Will's reach, almost not moving at all, but not entirely not moving, and then a silent disappearance, over the edge, gone.

"Shit."

His mind is hopping around all the ways that this is a problem, a dozen issues converging in his consciousness in a single second while he kneels there on the hot metal deck, the photos for the CIA, his digital train tickets, his two thousand contacts—how many are backed up?—and the unresolved emails and the text message from the general manager of the hotel in Salamanca, and how is Will going to replace this lifeline, and how is Miloshevsky going to respond?

"Am sorry." Miloshevsky doesn't look all that sorry.

Will turns toward the edge, no railing here. He leans forward, and looks down, expecting to see the churning sea. But that's not what's im-mediately below, which is another deck, high-gloss white fiberglass, a seating arrangement, couches and chaises and a couple of ottomans, on one of which sits Will's phone, safe and sound.

It's late. Will opens the wrong door. This cabin is done up like a bachelor pad from the 1960s, or rather a Las Vegas hotel's re-creation of one, with low furniture and organic shapes and a white shag carpet, on which a young woman kneels on all fours, completely naked, with a bald man behind her on his knees, fully clothed except for his fly unzipped and his silk shirt unbuttoned to his stomach, a matt of white chest fur, one of his hands grasping her long black hair and the other pushing down on the small of her back, for leverage.

Both copulating people notice Will in the doorway. The woman winces at the shame of it, but the man thrusts out his chin in defiance of Will's intrusion, continues to pivot his pelvis forward, taking a harder yank on the woman's hair, a bonus degradation.

"I'm sorry," Will says. As he pulls the door closed, he can see the woman's eyes fall back to the carpet, to whatever world she's trying to imagine instead of the one she inhabits.

Will is looking for the young British couple and an older Brit, also a Lord Something, they all wanted to sit down, and Lucia-Elena was going to find a place to watch a DVD of a situation comedy that they'd all been raving about, there was a screening room somewhere, but Will said he'd meet them, first he needed the restroom.

It wasn't the toilet he'd wanted, it was the privacy. The chance to upload tonight's photos to the cloud-based server using a complex set of instructions that Elle had made him memorize. But in the privacy of the neat little washroom Will discovered that the boat was too far from shore, too far from cell towers; there was no reception. Will couldn't help but wonder if that, too, was purposeful, along with the near destruction of his phone, whose screen was cracked from hitting the helicopter pad.

Will is reluctant to open any more doors onto any more indignities, but he manages to stumble across the door with the CINÉMA plaque. Unfortunately, inside are a handful of tough guys watching *The Godfather*, as tough guys do.

Back outside, breezy and cool, house music, lots and lots of inebriated people.

"Do you see anything you like?" Lucia-Elena has found him. "Anything you want?"

Will is not sure what he's being offered.

"There is Suzanna"—she nods in the direction of a tall blonde—"who is from the Czech Republic. And the full woman wearing the white bikini, she is Francesca, born in Italy. If these are not your preference, there are other girls"—Lucia-Elena looks around—"but I cannot see any now."

"Um, I don't . . ."

"Gratis, of course. Señor Miloshevsky would be happy to make this offer to you, as an apology, for the damages of your phone. And of course he will replace the phone. You are staying at the Hotel Atlántico, that is correct?"

Will doesn't demur, but neither does he confirm. He's pretty certain he didn't provide this information to anyone in Miloshevsky's employ.

"A new phone will arrive tomorrow, by noon."

"Oh, that's not necessary."

"It is fair. Señor Miloshevsky has not achieved his level of success by being unfair."

Will can tell that Lucia-Elena is intelligent, quick-witted, clear-thinking. She knows that what she's saying is the opposite of true.

"Suzanna, then? Or Francesca? I have been told that Francesca is unusually skillful."

The yacht docks at 2:00 A.M. Cars are waiting to shuttle the partygoers who are departing—quite a few are not—to whatever passes for home, grand hotels, Art Nouveau apartments in Eixample, tile-roofed houses commanding turquoise lagoons up the Costa Brava.

None of the cars is for Will. Plus he seems to have lost track of Lucia-Elena, who offered a ride, though maybe that's for the best. He wants to get back to his hotel and go to sleep, without being forced to decline anything further. He feels like he has spent the past three hours saying no to things, drinks and drugs and hookers.

The carless make a mad drunken dash for the handful of taxis that have gathered, smelling expensive fares and exorbitant tips like sharks. There are more passengers than taxis, and within a minute the fleet has been hired.

The remaining partygoers whip out phones, calling for pickups, but Will decides to walk. Barcelona is a late place, compulsory naps in the evening, dinner at eleven. Two in the morning is early here. These streets are busy.

He strolls through La Barceloneta and into the Barrio Gótico. The medieval streets close around him, tight and dark and resonant with centuries of late-night revelry. In a small square, vagrants have established a community, smoke and music and untethered dogs, the sounds of amusement mixing with an aura of menace.

Will is aware of footsteps behind him, but he doesn't want to turn to look. Chances are that it's benign, and he shares with most men a deep antipathy against looking skittish.

At the end of a curving street he slows, not positive which way to turn, the curve disorienting his directional sense. He stops. Takes out his phone to consult the map. He doesn't want to make the wrong turn, not at this time of night, at this level of fatigue.

The footsteps behind him have also stopped.

He holds up his phone, which now features a jagged Y-shaped crack on the screen. He forces his eyes into soft focus, trying to locate the reflection of the real world behind the graphic representation of it, behind the white streets and gray buildings and green parks.

There. There they are, two men, quarter-turned toward each other, one oval face clearly in Will's direction. Fifty yards back? Seventy-five?

Will refocuses on the map, the streets, his hotel a half-kilometer away, maybe less, five minutes if he's walking quickly and taking the shortest route. But that's not what he's going to do. His eyes follow a longer, circuitous route, a handful of turns, a kilometer. He memorizes the decisions, grateful that he stopped accepting alcohol two hours ago.

He sets off again, a right turn at the T, setting a quick walking pace.

Behind him, the footsteps resume clicking on the stones.

Will takes a turn down a very narrow street. Out of view of his pursuers, he breaks into a jog, setting a pace of ten miles per hour, perhaps six minutes to his hotel, and he won't tire, in fact he'll be able to speed up at the moment when his pursuers will be slowing; he has more adrenaline, and he's a runner. His pursuers are paid to be strong, not fast.

He runs past the hippie-ish encampment again, feeling himself speeding up. A few of the smokers at the edge of the square cheer for him, or jeer.

The footsteps are still pursuing, but they're not close, and not getting closer. They're keeping his pace. But he'll outlast them. He speeds up. Another turn at another quiet narrow street. His feet are not feeling great, sliding around in the thin dress socks. But at least the soles are rubber. This would suck in leather-soled shoes with hard heels.

Will accelerates again, now going maybe twelve miles per hour, a faster pace than a nonrunner will be able to maintain for more than a minute. His pursuers' footsteps are falling farther behind.

This is his last turn, onto the narrow sidewalk of a street that's busy during most of the day, but not now, quiet and nearly deserted, just a few souls in sight, the lights of one restaurant and a couple of hotels, a taxi idling.

Will has made it. Just another twenty seconds to his hotel door, to the desk clerk, a witness. Will starts to slow, takes a deep breath, filling his straining lungs with air.

That's when the man steps into his path, just a few yards ahead, short of breath but otherwise big, tall, scary. Will comes to a stop.

These men must have known where Will was going, which hotel. That means they're not muggers. They're Miloshevsky's men, people who'd known where Will was going; Lucia-Elena did. So why not simply wait for him at his hotel? Perhaps they weren't sure he'd be returning to his hotel, and wanted to see where he went, wanted to monitor him. But they also wanted to capture him, didn't they? Or why else would they chase him through the streets?

What can they want? If they wanted to kill him, they would have.

It has to be the phone. They're supposed to steal Will's phone, make it look like a run-of-the-mill late-night mugging. Maybe treat him to a nonlethal beating in the bargain, to lend an air of authenticity, plus teach him a lesson.

This is all racing through Will's mind, the brain astronomically fast, all these thoughts and calculations occurring so quickly, arguments begun and developed and dismissed in less than a second, including the argument that his brain doesn't have the time to pursue that wonderment, not right now.

So what if they take his phone? Beat him up? Besides the physical, emotional, and metaphorical black eyes, what will happen? Someone who works for Miloshevsky will find the clandestine apps, the photos, the furtive surveillance of the party. They will suspect Will of working for—what?—the CIA? Maybe. Or one of Miloshevsky's business competitors. Or Interpol. They will have no idea whom Will is working for, and no way of finding out.

And if they guess correctly? If Will's cover is blown? Then maybe he'll no longer be a useful asset. He'll be let go, retired. Would the CIA have to kill him? No. Would they allow him to simply stop working for them, go back to his life, ten thousand dollars per month poorer, but simpler? Yes, that's exactly what would happen. Probably.

He can just stand here, and get mugged. Maybe punched in the face and kicked in the shin, a few stitches in a Spanish emergency room, a frustrating hour in a sleepy police station, a morning visit to the consulate.

Then what? Then he'll be finished. Finished with tradecraft and secret phones, with countersurveillance exercises and hidden compartments, finished memorizing faces and names and places, finished taking encoded notes and sending encrypted messages, finished with the CIA, finished with Roger, finished with Elle.

While all these considerations are firing, his cerebellum is pursuing its own involuntary agenda. It turns out that it's nearly impossible to voluntarily accept physical peril, to pursue a path of pain and possibly death if you can avoid it.

He hears a sound behind him. He glances over his shoulder, sees the lone runner turn the corner, a pose of exhaustion.

Will is running out of time. He turns to the man blocking the sidewalk. And he attacks.

19

t's after 3:00 A.M. when Will tiptoes down the hotel hall. There's no light visible from under his room's door, no noise audible. He pauses, his ear against the wood, straining to hear any sign of anything. Down the hall, a man is snoring; on another floor, a toilet flushes.

Will presses his body against the wall. Extends his arm to wave his keycard across the sensor. The lock releases, but Will doesn't open the door. He pulls back his arm, tensed and ready, and waits, listening intently. He hears nothing until the click of the door relocking.

He continues to wait, and listen, for another minute. Nothing.

He shouldn't linger. The night clerk was quite possibly in on it, dialing his phone this very instant, reporting that the American has just returned to his room. Will needs to get in and get out quickly.

He unlocks the door again, and this time opens it. Unsurprisingly, the room has been tossed, his clothes strewn everywhere, suitcase ripped open. The mattress has been tipped over, chairs upended. A thorough job, its intention undisguised.

Whatever they were looking for, they didn't find it, because there was nothing to find. But they wanted Will to know they'd looked.

He quickly repacks his damaged luggage, exits the wrecked room. How is he going to explain this downstairs? *Is* he going to explain this? Or should he flee with no explanation, accept the exorbitant damage charge on his credit card, hope that *Travelers*—or the CIA?—covers it? Or should he not worry about the money, because his life is in danger?

Will doesn't want the elevator call to attract any attention, so he takes the stairs. The lobby is still empty except for the clerk, who'd given Will a dubious once-over when he walked in, disheveled, very late. The clerk is obviously considering whether to intervene in this guest's hasty, unscheduled early-morning departure. By the time Will walks through the front door, the guy still hasn't decided what if any action to take, his moment to be a hero past. Night clerks are probably not, as a rule, go-getters.

The street is deserted. Will glances across to the alley entrance where he'd been lurking for a half-hour, watching the hotel for comings and go-ings, for anything suspicious. This is a location he'd scouted right after he checked in, garbage cans and motorbikes and nothing much in the way of light, a few deep doorways in which he could disappear into darkness, a second entrance on the next street to the north, which is how he accessed the alley, just a minute after he dispatched his assailant.

"There's very little substitute," Will's martial-arts instructor ex-plained, "for a swift kick to the groin. If someone doesn't know you're going to attack, this is the way to go. Lots of people make the mistake of trying to punch adversaries in the face. This is hard to land effectively, and easy to see coming, easy to get out of the way. A kick to the balls, though? Easy to get that right. Very difficult to defend against."

So that's exactly what Will did to the man who was blocking the side-walk. And as the guy was still in the process of doubling over in excep-tional pain, seeing stars, Will planted his groin-kicking leg, and brought his other leg up swiftly, kneeing the man in the face. He toppled over, writhing in agony, blood pouring from a broken nose.

Will sprinted away. There was no way for the second pursuer to catch up: the guy was obviously a slow runner, plus exhausted after running a kilometer at a rapid pace. And probably at least a little scared, with his companion lying on the sidewalk, bleeding profusely from the face. This second guy wouldn't be too eager to resume chasing someone he couldn't catch, and who might break his nose if he did.

At the end of the block Will turned right, then took another right, another, entered the alley from the far side. He crept down the damp pas-sage to the deep dark shadows next to the delivery door of an espadrille shop. He watched his panting pursuer tend to the injured one, then make a phone call. A minute later a Mercedes arrived, and the two men climbed in, and sped away.

Will uploaded the photos to the server, and sent an SOS message using the codes he'd memorized on the Eastern Shore of Virginia. Then he waited. He examined every car parked on the block, every pedestrian, every motorcycle rider and taxi driver, everyone a potential adversary, a man passed out behind the wheel of a sedan, a streetwalker who strolled by a few times. Will allowed an uneventful hour to pass, then retreated to the far end of the alley, and eventually found a taxi, which he took around the block to the hotel.

That taxi is still idling on the wide boulevard around the corner, as guaranteed by a torn-in-half hundred-euro note. Will climbs in. They speed through early-morning Barcelona, weaving past the trucks that are converging on the big food market, and the first commuters of the day riding bicycles and mopeds and fuel-efficient little cars.

Will reclines in the taxi's backseat, and can't help but smile.

NEW YORK CITY

Stacey and Eric are the last to leave, both seven-figure-per-year attorneys, sixty-hour workweeks, one night a month when they can manage to leave their offices in time for dinner together, desperate to make it count, sure-I'll-have-another. But still Malcolm finds Stacey in the hall, typing on her phone, thumbs flying furiously. "Work," she says, shrugging an apology. "Don't tell Eric, please."

Malcolm can't imagine what secret Stacey thinks she's keeping from her second husband. But he agrees anyway. "Why would I?"

They finally leave at eleven, cheek-kisses handshakes this-was-greats. Then it's time to deal with the mess. "I got this," Malcolm says, removing his watch and rolling up his sleeves, taking stock. He doesn't mind this after-dinner-party cleanup with his wife, moving silently through the kitchen in a dance of divided responsibilities, staying out of each other's way, taking care of what needs to be done, together. Marriage.

"Do those two really strategize their Facebook posts?" he asks.

"I guess."

"They actually discuss what they're going to post? And which posts they should share? And like? That's *insane*."

Allison seems to be ripping sheets of aluminum foil with an excess of ferocity. "Malcolm, did you remember the tuition bill?"

"Tuition is due?" More than a hundred thousand's worth of salary, poof. Like buying a new car every six months, every year, forever.

"Was. *Was* due, last week."

"I'll take care of it tomorrow."

She snorts, dismissive, as if it's impossible that he'll remember to do it tomorrow. She isn't necessarily wrong.

"All right, I'll take care of it after the dishes." He fleetingly worries about the sum, realizes what he'll need to do. "But in the meantime, do you want to tell me what's bothering you?" Malcolm has had a few glasses of wine in addition to his few glasses of scotch. Otherwise, he doesn't have the courage, or the energy, or the whatever he needs to confront his wife point-blank with a question like this.

"Is it something I did? Or didn't do, that I was supposed to? I mean, besides the tuition?"

She shakes her head, hammers the heel of her hand against a plastic container. "I am not just some . . . *house*wife."

"No," he says, knee-jerk. "Of course not."

"I have a master's degree."

He's heard this before, and not just from his wife. There's no shortage of women whose graduate degrees have transmogrified into heavy chips on their Pilate'd shoulders.

When they're finished cleaning, Allison says, "I'm going to watch TV," disappears.

There was a time when sex always followed a dinner party; that aspect of being a couple turned Allison on. But now it's the opposite. Allison is going through a bad time, and Malcolm doesn't know how to help her fix it.

He wonders if his wife loves him enough to make it—what?—another thirty years with him? Forty? Or if he loves her enough? Or if they're going to agree—five or ten or twenty years from now, the kids grown, gone—that enough is enough, good-bye. Or maybe they won't agree. But although it takes two people to marry, only one is needed to split.

There's really nothing encouraging that he could say to Allison, trying to figure out what to do with the rest of her life, that wouldn't be some sort of lie. Lord knows he already does more than enough lying to his wife.

He walks to the office. Above the desk, the bulletin board is festooned with the normal home-bulletin-board flotsam, children's drawings and an after-school activity checklist, tickets to the opera and the Montauk-line train schedule, the odds and ends of life, punctured with pushpins.

He can hear the hum of the television, theme music, canned laughter.

Malcolm pushes the left edge of the bulletin board's frame into the wall, releasing a magnetic catch. The board swivels open from hinges, revealing the rotary dial of an in-wall safe.

This is not a very high-tech setup, as security measures go. Malcolm doesn't want too high-end of a safe here, where if discovered it would arouse suspicion. Why, Mr. Somers, do you have such a sophisticated safe? What is it you're protecting? Afraid of?

He opens the safe. There's not much inside, nothing particularly incriminating. He removes a little device that looks like a thumb drive, but isn't.

Malcolm sits down at the computer. He punches in the password, then signs out of the family account, and logs in under a different alias. He launches an obscure web browser, an application that's buried in an irrelevant-looking subfolder. Types in a URL, then a long user ID. He picks up the device from the safe, and hits a button. On the device's small screen, a long string of digits appears, a random-generated passcode that refreshes itself every sixty seconds. He uses this code to access the account, and initiates the transfer, moving tuition money to his checking account in the United States from this ultrasecure account in Switzerland, a numbered account that his wife has no idea exists.

BARCELONA

There's always something shocking about the bustling alertness of a big-city airport at seven in the morning, when everything else is asleep or drowsy, sparsely populated, but here in some suburb off a highway there are tens of thousands of busy people.

Will doesn't know whom to expect; that was never specified. But he certainly didn't think it would be Elle he'd see walking up to the ticket counter. She exchanges a couple of sentences with the Iberian Air rep, then both women laugh, and Elle walks away.

When she has almost disappeared into the crowd, Will sets off in her wake, following her across the terminal to a café's queue, which he joins, standing a few customers behind her, amid roll-aboards and hand luggage and a stroller with a peacefully sleeping baby.

How should he act? How should he play this?

On the one hand, he's furious that he was so irresponsibly put in such extreme danger. Really, what the hell? He could've been killed. Maybe. He's not actually certain what risk he was at, what those thugs wanted, what they would've done to get it.

On the other hand, he acquitted himself admirably at every stage, from his surreptitious surveillance on the boat and the mortifying inter-action with Miloshevsky to the well-executed flight through the Barrio Gótico and his decidedly competent self-defense, all the way up to his by-the-book SOS message and this meet right here, waiting patiently in this café queue. Will has done absolutely everything he was supposed to do, exactly as he was supposed to do it. And it has felt *good*, vigorous and exciting and satisfying. Like sex.

Will collects his espresso, and scans the seating area. Elle is standing at a tall round table, and she meets his eye indubitably, the signal clear. *"Buenos días,"* he says, approaching, inclining his head at the expanse of empty table, the universal is-this-spot-taken? gesture.

"Yo no hablo español," she says in a thickly American-accented version of a language that, Will knows, she speaks fluently. "Do you speak English?"

"Yes," he says. "I'm American."

"Oh goody."

He takes a seat.

"So why are we here?" She speaks in a quiet but normal voice, not a whisper. There's plenty of ambient noise in here to cloak their conversation; it's whispering that would be noticeable.

He reaches into his pocket, extracts a typical traveler's pile, guidebook and map, slips of scrawled-upon hotel stationery, a page ripped from a notebook.

"The top piece of paper," Will says, glancing down at his densely packed but neat handwriting, a narrative he composed in the back of the taxi during the ninety minutes that they drove around before Will thought he should arrive at the airport, not wanting to be too early, to spend too much time lurking around in public. He'd told the driver that he wanted to see sights, just show me around for a while, wherever you think is best.

The page is already facing Elle. She doesn't need to touch it, doesn't need to make any visible effort other than to lower her eyes and start reading the carefully summarized story of Will's past twelve hours. Meanwhile he pretends to read his guidebook. They're just two strangers, sharing a cluttered table at a busy airport café.

"Wow," she mutters, but she doesn't seem terribly surprised.

"What are you doing here?" he asks. "You're following me?"

"Of course I'm following you. This was your first active operation. We needed to make sure you were safe."

"Then why weren't you there last night?"

"What makes you sure we weren't?"

Will thinks back to the streets, taxi drivers and vagrant hippies, the sleeping driver and the working girl. "Who?"

"It doesn't matter." She shrugs. "You were never in any real danger. And if you had been, we would have helped you."

"And Miloshevsky's thugs? What was that about?"

"They wanted your phone. To wipe your documentation of the party-goers. But Miloshevsky didn't take you seriously, and he didn't give serious orders, so those weren't serious thugs. That was just his casual everyday security. You took care of them yourself, didn't you? But today he'll take you more seriously, so it's best for you to leave."

She taps the piece of paper on the table in front of her. "You should get yourself through security ASAP. Like, don't use the men's room out here. Don't step outside for a smoke."

"Smoke? I don't—"

"I know, I'm kidding." She takes a sip of her coffee. "You all right?"

He nods.

"Good." She knocks back her coffee, puts the cup in its saucer, a little clang. "And you did good, Will. Nice work."

He watches Elle walk away, and wonders if this is really the first time she has followed him abroad. Or has she been tailing him for months? Could he somehow be worth that type of effort, that type of expense?

◆ ◆ ◆

Elle climbs out of the taxi and into the bright sunshine, another hot day on the way in Catalonia. A bellhop holds the door, and she strides across the cool lobby, closes herself inside the small elevator.

Upstairs, the hall is long, dead-quiet, no room-service trays, no chambermaid carts, no nothing. The elevator doors whish closed behind her, and she stands unmoving, listening. She's spooked. She really didn't expect any of that to happen last night. Just as she didn't expect Will to be interrogated in Dublin. It certainly seems like he's drawing the intense curiosity of excessively prudent people. Which in a way is good: it means the op is working. But in another way is bad: Will may very well get himself into real trouble, the sort that Elle couldn't mitigate.

She walks down the corridor, swipes the key, opens the door. Roger is sitting inside at the desk, a laptop in front of him. "He's on a plane?"

She nods.

"That sure was close, wasn't it?"

Elle takes a seat on the bed, kicks off her shoes.

"We could've gotten him killed."

"I don't know about *killed*," she says, rubbing the sole of her foot. "But anyway, it worked. Look at all the phone numbers we captured, all the calls that those people made after encountering Rhodes. This giant network, one, two degrees of separation . . ."

On Roger's screen, there's a tree of phone numbers, with branches that extend all around the world.

"Has everything been uploaded to the server?"

"Yes, already being analyzed in Virginia."

Besides Elle, Roger is the only one on the team who has any contact whatsoever with Virginia, where all the data is collected, analyzed, and disseminated back out to the field, keeping the operatives in the loop about the past, present, and future locations of the mission's assets and targets. This is how Elle knows where Will is traveling—his flight number and seat assignment, terminal and gate, hotel and restaurant, train reservation and rental car. Whom he calls, texts, emails. What he buys for his wife, where. Every piece of information in his vast digital footprint, constantly monitored in real time.

"Look," Roger says, "there's one update now." A small window appears next to a number, with a name, a headshot. It's a man in Abu Dhabi.

"You think this is going to work?" Roger asks.

Miloshevsky's party guests were exactly the sorts of people who can provide what Elle is looking for. This operation has been active for months already, with no real progress. Some ops get more secure and more fruitful the longer they go on; longevity is the actual goal. This isn't one of them. This op is always on the verge of falling apart, every day a fresh opportunity to fail.

But that's not what she says, which is "Yes, I do," and she tries to convince herself it's true.

20

"I was terrified," Will says.

Gabriella is leaning on Will's doorjamb, clutching a notepad, and a folder with spreadsheets and schedules, and her phone, screen facing up, poised to alert her to whatever crisis will arise next, even though the day is over for most people. Gabriella's day is never over.

What is it about her job that makes her an editor? Most days it's hard to identify. Unless she revises the editorial functions of being an editor—*edits* out the editing—from her conception of her job, and recognizes that what she has is a management position, a job that's exactly about these things she's carrying around—budgets and schedules and crises—and not about the things she imagines, the things she used to do.

She finally complained to Malcolm. "You're looking at it the wrong way," he said, shaking his head. "These meetings that you attend—meetings about process, about finances—and these hours you spend helping people with their problems, and these advertiser dinners and industry conferences ... All these are not things that are *interrupting* your real work. They *are* your real work. Your job is about other people. Their performance *is* your performance."

And so she's in Will's doorway. "God," she says, "that sounds awful," trying to project sympathy, which she genuinely feels. Gabriella has been there herself, far from home, worried, alone, no one within hundreds of miles upon whom she could rely for anything. But not recently. Not since she became this type of suit. "Terrified of anything specific?"

"Ebola, SARS." Will smiles. "I don't know, cholera. Typhoid. Whatever global epidemic is next."

"So what made you get on a *plane*?" She takes a seat in Will's guest chair, looks around the always-spotless office.

"Honestly, I just didn't want to go to a hospital abroad. If I had something serious—if I was patient zero of the next contagion—I wanted to get diagnosed in New York. Get treated here. Quarantined here."

"And you did?"

"Well, by the time I got home . . ."

"You were better?"

"Mostly. I still didn't feel great, but I was no longer worried about dying."

"There's always next time."

"Yup."

"So besides your contagion, you okay, Will?"

He gives her a quizzical look, trying to pretend he doesn't know what she's talking about, but she knows he does. She allows him his silent dishonesty without calling him out. "You seem, I don't know, *off* these days. You angry at me about something?"

"Not at all."

"Then what's up?"

They've been friends for a dozen years. But Will's marriage put up a wall, a much taller wall than Gabs's own marriage had. There had always been a sexual tension between Will and Gabs, a real one, not just a reaction from her free-floating flirtations. There were a few near misses, late nights in faraway places, interrupted by other people, other circumstances. Nothing ever happened. But it could have, and—who knows?—maybe will. Life is long; marriages aren't, not always. Hers wasn't.

"Nothing," Will says. Gabriella is pretty sure he's still lying. But now isn't the time to confront him, and she's probably not the one to do it.

It's a peculiar relationship between colleagues who are similar ages, with similar levels of experience, similar job responsibilities: sometimes allies, but also rivals. People can talk about teams, but every colleague is one of three things: a boss, an underling, or a rival. Will is neither a boss nor an underling.

"Okay Will." She gets up, walks to the door. "Tell Chloe I say hi."

Gabriella walks around the corner to reception, steps into the elevator. She examines herself in the wall of mirrors in there, aligns the slit of her skirt, fluffs her hair.

Down on twenty-eight, with the archives and accounting, legal and IT, she nods at a couple of men she doesn't really know, gives them the smile they want. She can practically feel their eyes follow her after she passes.

She turns a corner, comes to a stop at the open door of an interior office. "Hey Stonely," she says, "you got a minute?"

"Sure thing."

She steps into the small cluttered room, its high shelves packed with keyboards, monitors, cords. "I'm wondering"—she shuts the door behind her, leans against it—"if you could take care of something for me."

It's a fine line between a rigorous workout and vomiting, and at least once a week Allison finds herself straddling that line. "Um," she says, unsure what to order now that she's standing at the juice-bar register.

That's when she sees the handsome headhunter, Steven Something-or-Other, a cleft chin, a lot of thick hair, you could lose solid objects in there. When they'd met, he'd introduced himself as executive VP of talent acquisition.

"Talent acquisition? That's a thing? A job function?"

"For me it is."

He's now staring down into his phone, fingers tapping away. He's taller than she remembered—he'd been sitting during their first and only meeting, and she'd been wearing heels when they'd shaken hands hello-pleased-to-meet-you and then again good-bye-I'll-be-in-touch. But then he hadn't, in fact, been in touch.

She might be too nauseated for this. But before she can decide anything—how to say hello, or maybe how to flee, to get the hell out of here—he looks up. "Oh, hello . . ."

"Allison," she helps him. "Allison Somers. Rabinowitz-Somers."

"Of course, hi Allison, nice to see you again. I'm Steven Roberts." He has an easy smile, a surfeit of big white teeth. Nice suit and tie, briefcase. The whole handsome-adult-guy-with-job package. "Listen," he says, "I can't really talk now"—glancing down at his phone—"but seeing you reminds me that we have something, just came up."

"Oh?"

He looks around, as if for eavesdroppers. "Would you be interested in educational publishing?"

She raises her eyebrows.

"It's okay if not—"

"No, I mean, yes. Yes, I'd be interested. Definitely." This is not strictly true, though since having kids she has become marginally less uninterested.

He smiles wide, all those teeth. He must've had a really great orthodontist, she wants to ask if it was someone in the city, she can already tell that corrective dentistry is in her kids' future. Waiting rooms, headgear, tears.

"I'm absolutely interested." She nods eagerly.

"Good. Can you make it for a drink tonight? Say, seven?"

Will has lost track of what day it is, what time, lulled into a languorous stupor by the first-class barrage of second-class sandwiches and third-class wines, things he'd never consume had they not been exorbitantly paid for. By the CIA. How bizarre.

Will walks into the sun that's hanging low at the end of crosstown streets, nearly blinding, baking the city in early-evening heat. He occasionally stops abruptly, pauses at a shop window, ducks into a deli, trying to flush out tails, to remember the individuals who constitute the crowds.

He has been increasingly successful at justifying his double life to himself. It's just a job. A series of tasks that an organization pays him to do, like his employment at *Travelers*. One of his employers is a private enterprise trying to generate profit; the other, the government trying to maintain national security.

But other aspects of his predicament still loom large. One is the lying— it makes Will feel dirty. And it has become a lot of lying, daily lying.

Another is the danger. He'd been taking self-defense classes in the same way that he was paying for flood insurance: protecting against long-shot disaster. Until Barcelona, it hadn't seriously occurred to Will that he'd actually need to defend himself against violent attackers; it didn't seem like that type of role he was playing. And he didn't wholly believe that Elle and her hidden colleagues could've kept him safe in the late-night streets of the Barrio Gótico. What if one of Miloshevsky's goons had pulled a gun?

Will is no longer confident that he knows what level of danger he's in. Nor whom he can trust to protect him. Can he really believe the CIA? What's more, is he definitely working for the CIA? There's a lot of information about the Central Intelligence Agency floating out there, but it's very difficult to know which of it is reliable. Will's most trusted sources have been books written by verifiable authors and published by large, presumably responsible publishing houses. So far, everything he has learned about his operation seems credible. What he can't find is any confirmation that Agency operatives have actual sex with potential assets; but he also hasn't come across any refutation.

Sometimes, the whole thing seems totally implausible. Sometimes, it seems completely credible. Either way, it increasingly seems dangerous, and indefensible.

"I can't do this anymore."

"Of course you can." Elle smiles reassuringly. "You're doing a great job."

They're sitting in a booth at the back of an O'Somebody's on the West Side, dank and cheap and geezer-filled. Will has already summarized his recollections of the yacht, the guests, his recital digitally recorded by the app on Elle's phone, sitting in full view, not a suspicious item. This type of meeting must have been a lot more difficult before smartphones.

The hard information—the photos of the guests, their names—has already been transmitted electronically. This meeting is sort of superfluous, overkill, which Will has begun to realize is the CIA's MO. Redundancy atop repetition.

"I could've been killed."

"Not so loud." She glares at Will as a guy walks by, a bit too near, a Latino wearing a cheap black suit and a dingy white shirt, looks like a hired-car driver, bathroom-bound.

"And what about Dublin? Have you found out what that was?"

"I'm looking into it."

"That's what you said last time. That's what you always say."

"Because that's what I'm doing."

"Not very well."

She doesn't respond to this insult.

Will glances across to the streaked mirror behind the bar, visible swirls where someone did a half-assed cleaning job. Will can't see himself in the mirror, just the reflection of the men on stools, hunched over their pints of beer and shots of rye, their disappointments and despair. The bored bartender seems like an AA guy, someone who does this job to remind himself every day why he can't drink, not even a cold one after a hard shift on a hot night.

Will turns back to Elle, his bile rising again, his disappointment in himself, that he allowed his needy ego to drag him into this whole morass. "Who was that woman I met in France?"

"That was me."

"Totally you? Only you? No acting?"

"Is there such a thing?"

"Of course there is."

"Really? Being completely natural, completely unguarded? No guile, no artifice, no agenda, no disingenuousness or dishonesty of any sort?"

"You've never been married."

"Is that right?" She actually laughs at him. "You're completely honest with your wife?"

"I used to be."

"Bullshit. Everyone is acting all the time. Smiling and laughing, great to meet you, that's awesome. Wearing this and not that, keeping quiet when you want to scream, saying things you know aren't true. You do it every day, Will, and you did it before you ever met me. We all do. That's what keeps society going. That's what life is. Acting."

"You are one fucked-up person."

"Maybe. But who isn't?"

"Oh whatever. You know what? I've had enough of this. Of you. I don't believe a damn thing you say about anything, and I don't think you have any idea what the hell you're doing, and you're going to get me killed. I'm out."

He starts to stand, but Elle grabs him by the wrist, yanks him back down. "Don't be ridiculous. You're safe. We're not going to let you get hurt."

"I want out."

"Do you really?" She leans closer to him, her face just inches away. He realizes that they look like lovers having a spat. "And you're willing to accept the consequences?"

Of course not. Will has let this confrontation escalate too much, emotions getting the best of him. He needs to back down. But not all the way. He needs something, some reassurance that this is all real.

"I want a sit-down with your boss."

Allison's first job-search meeting, with a career coach, began inauspiciously.

"I don't think," Judah said, "that a director-level position is, um, a *realistic* expectation."

She glanced down at her résumé, one page, her professional life, a big ALLISON RABINOWITZ-SOMERS at the top. Malcolm had been dead-set against the hyphenate—"it sounds like the name of one of those Catskills camps: Rabinowitz Summers"—and had even offered, in a moment of inebriated chivalry, for their future children to use her name.

"It would be one thing if you were a doctor. Or a teacher, or a, I don't know, a carpenter."

A carpenter?

"Those professions don't change. But you worked"—past tense, brutal—"in marketing." Judah shook his head. "You know, the last time you were really *in* an office, there was *no such thing* as social media. Do you understand how big that has become?"

"Of course I do, Judah. I participate in the world."

"Have you given any thought to an internship?"

The urge to punch Judah in the face was almost uncontrollable. She'd been taking boxing classes, combining her passion for vigorous exercise with her acute misanthropy.

"An internship can be a wonderful experience, for someone in midlife transition."

She almost threw up, right then and there, expelling her all-greens juice onto his pleats.

Then her second career-development meeting was with the handsome headhunter in the hotel coffee shop. The third is here, an elegant place with a long well-lit aggressively serviced bar, twenty-two-dollar glasses of Montrachet, high-quality mixed nuts, plush upholstered barstools, middle-aged people in suits and skirts, nothing seedy about it. Lovers don't meet here. This is a place for business drinks, celebratory dinners, expense-account Bordeaux.

Steven gets down to business immediately, and a half-hour passes quickly, during which Allison believes she's at her most charming. Then suddenly, "I've gotta run." He's glancing at his phone; one of those obsessive phone-glancers. He tells her that she should make some small changes to her CV—"just a shift of focus." Tomorrow would be better than the day after.

Steven picks up the check, of course, please don't be silly. Allison doesn't quite understand who is working for whom, who's the client, how he gets paid—by her, somehow, at some point? She has never known anything about headhunters.

As she dismounts the barstool, she thinks she catches him checking out her legs, and she feels herself flush. He rests his hand on her upper arm, kisses her cheek. She feels the fine-grit sandpaper of his five-o'clock shadow as well as a small surprising thrill, which maybe isn't so small after all, nor for that matter surprising.

"I'll see you tomorrow?" he asks, eyebrows raised, hopeful, though she's not sure for what, exactly.

"Definitely."

"Good." He smiles, all those white teeth again, plus that little chin cleft, she can imagine putting the tip of her tongue in there, *God*, did she really just think that?

A man takes the empty subway seat beside Stonely. It's a long stretch before the next station, a full mile, and the subway picks up speed, rocks back and forth. Then the train begins to slow into West Fourth Street, and Stonely glances over to confirm who's next to him, but that's unnecessary, because what other person would voluntarily take a seat next to anyone at this hour—at any hour—when there's a car full of empty seats?

The envelope that's already in Stonely's hand contains a small stack of cash and a Post-it with an address. Stonely lets the envelope slide into the space between his thigh and the man's.

The subway stops.

The man rises, the envelope now in his hand, and leaves.

The train starts to move again, and Stonely catches a glimpse of the guy, walking toward the exit at the end of the platform. They catch each other's eyes before Stonely's car gets sucked into the dark tunnel, speeding him toward his home and family.

"Chloe? You here?"

Even though Will has arrived home two hours later than expected, Chloe appears to be out. He breathes a sigh of relief.

How awful. Has it really come to this? He's *happy* that his wife isn't home?

He hustles upstairs to his office, gropes in the dark for the pull to the bare bulb that's hanging from the rosette in the middle of the room. Will has identified fourteen spots in this house where he intends to install new light fixtures—chandeliers and sconces, a wall-mounted swing-arm here in this room, to illuminate the desk. A junction box is exposed in a cutout of the plaster wall, at the spot where that lamp will eventually be installed. But the lamp is an item that Will would rank somewhere between two hundred and three hundred on a list of punch-list priorities, if he were willing to undergo the painful process of enumerating the unfinished jobs, and ranking their importance, an exercise that would thrust him into a pit of utter despair. So he doesn't do it.

Will pulls a shoebox from a high shelf, removes the lid. The box is filled with vintage hotel labels collected at flea markets in Bruges and Singapore, Sharm al-Sheikh and Rio de Janeiro. One day they will all be framed, hung from walls yet unpainted, another of his theoretical projects, awaiting their abstract perfections.

He removes the labels, careful with the thin waxy bags and glassine coverings, and sets the stack aside. He picks up a letter opener. He hears the door close downstairs.

"Chloe?"

"Hi!"

He hurries now, using the letter opener to pry up the false bottom of the shoebox. He can hear Chloe's bag drop on the foyer floor, thud. Her feet clacking on the parquet.

Will reaches into his jacket, and removes the envelope with his latest payment, adds it to the rest of his secret trove, a few piles of hundred-dollar bills.

Chloe is trudging up the stairs, one loud step at a time.

Will is having trouble replacing the false bottom, his hands shaking.

He hears Chloe arrive at the top of the stairs, and now she's walking down the hall. He tosses the glassine bags back into the box, but he's not going to make it, he's not going to have time to get this straightened out before she walks in the door.

"Hey," she says.

Will's back is to the door. He turns. "Hi," he says, walking to greet her, mostly to prevent her from entering the room, seeing what he's doing.

"What are—?"

He kisses her on the mouth, breathing in her question, swallowing it. He wraps his arms around his wife, tightly. Squeezes.

Then he asks, "How was Washington?"

"Bureaucratic. How was Spain?"

What can Will tell her about Spain? "It was fine. Except when I was throwing up."

"Right. Sorry. What was it? Food poisoning?"

"I guess."

Did she just look over his shoulder, to see what he'd been doing?

"But I haven't seen my wife in more than a week, and believe it or not"—he drops one of his hands down, below the small of her back—"talk of vomit is not what I missed about her." With his other hand he takes Chloe's, and leads her away from his half-hidden secrets.

It's only a dozen feet to their bedroom door, just a couple of seconds of furious calculating for him to come to the conclusion that he'll have to feign extra-urgent desire here, he'll have to pretend that he simply cannot control himself, he *needs* to be on top the whole time, despite Chloe's preference. Today he'll have to be selfish. Because he needs to be the first to get up from the bed after sex, so he can return to the office before she has the chance.

21

nother day has slipped away, and here it is nine-thirty, and Malcolm has never gotten around to calling his wife and kids, never had the chance to do half the things he thought he'd do, including check the security footage, which he should do every other day at the least, but now it's been nearly a week, and tomorrow isn't going to get less busy, so, fuck it, he'll do it now. It's too late anyway to score points for coming home; the kids are already asleep. He might as well try to bank whatever he can for being a workaholic.

Malcolm walks down the hall, nearing the predictably occupied office of the man whose nameplate says VITO PARNELL but whom everyone calls Veal Parmesan, a play on not only his name and his profession but also on his long-ago mistake of admitting that he loved the Italian-American breaded cutlet.

Vito is a food writer from back before food writing was fashionable, as well as the director of the test kitchen. Vito is a legend, well known throughout the industry for meticulous prose and exacting research, and famous in this building for his snail-like velocity. There is no piece of text, no matter how short and trivial, that Vito can dispatch quickly. He arrives at the office early and departs late.

"Veal," Malcolm says from the doorway, not quite stopped. No one who's still in the office at this hour wants to chitchat.

"Malcolm."

At the end of the hall, the boss shuts his office door behind him, locks it. He doesn't turn on the overheads. There's plenty of light streaming through the floor-to-ceiling windows that face the Avenue of the Americas, shining from the buildings across the avenue whose own windows present something like a performance-art exhibit of lonely late-night labor, aproned cleaning ladies pushing vacuum cleaners, and jumpsuited maintenance men on ladders, and bankers at desks with sentient-looking

Equipoise lamps, takeout containers and partially crumpled cans of Diet Coke that didn't quite make it to the trash bin, all of it a silent pantomime of isolation and alienation.

Malcolm unlocks the clandestine inner sanctum. He takes a seat at the small metal desk, opens the laptop. He accesses the folders for the compressed video files, and opens the first one, Monday's. He doesn't as a rule check the weekend footage.

He waits a few seconds for the file to decompress, then the video starts to play. It's a static view of his guest room–cum–home office, captured from a lens that sits in an air vent in the crown molding, aimed at his desk, motion-activated.

Nearly all the motion is his wife, walking back and forth across the carpeted room, tending to a basket of laundry, yanking open curtains, tidying throw pillows. Late in the day he sees himself sitting at the desk, opening the computer, then a minute later closing it, lights out. That's Monday.

Tuesday is not different in any meaningful way, except that for ten minutes Allison lies on the sofa, talking on the phone. After the call ends she continues to lie there doing nothing for a minute, staring into space, smiling. Malcolm wonders if she is smoking weed again.

Viewed in fast-forward, eliding the nonmoving unoccupied bits, it's clear that this room is barely used, like an impulse purchase at a sample sale, whoops, we didn't really need that.

Nothing on Wednesday until Allison enters the room at midday, crosses it, the images racing along, skipping most of the frames, which is why it takes Malcolm a moment to process what he's seeing.

Fuck. Did he really just see what he thinks he saw?

He returns this video segment back to the beginning, the door opening. His wife enters. She is tugging on a hand, whose attached arm enters the frame, followed by the rest of the person, a man. Malcolm hits Pause to examine him, completely 100 percent unfamiliar. Who is this guy?

Malcolm hits Play. The two people walk to the sofa, where they undress urgently, frantically grabbing body parts, tossing aside clothing, belt unbuckling, panties unfurling, garments hitting the carpet one after another, a hailstorm.

Allison lies back on the furniture while the man grabs her calves, hoists them in the air, opens her legs. He falls to his knees on the floor, and his face disappears between her thighs. The top half of her body is out of the camera frame, which was installed to monitor the desk, and the safe. Not the sofa.

Then the man stands, starkly naked, disturbingly erect.

Allison brings herself to a seat at the edge of the sofa, leans down, opens her mouth. Her tongue works up and down, then her head bobs while the man strokes her hair, her ears.

Malcolm has seen pornography before, of course he has, but he's never seen anything like this, real. And it's *his goddamned wife.*

She unmouths the guy, moves her face away, says something—thankfully there's no audio to accompany this video, Malcolm isn't sure he could stand sound—and lies down again, on her back again, and this man—who the fuck is this man?—climbs on top of her.

Malcolm increases the fast-forward speed, the images once again herky-jerky, less graphic because of all the skipped frames. The two characters in this film shift positions—she gets on top, then climbs off, turns around, presents her rear in the air, creating an unfortunate view of this other man's ass as he stands on the floor, fucking Malcolm's wife doggy-style at 11:48 on a Wednesday morning. *This* morning.

Finally the two decouple, re-dress, retreat from the room, the whole disrobing episode replaying in reverse, until the screen appears to freeze, a view on an unoccupied room, then cuts to nothingness. The next scene is a half-hour later, Allison alone, looking for something, then locating it, something small on the sofa, an earring that she reinserts in her right ear.

Come to think of it, Malcolm didn't notice any goddamned condom in that sex tape.

He shuts the computer. He sits in the dim light, staring at the wall in front of him, the giant outdated map of the irrelevant world.

This is hugely dispiriting. But now that the event has happened, it's not shocking. His wife is, obviously, bored out of her skull. She is lonely. Malcolm isn't surprised that she wants an adventure, and by definition her husband is not. But what is surprising is that she needs the adventure so much that she went out and found it, brought it home; that she's so desperate for it she's willing to do this, this forbidden thing.

Malcolm realizes that there's no longer any reason for him to be in the glum little windowless room, which doesn't have a damn thing to do with his adulterous wife.

But—oh shit, it suddenly occurs to him: what if it does?

Will is jolted awake, confused. "What's that?"

"Huh?"

"*Shhh.*" Will is bolt upright in bed, head cocked. "I think there's someone in the house," he whispers.

"*What?*"

"*Shhhhhh.*"

"Why? Shouldn't we make noise? Like with bears?"

Will looks over at his wife in the eerie half-light. Bears? Or maybe she's right. Maybe the best course of action is to make the intruder aware of their presence.

He gets out of bed.

"What the fuck are you doing, Will? Don't go out there."

Will looks around the room for a weapon. A pointy high-heeled shoe is the most dangerous thing he can see, and he's not going to defend himself with a woman's shoe. He steps into the hall, unarmed. Looks left, right. Tiptoes toward the stairs that lead to the parlor floor. Peers over the banister, trying to—

"*Hey!*" he can hear Chloe scream, from the bedroom. Will turns just in time to see the man running directly at him—

Will braces for impact as the man lowers his shoulder, slams into Will like a fullback trying to barrel over a cornerback. Will feels himself flying off his feet, tumbling head over foot down the stairs, tangled up in the legs of the intruder, who steps on one of Will's hands, kicks him in the thigh, then vaults over Will, who's sliding headfirst, bumping against the stairs, tailbone and shoulder and the back of his skull, and Will is still in the process of getting injured when he realizes he's thankful he's not getting shot, and he comes to a stop, in a crumpled heap of pain, halfway down the stairs, from where he can see the man running through the front hall, and grabbing a couple of bags as he dashes out the door.

◆ ◆ ◆

Malcolm can hear Allison clattering around in the kitchen, doing God-only-knows-what at eleven at night. Probably nothing more culinary than avoiding going to bed with her husband; it must be horrifying to contemplate having sex with both your lover and your husband in the same day. Malcolm's not sure how he and Allie are ever going to have sex again.

He wishes he could've learned about the affair without the visual evidence. It'd be more like having a broken bone, something that will heal over time. But this is like a cancer, pain from within, no cure.

Malcolm walks into the office, looks at the couch. At least Allison had the courtesy to keep it out of their bedroom. Or did she? Who knows? There's no camera in the bedroom.

She is still, loudly, in the kitchen.

Malcolm opens the safe, removes a thumb drive. He types the password into the computer. Plugs in the little drive, and swaps out a half-dozen of the hard drive's sensitive files with different versions of the same files from the stick, which he slips into his pocket. He'll keep that on his person for a while, till he figures out what's going on.

And of course now there are other security measures he'll need to take. He runs through the list in his mind, checking off items, a timeline. What a nightmare.

Who *is* this man? Malcolm needs to find out. Then what? Malcolm isn't going to kill this man for fucking his wife. But that doesn't mean Malcolm isn't going to kill this man.

"So this is it?" The policeman looks down at the list of items that were in the stolen bags, Will's and Chloe's. "Nothin' from upstairs?"

"No," Will says, "it doesn't look like it."

"And you say the intruder was on the third floor? Did you see him descend, ma'am?"

"No. I saw him run past our bedroom. He could've been coming down from the third floor. Or he could've been in the home office."

"Home office? Whatcha got in there?"

"Not much," Will says. "The printer is the most valuable thing."

"What about paperwork? Files? Where do you keep your passports? The deed? You own this house?" The cop looks around with a frown, unimpressed. He has a thick outer-borough New York accent, the type of accent that Will remembers from his childhood visits to see his uncle in Brooklyn, the diction of cops and firefighters and plumbers and doormen, of certified public accountants and registered nurses, fourth-generation Irish and Italians and Poles and Germans, the Ellis Island crowd, plus blacks who migrated from the Deep South two or three generations ago, recolonizing the old European-immigrant neighborhoods in the Bronx and Brooklyn.

This is what New York used to sound like, not very long ago, when the city was populated mostly by people whose parents and grandparents were born here. But now the city is filled with other sorts of immigrants and other American transplants, just like Will, who sounds like he could be from anywhere. This cop could only be from here. His partner too, who's outside taking statements from neighbors.

"The office is untouched," Will says. He really doesn't want anyone to start snooping around up there. "I'm sure of it."

"Oh yeah?" the cop asks.

Chloe is looking on, observing the exchange. Maybe Will is overplaying his hand. "Pretty sure," he says. "Our passports are definitely still there. But I didn't do a complete inventory."

"You should," the cop says, putting away his notebook. "You never know what people are after these days, what with identity theft, things like that." He shrugs, the modern world, who can figure it out.

"That's a good point. I will."

"You're lucky," the cop says. "Very lucky. You know that?"

"Why did you do that?"

They're lying in bed on their backs, staring at the ceiling, still wired from the break-in, the police, the busyness of a crime scene, however petty. The cop's ignorant assertion is still ringing in Will's ears. *Lucky?*

"Do what?"

"Run after him, Will? You could have been killed. You're not that type of man."

"Oh no? What type of man is that?"

"The type who does something stupid, something that can get him killed." She leans on her elbow, stares at him in the low light. Will wonders what she sees.

"Were you really worried about what that guy could steal?"

"I guess not."

"Then why? Were you worried about what I'd think if you didn't do something? I hope not."

Why *did* he do that? What was he trying to protect? Was he worried about his stash of cash, his burner phone, the revelation of his secret life? That's how people get caught in crime, in extramarital affairs: the freak unrelated accident that exposes everything.

No, he realizes, that wasn't it, not at all. What he was worried about was his wife.

But now that he thinks about it: was this really a freak unrelated accident?

22

C hloe cuts her eyes away, dodging the question.

"*That* bad?"

"Noooo," Chloe protests, but she doesn't sound compelling, a trace of up-speak at the end of the drawn-out vowel, inserting a question there, self-asserting her own doubt to her own response.

"Oh my God, Chlo, do you think Will is *cheating* on you?"

It's a good thing that Allie Somers will never rise to any position of power. Her first instinct, always, is to activate the nuclear warheads.

Chloe had arrived at the same conclusion a lot slower, after months of vague suspicion. So on an evening when Will had mentioned a drinks date but didn't specify with whom, Chloe decided to find out.

She pulled her hair into a ponytail, tucked her head into a Mets cap, a freebie from some event a few years ago; she's a Yankees fan. She wore sunglasses under the cap. It's hard to distinguish anyone wearing glasses and a cap, an effective disguise that also has the benefit of being deniable. There's no excuse for wearing a wig.

Chloe took the subway into Manhattan. She changed lines unnecessarily. She walked a quarter-mile, then parked herself in the sweltering late-afternoon heat across the street from the *Travelers* building, on the uptown corner of a very busy thoroughfare. Chances were high that Will would exit the building and walk downtown.

He did.

From a safe distance, Chloe followed her husband around a corner, across a crowded side street, traffic at a standstill, drivers honking, futile noise pollution atop the air pollution. She let him get a long lead.

Will was walking strangely. He paused in the middle of a block to tie a shoe that didn't appear untied. On the next block he raced ahead to catch a traffic light, though he'd been in no rush beforehand. He walked into a news shop and emerged with nothing. He reversed course, backtracking a half-block before turning.

Either he's going insane, she thought, or he's trying to determine if he's being followed. Wow, she thought, that's strange.

Or maybe not.

Chloe scanned the crowd, trying to memorize hats, hairstyles, dresses, suits. But it was impossible to be thorough: there were hundreds of people on the sidewalk, maybe thousands, rush hour.

Will turned onto another avenue. Chloe continued to scan—a white mop of middle-aged head, a Southern-belle helmet hair, the unmistakable signifiers of red Prada stripes and beige Burberry plaids.

Then suddenly Will was gone. She'd lost him.

Chloe ducked into a cramped convenience store, stood there looking out the window. Nothing.

She took out her phone. Opened an app that was the companion to one she'd secretly installed on Will's phone, the type of GPS-tracking system that parents use to locate their untrustworthy teenage children. A couple of weeks earlier, she'd confiscated his phone while he was asleep. He hadn't changed his password recently—it was still their wedding date—which was an encouraging sign. If he was calling or texting or sexting someone who wasn't her, he'd change his password, right?

She scrolled through his text messages, all of them innocent. Glanced through his emails, found nothing suspicious. She examined all his recent calls—Malcolm and Gabriella, the office line and the barbershop, Dean Fowler, a couple of old college friends whom she didn't much like, his dad. There were a handful of numbers that weren't saved as contacts, all of them with 212 and 718 area codes, local. She wrote down these numbers, which the next morning she checked from a pay phone in another neighborhood. They were all restaurants.

Then Will went to Spain, where she couldn't follow him in any useful way. But now he was here, apparently on this block somewhere, unmoving.

Chloe watched the screen, the blue dot on the map pulsing, immobile.

He began to move again, south along the avenue. She waited a minute for him to cross the street, to establish distance. Then she followed. After two blocks she could see him turn into a building, but she couldn't see what it was, her eyes darting around to identify landmarks, the no-parking sign, the red sports car, the fire hydrant. A minute later she arrived at it: an Irish bar next to a check-cashing business, payday loans and bulletproof glass, probably a front for a fencing operation, or pills.

Will Rhodes did not belong on this block, in this bar.

Chloe saw a handful of the usual boozers in there, plus a youngish-looking blonde sitting off by herself. That must be her. But Chloe couldn't get a good look, not without drawing attention.

She continued walking to the corner. Here there was no mass of humanity into which she could disappear. Loitering here, she'd be noticed if someone was watching, and she expected someone was.

Chloe entered a pizza shop, ordered a slice, don't heat it up please. She used her phone to order a black car, which arrived in two minutes. She jumped into the dark cool backseat.

"Where to, miss?"

"Just turn the corner, then pull up over there. I've got to wait for someone."

They parked across the street from the bar.

"How long's it gonna be?"

She reached into her wallet, extracted a twenty, handed it across the backseat. "However long it is. How much does this buy me?"

"Ten minutes?"

"Fifteen?"

"Okay. Mind if I step out for a smoke?"

"Sure." She glanced at the hack license. "Could I ask a favor, Pedro?"

He regarded her skeptically in the rearview, not committing to any favor.

"I'll be honest with you," she said. "I think my husband's cheating on me."

Pedro raised his eyebrows slightly, probably wondering what type of lunatic had climbed into his Lincoln to park in Hell's Kitchen. But he had the tact, as well as the profit motive, to remain silent.

"And I think he's in that bar with her."

Pedro glanced across the street, snorted. "That's a sad-ass affair they're having, if they're having it in a shithole like that."

"Aren't all affairs sad-ass?"

"Never been married, myself. Not a, um, *connoisseur* of monogamy."

Chloe scrolled through her phone's photo stream, found a close-up of Will. She leaned forward, showed Pedro the screen. "That's him."

"Uh-huh." He obviously didn't care for the direction in which their interaction was heading.

"I suspect your lighter is dead, Pedro, and you need to collect a book of matches for your cancer stick. Smoking kills, you know."

"Yeah, I think I heard something 'bout that."

"That bar looks like they might have some matches. I'm willing to bet the matchbook will be orange and green. Irish flag." She extracted another twenty. "You wanna bet?"

Pedro took the twenty, didn't comment on the wager offer. He cracked the windows, turned off the engine, removed the keys from the ignition.

"What? You think I'm going to steal your car, Pedro? Come on, keep the AC going."

He turned around to face her. "I don't know you," he said. "Crazy chick using me to stalk some dude in a bar."

"Not some dude. My husband."

"Sez you. Just 'cause you got a picture some dude on your phone, don't make it your husband. Nah, lady, I'm not leaving you with my car keys."

"Come on."

"In *fact*, you need to give *me* your driver's license."

"What?"

"Give. Me. Your. Driver's. *License*. I need some collateral. Case I'm walking into a trap."

"A trap? Why would I be trapping you?"

"How should I know? Because you're a crazy chick."

She handed over her license.

"This your current address? You live on the Lower East Side?"

She saw no upside to admitting the truth, so she nodded.

"All right then." He opened the door.

"Hey!" she said. "You know what it is I want you to do?"

"The fuck I look like? A idiot?" He climbed out, cigarette pack in hand, patting the pockets of his cheap black suit as if searching for a lighter. He looked around, pretended to notice the bar. He's a good actor, for a livery driver. Maybe he really is an actor.

Pedro jogged across the street, pulled the door open, disappeared into the darkness. Chloe watched for a minute, two minutes, longer than necessary to collect matches; she was getting worried.

She looked down at her phone, the surreptitious tracking of her husband's device. No blue dot. She closed the app and reopened it: still no dot. How was that possible? Only if Will had disconnected his phone from its power source. Why would he do that?

Finally Pedro emerged, stood in the bar's doorway, lit his cigarette. He smoked casually, in no hurry, checking out the women who walked by. Cigarettes offer a broad range of opportunities to interact with strangers, to get into other people's business.

Pedro tossed his butt into the gutter, and sauntered across the street. He climbed into the driver's seat, restarted the car to get the AC flowing.

"What took you so long?"

"I had a shot of Jack."

"Why?"

"Why not?"

Well, for starters, your job is to *drive a car*, she thought, but did not say.

"Plus, the drink gave me a chance and a reason to take a piss, so I could walk to the bathroom, so I could see this dude of yours, who's sitting in the back, with a blonde."

"She good-looking?"

"That's a matter of opinion."

"Do they look like they're, y'know . . . ?"

"Look to me like they having a fight."

"How's that look?"

"Like two people having a fight. I'm guessing you ain't entirely unfamiliar with that."

They waited another fifteen minutes, and Chloe handed over another twenty. The bar's door opened a handful of times, admitting sober people and discharging drunk ones—reverse rehab, dehab—before Will emerged.

"You want I should follow him?"

She looked down at her phone, his blue dot active again, moving again, no doubt headed toward the subway, toward home, toward her. "No. I know where he's going."

Chloe could see Pedro nod, okay, if you say so, lady. But he held his tongue again.

It took five more minutes before the woman stepped out, a curious gap. Chloe had more than one unusual app on her phone, and she opened another, a camera with a special lens, a far superior zoom than standard-issue, a higher resolution. She took a burst of photos of this blonde, then another burst, a dozen frames in rapid succession.

"That's her," Pedro said. Then he gave Chloe a half-minute of silence—a woman scorned needs a little room—before asking, "Where to?"

"Let's go to Brooklyn," she said. "I'm going to visit a friend." She gave him her address, and sat there in the comfortable leather and air-conditioning in the horrible traffic, considering all the angles of this development, the woman, Will's secretiveness, his evasive maneuvers, his unbatteried phone.

"So you gonna confront him or what?" Pedro asked, counting the cash in front of the Brooklyn house, a few lights on. Will's subway had apparently made better time than Pedro's car, for one-tenth the price.

"I don't know what I'm going to do," she said, lying to a stranger.

That was Monday night. And "I don't know" is also what she tells Allison right now, lying again, this time to a friend.

"My God, Chlo: is there someone you think he's having an affair with?"

Chloe leans on the marble table, fingering her glass of midday wine, enacting the cliché. "Maybe," she says. She fights back a tear, wipes her eye. And she realizes that she isn't entirely sure if she's acting or not.

Allison wraps her legs around Steven's back, locks her ankles, and pulls him in deeper, feeling a bit like she's trying to break his back, to kill him in some sexual ninja move, even though what she's trying to accomplish is simply to make him finish.

"Ohhh," she pants. She rakes her fingernails across his back, pressing hard enough for him to feel, but not enough to break the skin. She doesn't know who else he's bedding—surely she's not the only one—and she doesn't particularly want to get him in any trouble. For all she knows he has a girlfriend, a fiancée, a wife.

"Oh God, yeah."

She already achieved what satisfaction she's going to achieve; Steven is adept with his tongue. Plus when he's going down on her she can't see anything except the top of his head, which helps revert this escapade to something more like an imaginary fantasy instead of a concrete enactment of adultery, with her lying on the couch in the family's home office, at two-something on a weekday afternoon, with some strange man's cock plunging inside her, and meanwhile she has to be at school in—how long? she glances at the clock—shit, twenty minutes.

"I want you to come," she whispers into his ear, "in my mouth." She really needs to get the hell out of here. "Are you ready?"

"Ungh."

She rolls him over and finishes him quickly, wetly, using both hands and her mouth and an excess of saliva. Sex can be an awfully disgusting business, if you pay attention too closely, all these viscous fluids, yeesh.

"I gotta get going," she says, getting up, repressing a shiver. "You want water?"

"I'd love some." Steven is smiling, pleased with himself. "With ice, if that's okay?"

She turns her back to him, not all that psyched that he gets to recline and watch her walk away. Allison knows exactly what she looks like full-frontal naked, and she's fine with that, sort of. But the rear view is not something she can ever see, and she's worried about it.

Then again, who gives a damn? She's not going to be doing this anymore. She arrived at this decision an hour ago, sitting in that restaurant while Chloe was on the verge of falling apart because she suspected Will of cheating—*Chloe*, the least likely woman to fall apart in the history of the world—and Allison was trying her best to pay attention to Chloe while not obsessing about herself. What the hell is she doing with this guy? And why?

She had no answers—no good answers—then, and she still doesn't now.

This is not exactly her proudest moment, standing naked in her kitchen, rinsing out her mouth at the sink, gargling and spitting, like at the dentist's.

Mostly what she wanted out of this—this what? affair? she's not sure it qualifies as something as grand as that—was simply being wanted, a deposit in the self-esteem bank, something she can consult whenever she's folding laundry. But on the debit side, Allie now has to be worried about the shape of her naked ass retreating to fetch ice water from the kitchen, which is not something that particularly concerns her with her husband.

Do the daytime doormen know what's going on up here? Of course they do. They're chuckling about it down there, cigarette breaks, you know about Mrs. Somers, yeah man.

She doesn't feel as bad as she might, as she suspected she would when she was riding up in the elevator that first time, thinking, huh, am I really going to do this?

But neither does she feel too good. There have been moments when she thought, there, this is justified, I'm getting back at Malcolm for his cheating, despite her lack of proof. She has long harbored a vague suspicion, one that she passively decided not to investigate.

Now look at her, here, the goddamned adulterer.

She has to end this carefully, gently.

Allison walks naked through her apartment, heading back to the man she wishes weren't there, the ice water tinkling in the tall frosted glass. Damn, she thinks: I should have brought a coaster.

23

Will marvels at the resilience of his rosebush. Despite the long summer's heat, despite the pollution of the city, despite his own passive neglect, the plant not only refuses to die, it even sprouts yet more fresh blooms, aggressively bright red, defying and taunting Will's inattention.

He pauses at the bottom of his stoop. How many times now has he trudged up these steps with a fresh lie? Every time, he's worried that it'll be his last, that this time, he'll be caught.

And this time, he is.

"Where were you Monday night?" Chloe is staring at him from the kitchen.

He shuts the door behind him, the heavy old glass shuddering in its decaying wood frame. "When?" He's not sure if he should join her in the kitchen or run away, claim to need the bathroom, buy himself some time to compose himself, his story.

"After work. Before home."

No, he can't flee. He walks toward her, slowly. "Having a drink."

"With?"

A couple of Chloe's friends are habitual cross-examiners, women who are constantly trying to extract unforthcoming information from their husbands and boyfriends. But Chloe has claimed to not understand the impulse; she has never been a digger into Will's business. Or at least not that he knows about.

"With Gabriella."

"Okay." Chloe folds her arms across her chest. "Let's try this again. And please, Will, this time I need you to go with the truth. Who. Were. You. With?"

Will can see that she's not taking her eyes away from his; she's watching him intently. She's not going to miss any detail, any nuance, in this conversation, this confrontation. She must know something.

"And before you answer, Will, I should tell you that I saw you with the blonde at the bar in Hell's Kitchen."

Ah—that's what she knows.

He stares down at the floor of his own private hell's kitchen. How did Chloe follow him? His surveillance-detection route was complicated, exhaustive, and *she's his wife*. Surely he could not have missed his wife following him? *For an hour?* He's not that inept, is he?

"I, uh . . ."

He has prepared for this, he has a lie ready. The woman lives in San Francisco, he didn't want to tell Chloe about the drink—or the coffee or the lunch or the whatever he was doing with Elle, whenever it was he got caught—because he knows he shouldn't really be seeing this woman, she's trouble, and their breakup wasn't clean.

This is designed to be a scenario that makes him wrong, makes him guilty, but that doesn't make Chloe leave.

"Listen." He shuts his eyes, pretending to gather his courage, or his concentration. "I'm sorry. Her name is Lillian, and we used to date. She lives in San Fran—"

Smack.

Will doesn't completely believe that just happened. Did his wife really hit him in the face? Or is he hallucinating?

He holds his hand up to his stinging cheek. Sure enough, that pain is real.

"Strike two, Will. So help me God, if you lie to me a third time, our marriage is *over*. Do you understand?"

No, he doesn't understand. What is it that Chloe knows? And how? And does he have any alternative to telling Chloe the truth? And if he *does* have an alternative, should he tell her the truth anyway? What exactly is he so worried about?

The worst of it is that he slept with Elle. And that's pretty goddamned bad. But is that marriage-ending bad? Maybe. Probably? Hard to tell.

What if he omits that damning detail from what's otherwise a completely true story? Is it a credible story without the sex?

And if Chloe knows enough to be positive that Elle isn't any ex-girlfriend from California, she might also know enough to be able to identify any part of his lie.

He doesn't want to lose his wife. He doesn't have a choice.

"Let's sit down," he says. "This is going to sound ridiculous."

Gabriella shuts the door behind her, walks across Malcolm's large office, takes a seat.

"Will's laptop is clean," she says.

"Do I want to know how you know?" Even as he's asking the question, he realizes how ridiculous it is.

Gabriella doesn't even deign to answer. "There's nothing there that shouldn't be," she says. "No *content*, that is."

"Oh?"

"But he's not very good about keychain security—"

"Gabs, you know I don't—"

She holds up her hand. "He uses relatively unprotected passwords. Including for their bank accounts. It looks like they've become a lot more solvent in the past few months."

"A lot?" Malcolm cocks his head. "Well, he did get a raise, but that should be—what?—a couple hundred more per paycheck?"

"It's more than that. What about Chloe?"

Malcolm doesn't want to answer. But he knows that if he doesn't, Gabriella isn't going to simply drop it. She'll be a pain in the ass, and she'll find out sooner or later anyway.

"Yeah. She did a big freelance job."

"For us?"

"Indirectly."

Gabriella wants him to explain, but Malcolm isn't going to. Chloe's new position is, by necessity, highly compartmentalized information.

"That's all you're going to tell me?"

"And I appreciate your understanding, Gabs."

She scowls. "Okay, I found one other thing: Will has been going to a gym."

"Good for him."

"It's an unregistered gym, Mal, just a guy in a warehouse, and it's very inconveniently located, rendered even more inconvenient because Will makes sure he's not being followed when he goes there."

Oh God, Will too? Why is everybody such a problem? "Wait," Malcolm says, "let me guess: Rhodes is trying to hide that he's learning to tap-dance."

"Mixed martial arts."

Chloe's mouth falls open. She's standing extra-upright, spine straight, shoulders back, one of those stances Will sees all the time now that apparently all women practice yoga regularly, even when they're not practicing yoga but instead are confronting their husbands with incontrovertible evidence of unacceptable duplicities.

"Well, not a spy, exactly," he says. "But I am working for the CIA. I was recruited to gather information. About the people I meet, when I'm abroad."

Will pauses, waiting for his wife to respond. It takes her a few seconds to say, "You understand that this sounds like utter horseshit, right?"

"Yes, Chlo, of course. And that's exactly why I haven't told you. But it's true. The woman you saw me with? She's my handler. My case officer. I report to her."

Chloe raises her eyebrows as far as she can. She looks around, as if for physical support, but all she sees is their half-finished kitchen, the centerpiece of their half-finished lives.

"Um, okay. I'll play along." But her facial expression doesn't look as if she's being magnanimous with her credulity. "When did this begin?"

"A few months ago."

He has been dreading this moment since he stood in that hallway in St-Émilion, the taste of Elle on his lips, and the possibility—the certainty—that sooner or later, Chloe would find out.

"They recruited me. When I was on a trip."

"Where?"

"Argentina."

"How?"

"There were two of them." He feels his eyes flick away, then back.

Damn, she'll know he's lying. "A woman who was pretending to be a journalist, she befriended me."

"*Befriended* you? What does that mean?"

"She was joined by a man. They made me a proposal: money, in exchange for information. That's where the money has been coming from, Chloe. Ten grand a month. That's how I got the windows done, and the kitchen . . ." He gestures around at the significant progress. "And, y'know, other things."

She crosses her arms, not looking any less dubious. "The CIA is paying you ten thousand dollars a month? To do what?"

"To tell them about the people I come across. The contacts from the *Travelers* files, and my own connections, and the people I meet, the expat Americans, the diplomats, the finance people, the mayors, the actors, the whoevers. Everyone who's anyone, anywhere." He watches as she processes this new paradigm.

"Why does the CIA care about any of these people?"

"I don't know."

"What do you mean?"

"I mean they won't tell me. I'm not supposed to know *why* I'm doing what I'm doing. They're not paying me to ask questions. They're paying me to tell them about influential people who live abroad."

"What about in New York?"

"No, not really."

"Meaning?"

"They've asked about the people who work at *Travelers*. About the office."

"Have they asked *a lot* about New York?"

"Yeah, actually. About the staff in the office, even the layouts."

"What about me? Have they asked about me?"

"Yes. I think they're trying to get a sense of me, my life. How I might get caught, maybe? How I might get manipulated. Honestly, I really don't know."

Chloe squints at her husband. "I'm finding this very, *very* difficult to believe."

"I understand that. I do, of course. But it's true."

"Uh-huh. So was it difficult to convince you to do this?"

"No, not really."

Again she waits for Will to continue, but he doesn't. He's trying to tell the truth; he doesn't want to intersperse lies in there, not if he doesn't have to.

"Why not?"

"It seemed benign. In fact, it seemed sort of like a good idea. And we needed the money; still do. I didn't see the harm."

"Why didn't you tell me?"

"I, uh . . ." This is one truth he cannot tell, and he has no idea how to answer. He should've prepared for this eventuality, he should have coached himself, rehearsed, sounded out the arguments, extended them to their logical conclusions. Why the hell didn't he anticipate this eventual conversation? Hubris.

"Because they ordered me not to" seems like the best answer.

"Ordered?"

"I should have told you anyway. And I'm very, very sorry."

She stares at Will, searching his face. "I don't believe you."

"About what?"

"About *what*? About *all* of this, Will. About this whole cockamamie story."

"What do you think is going on?"

Chloe laughs. "I think you're fucking her, that's what I think."

"Then why did we meet in a dumpy bar and then not leave together? What type of tryst is that? Why would we do that?"

"I don't know, Will, you tell me."

"Because I'm not fucking her! That's why. Because I'm working for her."

Chloe shakes her head.

"But it's true," he implores. "I know it sounds ludicrous. But it's all true. I'm sorry for not telling you before. But I'm telling you now."

What a catastrophe.

Malcolm has left the frying pan out there with Gabriella, with whatever the hell is going on with Will, and into the fire that's burning on the computer here in the secret office in the wall.

How did he allow this to happen? How is he going to find out what exactly happened? Does it even matter how?

He hits Rewind, and stops the herky-jerky reverse-action images when his wife gets off the couch. He hits Play, watches her cross the screen, naked. A second after Allison disappears from the frame, here he comes, this guy—who *is* this guy?—practically sprinting across the room, his still-semi-hard dick flopping around, bending down to reach into the pocket of his pants, removing a little something from the cloth. He takes a few quick steps to the desk, in the center of this footage's frame. He bends over the computer, and inserts that thing—a duplicating device? a worm installation?—into a port in Malcolm's laptop.

The guy stands there and stares at his watch, the timepieced left hand held up at a right angle, the other on his hip, naked. If this weren't deadly serious, it might be hilarious, a Monty Python skit, a laugh track, the crowd titters after ten seconds when the man yanks out the drive, chuckles as he replaces the device in his pants pocket, a more full laugh as he leaps back onto the couch. This guy is one athletic motherfucker. A literal motherfucker.

Uproarious laugh, sustained applause, but then it dies down as we await the return of the clueless cuckolder, the woman who was seduced to be taken advantage of. Whatever reasons that compelled Allison to sleep with this man, whatever sadness and disappointment and dissatisfaction were behind that decision, this reality is worse, exponentially worse, immeasurably heartbreaking. The audience absorbs this reality, grows silent. Someone coughs.

There's almost no negative emotion that Malcolm isn't feeling.

He stares at the wall, at that outdated world map, his eyes hopping around all those cities and countries that don't matter anymore. Bulgaria? It's hard to believe that Bulgaria was once considered critical to America, a domino that needed to be propped upright. And now? Now what's important to America? Is there even such a construct anymore? Or is there only what's important to Halliburton or ExxonMobil, to Microsoft or Apple, to Coca-Cola and Walmart.

Does anybody care? Does Malcolm?

Or is there only what's important to Malcolm Somers? Which is this, now.

Malcolm picks up the landline, the big clunky handset attached by an accordion cord to the heavy base, a touch-tone keypad, a little protruding nub to release the connection. He dials the long string of digits, the call he's been dreading. As each day has gone by, Malcolm has become more and more certain he'd have to make this call, while at the same time more and more unwilling to actually do it until he was 100 percent. So in the meantime he'd had his apartment swept—clean—by a pair of guys pretending to be measuring radon levels, and he has been checking the video feed obsessively, three, four times per day. And he's been keeping a fairly close eye on his wife. But he can no longer keep this to himself. That's the type of dishonesty that gets people like Malcolm killed.

"Yes?"

"Hi," Malcolm says. "I've been compromised."

Malcolm can hear the man sigh audibly. "By?"

"I don't know yet."

Silence.

"Data has been stolen from my home computer."

"Oh sweet Jesus."

Malcolm reaches back into his memory, plucks out the coded phrase that he'd never before had occasion to use, not in this context. "It's an unmitigated disaster," he says.

This phone is supposedly as secure a landline as exists in the world, but Malcolm doesn't believe there's any such thing as a totally secure phone line, just as there's no such thing as a secure email, a secure digital file, a secure computer. Which is the whole point of all of this, of everything.

Nor for that matter a totally secure marriage.

The man doesn't respond to this code, but Malcolm has to assume that he understands what's being communicated. That's the way codes work, and you can't double-check that they're working as intended.

"Do you have any idea how this happened?"

"Oh, I know exactly how."

"Has that problem been solved?"

"Er, not exactly. That problem is complex."

"Aren't they all?"

Malcolm doesn't want to explain the problem. "No," he says, "the problem has not been solved. But it is being managed. Monitored."

"Hmm."

"Seriously, I've got it."

"You'll ask for help if you need it?"

"I will. But it's under control."

"Are you sure? It doesn't sound like it."

Yes, Malcolm thinks, I'm sure: I'm sure I'm lying. Nothing is under control; nothing is ever under control. But if there's one thing Malcolm has learned, it's that no one wants to hear this, ever. "Yes," he says, "I'm sure."

ÞINGVELLIR, ICELAND

Over the course of his career, the American had occasion to use a variety of aliases. It had been challenging to remember what name he was supposed to use when, where, with whom. He always used generic American names, the one-syllable abridgements of biblical figures, Jim and Tom, Matt and Mike. But recently it had been Joe, an Average Joe, which was not him at all, and part of the private humor of it.

Joe is probably what he'll be till he dies. It is refreshing, relaxing, to not have to think about how to answer "What's your name?"

"I'm Joe," he says to the young woman with a camera. "Nice to meet you."

They are standing in the seam between the tectonic plates of North America and Eurasia, a deep wide fissure between giant pieces of planet. On one side, the plate stretches all the way to the west coast of North America; on the other, the mass is uninterrupted till the Pacific Rim of Asia. Earthquakes rock California and Japan because these two plates here, on this volcanic protrusion jutting out of the North Atlantic, are pulling apart. The rift he's standing in widens every year, and so does the island, growing incrementally, accompanied by earthquakes and volcanic eruptions, by massive disturbances to the geological peace, all for the sake of a few millimeters per year.

This spot is also the site of the world's very first parliament, established A.D. 930, a settlement with a church, hiking trails, bridges over the waters of Lake Þingvallavatn. It's photogenic here. There are always tourists, even in crappy weather like today. There's a lot of crappy weather in Iceland.

When he doesn't live in a bustling Scandinavian city, he lives in the middle of Scandinavian nowhere. And he occasionally visits places like this, or the capital, or the geyser. He is always researching or rehearsing escape routes, contingency plans, alternative exits. He has no job, no responsibilities, other than to keep himself alive. He is fairly confident that one day, someone will come for him. Every single day, he wakes up prepared for that one day to be today.

24

The note is simple:

Need time to think. Gone to visit Mom. —C

Will flings aside the paper, which flutters past his wife's unoccupied pillow in a miasma of dust particles, a miniature little snowstorm in the bright early-morning sunlight.

He'd been up half the night, worried about what his wife was going to end up doing, or saying. After a certain point she'd been unwilling to continue talking about it, unwilling to listen to Will try to prove he was telling the truth, unwilling to absorb the details of his meetings, his countersurveillance training, his operations in Europe. He possessed so very much proof that he was a CIA asset, but she was unwilling to let him provide it.

"Stop," she'd said. "Enough. I'm going to bed."

"May I come?"

She'd stared at him, making it clear that she was debating it. "I don't want to continue talking about this. And I hope it's obvious that you're not welcome to touch me."

He'd tossed and turned till two, maybe three, before falling into fitful sleep. But apparently not fitful enough to notice Chloe wake up, get out of bed, pack a bag, and walk out the door.

His wife had left him.

Chloe had always been a leaver, fleeing confrontations, fleeing uncomfortable situations, fleeing parties and movies and picnics, anything that she wasn't enjoying. She apparently used to flee relationships too, at the first sign of trouble; she admitted fleeing from a couple of one-night stands, disappearing in the wee hours, and for one—in college—she actually climbed out of a window.

But she wouldn't flee a marriage, would she?

Chloe would come back. Or Will would go get her.

It has been a long time since Malcolm waited for a weekend-schedule F train, which seems to be inhabited almost exclusively by men with beards. *Hey, guys w big bushy beards!* He two-thumbed-types. *We get it – you're virile! Enough already. Time to shave.*

It's a slow ride, followed by a long, hot, monotonous walk from the station. He has plenty of time to consider what to do about the Allison aspect of her adultery.

What he really wants is to contrive to catch her in the act. Outrage— "Oh my God! What's going on here?!" But that might get violent. Plus her lover—ugh, he really hates that word—would then obviously know that they'd been caught, and might suspect that in actuality they'd been caught earlier, and wonder what that might mean . . . So that's not a great plan. Instead:

One: he could simply ask her. "Are you having an affair?" She'd deny it to Malcolm, but after the confrontation she'd be worried, she'd have doubts. She'd end up saying, "My husband suspects something, I'm sorry, I can't do this anymore . . ."

Two: Malcolm could try to bring about the affair's conclusion from the male side of the equation. He could probably figure out some indirect way to dissuade this guy from continuing this relationship.

Three: he could ignore it. Hope that the affair will fizzle of its own accord, as these things probably do. Except when they don't, when they evolve into something else.

But that won't happen with this affair: it's not possible that Allie will leave Malcolm, even if she wants to. This is perhaps the most degrading element of this whole situation, which is degrading on so many levels: the guy doesn't even want Allison. When he's finished with her—and for all Malcolm knows, the guy may be finished with her already, having already attempted to hack Malcolm's computer—he's going to toss her away. Will she be brokenhearted? Mildly disappointed? Are things going to get better for her? Worse?

Allison is gone for the weekend, out in Bridgehampton with the children and their activities, their play dates, kids in swimming pools, moms in rosé. In a week all three of them will move out east for the duration of the summer, surfing camp and tennis lessons, benefits at the library and the museum, parties for the horse show and the celebrity softball game. Maybe her affair will wither in the neglect of the hot summer sun.

This weekend, Malcolm begged off going east. "I'm sorry. I've fallen behind, and we're closing on Wednesday." He could see her suppress a giant shrug. The extent to which Allison gives a shit is limited to the minuscule embarrassment of her husband's absence from whoever's catered dinner party is on Saturday night. Tonight.

On the other hand, many in Allison's crowd of Hamptons housewives basically compete about their husbands' relative importance. Weekends "trapped in the city" are offered as evidence of the man's exalted position in the firmament—a deal closing, a trial. In the midst of all the standard-issue Wall Street, Malcolm knows that Allison relishes being able to say, "He has to close an issue," accruing a certain social currency via her husband's marginally creative career. It's what she has instead of actual currency.

Malcolm wonders if this is part of what's bothering his wife: their relative lack of money. Money is nothing if not relative.

The idea of solvency reminds him to call Will; Malcolm has to get to the bottom of that. No answer. "Hey Rhodes, I'm in town this weekend, want to get a drink? Call me back."

Malcolm surveys the massive complex of baseball diamonds and soccer fields, small portable grills and big orange coolers, taco trucks and shaved-ice carts, toddlers running around shrieking, red-faced middle-aged men leaning against chain-link fences clutching tallboys wrapped in crinkled brown bags, and everywhere the sounds of games, referee whistles and the cracks of bats, the groans of teammates and the cheers of spectators, and grown men in brightly colored soccer shorts and dingy dirty baseball pants, and nowhere in these fifty acres—in the geographical center of the most populous English-speaking city in the world—is anyone speaking a word of English.

PROVIDENCE

When the train pulls out of the station, the wi-fi connection revives itself, solid arcs on her laptop's icon, and Chloe is able to complete her purchase, a round-trip ticket to Punta Cana, sugar-sand beaches and bath-temperature seawater, towering palms and frozen cocktails. It's an unlikely destination for midsummer travelers from the American Northeast, so the plane tickets and hotel room are inexpensive.

She types in her Trusted Traveler number, her passport number, her telephone number. When it comes to her emergency contact, she automatically starts to type Will's mobile number, then pauses, her fingers hovering—

No. She backspaces to the beginning.

FALLS CHURCH

As it turns out, Raji's health insurance isn't nearly as ironclad as he'd been led to believe. The HMO is now asserting that Raji's heart problem is a preexisting condition, which of course is true. But isn't nearly everything, in some way, a preexisting condition?

So Raji is now working for his thirteenth straight day, trying to amass overtime, to pay for the procedure. It has been easier to get OT approved since his watch list was winnowed down, with a vastly increased level of thoroughness. It's a lot of work, at all hours, every day.

And this particular woman? She began her day very early, entering the New York City subway system via a MetroCard that she'd purchased a week earlier using an American Express card. Twenty-one minutes later, at Pennsylvania Station, she purchased a one-way Amtrak ticket to Portland, Maine. Aboard the train, she registered her computer with the wi-fi provider, then bought a plane ticket for a few days in the future, which are the details that Raji enters now:

U.S. PASSPORT NUMBER: 10414962
FLIGHT: 83 BOS to GUA

TICKET CATEGORY: D2
SEAT: 39D
ALERT CODE: 2

Raji pulls up this woman's image on the screen. He remembers her from when he first started working here, tracking untrusted travelers, a couple of years ago. This woman used to travel a lot more, all over the world. But then she cut back dramatically, just a couple of international trips in the past year. Raji wondered what had happened to her, if she was okay. He's relieved to see her on the move again.

She books a room at an all-inclusive resort. The hotel takes care of airport transfers, so Raji doesn't expect that she'll book ground transportation, and she probably won't rent a car. For some trips, there can be a lot of reservations, a lot of deposits, a lot of prepaid—

Raji suddenly realizes something strange about her previous international trip. He does a quick search to confirm, then sits there staring at his screen, trying to figure it out.

He exits his cubicle. Halfway to Brock's office, he pauses, thinking through again, reconsidering, but this time from another viewpoint: what's in it for him? Why should he go out of his way, above and beyond the call? Open himself up to being wrong? To criticism? Or conversely to pressure, to a rush, to anxiety? Why? He has plenty of other problems.

He stands in the taupe corridor, surrounded by all this blandness, all these bland people doing all this bland work, his bland life. He turns back to his bland cubicle. To hell with them, he thinks. To hell with this.

Then he changes his mind again. He doesn't have it in him to shirk responsibilities, even if no one gives a damn.

"Boss?" He raps on the door, soft knuckles.

Brock looks up, a scowl, interrupted from doing whatever the hell Brock does in here, which everyone suspects is watch porn, all day, every day.

"What's up, Raj-man?"

"I think I found something."

NEW YORK CITY

Stonely takes a few handfuls of ice cubes from the beer cooler. He puts the ice into a plastic deli bag, cinches a knot. He swings the bag against the fencepost, and again, a third time, crushing the ice, while glancing beyond the chain-link fence, taking a mental inventory of teammates, opponents, friends who are about to see him interact with this dude whom it's impossible not to notice.

He presses this icepack against his aching misshapen finger, which he broke halfway through his second year at Triple-A, the season when he had his best shot, but not if he sat on the DL for two months. He'd known immediately that this finger was broken. But he refused to admit it, and just kind of hoped the finger would heal itself. It didn't, of course. So when he eventually owned up to it, people started calling him Stonely, based on this ridiculous lie, this bogus macho, when it was really just fear and denial, aka being a pussy, which is the opposite of being hard as a stone-faced killer.

When the following season ended, riding the bus back from Toledo, he knelt beside Coach, sitting at the front, surrounded by paperwork. "Hey skip, I was wondering if you'd write me a recommendation letter?"

After a long-ass Greyhound-bus ride—from Louisville through Cincinnati and Columbus and Philly, twenty hours—and a few weeks of looking, he landed a temp job in a mailroom, then started taking computer classes. He got promoted, and promoted again. That was thirteen years ago.

"Hey boss. You came out to Brooklyn 'cause you need baseball but the Yanks are in Baltimore and you hate the Mets?"

Malcolm's smile is the sort of a guy about to deliver bad news.

"You remember last year, Stonely, I asked you to take care of that thing?"

Stonely looks down at his dirty pants, his spikes, the mangy grass. There's a cigarette butt down there, and a crushed piece of plastic that might be the cap to a crack vial. "Sure. How could I forget."

"Well, I need you to do that again. Same type of thing."

Stonely looks Malcolm Somers in the eye. He doesn't like being a brown-skinned dude being hired by a white-skinned dude to commit a crime. But Stonely needs this job, and Malcolm is the one who keeps him in it, and Stonely likes Malcolm. Plus he could use the extra money. So of course he's going to do it. But still, he doesn't have to like it. That's what makes it a job. "Who is it?"

"Some asshole who's fucking my wife."

Stonely can't hide the look of surprise. "No shit?"

"No shit."

"You sure this is a good idea, boss?"

"I'm pretty sure it's not. But we're going to do it anyway."

Stonely doesn't want this. But although Malcolm has a choice, now that Malcolm has made it, Stonely really doesn't. "When?"

"As soon as you can manage."

BOSTON

When the train pulls out of the station, her phone starts to ring again, or rather to vibrate, illuminated, an insistent plea for attention. Will is calling again.

Chloe hits Ignore again. She doesn't want to talk to her husband, to listen to him beg, *Please believe me, it's the truth, please.*

Chloe is furious, and she doesn't want to talk to anyone, not until she figures out exactly what she's going to do about it. Her options are limited.

She doesn't want to be reachable, doesn't want to be findable, and that's not so easy. It was only fifteen years ago when people used to go on vacations and weren't heard from for a week or two, in Guatemala or Tanzania or New Zealand, or not even so exotic, just a weeklong rental in Rehoboth, camping in the Poconos. They didn't post pictures on social media, they didn't answer calls or emails or text messages. Vacation meant you were just not around. Perhaps you were missed or needed or wanted, perhaps not, but either way, everyone dealt with it.

Chloe rises from her seat, walks down the aisle, holding seatbacks for balance, the train rocking back and forth, hurtling into New Hampshire. She slides the restroom door open, bolts the lock. Her phone rings again, Malcolm this time, that shit-heel.

They had a deal, and it was straightforward: Chloe would leave the staff, and would instead take responsibility for the important freelance work that *Travelers* needed—probably just one or two assignments per year, but done carefully, perfectly. In return, Malcolm would leave Will completely out of it. This deal was struck in a conversation that wasn't opaque, not open to interpretation or misunderstanding. Chloe had made sure of that.

She had been given only one assignment so far. It had been the most difficult thing she'd ever done in her life, by far. But she'd done it well. She was living up to her end. Malcolm obviously wasn't.

She drops her vibrating phone to the floor, and raises her foot to stomp on it, to stop the harassment. She's going to hammer the SIM card with the cracked-up phone, then throw all the little bits of plastic off the train, one by one.

But no. She may very well need this phone. So instead of destroying it, she'll do what Will did when Chloe was following him to his illicit meeting. She kneels down and picks up this lifeline, this tracking device we all carry with us, wherever we go. She disables it.

FALLS CHURCH

"Here is what is odd," Raji says. "This woman, this Chloe Rhodes, she took a taxi to the New York airport, which she paid for with a credit card. She checked into her flight—no bags—then used this same plastic in the airport to buy stuff. Look."

Brock leans forward, plants his palm on Raji's desk, flexing the muscles on his forearm, sending the SEMPER FI tattoo into ripples. Brock never misses an opportunity to flex his muscles, nor to remind people that he was a marine.

Raji plays two video clips of surveillance footage from two different airport-security cameras, a woman buying a boxed salad and a drink from one vendor, then chewing gum and a couple of magazines from another.

"And here she is, boarding." From a third camera, the woman hands a pass to a gate agent, then disappears down a gangway.

"Here she is at the other end, at immigration." Click. "And exiting the terminal."

"She's hot."

"Yes. There are two strange things about this trip. First, when she boarded the return flight to New York, she didn't reenter this terminal."

There's a pause while Brock considers what Raji means. "You sure?"

"Not one hundred percent, but yes. So she must've returned to the terminal via another flight, from somewhere else. I still haven't found any footage of her deplaning another flight, and her name doesn't appear on any other manifests, but I'll continue to look. She *must* have returned to the terminal somehow, right?"

"Uh-huh."

"She flew all the way to Europe for a few days, *and* took another round-trip flight somewhere else. That's a tremendous amount of flying."

"You're right about that, Raj-man."

"And the second strange thing is this: she doesn't use that credit card anywhere nearby—not in Turkey, not in Greece, not in Bulgaria. What's even stranger, she doesn't use *any other* card. She's over there for three days, getting on some other flight, and she doesn't swipe any bank card, anywhere. Not once."

"Huh."

"Not for a taxi, not a hotel, not a restaurant. She begins this trip using a credit card in New York, but then doesn't use plastic for a single purchase of any sort. She also doesn't use any bank card—or at least none I've been able to ID—to withdraw any cash."

"Is it possible that she went over there holding sufficient Turkish, um . . ."

"Lira."

". . . lira to keep her alive for three days?"

"Sure, that's possible. But wouldn't it be very strange?"

"I guess so. Do you have a theory, Raj-man?"

"Yes. Either someone else was paying for everything she did, while she was there."

"That's plausible. Or?"

"Or her destination was not Istanbul."

25

Sunday night, Will is still alone, hoping to not be, expecting that Chloe will come home in time to go to work tomorrow. She's not the type who calls in sick, and he doesn't think she's willing to be a no-show. So she'll be back. Tonight.

When Will was single, he hated Sunday nights. On weeknights he never felt bad being alone—going to sleep alone, waking up alone, that felt like part of work, part of his work ethic. And then Fridays and Saturdays, there'd be parties, or dates. But Sunday mornings he'd usually wake up alone, tired, possibly hungover. He'd sometimes spend the entire day alone, taking care of errands, laundry, groceries, cleaning, exercising. By bedtime he'd be depressed. Which he is now.

He should get out of here, this broken home of his. He should go get a drink, is what he should do. And he should do it at Ebbets Field.

Then another idea occurs to him, something else he can look for at Dean's bar.

Dean is in a conspiratorial huddle with the bartender, their heads inches apart, when he notices Will. "Mr. William Rhodes, always a pleasure. Please have a seat. How's that hot wife of yours?"

"I'm not bad. She's, um, she's not bad either."

"I've been wondering, Will, what's up with Gabriella Rivera?"

"Not sure what you're asking."

"Did you ever, y'know . . ."

"Uh, no."

"What's her story? She single?"

"She's a widow, Dean. Remember Terry Sanders? That was her husband."

"Oh shit, really?"

"Really. But listen, Dean, can I ask a favor?"

Dean has always been widely known as a man who can procure all sorts of things while daring the world to either catch him or reward him. Mostly it has been the latter.

"Always."

Will looks around, assessing their privacy. Marlon the ultraserious barkeep is at the far end, in deep conversation with a shady-looking character. No one else is in earshot, not above the background music.

"This is going to sound strange."

"Already does."

"I'd like to buy a fake passport."

Dean smiles broadly. "What are you *up* to, Will Rhodes?"

"This is just an insurance policy."

"Insurance? Against what?"

"What's insurance ever against, Dean? Bad things happening."

The following night Will finds himself in another bar, a divier bar, in a dicier neighborhood, fewer brownstone townhouses and more mechanics' garages, less reliable access to taxis, to fresh produce, to responsive police. He shakes hands with a toothpick-wielding guy who takes his rock-and-roll cred very seriously, painted-on black jeans and Doc Martens, tats and piercings and studded leather jacket, a Ramones tee shirt. It's always the Ramones. Except when it's the Clash.

"It's five thousand for Canadian, ten thousand for American."

"Okay," Will says, "I'll take the Canadian."

The toothpick dances around. "Yeah, Canadian's good for getting out of the States. Might be a problem getting back in, though."

Maybe, but that wouldn't be Will's problem. He'd be coming back under his own name, or he wouldn't be coming back at all. He looks down at the Canadian passport, turns the pages, fingers the paper, examines the details. The name is Douglas Davis.

"Who's this?"

"You care?"

"Not in an existential way. But in a practical way, yeah."

"Some meth-head who lives near Hamilton, Ontario. Sold this with the guarantee that he wouldn't report it missing till, um"—the guy checks a notebook—"next April."

"What if he reports it earlier?"

"Then I'll tell the guy I bought it from, and he'll go break the mother-fucker's legs."

"But meanwhile I'll be in jail."

"Yeah, that's definitely a risk." The look on his face asks, what do you want me to tell you? Will doesn't have any idea what sort of remedy he would have expected.

"You'll take care of changing the picture?"

"Of course. The book can be ready for you tomorrow. You brought the cash?"

Will looks around the dumpy room populated by an untrustworthy crowd. "No, I'll bring it tomorrow."

"Okay, that's cool."

Will feels the need to assert himself here, indicate that he isn't any-one's sucker. He's putting himself in a bad position, needing to trust a stranger, and not just any stranger but a criminal stranger, at a significant level of trust.

"And," Will says, trying his best to look tough, "we'll meet somewhere else."

"No problem." The man is surprisingly easygoing. Too easygoing? "Also, for an extra thousand, you want the guy's driver's license?"

On Monday Will managed to avoid everyone, spending most of the day hiding in the archives, grunting monosyllables at Stonely Rodriguez, lunching on a pint of soup at the little table, crumbled-up saltines, a fine dusting of crumbs that he swept away with his hand. After work he paid for his fake passport with his CIA-informant cash, then sat home, sulking about this new life of his.

Tuesday, he can't hide. He has a status meeting with Gabriella, an art meeting with Jean, a sidebar to revise, on tight deadline.

Then Malcolm stops by. "You okay, Rhodes? You look like shit."

A weekend has come and gone, the workweek has restarted, and Chloe still hasn't responded to any of Will's calls, or texts, or emails. She hasn't gone back to work, and it doesn't seem like she's coming home anytime soon.

Will doesn't particularly want to discuss this with Malcolm, or with anyone. It's humiliating, it's uncomfortable. And telling the truth will require inventing yet more lies, a whole new layer of deception, lying about the lying.

But Chloe's absence isn't a secret he can keep forever. The longer he waits to tell Malcolm, the more insulted Malcolm is going to end up being that Will didn't say something sooner. They're close friends. It might as well be now.

"I think Chloe left me."

"*What?*" Malcolm walks into the office, sits down.

"We've been bickering, more and more, about everything." This sounds credible. Universal, even. "And she just decided to leave. To go stay with her mother."

"When?"

"Late last week."

"Have you spoken to her?"

"She's not answering my calls."

"Holy shit, that's awful. Did something happen? A big blowup?"

"No. I think it was a combination of all the little fights. Or honestly I don't know what the fuck it was, Mal. What it *is*. I really don't know."

"Do you think there's someone else?"

Will is not surprised that this is Malcolm's theory. For Malcolm, everything is about sex.

"It's possible, I guess. But then I don't know why she'd go to Maine." It's not until he says this aloud that he considers the possibility that she hasn't gone to Maine. Could Chloe's departure have been instigated by something other than Will's behavior? Now he has a whole new set of worries to keep him up at night.

In the late afternoon, he does manage to get Chloe's mom on the phone. "Come on, Connie," he says. "I know she's there."

"Oh, Will, I'm sorry but she's just not going to speak to you. She won't tell me why. What did you do?"

He doesn't have a good answer for her, not something he can explain in a sentence or two. So he doesn't.

"Please tell her I love her."

Malcolm dials the number from memory, but the call goes immediately to voice mail.

"Hi," he says. "Listen, I hear you left your husband. I can't help but think this has something to do with our, um, arrangement."

Malcolm doesn't know who's going to pick up this voice mail, listen to this call. He has to be careful, but he also has to be credible. He doesn't want to sound like someone who's trying to keep the secret he's trying to keep. He'd rather sound like someone who's trying to keep a completely different sort of secret.

"But I really need to talk to you." He leaves his number, as if she doesn't know it. Then he hangs up, stares at the phone, tries to puzzle through what could be going on. Things are out of control.

Will decides to walk home. It'll be about six miles, two hours. It's perfect weather, warm but dry and cloudless, a nice breeze.

Maybe he'll walk but not go home. Maybe instead he'll stroll into some singles bar, hit on nose-ringed young women, hey, wanna-get-outta-here? Become the cheating son of a bitch his wife already thinks he is. Elle will have become his gateway drug to a debauched life.

Will marches down the busy avenues, lost in his head, past Bryant Park and Herald Square, Madison Square and the Flatiron Building, through Union Square and Washington Square Park, people everywhere. His feet begin to hurt in SoHo, but he keeps going through Chinatown, into the Civic Center, past all the classical architecture, the columns and porticoes and broad-minded expanses of limestone.

He turns onto the Brooklyn Bridge, walks up into the sky. The sun is beginning to set, the spectacular view glowing in the gloaming, the harbor and lower Manhattan and downtown Brooklyn, the Manhattan Bridge and the Midtown skyscrapers.

Near the far side of the river, he stops dead in his tracks.

"What do you want?" he asks.

Elle is standing in the middle of the wide-planked wooden walkway. Bicycles are flying by one side of her, pedestrians marching up the other. In front of her is the borough where Will works; behind her is where he lives. Elle is in the way.

"I've been calling you."

"You sure have." Four times in the past three days, one summons after another, meetings to which Will did not show, again and again. He resumes walking, fast, and she races to catch up. "What do you want?" he asks.

"I want you to answer your goddamned phone."

"My phone?" He digs it out of his pocket, holds it up. "This phone?"

Elle doesn't answer.

Will nods, then tosses the phone down onto the roadway, where it bounces twice before getting flattened by a beat-up van. He keeps walking, even faster on the downhill slope.

"What do you think you're doing?"

"Well, that's a good question," he says. "What *am* I doing? I've been working for you for five months—"

"You're not working *for* me, like a personal assistant."

"Oh, whatever. I've been reporting every step I take, for a half-year. Lying to everyone around me. Doing a shitty job of my job, a shittier job of being a husband. And you know what? She left me."

"Chloe? When?"

"So if you want to track her down, and show her our little X-rated video, be my guest. You've already ruined my life. Well done. I hope you're proud."

Underfoot, the soft pliable wooden planks give way to sturdy unforgiving concrete.

"I'm finished," he says. "I quit."

"*Quit?*" She laughs. "This isn't Denny's. What makes you think you can *quit?*"

Will didn't intend to do this; this isn't what he planned for this evening, or planned at all. It's just happening, as if beyond his control.

"Will, come on. Stop."

He feels a hand wrap around his arm from behind.

"Go to hell," he says, and wrests his arm away. The end of the bridge comes on suddenly. He descends the dark stairs that lead to the street.

"*Stop.*"

"Or what?" He spins around. Here under the bridge's ramp, it's night-time, streetlights on, headlights. "What are you going to do? Shoot me?" He holds his hands open high and wide, go ahead.

"No, Will. I'm going to tell you the truth."

"Okay. Start talking."

"Not here." They're standing on a dark sidewalk, under the pulsating thrum of the traffic on the bridge overhead; down here the sounds of the traffic are loud and echoing, bouncing off the stone and concrete.

"Why not?"

"You're not an idiot, Will. Don't act like one. We can't talk in public."

"Why not? National security?" He snorts. "I don't even believe you're *in* the CIA."

She glares at him.

"Why haven't I met your boss?"

"Because he has other things to do. He's not at your beck and call. Come on." She holds out her hand, like a mother beckoning her toddler to climb out of the sandbox. "Let's go."

"Oh fuck you," he says, and starts to turn away.

Then two things happen more or less simultaneously: a car screeches to a halt at the curb, with one of its rear doors flying open; and someone grabs him from behind, firmly.

Will tries to turn around, but whoever's holding him is big, and strong. Will can't spin, can't punch, can barely move his arms. Instead, he raises one knee high, then brings down his heel with all his strength, stomping his abductor's foot. The man's grasp eases—not a full release, but enough for Will to wriggle his arm semi-free, to thrust back his elbow, which sinks into the man's gut with a loud "Oof."

Now Will can spin around. Rears his right arm back, ready—eager—to hit this person—Roger, of course it's Roger—as hard as he can, again.

But that's when the woman who calls herself Elle Hardwick punches Will in the face, laying him out for the second time in their brief, tumul-tuous relationship.

26

Will's hood is yanked off.

He looks around, squinting in the brightness of overhead fluorescents. He's seated at a conference table, with a complicated-looking phone in the middle. A credenza is stacked with office supplies, a few reams of paper, a box of binder clips.

There are no windows. A dormant LED screen dominates one wall; on another is a framed photograph of the president of the United States; a third wall contains the door, flanked by frosted glass panels. Hanging on the fourth wall is a three-foot-diameter laminated-cardboard circle, blue ringed in gold, an eagle in profile, a white shield with a red starburst, the words UNITED STATES OF AMERICA across the bottom arc. Along the top, CENTRAL INTELLIGENCE AGENCY.

Roger is at the far end of the table, holding the felt hood, which had been pulled over Will's head in the back of the car for a fifteen-minute ride, which felt and sounded like a journey back over the bridge, then onto Manhattan streets, potholes and short stops, a sharp turn then a steep slope, probably the ramp to an underground garage.

At the beginning of the ride, Elle had made a quick phone call. "Sorry to bother you," she said, "but we're on our way in." She then listened for the space of a couple of sentences. "Again, I'm sorry, but it has to be tonight."

Will was pulled from the car, led to an elevator, a whoosh, a ding. Guided by the elbow to walk thirty paces, with a trio of ninety-degree turns, before being deposited into this chair, and his vision returned, a gift.

Now someone knocks on the door. Roger rises, leans his large frame through the door's, collects something.

"Here." Roger gives Will a makeshift icepack, paper towels cinched with a rubber band. Will brings this up to his face, to his nose, which he now realizes is bleeding; his lip seems to be split; and it feels like a tooth might be loose. It's almost funny: these people keep punching him in the face, then giving him ice.

Ten minutes later, the door opens. Elle walks in, followed by an unfamiliar man who's wearing a suit but no tie.

"Will Rhodes," the man says, "I understand that you have, uh, *adamantly requested* to meet C/O Hardwick's supervisor. Correct?"

Will glances at Elle, who's taking a seat at the far end of the table. She doesn't speak, but she does make a face that says, Well, go ahead, you asked for this.

"That's right."

"My name is Mike Russell." Holding out his hand. "Pleasure to meet you."

Will shakes the guy's hand without getting out of his seat. "Are you going to tell me your job title?" Will puts down the ice pack. "Give me your business card?"

"I'm afraid not."

"And if I call the CIA tomorrow, and ask to speak to Mike Russell? Are they going to put me through to your line?"

"That's not the way it works, Mr. Rhodes."

This Mike character is wearing an ill-fitting suit, taupe, low-cut single-lapel, two-button. It's a starkly unfashionable suit, a poorly paid bureaucrat's suit, ninety-nine dollars at one of those discount emporiums that surround the bureaucracies' offices. It's a caricature of a bad suit.

"You want something to drink, Mr. Rhodes? Some water?" Mike indicates his own plastic bottle, a sweating little price sticker at the neck, $1.29, a corner-deli bottle.

Will shakes his head.

Mike sits down, halfway between Will and Elle, who says, "I'm afraid I haven't been completely honest with you."

Will snorts, no shit.

"I've given you the impression that you were recruited to provide info about the people you meet during your travels abroad. People who might turn out to be valuable intelligence targets. Well, that's part of the story. A small part. Actually, it's an insignificant part of what we really want from you, Will."

Will glances again at Mike. It's unclear whether the guy's shirt was at one point white or whether it's supposed to be this color, a sort of washed-out yellowish gray. It's a hideous shirt, under a cheap suit. The type of outfit that a Hollywood wardrobe department would create for a central-casting character one-word-described as *loser.*

And from this angle, it seems that Mike is sporting a once-pierced earlobe, which doesn't really go with the rest of the persona. But everybody had his youth.

"The real target of our operation—*your* operation, Will—is much closer to home, and much more finite: it's *Travelers.*"

Will can feel his eyebrows climb his forehead.

"We recruited you because you were new to the magazine. So we knew you hadn't yet been admitted to the inner circle. You didn't really know what was going on, and you weren't yet fully invested in feeding the beast."

"Huh?"

"Organizations are like organisms, Will. They have deeply ingrained survival instincts. Which isn't surprising, is it? After all, organizations are made up of people, and people are motivated by self-interest. We're all self-preservationists. First and foremost, what people want is what's best for themselves. We want to survive, we want to flourish. We get jobs, then we develop loyalty to our employers, and our loyalty helps our employers achieve success, which in turn helps us people survive. It's a symbiotic relationship."

"What are you talking about?"

"I work for the U.S. Central Intelligence Agency, Will. I'm loyal to the Agency, not just because the CIA does important work, for an important cause, but because it provides my livelihood. I want the Agency to succeed, because that's how I survive."

The ice begins to burn.

"I'm sure Malcolm Somers feels the same way about *Travelers.* He's been working there a long time. Gabriella Rivera too. I have no doubt both of them are loyal to *Travelers,* because their loyalty helps the magazine stay in business, which helps them survive. You follow?"

"This isn't exactly quantum theory."

"Sometimes, our divergent goals of self-preservation put us into conflict with one another. You can assign value judgments to these conflicts, or not. But moral or ethical opinions don't change the essence of the situation, which is conflict. Simple. Universal."

"Are you going to get to the point anytime soon?"

"You got somewhere you need to be, Will? Date night with the wife?"

"Fuck you very much."

Will thinks he catches Mike suppress a smile.

"You're very welcome," Elle says. "So the CIA and *Travelers* are in conflict with each other, Will. Because one of these organizations is a governmental agency that collects and analyzes intelligence that's essential to the national security of the United States of America. And the other is sort of the opposite."

The secret office has no windows, no natural light, no time of day, no year. It's buffered from the world by the more public office, the big airy light-filled room lined with shelves packed with books, and walls decorated with blowups of magazine covers, and the Wall itself, a forty-square-foot schematic of the future.

But not in here. This little room is the past, just as it has always been, since the inception of *Travelers* three-quarters of a century ago. A place to communicate with one other place, a space invented for one man to talk to one other man.

"My problems," Malcolm says, "seem to be multiplying."

"Tell me what you need to solve them."

"I need to bring Rhodes inside."

"Are you sure that's a good idea?"

"It's necessary."

"What if he balks? Decides to talk?"

Malcolm would like to say something along the lines of "We'll cross that bridge if we come to it," but that's not the way this world works. "We'll detain him. Until he changes his mind."

"And if he doesn't?"

"I know what we need to do."

"You sure?"

"I'm sure."

"All right. When?"

"Tomorrow."

"Not tonight?"

Tonight there's a piano recital that Malcolm has to attend, a command performance to make up for one he had to miss, months ago. Sylvie has begun using the pedals as well as both hands. He can't reschedule.

"Tomorrow," Malcolm says, "will be better."

There's a complex lie he could tell to justify this statement, but better not to, unless he's asked. He's not.

"That's preposterous."

"Is it really, Will?" Elle stares at him for a second, perhaps waiting for an answer. Then she continues, "Do you carry sealed envelopes across international borders? Envelopes stamped *Personal and Confidential*?"

"No one would hide anything in envelopes that scream out *secrets!*"

"Oh no? Isn't that exactly where it might make sense to hide something? And you've given these envelopes to people you don't know. People in Paris and Dublin and Stockholm, in Berlin and Athens. People in *Cairo*, Will. In *Beirut*."

Will still doesn't say anything.

"Some of these envelopes come back. And you're under strict orders to deliver them directly to Somers, and to Somers only. Why, Will? If these are human-resources forms, why not deliver them to human resources? Why is the editor-in-chief serving as an intermediary between foreign personnel and HR?"

Elle seems to be waiting for an answer to this question. "I don't know."

"I do: because what's in the envelopes doesn't have anything to do with HR forms."

"Then what *is* in the envelopes?"

"What do you think, Will?"

"*I* don't know."

Elle stares, waiting for Will to hazard a guess.

"What do you people want me to say?" he asks. "This is your ridiculous theory."

"How do you think *Travelers* stays in business? Ad pages are off by forty percent in the past five years. Subscriptions dropped by half. Newsstand sales . . . ? *Pfft*. The business is in free fall. Yet there have been no budget cuts, have there? Is there something in particular that you think *Travelers* is doing right that all other magazines are doing wrong? Some special way that your employer—a *print magazine*, with an ancillary business in *bricks-and-mortar travel agencies*—is maintaining profitability?"

Will doesn't know. The business of the business is not his business.

"And let's for a minute consider Malcolm Somers himself. Your boss seems to have more money than a magazine editor should, don't you think? That's a fancy apartment he lives in, when he's not at his summer house in the Hamptons."

"That's just a rent—"

"His wife hasn't worked in—what?—a decade? Yet two children in private school. You know what the tuition is, Will? Forty-three K per year, per kid. Those must be some *good* lunches."

Will always assumed there was another source of income. Maybe Allison came from money? Personal finance is not something Will ever discusses, not even with his own wife.

"And what about Gabriella? She's at a professional level that's similar to yours, so I'd expect her to be earning about what you earn. But she has a more exalted job title, so maybe a little more?"

Will is not going to give Elle the satisfaction of agreeing with her. But she's right.

"Yet she too seems to be living a lifestyle that's notably different from yours. Big apartment—*huge*—on the Upper East Side. No debt."

Will knows that her apartment is somehow connected to her dead husband's family; it's affordable for some reason. Or maybe that's just what Gabs has always claimed . . . ?

"But you, Will? You live in a house that I think may actually be *condemned*. Is it?"

Will doesn't answer.

"In a neighborhood in Brooklyn that—let's face it—is a borderline slum. Plus you're up to your eyeballs in debt. Why should this be? This *gap* between your lifestyle and Gabriella's?"

Elle waits for an answer. Or waits for these details to sink in, to form a narrative.

"Are you getting a clearer picture, Will?"

Will catches movement from Mike, who's merely checking his wristwatch, a guy dragged out of his life to sit here and bear witness to a meeting. Will can barely make out the time on the white face of the watch, pale numbers, delicate hands: it's about a quarter to nine. He can't read the maker's name, but the logo looks like J. Lindeberg's, the *J* and the *L* back-to-back mirror images, *JL*. Mike doesn't seem like the type of guy who'd wear a watch from a Swedish youth-oriented fashion label. It must be something else.

"What do you think happened to Jonathan Mongeleach?" Elle asks.

"Huh?" Will is still staring at the guy's wrist.

"A man like that, well known, well liked. Very social person, lots of friends, leading a big life. The type of life that gets reported in the papers, on Page Six and the, um, *Styles* section." As if it's distasteful. "A man like this just disappears?"

Will shrugs.

"This man who spent his entire career at the magazine, half of it in charge. And this man just one day vanishes. Does that make any sense to you?"

"I don't know anything about Jonathan."

"You must've had some guesses, though? This must've been something you and Somers discussed. After all, Jonathan's disappearance did get the both of you new jobs, right? This was not an irrelevant event in your life."

"There were a lot of rumors." Most of the rumors centered around Jonathan's love life—he was known to have a taste for blondes of the Scandinavian sort—but of course the popular rumors would be about sex. Sex is popular. "I had no way of judging them."

"Sure, Will. But what seemed *most* likely?"

Will had never come to any conclusion about Jonathan. "Listen, why don't you just tell me what you're driving at?"

"Because we want you to figure it out yourself, Will. Surely you—"

"*What the fuck do you want from me?*" Will screams this, and everyone at the table jumps. "Jesus fucking Christ, will you just tell me what's going on? Please?"

Elle leans away from the table, wearing a victorious smile. "*Travelers* is in the business," she says, "of acquiring and selling stolen intelligence. That's who you work for, Will: a mercenary spy ring."

Will doesn't know how to refute this. It sounds true.

"Which makes you guilty of treason. You know the penalty for treason against the United States, Will?"

PART

IV

27

Will approaches his dark house slowly, warily.

The streetlamp has failed to ignite tonight, and the sconces on either side of the front door are still not installed, and there's been no one home to turn on any lights. The house is creepy.

Will finds his keys, looks over both shoulders before climbing the stoop, the very picture of the spooked-out urban dweller, eyes wide, shoulders tensed.

Inside he turns on every light switch he passes. He pours himself three fingers of an eighteen-year-old single-malt from an obscure producer, swag from some party or presser or who-the-hell-knows. Will's life is filled with swag, with booze bottles and beach towels, sunglasses and baseball caps, hotel rooms and tasting menus and all-inclusive luxury-resort weekends. But none of this shit-we-all-get pays the bills.

He takes a big gulp, clunks the glass down on the island, honed black granite, quarter-inch corner radius, an extra hole drilled for the soap dispenser that Will still hasn't procured, plugged with a wine cork. Will found the barstool on the street, large-refuse-collection night, a Post-it marked FREE! He lugged it home and washed it up, replaced the missing screw that was making the seat wobbly, perhaps the reason someone had thrown it away, too lazy or too indifferent to bother diagnosing such an easily treatable ailment. Or maybe they didn't like the damn thing. It's not particularly comfortable.

Will can't wrap his mind around the enormity of the CIA's allegations: that Jonathan Mongeleach became a traitor-for-hire to support his extravagant habits—the women and gambling and parties and drugs, the whole big lifestyle, in a city populated by millionaires and billionaires and trust-fund babies and European nobility, where Jonathan's magazine salary—inflated as it eventually became—never really amounted to more than a pittance, not in the milieus in which he circulated.

During Reagan's all-out dash to the Cold War's finish, in the midst of the pervasive greed of the eighties, an opportunity presented itself to Jonathan, in the same way that many opportunities present themselves to profiteers—to weapons manufacturers and aerospace engineers, to Central Asian drug dealers and Latin American labor leaders, and to the occasional opportunistic American civilian. War, even the cold sort, is always a boon to someone.

No one knows if it bothered Jonathan—or encouraged him—that his opportunity came from the Soviets. He never made his political views known, not in speech. But in action, he became a traitor: a courier of purloined intelligence from Washington to Moscow, from crooked diplomats and compromised CIA operatives in foreign cities to their opposite numbers in Soviet embassies.

Before long he expanded his role to include the ever-important service of collecting and reporting gossip: who was screwing whom, who had a problem with blow or junk, who was a closet queer. Jonathan became an indispensably well-placed, well-traveled source in the KGB's permanent quest to ID vulnerable high-value targets, in exchange for money. It was a simple arrangement.

When he ascended to the editorship of *Travelers*, it became more complicated. He was able to expand both the courier and intel-gathering operations to encompass the staff. The whole magazine became cover, its employees operatives—perhaps unaware of it, perhaps not. Jonathan recruited Malcolm; possibly Gabriella; maybe others.

When the Cold War ended, and the Soviet Union collapsed, Moscow didn't become any less eager to buy whatever could be stolen from Langley. If anything, the post-Communist bureaucrats were even more avid consumers of other people's secrets than the Soviet apparatchiks. This was a cadre who'd stolen their country's wealth and power; these people saw stealing as a best practice, not as a last resort.

According to Elle, the operation had been active for at least thirty years, during which Moscow had become reliant on—addicted to—an uninterrupted flow of pilfered CIA intel via *Travelers*. The Russians weren't satisfied to let this river dry up; they took measures to ensure that it wouldn't. When Jonathan began contemplating his eventual retirement, he started grooming Malcolm. And last year, Jonathan either met his demise or he demised himself. Either way, Malcolm stepped in, and soon hired Will, who became another in a possibly long line of unwitting spies.

It all sounded thoroughly credible. Yet also completely implausible. And Will has no one to turn to, no one who can help him figure out whether it's true. The one person he would want to ask—Malcolm—is the one person whose answer Will wouldn't be able to believe.

Will's phone dings. Is it possible that Chloe is finally calling him back? No, it's just the alarm, alerting him that his face has had fifteen minutes off. He replaces the ice bag against his aching jaw.

When Elle finished her long recitation, Will stared at the wall, his eyes drawn to the large CIA seal hanging there, why, exactly? Reminding people where they worked?

"So what happened to Jonathan?" Will asked.

"We don't know," Elle said. "It's possible he got spooked, afraid we were going to catch him. So he fled."

"To Russia?"

"He doesn't seem like the type of guy who'd live in Russia, does he?"

Will didn't know what type of guy Jonathan Mongeleach is. Or was.

"It's possible that he outlived his usefulness, or his reliability. That he was eliminated."

They all sat silent for a minute. Will had now gotten what he'd asked for: a meeting with the boss, and an explanation of what he'd become involved in. He didn't know what else he should ask, what else he could expect.

"Okay," he said. "What is it you want from me?"

They all exhale as if they've been holding their breath for hours.

"Wow," Roger says.

Elle nods.

"Do you think it worked?" he asks.

"Definitely." Elle doesn't believe this. But what is she going to say to these guys here, now? Criticism wouldn't be constructive, not at this point.

"That was close." Roger is wearing a small smile, shaking his head in wonderment.

"Yes, it certainly was." She turns to face the other man. "Hey, Mike, thanks for getting here on such short notice."

"No problem. We were going to do this next week anyway, right?"

"Right." She smiles, but can't help but glance again at his watch, his mistake. Mike had been in a bar when Elle had called, and he'd gone home to change into this suit, but he hadn't had the presence of mind to remove his watch. Is this something Will would notice?

"You think he's going to do it?" Roger asks.

"We'll find out soon enough."

Will hides from daylight under a pillow. He manages to push past seven o'clock, eight, in and out of fitful sleep, bothered by his swollen punched-in-the-face jaw and his dehydrated five-glasses-of-scotch head and his bewildered paradigm-shattered consciousness.

He rousts himself at nine. The full-bore bustle of the *Travelers* day starts in earnest at ten, and by that hour he should be in his office. He doesn't want to arouse any suspicion, any questions. Not after what he learned last night. Not after what he's supposed to do today.

Will roots around in the medicine cabinet. What is all this crap? Creams and lotions and gels, anti-histamines and anti-inflammatories and anti-septics and little blue anti-anxiety pills, hundreds—thousands?—of dollars' worth of pharmaceuticals, but *where the fuck* are the painkillers? His jaw hurts like hell. He would really like to stop getting punched in the face.

He locates the amber bottle in a far corner, a prescription from dental work that turned out to involve more excavating than expected. He wrenches off the cap, and finds . . . only one pill left. He swallows it. The label says one refill, and he'll need it. He calls the pharmacy, the one on the Lower East Side that he and Chloe had been using for years. He hasn't needed a pharmacist since they moved to Brooklyn, so he hasn't yet found one.

The pills will be ready in a couple of hours; he'll collect them at lunchtime.

While he's holding his phone he tries Chloe's, but once again the call goes immediately to voice mail. He calls her mom's landline again, and has another brief, unsatisfying conversation.

"Please tell her I called."

"Of course," Connie says. Then, "Keep trying, Will."

He repacks the new device, handed to him last night in the CIA office, wedging it between a couple of magazines in his canvas-and-leather satchel. He learned a lot about this device last night, up very late. He couldn't find an online user's manual for this exact model. But he got the general gist. Enough, he hopes, to do what he needs to do.

"Does everybody remember that revised bios are due by Friday?" Gabriella looks around the conference table pointedly at a few of the most likely to ignore this deadline, this tiresome task. Everyone is required to sit for new headshots, to write exhaustively and shamelessly about themselves, to collect links to their TV clips and old articles, their author pages and personal websites, all this content shoveled onto the heaping pile of the magazine's redesigned website, trying to make personalities out of staff, to celebritize themselves, puffing out their chests to appear more relevant, less shut-down-able.

Will looks at Gabriella, presiding over the status meeting, a responsibility that Malcolm handed to her a few months ago, an augmentation of her managerial role. She was promoted to deputy editor when she came in from the field; she'd been the European correspondent before Will. But after what happened to her husband in Africa, she was no longer excited to hop on a plane tomorrow to anywhere, to wander the dark backstreets of questionable quarters. No longer enjoying it. No longer good at it.

So she came in. She relinquished her correspondent responsibilities to newly hired Will, and took up scheduling responsibilities, logistics, budgets. She also became the promotional face of the magazine, at advertiser conferences, trade shows, TV studios. She collected a bigger paycheck, and she slept in her own bed nearly every night.

But did she give up her job of shuttling state secrets to foreign agents? Does she now have other espionage responsibilities? Does she come to work every day and lie to everyone?

Will had made a lifetime habit of giving people the benefit of the doubt, getting to know strangers, however briefly, trying to see the world through their eyes. He'd been almost universally relieved to find the essential humanity in even the most disagreeable-seeming people, his optimism warranted. But not anymore. Now all around him he sees distrust, liars, betrayals. His world is ruined. And he is too.

"Have we decided yet," Vito asks, "what's going to be the next special, after food?"

Gabriella directs her gaze to the other end of the table, and all eyes follow. Malcolm looks up. "I think you all know that no one finds this more distasteful than I. But in March"—he takes off his reading glasses, like Cronkite announcing Kennedy's death—"we'll be publishing our first-ever luxury issue."

Groans all around.

"What can I tell you? This is the world we live in."

Back in his neat little office, Will removes the device from his bag. It seems even larger now than it did last night, more noticeable.

He looks at his watch, 11:52.

His phone is ringing—an art-department assistant—but he doesn't pick up. He grabs a handful of books from a shelf, puts them on his desk. He tucks the device into the middle of this stack, just another book. Takes out some files, strews them around, along with pens, issues of a competing magazine, a dictionary and a style manual, both open. Trying to manufacture disarray, in what's normally a tidy environment.

Will crosses the small room to the threshold of the door. He examines his work. The faux clutter doesn't look quite right, but maybe that's just because he knows it isn't.

It's 11:54.

His bag is open, on the floor next to his chair. He reaches into the bag, feeling around for the cord, but his hand doesn't find it. Is it possible he left it at home? Shit.

Will's mind is racing through last night, and this morning: when might he have removed this cord from his bag? Where? And for the love of God why? Shit shit shit.

His eyes dart around in panic, and that's when he sees it: sitting on his desk, amid the clutter. He allowed himself to be distracted by his own ruse.

He looks at the door; no one there. Glances at his watch: 11:55.

The phone rings again, Jean the art director. Not now.

Will plugs one end of the cord into the back of his CPU, and turns again to the door before plugging in the other end. Then he takes a seat, and looks up—

Malcolm is standing in the doorway.

28

E lle slid the device across the table. It looked like a hardcover novel, with an effusive blurb across the front, metallic paper, bright colors, an attempt to communicate urgency, peril.

It seemed like they'd been sitting in the conference room for years. Will was completely disoriented about the time of day, and the location, and who these people were, and what they wanted from him. About everything, really.

"What's this?" Will asked.

"Sort of a computer."

"Sort of?"

Although there was a dust jacket wrapped around something, the book-shaped thing underneath wasn't made of paper and cardboard and glue. The dust jacket was wrapped around a cardboard casing of a metal object. "It connects to a port with this wire. Here."

"That ruins the disguise, doesn't it?"

"Yes, when the device is connected, it becomes obvious that it's not a book. But when it's not connected, it's not obvious."

"Uh-huh."

"At five P.M. every day, the *Travelers* server initiates the daily backup of all the files of every user's account. *Every* user. You understand?"

"You're saying some members of the staff, but not all of them."

She scowled at him. "This device here"—she tapped it—"is a powerful hard drive. It has the ability to hold every file at *Travelers*."

Will looked down at the thing.

"But in order to piggyback on the system-wide backup, first it needs to break a security code. Which might take thirty minutes, or as long as four or five hours. That depends partially on chance. We have no way of knowing. So you need to connect this device to your computer by noon, and leave it there till five-thirty. Then disconnect it, and deliver it to me immediately. You don't want this in your office longer than necessary."

Will's mind jumped around the personnel who might invade his office—Malcolm and Gabriella, the art director and copy editor, cleaning staff. "What if someone sees it?"

"That depends on who that someone is, doesn't it?"

"Malcolm. What if Malcolm sees it?"

"Then we're fucked. That is, *you're* fucked; Malcolm doesn't know who I am."

"What am I supposed to do about that?"

"Don't let it happen."

"That simple?"

"What do you want me to tell you, Will?"

"Is there any reason this needs to happen tomorrow?"

"Any reason it shouldn't?"

Will didn't answer.

"Listen, Will, you're the one who accelerated the process. You're the one who made this"—she gestured around the room—"happen. You're the one who forced us to cut to the chase. This, Will? This is the chase. This is what we need: proof of the operation."

He nodded.

"And Will? Don't trust *anyone* who has anything do with *Travelers*."

He snorts. "My wife works for *Travelers*."

"Yeah," Elle says, "I know."

Will's heart is in his stomach. It takes absolutely all his focus to not look at the cord connecting a fake book to his computer, to not check to see if this is noticeable to the man in the doorway, boss and friend and clandestine operative and, possibly, enemy.

"You okay, Will?" Malcolm looks worried. Will isn't sure if it's because of a legitimate concern for his well-being, or something else. "You didn't get into *another* bar fight?"

"No." Will reaches up to his jaw. "Well, actually, yeah. But the bar was in my house, and my adversary was the banister."

"Will." Tsk-tsk. "You should tell me when you're getting drunk by yourself. I'll keep you company." Malcolm hovers in the doorway, looking around at the disarray. He is fully aware of Will's passion for neatness and order. Everyone is. "You sure everything's okay?"

No, Will thinks. Absolutely not.

"Any word from Chloe?"

Will shakes his head.

"Listen, Rhodes, do you have a minute?" Malcolm's hand is on the doorknob, and it looks like he's thinking about pulling the door closed behind him. Oh fuck no, this can't really be happening—

"Um."

Then someone else is suddenly in the doorway. "Will? We've been calling. Jean needs you immediately. We've got to get art to the printer today."

Will turns his eyes back to Malcolm, who has pursed his lips, is considering whether to assert his authority and detain Will, or to let him go where he's needed.

Malcolm checks his watch, sighs. "Okay, Rhodes, go ahead. But can we grab a drink tonight? There's something I need to talk to you about."

Will absolutely does not want to do this. But what can he say? "Sure Mal." He stands up, fighting the urge to rearrange his staged disarray. "I'd love to."

The art department occupies an open-plan room, big white workspaces, oversized monitors and printers and scanners, all looking like a secondary school's technology room, complete with grown-ups who are making a concerted effort to look like kids, sneakers and tee shirts and jeans, headphones, even a skateboard.

"Will, thanks for coming over." Jean moves to a large monitor, in front of which Vito is sitting, clicking through photos. "Veal? Can I help you?"

"Oh, I'm just waiting for Penelope. We have to—"

"Honestly Veal, I don't care." Jean is not known for his gentle touch with office politics. "But could you move, please?"

Veal cedes his space.

"You see the top row?" Jean indicates a half-dozen images, glowing bright green. "Are those all the same mountains? I can't tell. Your ID list isn't clear about this."

Will leans over, examines each image. "Yes. It's outside of Edinburgh."

"Scotland?" Vito asks.

"Is there another Edinburgh?"

"I could've sworn these photos were from Iceland."

"You've been to Iceland, Veal?" Will can't quite imagine this giant African-American man roaming around the small, extremely Scandinavian island.

Vito shakes his head. "Worked on a story. Lots of art."

"We've never run an Iceland story."

"We most certainly have."

Will searches his memory, comes up blank. "I've looked through all the archives. I never came across an Iceland story."

"You must've missed it. Or someone must've removed the issue. Which would not be a surprise, the way people treat things around here." Vito is forever up in arms about the various levels of disrespect that his colleagues display for one another's property, and time, and effort. The world is not nearly as considerate as Vito thinks it ought to be.

"Do you remember when this was, Veal?"

"As a matter of fact, I can tell you exactly when it was: late 1994. It was my first year here, I was an assistant, and it was my very first experience working with Jonathan."

Will uses both hands to pull down the binder for the second half of 1994, lugs it over to the table, a typing stand that someone discarded, back when typewriters and their stands were being discarded.

The issues are wired together between rigid cardboard, but it's easy to find the covers. Will's thumb flicks across each, July . . . August . . . September . . . October . . .

December.

Will looks more carefully, scanning the page-number sequence, making sure he's not making a mistake here . . .

He's not. November 1994 isn't here.

Will turns over the binder, examines the wire system, the covers. It's not an easy apparatus to disassemble. Someone went to significant effort to extract November 1994. Maybe other issues?

Will flips through the binders, one after another, month after month, year after year. They're all here but two: the issue that features an article about Iceland written by Jonathan Mongeleach, from November 1994. And another from May 1992.

"This is good, Hector." Malcolm looks around the leafy street, a quarter-mile from his home. He's rarely in his residential neighborhood during daylight, and practically never on a weekday. It's nice. Quiet. Romantic. "I'll get out here. Thanks."

Malcolm watches Hector make the turn uptown, around the corner, out of sight. Malcolm keeps walking, halfway down the next block, where he climbs into the backseat of a silver SUV with no license plates, tinted windows in the rear.

"What's going on?" Malcolm asks.

"She's been in that coffee shop for, um"—Stonely, sitting behind the wheel, consults his watch—"twelve minutes."

Of all the fucked-up things Malcolm thought he'd ever do, he never imagined this. He and Stonely sit in silence for a couple of minutes. Malcolm can't imagine what Stonely is thinking, but he's grateful there's no small talk.

The café door opens again, and Allison and the man exit the coffee shop. They don't especially look like people who're having an affair.

"Is that him?" Stonely asks.

"Yup."

Stonely picks up his phone, hits a button, waits a second, says, "That's him."

Malcolm watches as a man falls into step behind the couple, on the other side of the street. "Okay," Malcolm says. "I'm out. Good luck."

"Thanks."

"Remember, we need to make sure she doesn't know anything. Doesn't see anything."

"Absolutely."

"And Stonely?"

"Yeah boss?"

"Make sure you stay hidden too. You're traceable to me."

"Understood." Stonely fires the ignition. "Don't worry about it."

If only Malcolm could not worry about it, that would be so fantastic. It was very recently that he had no idea that this was even a thing he could worry about.

He climbs out of the backseat, facing away from his wife. He hustles around the corner, out of sight, back to his other life, his office life, which has invaded his family life. Now he is launching his counterattack.

The main branch of the New York Public Library seems to have become more of a photo op than a functioning library, another backdrop for self-ies, tourists draping themselves around the famous lions, lounging on the steps sipping Starbucks, staring down at screens.

It takes a long time for the sets of magazines to be delivered to the periodical desk. Then Will stands at the wide counter, looking down at another set of *Travelers* magazine, 1994. Another incomplete set.

"The issues I'm looking for aren't here."

The librarian examines Will over her reading glasses. "Well that's peculiar."

"Yes, it is." Will doesn't expect her to be able to provide any meaningful answers to any of his important questions. What could she possibly know? "Do you think any other branches might have them?"

"Honestly, I wouldn't have the foggiest. This is *Travel + Leisure*?"

"No. *Travelers*."

"They're based in New York, aren't they? Have you tried their offices?"

Will smiles. "I have."

He finds the computers, hunches over a keyboard, conducts searches for back issues, which are being sold by dozens of people, at a wide variety of price points—pristine editions for collectors, stacks of undifferentiated issues from junk peddlers. After clicking through to a dozen prospects that all turn out to be unpromising, he identifies a dealer who claims to have full sets of magazines. "Please enquire!"

So Will sends an email. For good measure he sends a few emails, to a few prospects: *Looking for TRAVELERS May 1992 and November 1994.*

He gets up, and walks away from the computer. Then he turns back. Sits down again. Wipes the browser history, and empties the cache, and for good measure powers down the computer.

"Well if it isn't Will Rhodes! How ya been?"

The pharmacist wears glasses low on his nose, yoked around his neck by a metal chain. He also wears a wide smile on his face, and an extra forty pounds around his waist, sitting low and frontal, like a woman pregnant with multiples.

"I'm not bad. You? How's business?"

Silverstein shrugs, the what-are-you-going-to-do shrug of the beleaguered small merchant, communicating in one fatalistic pantomime the rising rents, the predatory pricing by online competitors, the federal-regulations paperwork and employee headaches and maybe a problem with rodents in the storage room.

"How's life in Brooklyn?" the pharmacist asks. "You happy that you abandoned the Lower East Side?"

Will shrugs.

"Just like generations of immigrants. One flees the Lower East Side for Brooklyn, the next abandons Brooklyn for the suburbs, the next leaves Long Island and comes back to the Lower East Side. An endless loop. Am I right?"

"You are right, Mr. Silverstein." The pharmacist is only a decade older than Will—Malcolm's age—but he acts of a completely different era, so he gets treated that way.

"*Or* you could skip all that *mishegoss*, and stay put, like my family. Been in the same neighborhood for a hundred twenty years." Silverstein rummages under the counter, opening drawers. "I bet you haven't found a pharmacist in Brooklyn as good, have you?"

"Honestly, I haven't needed one."

"You're lucky."

"I'm young."

"Same thing." Silverstein finally locates Will's pills, holds up the bottle, gives it a shake-rattle. "Every four hours, not to exceed four doses in twenty-four hours. This is important, Will." The guy actually wags his finger. "These things are habit-forming."

"Got it."

"I'm surprised this prescription is even refillable. Oh, I see, it was only a dozen pills to begin with."

The pharmacist peers at Will over his glasses, then turns to his computer, makes a few keyboard strokes, frowns at his screen. This is a man who clearly hates his computer.

"Co-pay is ten. Decline counseling? Please sign."

Will signs the digital screen with the stylus.

"It's good to see you, Will. You take care."

"You too, Mr. Silverstein."

Will turns, walks past the floor-to-ceiling oak shelves with library ladders, toward the glass door with a brass bell, the meticulously hand-painted business name, SILVERSTEIN & SONS PHARMACISTS SINCE 1922, all the things you expect but don't necessarily get anymore.

"Oh Will? You wanna pick up your wife's refill also?"

"My wife's?"

"Yeah. We called her . . . looks like . . . twice. She outta town?"

"Um . . ."

Will's body is frozen, half-twisted back toward the interior of the store, his feet still facing the exterior. His imagination conjures a half-dozen explanations in one second. Antibiotic for a lingering cough, but was there one? Muscle relaxer after a back strained in yoga. Nasal inhaler for inflamed sinuses, skin ointment for a fungal rash, antidepressants for a hitherto secret depression. One plausible possibility after another.

"Yes, she is out of town."

"I know it's hard to get here, since you guys moved."

Silverstein pulls open a drawer, then another, then removes a little paper bag.

Will glances at the prescription slip stapled to the front, just to confirm that it's his wife's name. But he forces himself not to read the label closely, not to identify the medication. Because until he reads it—until he opens the box and actually observes Schrödinger's cat, firsthand—his world is still suspended between two possibilities: it's alive or it's dead, the abstract cat, and his concrete marriage.

"Here." Roger reached out, handed Will the black hood. They were finished in the conference room with the big seal hanging on the wall. Will put on the hood for the hallway, the elevator, the garage, into the back of the car again, moving slowly, navigating a parking lot.

"Why'd she leave you?" Elle asked. "What prompted it?"

Will summarized the confrontation with Chloe. Elle didn't say anything, didn't interrupt, didn't ask anything. Just listened to Will talk for five minutes, sitting there in the backseat, blind.

"Do you think she believed you?"

"About what?"

"That you're working for the CIA?"

"I couldn't tell."

"Did you tell her that I asked you about *Travelers*? About Malcolm? Gabriella?"

Will felt the knot growing in his stomach, tighter, like someone was twisting his insides. The someone sitting next to him.

"Are you sure she left because of this, Will? Or could it have been something else?"

PORTLAND, MAINE

Chloe walks out to the dock, stares off at the water, the islands out there. She feels a hand on her shoulder, hears a deep-voiced man saying, "Well hello, you." She turns, wraps her arms around this man, squeezes tight.

"It's great to see you," he says.

She beams at him, and he rubs her upper arm, an intimate gesture, but not too intimate, and not sexual. Anyone watching would think that they're old friends, maybe college classmates, or they'd been neighbors as kids, or they're cousins, used to see each other all the time. But none of this is what they are.

"Thanks for coming all this way." She smiles. "Your flight okay?"

He nods. "So how have you been? Everything okay?"

"Not really."

The man nods again, but doesn't say anything.

"Listen, this may sound absurd to you. In fact, it sounds absurd to me." They're facing the choppy water, the stiff wind. "Will told me that while he was on a trip, two people—a woman and a man—claimed to work for the CIA, and offered him ten thousand dollars per month to be an asset when he's traveling overseas."

"Really? To do what, exactly?"

"To tell them about the people he meets, the places he goes. The embassies, parties, politicians. To help identify recruitment candidates."

"I don't know," the man says. "I guess it's . . . not impossible. When did this start?"

"A few months ago."

"And he's been receiving money?"

"In cash. And signing receipts from someone he calls his C/O."

The man raises his eyebrows. "You have any idea who these people are?"

Chloe takes out her phone, hands it to him. "I have a picture of the woman."

He glances down, furrows his brow, shakes his head. "Don't know her. But text it to me. Then give me a few hours."

NEW YORK CITY

Will stares at the little plastic dispenser, like a baby roulette wheel, albeit anti-baby, and explicitly not a game of chance, so more like the opposite of roulette. The days of the week, the different colored pills, the tinny rattle that Will hasn't heard in the past year, not since they've been trying to get pregnant. *Supposedly* trying to get pregnant.

His mind is reeling, grasping at different implications. Chloe would hardly be the first woman who pretended to be trying to conceive while at the same time taking steps to prevent it. Why? Is she having an affair? Is she using his deceits as an excuse? Is she planning to leave Will? For someone else? Has that in fact already happened?

Is Chloe really in Maine? Will keeps calling, and Connie keeps telling him that Chloe is out, and Will has assumed that his wife simply doesn't want to talk to him. But maybe Connie's covering. Maybe Chloe is somewhere else, with another man. Maybe that's why she has been so elusive, so evasive, for so long. Why she rarely answers his phone calls. Why she has been on such an aggressive exercise regimen: to look better naked, for someone else.

Maybe the adultery he needed to worry about wasn't his own. Maybe he has completely misunderstood the nature of the problem he's facing.

29

Will's phone rings, an unfamiliar number with a 718 area code.

"Hello, this is Will Rhodes."

"Who?"

"Will Rhodes. Who's this?"

"Hah?"

"I'm Will Rhodes. Who are you?"

"Can you speak up? I can't hear you."

"My name is Will." Loudly, slowly. "You called me. How can I help you?"

"I'm Bernie Katz."

"Do we know each other?"

"I'm the guy you contacted about the old magazines."

"Oh! Oh, thanks for getting back to me."

"So I got what you're looking for."

"*Travelers,* May 1992 and November 1994 issues?"

"*Travelers,* every issue."

"You're positive you have May '92? And November '94?"

"I got all of 'em."

"Super. How much are you asking for them?"

"For all of 'em?"

"No. For the one issue. I mean the two of them. Apiece."

"Ten?"

"Ten dollars?"

"No, ten *thousand* dollars."

Will is stunned.

"I'm kidding. Yeah, ten dollars apiece. Plus shipping."

"Shipping? Can I just pick it up? I'm also in New York."

"Uh, how do you know where I am?"

"Your area code."

"Oh, right . . . Sure. I'm in what you people now call Prospect Heights."

"You people?"

The guy doesn't respond. But Will doesn't want to pick a fight with him. "I can be there in thirty minutes." Then Will hears cackling through the phone. "What's so funny?"

"I'm eighty-one years old . . ." More laughter. "And this is the first time in my life . . . I've ever found myself . . . in a back-issue . . . emergency."

Stonely watches the woman he knows as Ray walk toward the target, tee-tering on high heels. She glances at the man a couple of times as they approach each other, fleeting eye contact, meant to distract him, put him off-guard, plus make him more likely to stop, when they're five feet apart, and this happens: she stumbles, hits the pavement.

"Oh my God." The man kneels in front of her, a gentleman. "You okay?"

That's when Alonso, who was just a few steps behind the target for the past block, sinks the needle into the guy's shoulder. The target collapses.

Stonely pulls the truck to a halt right next to them, remains at the wheel while Julio hops out of the back. Three people drag the target into the truck, then climb in themselves, bind the guy's hands with the same sort of plastic ties that the police now use for handcuffs, pull a pillowcase over his eyes.

"We good?" Stonely asks. Even though he wasn't out there on the side-walk, still his heart is racing like crazy. He looks in the rearview and side-view mirrors, can't see any sign of anyone who could've noticed anything.

Everyone grunts. Everyone except the target, who will remain uncon-scious until he's dragged out of the truck again, and deposited in a forti-fied room in a dank basement seven miles away, in another universe. The guy's old universe no longer exists.

It's a particular type of New York apartment building, a sunken lobby between two wings, dueling elevators, a neglected courtyard, cantilevered fire escapes, marble floors and plaster walls and ornate moldings, everything down-at-the-heels, chipped stone and cracked glass, wires in the porthole windows of the elevator, which is so slow that Will almost can't believe it's moving at all, a control panel with round Bakelite buttons and brass switches, a mechanical door that groans open, then you have to push a secondary safety door into the hallway that smells of boiled cabbage, the A and B lines in the front and C in the middle and D and E in the back, every toilet a powerful flushometer that makes you imagine the waste being sucked directly into outer space via pneumatic tube, nearly every doorway adorned with a mezuzah, even if the current occupants aren't Jewish, because once they were, and who the hell goes through the trouble of removing these things from the jambs?

Will rings the doorbell, Katz. He waits, then rings again.

"I'm comin'," he hears from inside. "Hold your horses, I'm comin'. Who's there?"

"It's Will Rhodes."

No response.

"The guy about the magazines?"

"Oh." The door opens. "Come on in."

The corridor is long and dark, and at the end is a living room that's an explosion of clutter, magazines and papers and books everywhere, some of the piles reinforced with vertically arranged three-quarter-inch planks, perhaps decommissioned shelving turned on end, and art-glass vases and framed drawings and stretched canvases and organic sculptures, musty rugs, the lingering aroma of pipe tobacco layered atop the fresh scent of takeout-Chinese garlic with undertones of litter box. This is the type of room Will has nightmares about.

"Wow." Will turns his attention more carefully to the piles of magazines, which he sees also include the more traditional horizontal shelving as well as vertical stacks. "Why do you have all these?"

"I'm a buff! I worked in the magazine business fifty years."

"Fifty?"

"Well, forty-eight."

"What did you do, Mr. Katz? If you don't mind me asking?"

"What *didn't* I do? Proofreading, layouts, photo editing, ad sales, you name it. I was even a managing editor! Believe you me, that was a shitty job. But eventually they shuffled me into a back room where I could just collect paychecks without breaking anything." The guy shrugs. "It wasn't so bad. Then they gave me a fancy watch, said good-bye, good luck."

"Is that the watch?"

"This? Nah. What they gave me was a Rolex, but I'm not a Rolex kinda guy. A watch says something, doesn't it? This thing you wear every day, whatever else you're wearing. It's like a part of you, it says something about you. I wanted something more, uh, *under*stated." The old man holds out his wrist, shows Will his timepiece, International Watch Company. Will has always been purposefully ignorant of watches, their levels of prestige. He buys old watches, in foreign places, inexpensively. But even he knows that IWC is expensive.

Will's senses are becoming more acclimated to the clutter, and details begin to emerge. The Heywood-Wakefield furniture, the original oil paintings and charcoal drawings, the Blondie concert poster that appears to be signed, in lipstick, by Debbie Harry.

The expensive watch casts everything in a different light. This man is not poor; this man is messy, eccentric.

"So the magazines?"

"Right!" He shuffles across the room, over to an upright piano that Will hadn't even noticed was there, pushed against built-in bookshelves. It takes Katz a good minute, but he finally locates both issues, double-checks the dates on the covers against the dates on the spines. Hands the two magazines over to Will, who in turn hands over a twenty.

"Does this break up your complete set?"

"Yeah, I guess it does."

"Why are you selling them?"

The guy holds up the bill, snaps it.

"Come on. Why are you *really* selling?"

Katz looks Will in the eye. "I been in this apartment since 1973. Rent-stabilized. I raised two kids in this apartment. My wife, she died in this apartment." He looks around at the accumulated possessions of a life. "The building's been sold. We're all getting kicked out. I'm never going to be able to afford anything bigger than a studio, and that studio's gonna be in, I don't know, *Queens*. If I'm lucky. So all this"—he sweeps his arm across his life—"has to go. I'd rather sell my things to people who want them than just put it all out on the sidewalk, to be picked up by scavengers."

Will thinks of the barstool he found on the street. Is he one of the scavengers?

"You wanna buy anything else? It's all for sale."

Will shakes his head. "Truth is I'm broke."

"Ha! Then you shouldn't go around buying old magazines from old men. Here." He thrusts the twenty back at Will. "Use it to buy some flowers for your wife. That's the only thing that really matters."

Will doesn't accept the money, so Katz shoves the bill into Will's breast pocket, crushing his pocket square.

"Thank you very much, Mr. Katz."

"Forget about it." They walk down the dark hall, the parquet creaking.

Will presses the elevator button, waits while the mechanics groan. He wonders where he should go sit while he scours those magazines, looking for the reasons they have been redacted. He glances at his watch, this obscure antique thing that he bought in Germany, and wonders what the watch says about him, what he hopes this accessory projects, the old man's words sinking in, but something else distracting him . . .

Another wristwatch . . .

"You again? What, you want some old *Vanity Fairs* now?"

Will shakes his head.

"Or I got a record player used to be owned by George Plimpton?"

"Mr. Katz, do you know a lot about watches?"

"A lot? I wouldn't go that far." The old man shrugs. "I know more than nothing."

"Can I show you something? I'd like to draw it."

Katz pulls the door open, and shuffles back to his cluttered living room.

Will remembers the symbol because it looked like something it probably wasn't. He scribbles down the *JL*, which he thought was for J. Lindeberg, however unlikely. Mike with the no-longer-pierced ear and the thick accent and the cheap suit wasn't a customer of a Swedish fashion label.

"You know what that is? I saw some guy wearing a watch with this logo."

"Sure. That's Jaeger-LeCoultre. Swiss."

"How fancy is that?"

"How fancy? Very fancy. Same league as this." The old man raises his arm a couple of inches, his wrist facing Will. "Starting prices probably seventy-five hundred, ten grand."

"Are there knockoffs?"

"I'm sure there are fakes of everything expensive."

"I mean Canal Street–type knockoffs."

"Doubt it. Jaeger's not a household-name luxury brand, not like Rolex or Gucci, all that fake crap you can buy anywhere. I'd be shocked if there's a market for people who want to buy hundred-dollar imitation Jaegers. No, if you saw a guy wearing a Jaeger, you saw a guy wearing a five-figure timepiece."

Will reemerges to the street, around a corner, into the tentacles of a movie shoot, the production assistants in their headsets and bell-bottoms, shunting pedestrians off to the side. The street is lined with gleaming vintage vehicles, late sixties or early seventies, tremendously long coupes with grooviness signifiers hanging from rearview mirrors, a delivery truck decorated with the names of bygone brands, a streamlined bicycle leaning against a fireplug.

"I'm sorry, we need everyone to keep moving. Keep moving, please."

Up close, Will can see that the cars' interiors are shabby—torn upholstery, rusted levers, missing glove-box doors. He wonders if these cars are even operable. Maybe they're just shells, exteriors that have been given fresh powder-coats and whitewalled tires but nonfunctioning engines. Nothing but artificial constructs, created to make people think something's going on that's not.

Will finds a hard seat in a crowded café, the high-decibel rattle of the bean grinder, the thrum of the espresso machine, the hiss of the steaming milk, clanking spoons and clattering cups, aggressively loud badinage at the table behind him, a man clearly trying to get into a woman's pants, tiresomely.

Will's phone rings, Malcolm calling. Will hits Ignore.

November 1994 was the Scandinavia issue. There's an article about every country, even Greenland. Fjords and fabrics, fermented shark and pickled herring, lingonberry compote and smoked puffin, summer cottages and the ice hotel, hot springs and geysers and volcanoes and glaciers, the midnight sun and the northern lights . . .

Will cares about only two of the articles, the ones written by Jonathan Mongeleach, and it doesn't take him long to find what he's looking for.

But the other issue, March 1992? No articles by Jonathan, none about Scandinavia, nothing that grabs Will's attention. Other than being the first issue that went to press after the collapse of the Soviet Union, Will can't see anything remarkable about March 1992.

He's missing something, he's sure of it. He turns back to the beginning.

Malcolm leaves a message—"Hey Will, Malcolm here, about that drink tonight: can we make it six o'clock? I'm out of the office for a couple hours, call me on my cell."

The car stops on a busy corner in East Midtown. Hector cranes his neck around, looking at the busy intersection. "You sure this is it, boss?"

"Yes, thanks Hector, this is it," Malcolm says. "See you tomorrow."

Malcolm climbs out of the car, turns the corner onto the side street, and climbs again into the silver SUV, which has another of Stonely's guys behind the wheel. Malcolm doesn't know this guy's name.

They drive down the river, over a bridge, into Brooklyn on an expressway. After a few miles they exit to traffic-free surface streets, bombed-out buildings, empty warehouses, vacant lots. The truck pulls to a stop in front of a decrepit row house, the front door plastered with stickers proclaiming CONDEMNED and ORDER OF SHERIFF, draped with a chained padlock.

Malcolm climbs out. In the distance he can see the full length of Manhattan's skyline, even the top of his own apartment building. That's a different city. Far more people live in this one.

He walks around to the rear of the building, a trash-strewn yard with the unlikely inclusion of a porta potty. Bangs on the reinforced steel door with the side of his fist, boom-boom. Sees the flash of the peephole before he hears the locks unclicking, a heavy deadbolt sliding, the squeak of the door opening.

A large man stands in the small, dark, tight vestibule, next to a barstool, with an electrical outlet occupied by a cell-phone charger, the phone itself on the floor; everybody everywhere is charging a cell phone. Alonso relocks the outer door, then uses a key to open the inner one.

Malcolm steps inside, and the door closes behind him with a firm slam, then click-clack-thud, locked again.

The windowless basement is spare, utilitarian. A boiler looms in the corner, with a hot-water heater, a big tank for something, all these pipes disconnected. A couple of buckets, a mop, electrical boxes spewing ganglia of frayed wires, a rubber garbage can.

In the middle, under a bare bulb, the guy who has been calling himself Steven Roberts is sitting on a wooden chair. His arms are bound to his body, his legs at the ankles and knees, all with copious lengths of duct tape. There's something in his mouth that looks like balled-up sweatsocks, held in place with more duct tape, which has a smear of blood on it that spilled, apparently, from his right nostril. His shoes and socks have been removed.

"Hi," Malcolm says. "My name is Malcolm Somers."

Steven's eyes widen in terror. A few feet in front of him is a folding table.

"As you are no doubt aware, you've been fucking my wife. I don't blame you for that. My wife is a very attractive woman, isn't she?"

The guy can't answer, of course.

"Should I call you Steven? Or is that a name you use only with Allison?"

The guy watches Malcolm walk to the folding table, look down at the items arrayed across the surface, an assortment of tools, a hammer, wire cutters, a wrench, pliers.

"Honestly, Steven, I guess I'd fuck her too, if I were you."

Malcolm picks up the wire cutters, holds them to his face. Watches the mechanism as he squeezes the handles. Puts down this tool, fingers the others. He picks up the hammer, hefts it, feeling the weight of the tool, its balance.

Steven has been sitting in this basement for three hours, with this table of tools in his field of vision, impossible to ignore. No one has said a word to him. He has been forced to imagine all the ways that his life can become a horror show, all the terrible disgusting things that can be done to his body parts with a hammer. With *pliers*. He has seen things on TV, in movies, maybe read them in congressional reports, maybe he's heard rumors about them in real life, or even witnessed these things firsthand. Malcolm wouldn't be completely surprised if this guy had participated in an enhanced interrogation before, from the other side.

Before he ever entered this room, and saw this table, this man already possessed an immense capacity to visualize the horrors that might be visited upon him by common household tools. The past hours have amplified that capacity. And now that he understands who has abducted him, he also has a pretty clear idea which of his body parts are likely to be targeted.

"In any case"—Malcolm starts walking toward him, the hammer hanging at his side—"this, um, fucking of my wife? That's not why you're here, Steven. That's not your crime."

Malcolm stops in front of the guy, eyes popping, squirming beneath his duct tape. "You know why you're here, don't you?"

Steven shakes his head.

"Of course you do. We both know that you know why you're here. So what is it we're here to find out?"

He continues to shake his head, more vigorously.

"I get the feeling you're not going to make this easy, are you?"

Still head-shaking.

"That's too bad, Steven. Then sorry to say, neither am I."

30

The city can look gigantic, eight-million-plus people, an overwhelming volume of life, of noise, of skyscrapers and traffic and the incessant collisions of worlds. But every metropolis is also a collection of small villages, some of them geographical, some professional, some social, some overlapping.

The women Will has dated in New York all lived inside his discrete little villages. He didn't go out with bankers or lawyers, with professors or doctors, with bus drivers or jewelry designers or elementary-school teachers. With one exception, every single woman Will went to bed with was college-educated, white, born in the seventies or eighties, living in Manhattan or Brooklyn, working in media or hospitality.

These villages aren't hugely populous. So Will runs into them all the time, the women he has slept with. Sometimes he finds himself literally surrounded by them, at parties or conferences, around someone's big dinner table in Brownstone Brooklyn.

Here comes one right now. This one, however, is the exception.

Will tries to remember what he was feeling when they met. Did he really believe that he was in love-at-first-sight with this woman? Does he remember correctly, that he was walking around France, lost in romantic reveries about the way she arched her eyebrow? How could he have been so goddamned delusional? He'll never trust his penis again.

"Hi Will," she says. She leans in, left-cheek kiss, right-cheek kiss, old friends, great to see you. Elle is carrying a cavernous bag that she drops on the floor next to Will's canvas satchel and a plastic shopping bag from a drugstore, one of those chains you can't walk three blocks without seeing. The streets of New York are beginning to look like a variation on the suburban four-lane thoroughfare, retail chains repeating one after another, an endless loop, up and down America's clogged arteries.

"Everything okay with you?" she asks, perching herself on a barstool. "You had a good day at the office?"

"Nothing went wrong, if that's what you're asking."

She laughs, probably for the benefit of other people.

The bartender asks if she wants something. "No thanks," she says, "I was just saying hi," They have nothing to talk about. This is not a debrief, not now. This is a handoff. "Nice running into you, Will."

"And you."

She leans down, collects her big handbag, as well as the ubiquitous drugstore bag, with the very unusual hard drive inside.

Well, he thinks, that was anticlimactic. Was that really the upshot of this whole convoluted operation? This wrecking of his entire life?

He assumes Elle will be bringing this package downtown straight-away, to her office, to whatever building they kidnapped him to last night, probably down near the other government buildings. It's rush-hour busy out there on the streets, so she'll probably take the subway, maybe a half-dozen stops, then perhaps a couple of blocks on foot. Fifteen minutes, twenty, before she plugs in the external drive. He doesn't know how long it's then going to take for her to fully examine the contents. Five minutes? Three days? But after she does, she's going to be angry, and she's going to come looking for him.

He doesn't have much time. Nowhere near enough for him to run a proper surveillance-detection route, nor for that matter even a half-assed SDR. Will has insufficient time to detect surveillance. He needs to elude it.

SCARBOROUGH, MAINE

Chloe climbs down the attic's folding stairs toting the dusty old backpack. It has been years—more than a decade—since she used the bag. Chloe still keeps things in her mom's attic. Maybe this is what it means to not be fully grown-up.

She doesn't want to bring a roll-aboard suitcase for the trip she's un-dertaking; that's not the type of traveler she wants to look like. She hoses down the backpack in the backyard, props it against a trellis to dry.

"I just need to get away, Mom. I'm going to spend a few days at a resort in the Dominican Republic—it's practically free, this time of year—and then I'll backpack. I've never been to Haiti."

Chloe doesn't have any intention of going anywhere near the Dominican Republic or Haiti. A few months ago she procured two passports for this type of clandestine travel. She ended up burning one of them in a trash can in Istanbul; the other is in her pocket.

"Just tell me if I can help. And please call sometime? Let me know you're alive?"

That was going to be hard, maybe impossible. "I'll try" is what Chloe says. "But don't hold your breath."

"All marriages have their problems, sweetheart."

Chloe doesn't respond to her mom's daytime-television platitudes. Connie had never seemed like she would become the type of retired person who'd spend too much time watching TV, but she has.

"I'd be surprised if your problems are unique, or insurmountable."

NEW YORK CITY

This is how a long-term operation can happen: it looks as if it'll go on forever—the months or years of planning, the interminable setup, the slow build of execution. Then one day something transpires, and, boom, it's over. For this op, that something may have just transpired; that one day could be today.

It has been a long year, and it began right here, just a few blocks away, where Elle spent a lonely night in a chain hotel in an unremarkable neighborhood. She'd been to the city only once before in her life, didn't know her way around, didn't much like the place, didn't want to try. The world was already populated with plenty of people who were awestruck by New York; the city didn't need another groupie.

The meeting was set for eleven A.M., but the location was unspecified until ten, when she received a text message with the name and address of a hotel, a room number.

She walked to the part of town that occupies a large space in the world's consciousness, where the greenery of Central Park meets the commerce of Fifth Avenue, horse-drawn carriages and sidewalk carica-turists, a golden statue and a tiered fountain and the Plaza Hotel, hordes of out-of-towner teenage girls posing for selfies in front of Abercrombie & Fitch, dowagers tottering into Bergdorf's to finger seven-thousand-dollar off-the-rack evening dresses.

It was immediately clear that this hotel was no normal level of swank, even though she'd never heard of it. Elle was familiar with only those New York hotels that appear in popular contemporary movies.

At the door, a black-suited bodyguard stood in a familiar pose. She wondered if this guy had been in the Sandbox at the same time as she had, if he too had returned stateside unprepared for twenty-first-century civil-ian employment, disillusioned by the disconnect between the military's promise of highly valued workplace skills and the private sector's actual valuation of those skills. So he'd secured himself one of the few available jobs that valued his particular skill set, with a concealed-carry permit and a bulletproof vest.

The bodyguard maintained a permanent grimace while he frisked her, then opened the door.

There's a certain type of good-looking man with perfect everything—perfect tailoring and skintone, perfect hair and shoeshine, posture and physique, smiling with a surfeit of white teeth and undisguised, untem-pered confidence, men who pay super-close attention to many details of their personal appearance. For women, it seems like the requirement is to try to look as good as you can look, seems like *not* making that effort is the contrarian statement. For men, though, Elle has always thought that the hyper-grooming is the exceptional statement, the aberration. She finds something appalling about these men.

This was one such man who was standing on the threshold, saying, "Thank you for coming." He closed the door behind Elle. "And thank you for your discretion."

She looked around the suite, which seemed to have been decorated by Liberace. "May I ask a question: Why are we meeting in New York? Isn't your office in Washington?"

Even before Elle had gotten the summons from his minion, before she'd followed up with hours of research, she'd already seen this man's face plenty of times, seen this smile again and again; he was well known. But still, she was unprepared for the brilliance of it, the quantity and alignment and brightness of his teeth, the shape of his mouth and the fullness of his lips, the squareness of his jaw. Elle had seen her fair share of extremely handsome men over the years, had even taken a couple of them to bed. But theirs had all been the attractiveness of youth and strength and toughness, and here this guy was in his mid-forties, none of those things, but still disarmingly good-looking.

"In a way, my office is a very public place. In fact, all of Washington is a small, gossipy town. But New York? New York can be very private, if you make a little effort."

Elle suddenly questioned the advisability of being in a hotel suite with a powerful man who had an armed bodyguard at the door.

"Plus what I have in mind would take place, mostly, here in New York. Mine is a project that will need a very specific type of manager, with not only a specific background and specific expertise, but also specific, uh, physical characteristics. You come very highly recommended. So highly, in fact, that you're the only candidate I'm currently interviewing."

"I appreciate your confidence," Elle said, but she didn't. Flattery like this called into question everything else. "But do you want to tell me what the hell you're talking about?"

He laughed. "No getting-to-know-you small talk for you, huh?"

"I'm pretty sure you've already gotten to know me, or I wouldn't be here. And you won't be surprised that I've gotten to know you."

"Be that as it may. I don't know everything I want to know."

"Oh no?"

"Why'd you get kicked out of the CIA?"

"Who says I got kicked out?"

He doesn't answer.

"Do you want to tell me why I'm here? Or should I leave now?"

He smiled patiently, leaned forward, looking earnest. "I'm in the middle stages of engineering the purchase of a group of magazines."

"Yes. The American Periodical Group."

He smiled. "That's right. You've been reading the financial-gossip mills?"

"You don't think I subscribe to *Forbes*? Just because I'm a broke blond thirty-two-year-old jarhead yokel?"

Elle had gone to two years of college, but she'd consistently discovered that the things she'd wanted to learn were not the things being taught in class; she preferred an autodidactic education, staying up all night to pursue one obsession or another, absorbing everything, then moving on.

"No, I don't think you read *Forbes* because it's for business professionals, and you're not one. Just as I wouldn't expect a cardiovascular surgeon or a rocket scientist or a Nobel-laureate mathematician to read *Forbes*. It's not because those people are stupid."

"Well, you're right. I don't read *Forbes*. But I did."

"Then I guess you know that if this deal ends up going through, it'll cost me somewhere north of two billion dollars."

"Well." She smirked. "*Cost* you?"

"What do you mean by that?"

"It's not as if you're cutting a personal check for two billion dollars, money that you scrimped and saved, taking the bus, eating jam sandwiches. I know how the world works."

"Please. Enlighten me."

"You're taking two billion dollars that you've borrowed from individual and institutional investors in the form of stock offerings and bank loans, on the backs of favorable regulations and legislation enacted by elected representatives to whom people like you contribute considerable sums to finance their campaigns so they can hold office and help you gain access to vast amounts of public and private money, of which you're reallocating two billion dollars from one corporate entity over which you exert control to another over which you'd like to. But it's not really your money—hell, it's not even really money—and you're not really spending it."

He stared at her for a second. "Okay, I'll put it another way," he said, undeterred. "I'm responsible for overseeing a multibillion-dollar business transaction, affecting the livelihood of thousands of people. Would you agree that this is a fair description?"

She shrugged.

"One aspect of my responsibility is due diligence. During which I learned, with a high degree of certainty, that one of the magazines is doing something illegal."

"Oh yeah? How'd you find this out?"

"You don't attain a position like mine without being able to learn things."

"Fair enough."

"So I'm required, as a legal matter of fiduciary responsibility, to exhaust every possible avenue of investigation to verify or disprove this allegation."

"But you're not required to report this illegal activity to law enforcement?"

He doesn't answer.

"If this activity bothers you, why not just walk away from the deal? You're right that I don't know much about business, but I'm pretty sure you'll survive fine if you continue to *not* own the American Periodical Group."

"I don't want to walk away, that's why."

"Is there something specific about APG that makes it so attractive to you? Something about the dregs of a dying industry that you find irresistible?"

"Because of the specific nature of the alleged activity," he said, ignoring her question, "I find myself unable to utilize the resources commonly used in this type of situation."

"Resources? Such as?"

"Forensic accounting. Mergers-and-acquisitions lawyers. Private detectives, the types with licenses."

"So what are these allegations?"

"I'm afraid I'm not at liberty to disclose those details, at this time. I'm sure you understand."

"No, I don't think I do."

He smiled again, a rich warm comforting smile, the type of smile that makes you want to curl up in it. "This isn't a situation in which a nondisclosure agreement would make any sense."

"Why not?"

"Nor is it a situation in which I'm willing to be, um, *trusting*. To a stranger such as yourself. No matter how highly recommended."

"Okay," she said, "how can I reassure you?"

"By accepting the job, and the fee that comes with it."

"And that fee would be?"

"A quarter now. Another quarter when the project is complete. It should take somewhere between six months and a year."

"Do you mean a total of a half-million dollars?"

"That's right."

"This is not a hit job, is it?"

He leaned back. "And if it is?"

They stared at each other for a few seconds. To replace her fleeting fear of physical assault, now she was assailed with the worry that she was being entrapped. But why would a man like this be involved in entrapping someone like her?

"No," he eventually said. "It's not a hit job."

"I'm not going to kill anyone?"

"I hope not."

That was not as definitive a refutation as she'd hoped. "A half-million dollars is a lot of money, to not kill anyone."

"As I've explained, it's a big deal."

"Of course. What's a half-million against two billion?"

"That's right. But as *you've* mentioned, that two billion isn't exactly my own money. The half-million is."

"So you're saying this fee is not negotiable?"

"Yes, that's what I'm saying."

She looked away from him, at the windows. She'd been expecting a sweeping view of Central Park, up here on a high floor on Fifth Avenue, but the shades were drawn. This guy must be one paranoid son of a bitch, to have the shades drawn in a situation like this.

"I'd like to think about it, but you haven't given me much to think about."

"As I mentioned, I'm not at—"

"—liberty. Yeah, I know."

Part of her was attracted to the payday, of course; a half-million was certainly a good amount of money. But the bigger part of her decision-making matrix was that she was bored. For a decade she'd been addicted to the adrenaline; then for the past year she'd been going through withdrawal, adhering to a life that was like a recovery's maintenance pro-gram, weaker substitutes and group meetings, affirmations and distrac-tions. But this? This sounded like the hard stuff.

What it didn't sound like was corporate espionage, as this guy was claiming. He wasn't telling her the truth about something, maybe about a lot of things. You didn't hire someone like her for corporate espionage. You hired someone like her for real espionage.

Since that first meeting, she'd expended a lot of effort trying to figure out why he so desperately wanted to acquire the magazines, and never did, not really. She discovered only what he'd been hoping to learn along the way. Not what he was going to do once he'd learned it.

This guy was undoubtedly good at what he did for a living, was very successful. But you know who else was really good at his job? Adolf Hitler. He was *really* good at being a fascist dictator, and came closer to conquer-ing the world than anyone in millennia. Good at your job does not equal admirable, nor trustworthy. She neither admired nor trusted this man. But she still wanted to do whatever this job was.

"Everything," she said, "is negotiable."

He raised his eyebrows.

"Make it a million," she answered his unspoken question, "and you have a deal."

31

Will boards the crowded downtown local to the East Broadway station on the fringe of Chinatown, where recent Asian immigrants mix with African-Americans and Latin-Americans and Orthodox Jews, a heterogeneity that looks almost stage-managed. The person here who stands out is Will. And whoever might be following Will.

He hustles alongside the park, pickup basketball and kids on tricycles, girls jumping rope and a few youths who might be dealing drugs, or want to look that way. He steps into a tiny deli, security bars across the windows, bulletproof glass separating the cashier from the people who might try to rob her. He buys a bottle of water, returns to the sidewalk, pauses in front of the store to take a sip, to look around. Not a Caucasian in sight.

The summer sun is lurking somewhere behind all these buildings, the low gritty ones in the foreground and the higher shiny ones that loom back there, a mile away—a very long mile—in the Financial District. Will walks quickly, making only a couple of turns and pausing once, almost positive that no one is following him.

He arrives at their old block, and his confidence ebbs away. This is a known location, a place where he might be looked for, if anyone is looking for him.

Will checks his watch: it's been eighteen minutes since Elle left him. She could be in her office this very minute, scanning the disk.

He enters another deli, buys a pack of gum. There's no metal on the windows here, no bulletproof glass inside, and Will has a clear unobstructed view out to the street, a commercial stretch of bars and restaurants and independent retailers, a grocer and a liquor store, secondhand clothing and vintage vinyl, eyewear and housewares. Plenty of people are loitering out there, a nice summer evening, smoking cigarettes and staring at phones, waiting for the bus or hailing taxis. Any of them might be looking for Will.

There's no way to tell if anyone is watching him. The only thing Will can hope to discover is if anyone looks familiar. It's not as if there's a team of hundreds of people who might be following Will; he's not a high-level Soviet defector, after all. How many people can be participating in this operation?

His old building looks unchanged, six stories of red bricks crisscrossed with metal fire escapes and decorated with no shortage of stone details—cornices and lintels and architraves, the type of superfluous ornamentation that was once universal, even for slum housing.

When the traffic light changes, Will dashes across the broad avenue midblock. The exterior door to the old building is always open, and he unlocks the interior door using the key that he never returned to the landlord. He was always finding strays in here, cold homeless people in the winter, kids smoking joints, drunk people groping, the occasional junkie with pockmarked skin and tattered clothing, just sprawled there on the grimy tiles. The building was dangerous, but romantic in a way that dangerous things can sometimes be, before they grow tiresome. Danger is exhausting.

The lobby is just a long hallway, a rack of battered brass mailboxes, ten of them, all with broken locks. Legal notices are pushpinned to the wall. A Post-it announces that because of necessary repairs, there won't be any hot water on Friday. The note is signed by Calvin, the elusive superintendant who works at a half-dozen buildings in this neighborhood, seemingly always on duty somewhere else.

Will walks to the back of the building, to the stairs that lead to the basement, steep and dark and dirty. Tenants don't have any business down there. No laundry room, no storage spaces, no rear exit, no nothing. Will would never have gone down here at all except he once needed to find a place to hide a large present for Chloe.

He'd scouted the basement on a weekday morning, worried that Calvin was going to catch him, carrying a flashlight like a cat burglar, looking guilty of more than his crime, which was nonexistent. Still, it felt wrong. That's how he'd found the spot under the stairs—dusty discarded bicycles, an old folding stroller, someone's box of Christmas ornaments—where he hid Chloe's skis.

The stairs are framed from underneath by iron I-beams, creating cavities with ledges, unlit and hard to access, occupied possibly by cockroaches or rats or carcinogenic piles of asbestos dust. No one would voluntarily reach back into this creepy subterranean darkness.

Will does. The third step from the bottom, slightly too low to be comfortable, for an extra measure of security. He feels around . . . left . . . right . . .

Panic sets in immediately, accelerated by the adrenaline that was already coursing through his body thanks to his flight from Midtown, his countersurveillance maneuvers, his outsize irrational fear of getting caught by the deadbeat absentee super.

His packet isn't here. How can that be?

He reaches again, leaning in farther, getting more complete coverage of the surface.

Shit.

He stands back, looks around. Is it possible that Calvin discovered his hiding spot? Someone else? His mind jumps to Elle, to Roger. To Chloe.

Will hears the front door slam upstairs. Heavy footsteps. He cocks his head like a dog, listening, scared out of his goddamned wits.

Why? What's he scared of?

Everything. This now, and all the things he has to do tonight, tomorrow, for the foreseeable future. This here is just the start, and it's already going wrong. Which might make it the end.

Will closes his eyes, takes a deep breath, counts to ten. Trying to calm himself down.

He opens his eyes. Turns his attention back to the iron underside of the stairs. Counts up from the bottom again.

Realizes that he'd been searching the wrong level for his go-bag, which is safely secured with duct tape, exactly where he placed it when he came back from Ireland, spooked. He rips off the tape.

Will's hand is on the front door, ready to push it open, to exit to the street, to get the hell out of this building before he runs into Calvin, or a resident, or the police. But he hesitates. He brings his face close to the diamond-shaped window in the door, security glass with a half-torn-off sticker for a twenty-four-hour locksmith, a smudge of what might be snot, in the best-case scenario.

There are just as many people outside as there were ten minutes ago, and a few look familiar: the crowd waiting for the bus is unchanged; the same scraggly middle-aged guy is hanging out in front of the liquor store, looking questionable, but it's the type of questionable that should concern the police, not Will.

Also a familiar-looking man in a lightweight suit, rubber-soled shoes, sunglasses that don't manage to hide the direction in which the man is staring: directly at Will's building. This guy would blend in perfectly in Midtown, but here on the Lower East Side? Sore thumb.

Will spins away from the door, back into the makeshift lobby. He climbs the first flight of stairs, the second, the third and fourth and fifth. Rounds the landing of the top floor, to the stairs that lead to the roof, closed off with a gate that claims FIRE EXIT ONLY: ALARM WILL SOUND IF OPENED.

He wonders if this gate is truly wired. This is the type of apparatus that doesn't necessarily work in a building like this. Broken, perhaps, or disabled, or never properly installed in the first place. Will had used this roof plenty of times, for impromptu spillover from parties, carrying ice and beer and bottles of wine, a tablecloth to serve as a picnic blanket, binoculars to watch Fourth of July fireworks. There'd been no such gate.

And if the alarm does work? Will it be audible on the street? And if it is, will the team following him understand what it means? Will they understand immediately?

He doesn't have much of a choice. Will pushes forward on the red lever, releasing the lock, opening the door, and . . . ?

And, yes: sounding the alarm. An ear-piercing scream, harshly bright light flashing here in the half-lit gloom of a tenement's top-floor hall, a full-scale sensory assault from a harmless-looking little box near the ceiling.

Will takes the steps two at a time. Opens the big metal door at the top, steps out onto the squishy tar. There are a few lawn chairs up here, a hibachi. No people.

He scampers to the front of the building, the very edge. Lies down on the tar. There are wide-diameter holes bored in the parapet, water drainage, little funnels that lead to gutters suspended on the façade. Will peers through one of these holes, locates the man in the suit across the street. He's looking up and down the block, apparently aware of the alarm. He glances up, scanning the roofline—does he see Will? No, there's no way. *No way.*

The man takes his phone out of his pocket, holds it up to his face, says something, nods. Then he starts to cross the street.

Will gets up. He jogs across the roof, climbs over a dividing wall, hops down onto an adjoining building. He does this again at the next one, and the next. Every building is six stories tall, the roofs all at similar heights, similar surfaces, similar evidence of unauthorized leisure use, cheap folding furniture and a big plastic bin, cigarette butts and beer bottles and a yellow cardboard condom box, ripped open jaggedly.

Will arrives at the end of a building and stops short, out of breath: it's a long drop down to the next rooftop, at least one full story. He looks around for a ladder, a rope, anything, but there's nothing.

He needs to get around this corner, needs to get off these rooftops and down to the ground and out to a stretch of street that isn't being monitored.

The volume of the fire alarm is suddenly louder, a grating layer atop the background hum of the city din, trucks and buses, a distant siren. He looks over his shoulder in the direction of the increased noise, sees the door swinging open.

He's out of time.

Will jumps.

"But you"—the man coughs, his throat dry—"you're the one who hired me."

"Excuse me?"

The guy was gagged for hours, and Malcolm has just uncorked him.

"Please, can I have some water?"

"No. What do you mean I'm the one who hired you?"

The man bound to the chair looks pleadingly at Malcolm. "Please."

"Tell me what the hell you're talking about."

"To get you out of your prenup."

Malcolm's mind is trying to imagine what this could possibly mean. He can't. And he shouldn't bother trying to get an honest answer now. First he needs to do something else.

He retreats to the door, knocks; it's locked from the outside. Click, clack, squeak, the door swings open. "Yeah?"

"It's time to do the fingers," Malcolm says.

"What?"

"Oye," Alonso cries out to the yard, *"ven acá."* Another guy trudges in, takes over as doorman. The door slams shut, the locks reengage loudly.

Alonso, who was hired because of his willingness to mete out violence, lumbers toward the guy sitting in the chair.

"What the hell do you mean, *do the fingers*?" The guy is panicking.

Alonso reaches into the rear pocket of his baggy oversize jeans, which hang low off his ass. He removes a big leather sheath.

"Oh God, no. *Please.*"

Alonso pulls a knife out of the sheath. A black leather handle, long thick blade, serrated on the back. This knife offers options, a lot of ways to cut different sorts of things, to slice and stab and saw things, animals, people. This is a scary-ass knife.

"Please," the man in the chair begs. "No . . ."

As he launches into the air, Will's mind flashes back to the long-ago weekend that he spent learning to skydive, another experience undertaken so he could write about it. The dull classroom instruction followed by the repetitive field training—jumping, tumbling, learning to land without breaking ankles or shins, flexed feet and soft knees, pitching forward and shoulder-rolling, spreading the impact across different bones, joints, muscle groups, bearing the load widely.

It's a long fall from one rooftop to another, and even as he's still rolling forward onto the tarmac he has begun to assess his injuries, the integrity of his joints. When he comes to a halt on one knee, it's his left ankle that doesn't feel great. He stands upright, flexes that ankle. It definitely hurts. But it's usable.

He runs to the front of the building: nothing here, no way down the fifty feet to the city street. He sprints to the rear. There's a ladder-and-stair fire-escape system back here, but it doesn't start until a floor below, and there's no way down to that top level, which is half-occupied by a collection of potted plants.

Can he jump down? What is it, ten feet? Sure. But what if he misses?

Will leans over the parapet, looking for a better option. Four houses up the block, there's a fire escape that reaches the very top. Does he have time to make it over there without being seen? Will needs to get the hell off this rooftop before his pursuer locates him and alerts his street-level partner—or is there more than one?—to Will's location.

No, he doesn't have time. Will has just a couple of seconds to get off this roof, out of sight.

Again, he has no choice. Again, he jumps.

32

Alonso holds the horror-film knife in front of the man who calls himself Steven.

"Please," the man begs. "Don't."

Malcolm ignores him, his fingers flying across his little touchscreen keyboard: *Sorry, Rhodes, running late, can we make it 7:00?* Then he slips the phone back into his pocket. "Come on," he says to Alonso. "Let's get this over with."

"No! *Please!*"

With a lightning-quick upward flick, Alonso slices through the duct tape that binds Steven's right hand to the chair. He repeats the maneuver for the left hand.

Steven glances at his free hands, looking for wounds, for evidence that he wasn't just unbound, but something worse.

Malcolm hands the small metal box to Alonso.

"What's this?" Steven asks, his imagination taking a 180-degree turn back toward terror, toward all the horrible things that could be inflicted upon him from this small metal box. What in the name of God could be in there?

Will is falling through the air on a wider horizontal trajectory than intended, getting much farther from the rear plane of the building than he wants, and he can tell that this is going to be a problem, possibly fatal, and he tries to reverse his body back toward the building but that doesn't work, and all this is happening *so fast*, and then somehow he does manage for his right foot to land directly on the handrail, midsole, and for a fraction of a second he's balanced there, midfoot, on an inch-wide strip of painted iron, three feet above the fire escape's landing, forty feet above the solid bone-crushing pavement of the backyard.

That balance is illusory. Will's momentum is carrying him forward, his weight shifting from the middle of the foot to the front, propelling his body away from the building, away from safety, out into free fall, obeying physics instead of volition, and there he goes, pitching into open air but reaching backward, his descent slowed and his angle altered as his hand fumbles for the railing, but his fingers can't find purchase, and he's dropping again, his hand grasping for anything, anything at all, and he feels metal in his palm, and he closes his fingers, and his forearm immediately begins to burn, even before he fully realizes that he is successfully hanging there, dangling from the corner of the fire escape, no longer falling, no longer about to die, at least not in the next second, not if he can manage to hold—

He flings his other arm into the same position, establishes a two-handed grip, more secure. He holds still. He gathers his strength. Swings his legs toward the building, then back out, then in again, his body a pendulum, and at the maximum amplitude he launches himself into open air again, but this time for a drop of just a few feet, clattering to the surface of the fire escape, crashing into a cardboard case filled with wine bottles.

A cat in the window screeches at him.

"Oh Gertrude"—it's a woman's voice inside—"what's wrong? What's out there?" This woman is not going to be happy to see Will on her fire escape; she's going to scream her ass off.

He hops out of the her sight line. Scuttles down to the next level, then down again, his feet clanking on the ladder, the whole structure jangling. Not making any attempt to be quiet here—let the residents scream, let them dial 911, let them gather their baseball bats and kitchen knives—but he's getting out of here.

It comes as absolutely no surprise that the final stretch of ladder down to ground level is stuck, unbudgeable, a code violation. Sometimes building codes are a bureaucratic pain in the ass, sometimes they're the difference between life and death.

Will swings his legs over this final railing, lowers himself, hangs from the bottom of the metalwork for a half-second. Lets go. Drops.

This fall is the one that hurts the most.

He limps through the yard, an open space common to a few buildings, unhealthy hostas and potted herbs interspersed with paved walkways and garbage cans, rat-bait dispensers and preschooler toys, and here's a low dark loggia, an exit to the side street.

Will peers up the block, back again. Just a few people are visible out here. None seems to be looking for him. Here comes an available taxi. Hand up, door opening, Will falling onto the sticky seat, ankle throbbing, not hearing himself announce his destination, hoping the words come out right.

The taxi turns onto the avenue, and—*shit!*—there's one of his pursuers, clear as day, a guy he recognizes from Midtown.

Will sinks low into the seat, turns away from the window. But the taxi is stopped now for a red light, and Will knows that he's in the guy's line of vision. Will sinks lower, brings his hand to his face, shielding his features with an imaginary phone.

"You okay mister?" The driver is watching him squirm in the rearview. "You ain't gonna be sick, are you?"

"No. Sick is not my problem."

"You got a different problem?"

The light changes, and the car pulls away, through the intersection, out of danger.

"Don't we all?"

He descends to the crowded subway platform, a train arriving, pushing hot stale air into the station, Will stumbling into the car and tumbling onto a bench. Across the car, a man is talking at least 25 percent louder than necessary, overly enunciating, his mouth making acrobatic-looking movements, as if to prove to his companion his theater training, his expertise in vocal projection. Like the occasional waitstaff in French restaurants, so exacting and precise in their pronunciations of pot-au-feu and bouillabaisse that practically no customers know what the hell is on offer.

Next to Will, a man is sighing heavily, one hand gripping his forehead in the classic woe-is-me pose, unashamed by his public display of distress, well past caring what anyone thinks of him.

Will looks down at his feet, away from all these people, their distractions. He's trying to follow the narrative he's still constructing in his mind, following the thread, like training his eye on the wandering line in a Miró canvas, weaving in and out of shapes and forms on its way to nowhere, the destination irrelevant, nonexistent, the journey everything.

He's pretty sure that the thing he's been told is going on isn't really the thing that's going on. Somebody has been lying to him—possibly everybody. It's time to find out who.

Will rides a few stops, consults the map over his shoulder. Yes, this is the spot.

Between stations, he stands. The sigher ignores him; the enunciator notices. Will walks to the end of the car. He fights the urge to look around at his fellow passengers; he doesn't particularly want to give anyone any reasons to notice him, to get a good look at him, to remember him when they're being interviewed by the police.

Will reaches up, takes hold of the emergency-brake handle, and pulls, and seven hundred thousand pounds of subway steel come to a screeching, shuddering halt.

Will opens the door at the end of the car, walks onto the ridged gangway between cars. He climbs over the safety rail made of chains, jumps down to the floor of the tunnel. Identifies the third rail, 625 volts, thankfully on the other side of the train. Walks toward the rear, in the small sooty space between subway and tunnel wall, his path illuminated by the lights through the windows.

At the back of the train he pauses, looks around. The station they just departed isn't far away, just a city block or two, its light intruding on the dark tunnel, a bright serum at the end of a dark syringe.

He sets off at a jog. Looks over his shoulder, doesn't see anyone following, no one peering through the rear window of the last car.

At the station, he walks up the steps, onto the platform. An Asian schoolgirl in a plaid uniform notices, but quickly turns her eyes back to the book she's holding. No one else pays him any mind.

He climbs the station stairs, transfers to another train that's just pulling in. He rides under the East River tube into Brooklyn, then sits for one stop after another, through Brooklyn Heights and Clinton Hill and Bedford-Stuyvesant, Brownsville and Ozone Park and Jamaica, a trip that seems to go on forever. In London, where you can't get anywhere quickly or cheaply, you can nevertheless take a nonstop train from Heathrow to Paddington in fifteen minutes. In New York you take the A train combined with the AirTrain for a slow, lurchy, and occasionally scary hour.

He assesses his injuries: a twisted ankle, abrasions on both hands, a gash in the shin.

"Yo, you all right? That looks nasty."

Will is dabbing at his bloody leg with the cuff of his jeans, trying to stanch the bleeding, though maybe all he's accomplishing is staining his pants.

"I'm okay," Will says, nodding at the guy across the car. He's finally on the loop that runs around the airport terminals, this strange subcity plopped onto the Jamaica Bay wetlands. Thirty-seven thousand people work at JFK, and this guy appears to be one of them, riding the AirTrain with no luggage. Just like Will.

He surveys the sprawling scrum of check-in—ticketing and bag-drop, customer service and security, thousands of people waiting, shuffling, complaining. All being observed by airline agents, by TSA personnel, by police, by surveillance cameras.

He approaches a self-serve check-in terminal. Takes his passport out of his pocket, swipes it through the slot. The screen informs him that it's *Searching our records . . . Searching our records . . .*

Will feels eyes all around him, and it takes every iota of his self-control to not look around.

Searching our records . . .

This is taking too long. His heart is accelerating, again.

This is taking *way* too long; something must be wrong. Maybe this kiosk is broken?

Will looks up from the screen. He scans the terminal, his eyes drawn like magnets to the guards, to the police, who themselves are scanning the terminal, looking for people who are looking at them.

Searching our—

The screen goes blank. *Shit.* What's about to happen?

—Record located

Will's hand is trembling as he hits the touchscreen, checking no bags, not traveling with any infants, agreeing to this and that safety measure, whatever, come *on*—

The kiosk finally spits out his boarding pass.

He realizes that he needs to clean himself off; he shouldn't go through security feeling like this, looking like this. He finds the restroom, washes the blood off his shin, his hands, applies some bandages from the first-aid kit in his go-bag. Runs water across his face, through this hair. Dabs himself dry with paper towels.

It's okay, he tells himself. I'm just a harried traveler, I'm sweating because it's hot and I've been rushing, not because I'm nervous, not because I'm hiding anything.

The queue is very short. He is, after all, a Trusted Traveler, according to the Transportation Security Administration's background check.

"Sir?"

He shuffles forward, keys and watch and coins in the little plastic basket, hands out of pockets, patting himself down. Backpack and jacket on conveyor belt. Nothing metal in there. Nothing, just . . . just what? Just illegal travel documents and a large sum of cash . . .

He should've kept his jacket on. He watches it glide into the X-ray machine.

Shit.

A TSA cop waves Will into the metal detector, and the thing starts beeping like mad. What? *What?*

"Sir, do you have a phone in your pocket?" Oh shit, yes. Into another basket, onto the conveyor belt, which almost immediately comes to a stop. With his bag and his jacket in there.

The X-ray operator is staring at the screen. The conveyor moves forward, then backward. The guy squints. Beckons over a colleague. They both stare at the screen. One says something to the other, who nods.

Shit shit *shit.*

The conveyor starts to move again.

"Sir?"

Oh good God. Will looks at the guards, these men standing between him and freedom. Who are these men? Why are they trustworthy? Who screened them? How? For whom do they work? Who are these people, to be given the power to hold Will's life in their hands?

"Sir? Is this duffel bag yours?"

Duffel? No, what duffel? I don't have any—

"Yes." It's the man standing next to Will who answers.

"Sir, do you have a cigarette lighter in this bag?"

Oh thank God. Will grabs his things, his contraband-stuffed jacket, and he gets the hell out of there, clutching his passport and boarding pass like life preservers.

Will gazes up at the departure board. The gate for the flight to Portland, Maine, is 34. Its status is boarding.

His phone vibrates again, yet another text message from Malcolm: *Hey Rhodes, what the fuck? Are we having a drink or what?*

He locks a stall in the men's room. Gets undressed, changes into his spare clothes, jeans, tee shirt, cap. He removes the padded envelope from the rear of his jeans, and slides his passport inside, keeping company with a thick wad of twenties, fifties, and hundreds.

Will extracts a different passport from the envelope, a Canadian document in the name of Douglas Davis. And a different boarding pass.

He examines the two thumb drives in his hand. He puts one in his front right pocket, the other in his rear.

He packs his old clothes into the bag, and exits the men's room.

"Paging Will Rhodes. Passenger Rhodes on the eight-fifteen bound for Portland. Please report to gate thirty-four immediately. This is your final call. Final call."

He looks up, locates gate thirty-four, a hundred yards to his right.

Will turns left.

SCARBOROUGH

"Hello?"

"Hey Chloe, it's Dean."

She doesn't respond. Is Dean really calling her? That takes a lot of nerve.

"Dean Fowler," he clarifies.

"Yes, believe it or not, you're the only Dean I know. Plus I recognize your voice."

"Glad to hear it. Listen, Chloe . . ."

"Yes?"

"Your husband came to me the other night, looking for something, um, unusual."

Oh. That's why he's calling. It's not to proposition her. Or at least not directly. Maybe Dean is taking a more indirect approach. "Just tell me, Dean."

"I don't have all the details, but I can probably get them, if you want."

"I'm sure I will."

NEW YORK CITY

He forces himself to stare at . . . at what? at his shoes? the back of the guy's neck in front of him? No. More natural, he needs to find something else to stare at, a good-looking woman is what he should ogle, there, on the adjoining queue in a different boarding group, short skirt and high heels, too lip-glossed, too tacky, but whatever: he'd rather people think he's a leering creep with bad taste than a fugitive.

His boarding pass is tucked into the passport with a name and ID number that all belong to someone else, someone who's not being hunted. Or at least that's what Will hopes. He has never before used this fake passport—*any* fake passport. Maybe that Canadian tweeker has already reported it stolen? Or maybe he got arrested, convicted of a crime, his travel documents voided. Maybe it wasn't a real passport to begin with. Or maybe it's the other guy who betrayed Will, Mr. Ramones who sold him the passport in the dive-bar backroom in Bed-Stuy. Maybe *he* got arrested, and opted to trade his secrets for a reduced sentence.

Maybe Will himself is about to get arrested right now, at an airport gate.

He hands his documents to the gate agent, his heart racing, racing, *racing.* She glances down at the passport, at the photo, up at Will's face.

He can actually hear his heartbeat thudding in his ears. Can she?

She puts the boarding pass down on the scanner, presses down to flatten the thermal paper's bar code, and Will waits to hear the pleasant beep, the nice soft sound that's coming from the adjoining station as the tanned woman passes, tossing Will a small smile, but instead of the nice beep he gets the deep buzz, the wrong-answer noise familiar to anyone who has ever seen a quiz show—

Oh damn, this is it, the alarms about to start blaring, the lights strobing, the SWAT team rushing in, weapons raised—

33

"Thanks again for taking care of this so quickly," Elle says, pulling the door closed behind her. She looks around Raji's sad little apartment, the pleather furniture, the humongous TV, the absence of any decoration of any sort hanging on any wall, the empty beer bottles that are arrayed on the kitchen pass-through, like troops defending a citadel. "Sorry about the hour."

"It is not a problem, you are the client, my job is to service you. Did you have a good dinner?"

"Yeah, it was fine." It was revolting. "Thanks for the suggestion."

Elle had noticed these bottles when she'd dropped off the disk drive, an hour ago. She'd decided to buy replacements, whose plastic bag she hoists now. "I come bearing gifts." While she puts the six-pack on the kitchen counter, she can hear Raji in the other room, the creaking of his desk chair, the clacking of his keyboard.

Elle uses a handkerchief to extract the cardboard container from the bag. Then she folds the plastic bag, puts it in her pocket, along with the handkerchief and her hands. She doesn't want to touch anything here. Keeping her hands in her pockets is a good way to avoid touching things. Plus she's wearing Band-Aids on the tips of her thumbs and forefingers.

"So Raji, tell me: what did you find?"

She can tell by his face that the news is not good.

"I am sorry to say that if the records are here, they are extremely well disguised."

"You're positive you've understood what I'm looking for?"

"You are looking for files that were created or updated by Malcolm Somers, files that might contain records of aliases that match up with other names, or that match names with monetary amounts, or that match names with any numbers that could conceivably be monetary amounts, or that match names with locations."

"And you've found nothing whatsoever like this?"

"No. Furthermore, I have found no files *at all* created or updated by Malcolm Somers."

"None?"

"None."

"That doesn't make sense. Is it possible that Somers doesn't actually have any files on his computer? Or on the server?"

"Yes. But what is *not* possible is that he would not have a folder. Here, let me show you."

Elle leans down, looks over the guy's shoulder at the screen.

"Do you see this organizational tree? These branches? Those are departments within the magazine. Editorial, design, pro—"

"I get it."

"Within each branch, the names of individual users. People."

"Yup."

"Here, freelancers. Here, archive."

"My God, archive is a big branch. *Huge*."

"Yes. Those folders contain files that have not been altered in three years, after which all files automatically migrate to archives. There are thousands of folders in that branch, representing any personnel who have ever created a file for this organization, since the advent of digital files, in 1988. There were very few back then, do you see, here?"

"Yes."

"This man, Malcolm Somers, he has been working for this organization for a decade?"

"That's correct." Her mind is racing to catch up with the likely explanation.

"Yet he has no folders," Raji continues. "None active. None archived."

"What can that mean?"

"Two possibilities. One is that for some reason he does not maintain files, and has asked his administrator to remove the folders with his name, folders that probably would have been generated automatically with his employment. So these folders—one for active, one for archives—would need to be manually deleted by someone with administrator privileges."

"What's the other possibility?"

"That the folders do exist on the server, but are not here on this external drive."

"Is it possible that this drive would fail to duplicate these folders, if they existed?"

"No."

"So the only way that those folders are not here is if they were deleted?"

"Correct. Either deleted directly from the mainframe source, or deleted from this drive after they were duplicated."

"Is there any way to tell which?"

"With a high degree of certainty, I can say that the folders were deleted from this drive after they were duplicated." Raji opens a new window, gibberish, strings of numbers. "Do you see this line?"

"Yes."

"That means that the drive completed its duplication at 14:09:51 today. And this?"

"Yes."

"That means that something was moved to the trash, and the trash emptied, at 16:20:11. This was an active function, initiated by a user. By a human being." Raji turns from his screen, looks at Elle. "Whoever was in possession of this drive at four-twenty this afternoon? That is the person who deleted the Malcolm Somers folders, and any files within."

That duplicitous bastard.

"And do you see this line?" He points at the screen again. "This means that before the data was moved to the trash, it was first copied to a different external device."

Huh? Will Rhodes copied the files and then deleted them? What the hell is he up to?

"But the files are not on this drive," Raji says. "I am sorry."

"It's not your fault."

None of this is his fault, poor guy. The entire operation has hinged on Raji's work, and he never knew it, and never will. Elle needed access to the satellites and databases and vast networks of nonstop surveillance of the American populace, which was not something she could arrange without the participation of a substantially plugged-in institution.

So the operation didn't really hinge on Raji himself; he's not a uniquely qualified individual. But his employer is a highly qualified outfit, and Raji is a uniquely disposable individual. He has been Elle's sole point-person since the inception of the project, working under the very specific, abundantly explicit mandate that he be the only person in his office with access to the operational details. Because although Virginia Data Associates takes great pride in its ability to gather secrets, and keep them, even VDA would have to comply with a court order, should it ever arrive. By keeping the VDA loop limited to just one person, Elle was simplifying the mitigation of that eventuality.

Raji is also the only person at VDA who has ever seen Elle.

"Your boss doesn't know anything about this, right?"

"About what?"

She points at the external drive. "These duplicated files."

"Absolutely not."

"Does he know anything about any of it, Raji?"

"Only the broad strokes: that I have been tracking the expenditures and movements of a small population of interconnected American citizens."

"Anything more specific than that?"

He's getting nervous. "Why do you ask?"

"Just to prepare my report. I didn't find what I'm looking for, and I'll need to explain why. But don't worry, my report won't reflect badly on you."

He doesn't look convinced.

"I promise, Raji. You've done a terrific job. But I do need to know if anyone else is aware of any sensitive details. I'm sure you understand."

Raji looks down. "I did consult my supervisor, but just one time. It was about that woman who took an undocumented trip to Italy when she seemed to be pretending to be in Turkey. Chloe Rhodes."

"Why?"

"I needed help. Although I'd figured out that the woman hadn't stayed in Turkey, I didn't have the personal bandwidth to spend the necessary time reviewing raw footage—*vast* amounts of footage, none of it high-quality, nor fresh—to find out where she *had* gone. Not without sacrificing all my other surveillance."

"So what did you do?"

"I requisitioned a team of freelancers. They reviewed the entire day's worth of footage from every available camera in the airport."

"What background information did they have?"

"Nothing. Just a picture of her face. They didn't have a name, an alias, a passport number, nothing. They were merely looking for a woman—here's what she looks like, please find her in the Istanbul airport, then tell me. That's it."

"And you're the one who tracked her to Capri?"

"Correct."

"So none of these freelancers—and your boss—none of them know anything specific?"

"That's right."

"Wow. I *really* appreciate your discretion, Raji. Great work." She turns toward the kitchen. "You want that beer now? I sure could use one myself."

"Yes, thank you." Raji starts to get up, but she stops him. "Please, it's my turn to do something for you." She walks to the counter. She removes two bottles with twist-off tops, which she twists off, puts the tops in her pocket.

From another pocket, Elle removes a tiny glassine bag that contains a single pill, small and white and seemingly benign, like any other prescription medication that someone might take to control hypertension or anxiety, for pain or allergies, to treat an infectious disease or prevent an unwanted pregnancy; the average American spends a thousand dollars per year on pharmaceuticals.

But this pill is different. The average American can't get a prescription for it, can't purchase it at a pharmacy, can't be reimbursed for it by any health-insurance plan, can't even buy it from the friendly neighborhood drug dealer.

Elle drops this harmless-looking little pill into one of the bottles.

NORTH ATLANTIC OCEAN

Will doesn't have his sleeping pills, on which he normally relies to knock him out on these red-eyes to Europe. And he doesn't want to put any liquor into his system. So his body is filled with unadulterated adrenaline, his imagination buzzing, keeping him alert, awake.

The loud horrible noise at the airport gate turned out to be nothing more than the exit-row protocol. But it nearly gave him a heart attack, and it takes hours for him to fully calm down. It's not until halfway across the Atlantic that he manages to pass out.

Then he awakes with a startle, just west of Ireland, his brain unwilling to accept sleep.

He retrieves the two old *Travelers* issues, whose archives were eradicated to prevent the casual observer from uncovering their secrets. Will is almost positive that the secret buried in November 1994 is that Jonathan Mongeleach is currently living in Scandinavia.

And what of May 1992? Will is pretty sure that the salient item is a one-page profile of Jean-Pierre Fourier, the man who opened the very first overseas bureau of *Travelers* in Paris back in 1949, on the occasion of his retirement, which coincided with his seventieth birthday, as well as the collapse of the Soviet Union. Monsieur Fourier had lived in the same apartment on the Île St-Louis for nearly his whole life, and he was planning on dying there. Which, as of last year, when he gave a quote to *Le Monde* for an article about elite hotel concierges, hadn't yet happened.

PORTLAND

"I have good news and bad news," he says. "Which do you want first?"

Chloe glances around at this restaurant, which looks like half the restaurants in Brooklyn, with all the handcrafted this and fusion that.

"This woman who claims to be Will's C/O? She doesn't work for the CIA."

Chloe assumes that this unsurprising revelation is what he means by good news, says "Okay" without any enthusiasm.

"But she did."

"When did she leave?"

"Well, she didn't *leave*, exactly. But her association, ah, self-terminated."

"Huh? What happened?"

"Here's the thing: she *died*. KIA, Libya, five years ago."

RESTON

Elle takes a sip from the beer in her right hand, extends the one in her left toward Raji, holding the bottle by its neck with the Band-Aided tips of her fingers.

"Again," he says, "I am sorry."

She takes a seat a few feet away from him. "Can I ask you a question, Raji?"

"Of course."

"Who is it you think you work for?"

"I work for Virginia Data Associates."

"Yes, but what do you think VDA is?"

His face is blank.

"Do you think it's a privately held company? Family owned? A subsidiary of a publicly traded corporation? A government contractor?" It doesn't make any difference what Raji thinks, but Elle is curious, and this will be her last chance to find out. "I guess what I'm asking is: who's benefiting from your work, Raji? Is it private profit? Or public good?"

He smiles shyly. "I have always sort of assumed that VDA is an arm of the NSA. Or perhaps the CIA."

There are plenty of Americans who have reason to think they might be working for their government—bodyguards for State Department personnel in Latin America, foot soldiers in the Middle East, data analysts in the D.C. suburbs—but aren't. This is another effect of the post-9/11 obsession with antiterrorism: untold billions funneled from taxpayers through the government to private contractors that employ the sorts of people who are drinking beer in this sad little apartment, clueless techs and cold-blooded mercenaries.

She takes another sip of beer, but doesn't say anything.

"Am I right?"

He's not. But she could see why he misunderstood. Because from any angle, VDA looks like it performs the types of functions that Americans would assume are the province of their government—that is, if Americans expect their government to monitor their travel, their phone calls, their text messages, their emails, their social-media interactions. To spy on them, in the name of national security. That doesn't seem like the type of domestic surveillance that would be entrusted to the private sector.

"Yes," she says. There's no reason to disabuse him. He beams back at her, proud.

Elle had researched Raji thoroughly before handpicking him to be her point person on this job. His personnel file at VDA didn't offer any especially useful information; it's amazing how slapdash the screening process can be. But Elle was diligent, and followed the trail of Raji's bank transactions to a hospital, to a cardiology practice, to a pharmacy, after which it wasn't difficult to figure out what was wrong with his heart, the type of preexisting medical condition that a job candidate certainly wouldn't divulge in a human-resources interview or questionnaire, nor something that would be detected in a routine employer-mandated urine test, whose primary concern is illegal drugs.

But Elle found it. It's important to have an exit strategy.

She holds up her beer, reaches across the arm of the sofa toward his outstretched hand, clink. "Cheers."

"Cheers." Raji smiles, pleased, working for the CIA, he knew it all along.

"You know what, Raji?"

He looks at her, has no idea what's coming.

"I think we should get drunk. What do you say?"

There's no way this man is going to say no, with his video-game library and his spare tire and his web cache filled with porn. He takes another long drink, the dissolved pill cascading into his stomach, where it'll take a minute or two to start being absorbed into his bloodstream. Then it'll be another minute for the blood to be pumped through the entire circulatory system, to the heart.

Raji puts his empty bottle down. He stands. "You ready for another?"

Elle nods.

He disappears into the kitchen. She can hear the two new bottles knocking together as he removes them from their cardboard packaging, then the fizz as he opens one of caps.

"*Aah,*" he says. "*Owww.*"

She should call out something like "Are you all right?" But he's not. And there's no reason to pretend, not anymore.

She jumps in her seat as one of the bottles crashes to the floor, then the other.

"*Ooooh.* I, uh—"

Everyone likes to imagine that what he or she is doing is noble, is good for humanity, for the planet. The parasitic bankers who congratulate themselves on their supposed creation of wealth, the health-insurance execs who pretend that their private jets aren't paid for by the premiums of struggling wage-earners.

Elle has a hard time justifying herself, a hard time sleeping. Tonight is going to be particularly bad. Long ago she resolved to try to banish the good-bad dichotomy from her awareness; that she was living in an awful world; that she was merely surviving till the end of her time in it; that if it wasn't her who did terrible things, it would only be someone else. The terrible things would still get done.

Elle looks around, scanning surfaces, double-checking that she didn't touch anything except the bottles, which she'll take with her, shatter far away. And the caps and bag, already in her pocket. And of course this worthless external drive, which she'll also be bringing with her, presenting to someone else. How the hell is she going to explain this colossal failure?

She hears a loud thud from the kitchen. It must be Raji toppling, and something hard—an elbow? his skull?—hitting the floor.

Glass crunching.

"*Aaaahhh.*"

Labored breathing.

She's relieved that this is happening in the other room, that she can sit on this cheap couch, not watching an innocent man experience severe cardiac arrest on the linoleum floor of his dingy kitchen.

This is how she describes it to herself, in her head: simplifying the mitigation of a disadvantageous eventuality.

It will take only a minute for Raji to die, from a cause that will appear to be completely natural, perhaps even inevitable.

PORTLAND

"Thanks for the info," Chloe says.

"What are you going to do?"

"I don't know. I think I'll travel for a bit."

"Do you want to tell me—?" The look on her face cuts off his question. "No," he says, "I guess not."

"Listen, I'll see you in the office in a couple of weeks, probably. Thanks again. This is a big help."

He turns to leave, takes a couple of steps, then turns around. "Oh by the way." He walks back until he's just a foot away from Chloe, and speaks very softly: "I just wanted to tell you: that was *nice* work in Italy. Very nice."

She's too surprised to respond. She didn't think anyone would discuss this. She didn't even think anyone would know.

"Really impressive how you managed to hide what you needed to hide without going to the trouble of hiding it. Brilliantly done."

She'd wanted it to take the Capri police as long as possible to find Taylor Lindhurst's body. Not merely so she'd have time to escape—to flee Italy, to clean her identity through Istanbul, to get back to America—but also to ensure that the crime would be infinitely harder to solve, with witness memories no longer fresh, with any physical evidence compromised or obliterated, with her own trail gone completely cold.

"No one in the office can believe it was your first. Was it really?"

Chloe fights back a smile; it seems gauche to gloat about this sort of compliment. She nods.

"Well," he says, "it looks like you're a natural."

PART

V

34

The Île St-Louis is just a few short blocks wide and a handful of blocks long. Some dozens of businesses, a couple hundred buildings, maybe a few thousand residents. This shouldn't be hard.

Will is exhausted but also wired. He stops at a café, pretends to read the newspaper, chitchats with the waiter, pays his bill with a forced cheerful *"Merci, monsieur!"*

"Merci à vous," the waiter answers, unenthusiastically. It's early morning on a weekday, very few customers, no one ordering anything more expensive than coffee. He'd had a long day already before he earned his first tip, which wasn't even a full euro.

"Monsieur, une question, s'il vous plaît? Parlez-vous anglais?"

"Bien sûr." The waiter drapes a dishrag across his shoulder.

"I'm looking for a man who used to work for the same magazine I do. It's called *Travelers*, it's an American magazine. Have you heard of it?"

The waiter looks like he didn't entirely understand the question.

"Anyway, this man I'm looking for, he's quite old, *quatre-vingt quinze*. He lives here on the Île St-Louis. His name is Jean-Pierre Fourier."

"Jean-Pierre? Fourier?"

Will is trying not to let hope get the better of him. This would be too easy. The waiter squints, as if searching his memory. Will slips a twenty-euro note onto the tray. The waiter picks up the tray, folds the bill carefully, puts it in his pocket. Then says, "I am sorry, *monsieur, mais non."* He shakes his head. "Ask Madame Bouchardeau, at the *épicerie*. She is working here forty, fifty years? She is knowing everyone on *l'île*."

Five minutes later, Will is confronting a clerk who's shaking his head. *"Je suis désolé, monsieur."* Apparently, Mme. Bouchardeau will not arrive until midafternoon; the clerk is unwilling to specify what hour exactly. Mme. Bouchardeau is old, her hours cannot be predicted. Nor her moods for strangers with questions.

Will wanders the streets of the neat little island, the Seine at the end of every street, views of Notre Dame. He looks at doorbells, but that's hopeless, or nearly so. He asks at the ice-cream shop, the brasserie, the wine shop, the cheesemonger. Some people have heard of M. Fourier; others know him personally. But no one knows where he lives.

NEW YORK CITY

"Hey, have you heard from Will?"

Gabriella looks up at her boss, away from her desk, a red pen poised above an article that's too long. She's trimming it down line by line, sometimes character by character. Every day she comes to the office and edits for space—cutting a sentence here, an adjective there, tighten the kerning on this line, boom, done, next.

"No, I haven't." She leans away from her print-magazine problem, considers her boss, this other problem. Problem after problem. "When's the last you heard from him?"

"Yesterday late morning. He was headed down to art. Haven't seen or heard from him since. He wasn't at the ed. meeting, then we were supposed to get a drink, and he blew me off. Not answering texts or calls."

That really doesn't sound like Will. "Did you try Chloe?"

"Not yet. They're, uh . . . She left him."

"Really? Why?"

"That's not clear to me. Do you know anything about it?"

"No. You need to call her, Malcolm. Or do you want me to do it?"

"You're right. I'll do it."

"You worried?"

"Definitely."

"About?"

He chuckles uneasily. "About everything. Okay"—he raps on the door frame—"thanks Gabs."

PARIS

Will's fingers keep finding the flash drive in his front pocket, and his mind keeps jumping to the one in the rear, the one he loaded yesterday afternoon, after his Prospect Heights sojourn to collect back issues from Bernie Katz. When Will returned to Midtown, he took an extra lap around the block, killing time to arrive at 4:05, by which point the weekly editorial meeting would be under way. He didn't want to run into anyone.

He followed the complicated protocol he'd memorized the night before, via instructions he'd tracked down on the web. He opened the external drive. Scanned through the folders, found Malcolm's files, and moved them from Elle's large device onto his own small drive. He didn't know what was going on between *Travelers* and the CIA, and until he figured it out he wasn't going to help, or harm, either.

The file titles were all named according to company guidelines. He opened a few—old articles and research notes, photographs and expense reports. Almost none of the files had been altered recently, except Malcolm's monthly front-of-book letters.

Will's attention was caught by a folder with spreadsheets, all of them titled oddly: beginning with a pair of uppercase letters followed by a long string of numbers in groups of four, separated by spaces. These file titles had anywhere from sixteen characters up through maybe thirty. This was a familiar-looking pattern, but Will couldn't place it.

He opened one of these files, found two columns. One was clearly dates; the other seemed to be currency amounts.

The same sort of thing was in a second file. And a third.

Will opened a dozen files, each containing two columns: dates and figures. Some of these spreadsheets had only a few lines, dating back a couple of years; others had hundreds of entries, going back decades.

These had to be financial records.

Will turned his attention to the file titles. They all started with a pair of letters, ES, GB, IL, GE, TR, CH . . .

Country codes! These were country codes. For what? Phone numbers? No, phone numbers would start with dialing codes. These had to be banking codes: IBAN numbers. Which meant that this was a record of bank accounts. And these bank accounts had to belong to people who were being paid by *Travelers*.

There were accounts in every country where *Travelers* maintained a bureau, but also in countries where the magazine had no presence. There were of course accounts here in FR, the headquarters of Europe. But as far as Will knew, only two people worked in the magazine department of the Paris bureau, with another three downstairs at the travel agency. But here were a few dozen FR accounts, many being paid on a regular basis.

Who were all these people?

He's sure that one is the old man who lives here, on this island. But no one seems to know where exactly. Until someone does. "*Oui, oui, certainement. Là-bas*"—it's Will's lunchtime waiter, pointing past the church. "*Sans doute.*"

Will pays the check in a hurry. He finds the doorbell—*Fourier!*—and buzzes. He forces patience upon himself, waits a full minute before he buzzes again. It's an old man, Will reminds himself, who might take a long time to get to the intercom.

No answer, again.

Will buzzes a third time.

The door to the street opens. It's an old woman. "*Oui?*"

"*Bonjour. Je cherche Monsieur Jean-Pierre Fourier.*"

The woman says nothing.

"Do you know Monsieur Fourier?" Will continues, lapsing into English.

"*Oui. Il était mon père.*"

In his excitement, Will doesn't notice the tense of her verb. "Could I speak with him? It's important."

She crosses her arms.

Will reaches into his pocket, removes a business card. "I work for *Travelers.*"

She examines the card.

"I'm trying to find a friend, a colleague of your father's. I was hoping he might help."

"I am sorry," she says. "But my father, he is dead."

NEW YORK CITY

Malcolm tries Chloe's cell again, straight to voice mail. This time he leaves a message. "Hey, Chloe, it's Malcolm. Sorry to hear that you and Will are, um . . . having a disagreement. But listen: Will has been AWOL for twenty-four hours, and I'm worried. Could you give me a call?"

He pockets the phone, looks out the car window. Literally everything is wrong here. The derelict Brooklyn street looks more like Baghdad in wartime than a New York that's enjoying the lowest crime rates and highest property values in recorded history. On this particular block, crime is high, and property is worthless.

Malcolm walks around to the rear of the condemned house. He descends into the basement, past the stoic guard, through the door.

Here's the man who's been missing from his life for a day. This man is no longer bound to the chair, and he has used his freedom to retreat to the far corner, where he's sitting on the floor, leaning against the masonry wall. He has been allowed to use the portable bathroom in the backyard; he has been given water and food; he is uninjured, physically. So far.

The man looks up as Malcolm enters, closes the door. Malcolm turns a chair around to face the man, takes a seat. "Your name is Timothy Dunne?"

The man nods.

"You're from Nashville?"

"Yes." Tears spring from his eyes.

A thorough search using the guy's fingerprints and Social Security number yielded a completely viable biography, one that matches the guy's claims in every detail. If this man is not actually who he's claiming to be, he has a remarkable legend and is a spectacularly skilled operative, one whose proficiency wouldn't be wasted on an operation so absurd. Certainly not within the borders of the United States, against a domestic target.

"Timothy Dunne from Nashville, you've gotten yourself into a bad situation."

"I know." He's obviously trying to control his crying, to contain his abject terror, but he's failing. "I'm sorry. But seriously, aren't *you* the one who hired me?"

Malcolm hasn't given this guy a chance to speak on his own behalf until now; he didn't want to hear the shit until he'd gotten at least a broad understanding of the bull's identity.

"That's simply not true, Timothy."

The guy now starts crying freely, floodgates wide open.

"Don't fall apart here, Timothy Dunne. I need you to hold it together." Malcolm is trying to sound encouraging and menacing at the same time. It's a tightrope. "You're going to tell me exactly what happened. From the beginning."

Timothy is nodding, wiping tears away from his cheeks, snot from his nose, a blubbering mess. "I came to New York six years a—"

"No, not the beginning of your whole adult life." In truth, Malcolm feels halfway bad for this guy. But now's not the time to show it. "How'd this, uh, situation with my wife start?"

"I'm an actor. I answered an ad in the trades, for a part in an indie film. 'Good-looking man,' the notice said. 'Late twenties to late thirties.' It was a woman holding auditions. She said her name was Nancy? I guess that's not her real name."

Malcolm rolls his eyes.

"There were a lot of us, open casting. I saw a few guys I knew."

"This was where?"

"Hotel suite, Theater District. My audition was five minutes, small talk, read a few lines. I filled out some paperwork. The film was going to be shot in Toronto, overseas travel, so the producers needed to make sure any actors were American taxpayers, with valid passports, whatever. There were forms."

Why? Why get a bunch of strangers' signatures and Social Security numbers and passport numbers? It must've been to do credit checks. And background checks. Assessments of financial stability, criminality. Looking for the right sort of candidate.

"You ever been convicted of a crime, Timothy?"

"Um . . . no."

"You sure?"

"I didn't say I've never been *arrested*. Down in Tennessee . . . it was complicated."

"Isn't it always? But I bet you can simplify it."

"I was arraigned on extortion charges. Really just a misunderstanding. I cooperated, pled out to misdemeanor."

So Timothy was a punk.

"That's when I left Nashville. Came to New York."

"Uh-huh. So, Timothy, back to the future: you got the part?"

"Yeah, I did. But work wouldn't be starting for another month."

"What did you do in the meantime? Any contact with this Nancy woman?"

"I kept my day job. Celebrated a bit. This was a big deal for me, my first film role. I've been in New York for six years, trying to do this . . . to act. Do you have any idea how hard it is? How many people come here to try this?"

"Yes, it's a well-known predicament. Did you start spending this money?"

Timothy nods. "The job was going to pay a thousand dollars per day, for probably ten days of shooting. That's a lot of money for me."

"Uh-huh."

"After a couple weeks she got back in touch, set another meeting. Now she told me something completely different: there was no film. She wasn't even a film producer. She was a private detective. Her client wanted to do something dicey, though not illegal, not really. This job would pay twice as much as the nonexistent acting role, and it would be easier. She wouldn't tell me exactly what I'd have to do until I accepted the job, signed a contract with an NDA, took some money."

This was brilliant. She set him up with the expectation of money, she made him count on it, then she took it away, while also promising more.

"I tried to get assurances that it wouldn't be violent—I'm not violent. I was in a bad spot. I'd already spent some of the money, I really needed it. She showed me an envelope with five grand in cash, tax-free. Right there in the room, for me to walk out with."

"So you accepted."

He nods. "The scheme was that her client was a rich man who wanted a divorce, but there was an ironclad prenup. The only way to void it was to catch the wife committing adultery."

"I see. So your job was to seduce my wife?"

Timothy's eyes widen again. "I'm sorry, man. I didn't know."

"Didn't know *what*?" Malcolm shakes his head. "Listen, don't try to justify yourself to me. Just tell me what happened, okay?"

Timothy nods.

"So how'd this work?"

"Another help-wanted. An advertising trade magazine. *Ad World? Ad Age?* Something like that. I guess it was a notice tailored to attract, um . . . what should I call her?"

"Who, my wife? What do you think your choices are?"

"Mrs. Somers? Allison? Your wife?" Timothy is obviously worried that making the wrong decision is going to get him hurt. "So she, um . . . Allison . . . had just met with a career counselor? And she'd taken out a subscription for this magazine, *Ad Whatever.* She was obviously looking to restart her career, which I'd guess she'd put on pause to, um . . ."

"To raise our children?"

"Yeah. So she responded to this ad, and we set up an interview."

"You used an office?"

"No, we met in a hotel. Not like a *hotel* hotel, but a hotel's coffee shop. A *nice* coffee shop. I was a headhunter, the type of person who meets in coffee shops, hotel lobbies. I told her she was a terrific candidate, but this position wasn't exactly right. But I was impressed with her, and I'd see if we could find something else. I let her dangle awhile."

"This was at your discretion?"

"No. It's what Nancy told me to do. Then I contrived to run into Allison, which supposedly jogged my memory about an opening. We met for drinks. Then lunch, where I told her that the position had already been filled, but I didn't cancel lunch because I really wanted to see her. That what I really wanted, more than anything . . . Do you really want to hear this?"

"I do."

"That I really wanted to see her again and again, every day. That I couldn't stop thinking about her . . . Listen, man, I really don't want to, um . . . *please* . . . I'm so, *so* sorry."

Malcolm waves it off. "Tell me about the thumb drive."

"Nancy said that in order to make absolutely sure that the prenup would be voided, her client needed to have his wife *admit* to infidelity. The husband knew that the wife kept a diary, electronic, which she typed on the computer in the home office." Timothy raises his eyes at Malcolm, asking if this is true. Malcolm shakes his head.

"Anyway, the computer was password-protected, and the client couldn't *ask* his wife for the password so he could snoop through her private shit."

"So you'd have to steal it."

"Right. I had to insert this thumb drive, wait ten seconds, and remove it. All the files would be copied. And that would be that."

"Was it?"

"Uh, yes, actually. When we met yesterday, I was all set to end it with her, to tell her that I'd crossed an unacceptable line, it was unprofessional, I could lose my whole career, et cetera. But I never got the chance."

"Why not?"

"She dumped me."

PARIS

"I'm so sorry, madame. When did your father die?"

"It was one month," says Mme. Fourier, with a resigned smile.

Will's heart sinks. Did someone kill this old man, to bury his secrets? "Was he very ill?"

"No, monsieur, he was very old."

"Did he happen to leave anything?"

"Of course. He left everything."

"I mean anything unusual; anything you wouldn't expect a man like him to have."

"I am surprised to find that he is having a mobile phone."

NEW YORK CITY

This backyard is as un-backyard-like as possible while still being a plot of land behind a house, which would be more accurately described as an ex-house. Malcolm didn't grow up wealthy—far from it—but there's a big difference between his working-class-suburb upbringing thirty miles east and this permanent-underclass urban hellscape here, ravaged by a half-century of abject poverty and drug epidemics, exacerbated by police brutality and its attendant backlashes, by the empty promises of pandering politicians and the irreversible trend of income disparity.

Alonso is out here smoking a cigarette, asks, "Want one?"

Malcolm shakes his head. Then changes his mind. "Actually, do you mind?"

Alonso knocks a smoke out of the pack, cups his hand over the lighter. Menthol, wow, that feels strange, and cigarettes are pretty strange to begin with.

"Thanks."

They stand in silence, both gazing out at the unmistakable arrangement of low-rise housing projects in the near distance.

"Where you from, Alonso?"

"Born in Mexico."

"Oh yeah? Where?"

"Campeche." Alonso spits. He's one of those recreational spitters, hocking up unnecessary phlegm every couple of minutes, as if to say, Hey, world, fuck you.

"That's the Yucatán, right?"

Malcolm suspects that Alonso doesn't want to make small talk with this guy who's his boss's boss's boss, this white guy doing strange shit to this other white guy, for something that doesn't seem to involve drugs or money. Alonso doesn't know what's going on, and doesn't want to.

"We're done here," Malcolm says, tossing the nearly finished cigarette. He's briefly afraid that his smoldering butt is going to start a fire, but that would be doing this place a goddamned favor. "Get rid of him," Malcolm says, "like we discussed."

PARIS

"No, I do not want it, certainly. I do not believe it is the phone of my father." She shrugs. "Keep it."

Will does. It takes a few minutes to revive the uncharged device at a small table in a crowded café, with a waiter who makes a big show of his forbearance for the American who needs an electrical outlet.

While Will waits, he uses an old pay phone near the restroom to try Chloe, yet again. She doesn't pick up.

"Hi," he says to the empty void of voice mail. "I miss you."

Will opens Fourier's flip phone, scrolls through the contacts. A dozen of them, most in Paris, except a number in New York City with a 347 area code, a relatively recently issued exchange. There's also a phone number in Iceland.

SCARBOROUGH

It's just a few minutes after the voice mail from Will—from an unrecognized number in Paris—that Chloe's phone rings again. This time she answers: "You're the last person I want to talk to."

"*Me?* What did I do?"

She turns away from the direction of her mother inside the shingled house, toward the bushes and trees, the obstructed view of the beach, the limitless ocean. "Don't give me that shit. You know exactly what you did."

"No I don't."

"Will told me."

"Told you? Will told you what?"

"You promised me, Malcolm. Promised you'd leave him out of it."

"And I have."

"Then what the hell was that new assignment you gave him?"

"Well, yeah, okay, I did do that. But seriously, Chloe, he doesn't know what that is. Far as he's concerned, that's just a new column, nothing more. I gave him a raise!"

"And the blonde? Who's that?"

Malcolm doesn't respond for a second. "Blonde?" Another silent beat. "Honestly, I don't know what you're talking about."

"And what's this shit about him being recruited?"

"*What?*"

Malcolm sounds legitimately surprised. Chloe almost believes him, but she can't. Malcolm is a professional liar. It's his actual job to lie—to the people he works with, the people he works for, his wife, his friends, everyone.

"You're telling me you don't know anything about this? About her?"

The wireless line is filled with a low static hum. Chloe wonders if Malcolm is trying to figure out whether or not to tell her the truth. Or maybe what he can say aloud, on the telephone.

"Mal?"

"Will hasn't been in the office since yesterday morning, Chlo. No one knows where he is."

She feels like she's going to throw up.

"No one has heard from him," Malcolm continues, explaining into Chloe's terrified silence. "He's not answering texts or calls." Making it worse and worse.

"He's not on assignment?" Chloe knows this is irrational, desperate. "Catching up on something old?"

"He was in the office yesterday, we spoke, he didn't say anything about going anywhere. We were supposed to have a drink. But he didn't show."

This is her worst nightmare: that her job will get her husband killed.

"I was going to tell him, Chlo. Bring him inside. *Last night.*"

"Tell him what?"

"Everything."

"About me?"

"No, everything else, but not that. That's your decision."

"Why? What happened, Mal?"

"I'm afraid we've been, uh, penetrated. Everything might be compromised."

Her fear turns to anger, as if one emotion says to the other, here, let me get out of your way: "You fucking asshole."

Malcolm doesn't defend himself.

"I put my life on hold, Mal. You know why?"

He still doesn't answer. She knows that he knows.

"Because I was worried that this is exactly what would happen. That you'd lie to me—"

"I didn't—"

"—and Will would end up lying to me, and my whole goddamned marriage would be ruined. My whole life, Mal."

This is why she'd been taking birth-control pills behind Will's back, unwilling to get pregnant while her husband was becoming immersed in the world of *Travelers*, and possibly drawn into all its ugly dangerous complications. She was worried that Will would get distorted, compromised. Worried even that he'd get killed, like Gabriella's husband: kidnapped abroad, held for ransom, murdered. At the time, Gabriella had just found out she was pregnant. The evening after Terrance's funeral, she suffered a miscarriage. Chloe sure as hell wasn't going to put herself through that. Certainly not for a job.

"Chloe, do you have any idea where he might be? I'm worried."

"Me too." But she doesn't think that telling Malcolm what she knows is going to be a solution; in fact, it might complicate the problem. So she says, "I have no idea where he is."

"You haven't heard from him?"

Chloe is halfway afraid she's walking into a trap here. Does Malcolm already know the truth? Has he been monitoring her cell phone?

"No," she says. "I haven't."

Chloe had tried to talk Will out of it, told him that if he joined *Travelers* she'd have to leave. So she did.

But she didn't leave the organization. She merely went to a different section, run out of a different office, with very different responsibilities.

35

"Hey boss?"

"Hi Stonely. Everything okay?"

"Uh, not really."

"Is it the guy?"

"No, boss, that's taken care of." The terrified kidnapped guy was dealt a perfunctory ass-whupping by that psychopath Alonso, then released on his own recognizance, with the promise of more serious violence unless he cooperated. "How do I cooperate?" he asked, through bleeding mouth.

"Disappear."

And to the guy's credit, that's what he did: packed his shit and got on a Greyhound bus. There was no guarantee he wouldn't be back, eventually, but Stonely suspected no one would care. Stonely certainly doesn't. Then again, Stonely doesn't know what the hell is really going on with this guy.

There's a lot Stonely doesn't know. He doesn't know why all the tight security for a magazine. Doesn't know why the secretive meetings with the boss. Doesn't understand the abductions and interrogations and break-ins—of their own staff. All Stonely knows is that these things are required by the boss. It's a very abstract concern, a generic version of the fundamental employment relationship.

It isn't completely satisfying to Stonely, being this much in the dark. But Stonely doesn't think that completely satisfying is a reasonable expectation. Even being a professional baseball player hadn't been completely satisfying. And here at *Travelers*, he has job security and health insurance, paid holidays and vacation, a 401(k) with matching contributions, no threat of physical injury, none of which was on offer in the minor-league system.

Almost everyone Stonely knows has a worse job.

◆ ◆ ◆

"No, boss," Stonely says, "it's something here in the office."

Oh good God, what now? Will has disappeared. Chloe has fled town and is lying to him. Allison got seduced by a guy who's trying to steal Malcolm's files. What the fuck else can happen?

"Yesterday, during the system's routine daily backup, someone copied all the files."

"All what files, Stonely?"

"All *our* files. Everything created by users here at *Travelers*, in every department. Including the archives."

"What? Who did this?"

"I don't know who, for certain. But I do know where: Will Rhodes's computer."

Stonely stands there, awaiting further instruction, but not asking.

"Okay Stonely, thanks. See you tomorrow."

Malcolm sits at his desk, head in hands, puzzling what this could mean, what he needs to do about it. Is it time to admit to his own boss that things have gotten out of control? What would happen to him?

He might be killed. And it might happen immediately. *Tonight.*

So no, that's not a great option.

He needs to try to solve this himself, quickly.

Malcolm unlocks the bookcase door, steps into the wall, shuts himself into the hidden office. He takes a seat at the narrow desk, and picks up the landline, hardwired to a dedicated line that falls through the wall cavity directly to the trunk in the basement, a line that's swept clean every week by a taciturn tech named Ivan, of all things.

Malcolm checks his watch. It's late, the first place he's calling. He's going to wake her up, which in a way is regrettable. But in another way it's not. It's sometimes useful to yank people from unconsciousness, to thrust them into a heightened form of consciousness, immediately hyperaware. Waking someone up sends a message, gets things done.

He dials the long number from memory, and waits a few seconds for the line to connect across the ocean.

She answers on the first ring.

PARIS

It's much later than Will intended. After he'd spent the better part of the day tromping around every inch of the Île St-Louis, his feet ached, his twisted ankle was swollen, his bruises were sore. He was unbearably tired. He found an hourly-rate hotel between Pigalle and the Gare St-Lazare, a tiny room facing an air shaft, a lumpy mattress on which he reclined, just for a few minutes, uninterrupted by any intrusion like turn-down service, devoid of street noise, a quiet cocoon in an unlikely location. A quick nap turned into a six-hour coma.

So now it's the middle of the night. Will has been standing in a deep doorway for fifteen minutes, watching the Paris bureau. No sign of life anywhere on this long quiet block.

He's wearing an oversize black cap with a stiff bill and a ridiculous logo, hiding not only his face but also disguising his personality; he looks like a thirty-something who's trying to look like a club kid.

His heartbeat quickens as he approaches the front door, keycard already out of his wallet, floating loose in his pocket. He waves the card against the surface of the reader, nothing.

He looks at the magnetic surface, waves the card again, and again, then remembers: he pushes the card flat against the reader. A click as the lock releases.

Through the door, up the grand staircase, around to the office door. He presses the button to release the second card reader, slides his card through the slot. Steps inside.

Alone in offices late at night, Will has always felt a little wrong, a sense of trespass, even in places where he belongs. Here, he feels even more wrong. He is.

Will strides to Inez's desk, takes a seat. His fingers hover above the lock's keypad, nervous. He's not sure how many chances he'll have to be wrong. Maybe none.

He'd practiced on the phone in his hotel room, hitting the touch-tone keys until he'd found the familiar-sounding sequence. He was reasonably confident that he'd narrowed it down to one of two possibilities, unsure of only the final note. But in truth he was unsure about the whole thing, worried that maybe his imagination had conflated the touch-tone sequence with the Pearl Jam phrase that he'd learned to pick on a guitar eighteen years ago.

He hits the first five notes with confidence, then pauses before the sixth. One or the other, 7 or 8. He hits 7.

It doesn't open. But neither does any alarm sound, not that he can hear.

He tries again, ending this time with 8.

Click.

He pulls open the drawer. His eyes scan the tabs, and he finds the files he wants.

Will removes one of them, opens it on the desktop, begins to copy information into his little notebook. For better or worse, there aren't that many contacts in this folder.

It's almost completely silent in here; he can hear his pen scratching on the paper.

And then something else, something louder, outside: a vehicle with a small motor. The sound grows louder, settles on a constant volume for a few seconds, then gets louder again, then dies.

What?

Will jumps out of the chair. A couple of strides to the window, a sidelong glance out to the street.

Damn.

What should he do? He doesn't want to steal these files—doesn't want their absence to be noticed—but he needs the information. Maybe Inez won't notice. Maybe her arrival is mundane: she lost her house key, and keeps a spare here in her desk. Or maybe it's New York who called her in, they need something—what? a photograph? an interview?—asap. Maybe she won't even open this drawer. Maybe this has absolutely nothing to do with him.

Will gathers his things, and some things that are not his: a couple of files, and, as an afterthought, Inez's extra-sharp letter opener.

Inez climbs off her Vespa, stows her helmet. She scans one way up the deserted street, then down the other. She yawns.

She lets herself in the front door. As she climbs to the *premier étage,* she thinks she hears a noise. She pauses, listening, turning her head this way, that, aiming her ears at who-knows-what.

Nothing.

She continues up the stairs, walking softer now, her heels making quieter clicks.

At the top of the stairs she pauses again. She looks both ways down the hall, a few closed doors, one lit sconce and two dark ones. She peers up to the second floor, back down to the ground floor.

She unlocks the door. She looks around, her vision flowing across the room, over surfaces, between pieces of furniture, to the windows, the chairs, the doors to the bathroom and kitchenette and coat closet and storage room. All looks correct.

Her large desk dominates the middle of the room, attracting clutter as if magnetically, pulling in piles of paper from the periphery. She powers on the computer. Punches in a keycode, reaches her right hand into the top drawer, plants her fingertips on the little scanner in there. On the monitor, a dialogue screen opens. She types in the first password, then another. The system admits her.

The first thing she does is locate Will Rhodes's personnel file. She prints out a few copies of his most recent contributor photo, full size, glossy paper, high quality. She looks through the other JPEGs in Will's folder, finds a profile shot, prints out copies of that too.

She checks the time. The others will start arriving soon.

Inez opens a different drawer, removes a toilet kit. At home she'd been too dazed to put herself together. But her day has now started, and she's going to be here for the next—who knows?—eighteen hours? She needs to brush her teeth, wash her face, apply some makeup. She doesn't want to look like she just rolled out of bed.

She steps into the bathroom and leaves the door open, because why wouldn't she?

It's an old door, big and heavy, six inset panels bordered by solid molding, brass hardware, a dented knob, a large figure-eight-shaped keyhole, which

Will looks through with one eye. He needs to move his entire head to change his angle of vision, watching feckless befreckled Inez carry what looks like a makeup bag to what must be the bathroom.

Will turns the knob slowly. Pushes the door gently, just wide enough to step through.

The sound of water running, a triangle of brighter light on the floor. She won't be able to hear him above the sound of the water, and he needs to take advantage of that, right this instant.

Will pushes the storage-closet door closed quickly, lets the lock engage. Rushes across the room, still careful not to clomp his feet, moving the purloined files from his right hand to his left, to facilitate opening the door and pulling it closed, but the handoff is not clean, and he drops the files.

He kneels, gathers the contents in an anxious rush, letter-size pages and three-by-five glossies, index cards, long folded-over sheets, fumbling, vibrating.

The sound of the water stops. A big glurp of a drip.

Will, crouched on the floor, looks over his shoulder. He doesn't know what he'll do if Inez emerges from that door.

He remains frozen, staring at the bathroom door. There's a shift in the triangle of light on the floor; she has moved in there.

Surely she's going to do something after the running-water task. What was that? Face-washing? Teeth-brushing?

He waits a second. Another. The light shifts again. But still no sound.

Will double-checks that the files are secure in his left hand. Stands up. It's only another couple of steps to the door. He lets his feet fall as gently as possible on the marble floor, rolling from heels to toes, as if blotting ink, careful not to smudge. He closes his hand around the knob, this one also brass, but smooth, undented, shiny, new.

Slowly, slowly. Silently.

A soft click as the lock disengages. He freezes, looks over his shoulder. Still nothing.

He pulls the knob. The door swings open silently. He takes a step, another. Pivots on his heel, pulling the door toward him now, closing it, but then he hears a different sort of click, and his eyes dart again to the bathroom door, where the triangle of light has suddenly disappeared—

He thinks he closed the door in time.

The office door opens, admitting Omar and Pyotr, "*Bonjour*" all around.

The two men live relatively near each other. Pyotr is the only one of the Paris bureau employees who's irrational enough to own a car, which does come in handy a few times a year, when on short notice Pyotr can give Omar a middle-of-the-night ride.

Pyotr busies himself in the corner, making a pot of coffee, a caffeine junkie.

Omar takes a seat across from Inez, leafs through yesterday's newspaper.

Then Parviz arrives, yawning, an explosion of bed-head hair and crooked eyeglasses and disheveled clothing, followed eventually by utterly fastidious Yang.

They all gather around Inez's desk, pulling chairs, rubbing eyes. It's 3:04 A.M.

"Okay," Inez says in English, "thank you all for coming so quickly." She distributes the photos to the assembled tech team. "This is Will Rhodes."

She's more than willing for anyone who visits to think that she's the secretary here, knows nothing, just the girl who hands out info packets that were put together by someone else, someone smarter, someone more important.

But there isn't any such someone. These four data techs all report directly to Inez. As does Barry, her American assistant here in Paris, as well as the chiefs of the eight other European bureaus, and by extension the vast network of hundreds of freelancers—train-station gypsies and tourist-spot panhandlers, taxi drivers and border functionaries, hotel concierges and crooked cops—who provide piecework information to the *Travelers* network in exchange for fifty euros here, a hundred quid there, a get-out-of-jail pass every now and then.

Inez is not the secretary, she's the director of European operations.

"Last night, Will Rhodes did not board his scheduled flight from New

York City to Maine. This afternoon, he left a voice-mail message for his wife, from a pay phone on the Île St-Louis. He is here. He is in Paris." She jabs a forefinger on Will's photograph. "Go find him."

Will is halfway down the stairs when he hears the front door opening again, the voices of two men. He spins on his heels, dashes up the stairs.

What the hell is going on? Are these colleagues of Inez? Or is it possible they're unconnected, going someplace else in this building, in the middle of the night?

No.

Will rushes down the hall, trying other door handles, but none open. He looks up the staircase. He has never been up there, has no idea.

Heels on the stairs, one of the men muttering something in French, indecipherable to Will, but getting louder.

He runs up the stairs.

There's a window at the landing between the floors, not a large window, but large enough. He pulls the brass latch. There's a small ledge out there. A downspout from the gutters. The ground is twenty-five feet below.

Not this again.

The voices grow louder.

Will removes his small backpack, tucks the purloined paperwork inside. He hops up on the sill, climbs out. As he's pulling the window closed behind him, he realizes he won't be able to engage the latch. If the men come up this way, they'll notice the unlocked latch. Which means Will can't simply hide out here. He has to flee. And he has to do it quickly.

He swings his leg to the far side of the gutter, grabs hold of it. Is this length of pipe sturdy enough? Secured to the wall sufficiently?

His thighs grip the steel tube, his ankles push in. He shimmies down, knee bumping against the wall, wrist getting snagged on a bolt, pain atop pain, adrenaline rushing, his feet hitting the pebbled ground with a crunch, falling backward onto his ass, careful to keep his head from thudding into the ground, again.

That was a lot of noise.

He hops up, looks around. It's dark. He doesn't see a way out of the backyard, but there must be one. He walks the perimeter, hugging the walls, and here, a wooden door, a breezeway.

It's pitch-black. He waits for his eyes to adjust, but there's no light, nothing to adjust to.

He shuffles his feet, hopefully in the right direction, hands in front of him, groping blindly. He finds a wall, a corner, another facet, a door, a handle. He turns it, and pulls, and pushes, but it won't budge.

He runs his palms over the surface, finds the deadbolt. He slides it open. Finds the knob again, pulls again, nothing. Pushes again. That does it.

The streetlight seems massively bright, the flash of a nuclear bomb. He leans his head out the door frame, surveying the sidewalk—

Shit!

Will ducks back inside, pulls the door closed behind him. There's someone else walking up the street, another man, his footsteps approaching the door. Louder, and louder.

The man is right in front of the door. His footsteps slow.

Will reaches into his pocket, retrieves Inez's sharp letter opener.

The footsteps stop.

God, he really does not want to do this.

For an eternal second, there's complete silence.

Then the footsteps resume. Will hears the big heavy door of the building swing open, then closed, with shuddering.

That's a lot of people upstairs, in the middle of the night, at what Will had thought was a sleepy little irrelevant outpost. They're looking for him, they must be, he's sure about it. Do they know that they have already found him? And why they are looking to begin with? Do these people work for Malcolm? Or is it Elle? Is it the CIA? Or the other side—whatever the other side might be?

And who the hell is Will himself working for?

PORTLAND

Whenever the door opens, a stench wafts in from the fish market across the alley, ice in the gutter, gulls shrieking, fighting over scraps.

Chloe nurses her beer and chowder, thin and bland, improved only slightly with a sprinkling of broken-up oyster crackers. In a town filled with great places to eat, this isn't one. On the other hand it's refreshing to be away from the vacationers and weekenders, the khakis and tattersall shirts and corporate-logo'd fleece vests favored by the white-haired captains of industry and finance who occupy her mother's corner of Vacationland.

A different sort of man struts up to the stool beside her. Run-of-the-mill small-town hood, tattoo sleeve on the steroid-enhanced muscles that push his arms out in a simian arc. He's wearing cargo shorts, flip-flops, a battered Red Sox cap, a belligerent sneer. He doesn't want anyone to make any mistake about his temperament.

He up-nods at the bartender. "Draft."

The drink is delivered, overflowing its foam. The guy swallows half the glass in one pull, belches. " 'Scuse me." He looks around. Satisfied that he has sufficient privacy, he leans toward Chloe. "You the girl that called Danny about the thing?"

"I am."

"Hey, how ya doin'." He gives her a once-over, and she returns it with an are-you-kidding? look.

"So the boat leaves at four in the morning, down at the end of the pier."

"What's the name of the boat?"

"*Artemis.*"

"And the skipper?"

"Connor."

"Anything else you can tell me?"

"Whaddya wanna know?"

"What do I need to know?"

While he ponders this question, he takes another couple of gulps of beer. "If you're the type to get seasick, you're prob'ly gonna get seasick."

"Uh-huh. Anything else?"

"It's gonna be cold."

"Okay."

"That's about it," he says, then drains the rest of his beer. "Beer's on you."

What a charmer.

"Oh," he says, "one more thing. The two grand?"

"Yeah?"

"Cash only."

36

Elle emerges from the brightly lit Tube into the dim gray of Knightsbridge, dingy bricks and narrow sidewalks, quotidian Topshop and Boots interspersed with the extravagances of Harrods and Harvey Nichols, hotels and embassies, royalty and riffraff, the ever-present possibility of getting run over by a red double-decker bus hurtling from an unexpected direction. Those LOOK LEFT and LOOK RIGHT signs painted on the pavement have the opposite effect on Elle, they make her turn first in the other direction, the wrong one, obeying some involuntary reaction to potential deception, a pathological level of distrust that she suspects might one day get her killed.

At a shop window she stops abruptly, pretends to consider the selection of shoes. Countersurveillance is always at its most tiresome when she's in a rush. And it's always pretty tedious.

She turns back in the direction from which she came, scanning the crowd, looking for familiarity but finding none, unsurprisingly. She has been running this SDR for ninety minutes, in a taxi and three separate Tube lines broken up by a frantic walk through the suffocating morning-rush multitudes of the City, then of Fleet Street, a three-minute pause on the landing of the wide enclosed stairway from Farringdon Street up to the Holborn Viaduct, faded yellow bricks, iron handrails with chipped red paint. No one who was following her could've failed to pass her there in that stairwell, and no one passed her.

Plus all this rigmarole was after her train ride from Heathrow, and a transatlantic flight from Washington. There's no way that anyone has followed her. Enough already.

This particular bazillion-star hotel is bedecked in plush red carpets and gleaming marble and enormous flower arrangements, a gaudy display of perishability. A horde of dark-skinned uniformed staff cast oblique eyes in her direction, unmoving in their stoic stances of subservience, but not unobservant.

Elle feels like a hooker. Walking through a hotel lobby, carrying no luggage, she always feels at least a little like a hooker. Which in a way she is. There are many ways to be a prostitute, and Elle has been almost all of them.

The list of things Elle wishes she hadn't done is long, and continuing to grow. Icky things and stupid things and ill-considered things, as well as a few things—perhaps more than a few—that would be described by most people as very bad, as evil things. She's beginning to suspect that what she's been doing for the past few months might be an unparalleled amalgamation of many of the ways that an endeavor can be regrettable.

She finds the ladies' lounge, redolent of roses and cleanliness, soft music, a nice place to take a nap. She scrubs herself clean of the plane and the train and the city soot, attacks her hair with a brush and a barrette, applies blush and lipstick, mascara and rouge, a pair of cheap earrings that could pass as not, a scarf with a pattern that's recognizable to the sorts of people who know these things; the sorts of people you run into at a hotel like this. She tightens her belt and loosens her blouse, leans in to the mirror, examines herself. Yes, she thinks, I just got as younger, as skinnier, and as prettier as I can get.

The elevator attendant is wearing a costume-party-looking suit with big brass buttons, an outfit whose point seems to be to degrade everyone involved. "Your room please, madam?"

"I'm visiting the, um"—she consults her phone—"Park View Suite."

"Of course." The attendant nods, not in agreement. "And the name of our guest?"

"Um . . . Chuck Worth." That's not the guy's name. But like most obscenely rich or household-famous people, the man she's visiting uses an alias at hotels, for security. If you're coming to a hotel to see Angelina Jolie or Bill Gates or this guy, you're asking for someone else.

"Very well, madam."

At the end of a short hall, a security guard—a new face—stands at the suite's door. "You are?"

"His eleven o'clock."

"Your name?"

"Elle." She hasn't really used any other name in the past year. She's beginning to wonder if she ever will.

"I'm going to have to frisk you."

She gives this goon a wry smile, as if he'd just told a joke that she'd already heard a thousand times. "Don't you fucking dare."

One of the doors opens partway. Both Elle and the guard turn to the gap, the man saying, "It's okay, Walt. Let her in." He glances down at her handbag, big and black and stuffed with who-knows-what threat. "Though I'm going to have to ask you to leave your bag out here."

She shrugs it off her shoulder, and Walt takes it.

"But I need that thing that looks like a book," she says.

Walt opens the bag, locates the odd device, holds it aloft for his boss, who nods.

Elle enters the vast suite, giant windows with a view to Hyde Park, plush upholstery, a cocktail table covered in silver service and a pastry platter and a bowl of beautiful fruit, food that no one's going to eat, the incessant wastefulness that's heaped upon the ultrarich, all the time, everywhere they go, plied with things they don't need, don't want.

"Please," he says, "have a seat. Your phone?"

She pops out the phone's battery, leaves the two pieces next to the pastries.

"This drive"—she taps the device—"contains the files from the *Travelers* server that were duplicated during the system-wide backup."

"Excellent. Shall we take a look?"

"Not so fast. It contains all the files *except* those belonging to Malcolm Somers. His files—his folders—were deleted. From this drive. Almost certainly by Will Rhodes. Who appears to have copied the files before he deleted them."

The man stares at Elle. "He found us out."

"It looks that way."

"How?"

"I really have no clue."

"Is it possible he knew all along?"

"I don't think so, no. He's not that good of an actor."

"How do you know? Maybe he's been inside all along. Maybe he was inside before you recruited him. Have you considered that possibility?"

She had. Way back at the beginning, when this operation was being planned, when she could've chosen anyone at *Travelers* to exploit. She'd investigated all of them thoroughly. The deputy editor with the dead husband, the IT guy with immigration issues, the gay African-American food editor who's been writing an unpublished novel forever, the pompous art director.

The main thing she was looking for was financial weakness. Many people assume that spies, traitors, and double agents are all motivated by political convictions. Not so. The vast majority of espionage is committed for a very simple reason: money.

Will was motivated. He was more broke than he should've been, had gotten himself in over his head with an untenable—and pretty much irreversible—real-estate decision. But otherwise he was clean, a normal civilian with no connection to any intelligence services anywhere.

Elle knew that Will might end up being untrustworthy, might turn out to be useless. But he definitely didn't start off as a double agent. She was as certain of that as anyone could be about any asset.

Will's wife, though? She was a different story. But Elle's plan, by definition, excluded Chloe's involvement.

"Will Rhodes wasn't anyone's spy," she says. "Not until I recruited him."

"So what happened?"

"Either he became suspicious of us—"

"Of *you*."

"Of me. Or Somers is the one who became suspicious, and clued in Rhodes."

"Which do you think happened?"

"Does it make a difference?"

"Maybe not. But don't you want to know if it was you who screwed it up?"

Elle looks away.

"Okay," the man says. "I guess it's time to terminate this aspect of the operation."

"Well, that's not going to be simple."

"Oh? Why not?"

"We can't find Will."

"What do you mean?"

"I'm not sure how to make my statement more clear. Which part didn't you understand?"

The man smiles again, wide and bright and ready-made for television. "When did Mr. Rhodes disappear?"

"Right after he handed over the drive."

"Well then, that's certainly damning, isn't it?"

"I also can't find Timothy Dunne."

"Am I supposed to know who that is?"

"The man we hired to seduce Somers's wife, to copy the contents of his home computer."

"Ah. Do you think this Timothy Dunne has also disappeared? Or maybe you just can't locate him momentarily?"

It's remotely possible that Timothy is on a bender, a struggling actor who compromised his morals for cash, and has taken a bus down to Atlantic City to drink and gamble away his blood money till he has spent it all, and can return to his New York squalor and pretend that he's just another broke artist, hardworking and idealistic and deserving of the fame and fortune that elude almost everyone.

What seems more likely, though, is that Timothy was discovered by Somers. That Somers abducted the actor. That Timothy was tortured, or threatened with torture, and that he cracked quickly, spilled the truth about his end of the operation.

Which means that Malcolm Somers knows that someone hired a handsome dim-witted actor to seduce his wife in order to steal his electronic files. And thus that Malcolm Somers is now aware that his entire operation is being pried open from the outside.

But not necessarily from the inside. Would Somers suspect that the attack was two-pronged? One of the goals of the dual prongs was to make the other seem unlikely, in the event of one's discovery.

"Timothy can't be tied to me," Elle says, "much less to you."

The man shakes his head in disgust. "What an epic waste of time and money."

Elle can't deny this. When Timothy presented her with the flash drive a week ago, Elle popped the thing into her laptop, which thankfully was protected with some of the most advanced malware-detection technology on the planet. Which is how the computer recognized that the drive contained a worm that instantaneously infested her hard drive. Somers was apparently prepared for this sort of intrusion. Aggressively prepared.

"*Shit!*" she yelled.

She yanked the device out of the port, her mind racing through all the bits of information that could have been remote-transmitted in the course of the few seconds between when the device was inserted and when it was removed, all the disasters that could befall her because of this bit of unprotected computer sex. Even her safe house was probably compromised, her secure location unsecured. She'd have to move, immediately. She'd have to destroy the computer. Everything went wrong, all at once.

"It's true," she admits, "that tactic turned out to have been ineffectual. We always knew that it was a low-percentage play. But no stone unturned, right?"

"Yes. But the duplication of the files? That was our *boulder*. And it looks like not only was there nothing under it, but now it's rolling down the mountain. At us." The man leans forward. "So what do you propose to do about it?"

PARIS

"I have something!" Unsurprisingly, it's Omar who's first.

Inez gets up from the little desk in the corner, the spare workstation. All the techs have big desks filled with expensive digital equipment, but this little surface contains only an old laptop, and barely enough room for a mug of herbal tea and a notepad. She leans over Omar's shoulder, examines footage from a security camera. "Where is this?"

"Charles de Gaulle." Omar hits a button, moves the cursor, opens another window, another. "This is footage from an arrivals gate, this morning. Or it is not today anymore. Yesterday morning."

"What passp—?"

"One moment." Omar is hitting keys frantically, one camera after another tracking Will through the terminal, corridors, escalators, and finally the queue at passport control, the window. But no camera has a good enough angle on the passport itself.

"*Quel dommage*," Omar says, continuing to hit keys.

"We need to access the records," Inez says. "Find his alias."

Omar shakes his head. "*C'est pas possible.*"

"Do not say that," she says. "Of course it is possible."

Omar turns to look at his boss.

"It is possible," she reiterates. "You need to figure out how, Omar; keep working on this. Parviz, pick up the physical trail."

Inez walks over to the desk of the Iranian, boarding school in England, university in Germany, a graduate degree from the Massachusetts Institute of Technology. Parviz is the most formally schooled of her techs, but also the least disciplined personally, late and erratic, hungover and sleep-deprived, an owl who sets an alarm for midnight, goes dancing at 2:00 A.M.

"Here, he is getting into this taxi."

"Are you sure that is him?"

Parviz opens another window, another, images of Will. "Yes."

"Okay, let us move to the satellites."

Parviz opens another application, a pull-down menu, then a screen full of prompts to enter specific data. "This is going to take a few minutes."

LONDON

"Me?" Elle snorts. "I propose to do nothing about it. My participation in this op has reached its conclusion."

"You've got to be kidding me."

"Absolutely not. This is a bust."

There had already been a few near-misses. First was when the actual CIA interrogated Will in Dublin; the whole thing could have blown up then. Second was when Will was nearly pulverized by Russian thugs in Barcelona, which Elle doubts she could have prevented, even if she were willing to try. Third, the infected files from Malcolm's home computer. Fourth, this compromised external drive. In fact, the whole goddamned op has been one failure after another. Almost as if it's jinxed.

"It's time to cut and run before something disastrous happens."

"Something disastrous has already happened."

"Not to me it hasn't. Nor to you. What's the disaster? That you wanted to gather some inside dope about a company you want to buy, and it didn't work out?"

Elle knows that there's a lot more to it than this cover story about sublegal due diligence of a corporate merger. But she doesn't know what, exactly. She'd allowed herself to get sucked into something she didn't understand. Always a mistake.

"Why is that a disaster?"

He doesn't answer.

"Are you going to tell me what the hell is actually going on?"

"No. *Not* telling you is why I'm paying you a million dollars—"

"Technically, you haven't. Not yet."

"—plus expenses, which I might add have been considerable. To pay your partner Roger, to pay the rest of your team. Five full-time people, is it?"

"Four."

"Plus an uncountable number of freelancers. And this missing actor, what's his name? Timothy? And hotel rooms all over the world, and apartments in New York, and plane tickets and rental cars, and food and gas, and the huge fees to VDA."

"Expenses are expenses. None of that is money in my pocket."

"But you'll walk away with a million dollars."

"*If* I walk away. That becomes less certain if I start killing Americans as a matter of course."

"Killing Americans? Who said anything about killing anyone? I certainly didn't ask you to do that."

Elle's stomach does a somersault. Why would he issue a denial like that? Fuck, she thinks: has this guy been recording this whole conversation? He looks incredulous, but she can't tell if it's genuine incredulity or Captain Renault's version of moral outrage.

"Just kidding," he says. "Of *course* you need to kill Rhodes. You know you do."

It hadn't previously occurred to her that this guy was a psychopath, just a very successful sociopath. Does he really think it's a joke to *not* kill someone?

She has been in plenty of dicey situations in her life, and she's beginning to believe that this hotel room is another. Is it possible that this man is not only a psychopath, but one who's going to try to kill her? Now?

No, she thinks, not here. Not in an ultra-luxury hotel suite in Kensington. But would he have someone else kill her, somewhere else? Yes, she thinks. Definitely. Obviously.

Elle had already considered the possibility that this operation might come to a fatal conclusion for her. In Virginia, after she permanently silenced the only person at VDA who could identify her and the details of her operation, she thought about fleeing this clusterfuck, driving the rental car on a bland American four-laner to the interstate, to the airport, to anywhere.

She had disappeared before. Disappearing would definitely be harder this time, with someone actively looking for her, someone who had already displayed an unwavering commitment to locating people who were trying to disappear. Hence this entire operation, a whole year of her life.

What she needed to do was make them *not* want to kill her. She needed to stand her ground, assert herself, protect herself with the force of her will and the strength of her character, try to intimidate the person who'd be trying to intimidate her. The person who's staring at her right now.

"What does Rhodes know?" she asks. "Nothing, really."

"But he can be tied to you. And he knows what's going on, doesn't he?"

This is probably true, she knows it, but she shakes her head. Although she'd rather kill Will than get killed herself, she really doesn't want to kill Will. Over the past months, she found herself growing fond of him. Fond enough, at least, that she doesn't want to kill him, not if she can avoid it. That's something.

"Are you saying there's no footage of you and Mr. Rhodes together somewhere?" the man continues. "That's not possible? Or that no one at the training camp would ever talk? No one in Falls Church? In France, in Argentina, in Spain? You're telling me that if he takes this story to Langley, no one on the sixth floor would ever believe him? No one would start looking for you? No one would find you?"

"I don't exist. That's why you hired me in the first place, wasn't it?"

"That's true only if the world continues to believe that you're dead. But if people start looking, and cross-checking postmortem photos against your pre-death records? Well then, your demise will prove to be unverifiable, won't it? And evidence to the contrary will mount."

"That isn't likely."

"He's a loose end, and you know it. And you know that you need to tie it up."

She pushes out a disgusted chortle, trying to sound dismissive, but she knows that this is a battle she's going to lose.

This operation has been a long one, with a vague time frame, an undisclosed objective, and a questionable outcome. But she certainly didn't expect it to come to this: afraid for her life, once again.

It has been five years since the dusty encampment in Libya where her unit got ambushed—it must've been a sellout—and half of them were killed. The other half scattered to the winds.

A few days later, she learned that she'd been presumed dead. She decided not to unscatter herself, at least not for the moment, not until she figured out what exactly had happened—who'd betrayed them, and why. But she never did find out. So she never did reemerge as alive.

Instead, she seized the opportunity of an undocumented existence, to become a more extreme version of the person she'd been tending toward, untethered from a name and Social Security number and tax returns, from rules and regulations, from forms and reports, from the lifelong slog of a wet-work operations career in the Central Intelligence Agency.

She let herself remain dead.

Little by little, word got out that there was this woman—this highly capable, morally flexible American woman—who could take care of things that other people couldn't, or wouldn't.

"Either Will Rhodes is the loose end"—he leans forward—"or you are."

37

"**G**ot him!"

Inez hustles to Parviz's workstation, leans toward the oversize monitor, where blurry satellite images offer disorienting views from directly above—the black spots of chimneys, the triangular shadows cast by pitched roofs and dormer windows, the dark green-blue of the Seine, the rectangles of cars, like this one, making a left turn off the Quai des Célestins.

"Merde," she mutters, realizing where it's going. The car crosses the Pont Marie, comes to a stop. The door opens. A person emerges.

Inez is surprised that Will Rhodes knows to go to the Île St-Louis but apparently not the exact location of Jean-Pierre Fourier's flat.

It is with difficulty that they continue to follow the figure's movements through the streets, in and out of buildings, crowds gathering. Eventually they lose him completely, midafternoon yesterday, when he becomes one of too many different possibilities to follow, small dots of persons, impossible to distinguish from one another. From hundreds of miles in the sky, all people look the same.

"Phone me if you discover anything," Inez says, walking out the door.

"Where are you going?"

"To find him."

The man is standing at the picture window overlooking the London park, turned away from Elle. She uses the opportunity of this semiprivacy to examine the silverware, wondering if she should palm a knife, a fork, something she could jam into someone's eye. She's getting a bad vibe.

"You're positive Rhodes is running?" he asks the window. Can he see her, in the reflection? Yes, probably.

"We've had round-the-clock on his home, office. He hasn't been to either. No electronic records—no credit cards, no passport swipes, no bank transactions. He's obviously traveling under an alias."

"Unless he's not traveling."

"Yes, but I'm fairly certain he is."

"Time is of the essence."

"Obviously."

"Where do you think he is?"

"I don't have any idea. None whatsoever. And I have no idea how to go about looking for him."

He doesn't respond.

"Listen," she says, "I know this operation isn't about any corporate takeover. And unless you tell me what the hell is really going on, I don't see how I can be of any further use." She stands up. "So start explaining, or I'm leaving."

He turns to her, a threatening pose.

She smiles. "And don't think I'll hesitate to kill Walt on my way out."

GULF OF MAINE

The fishing boat is heading in the direction of the barely lightening horizon. It's a cluttered arrangement of gear and men out there on the deck, and Chloe is relieved to be in the cabin, wrapped in a moth-holed woolen blanket, out of the way, out of the cold wind.

She notices something on the horizon, up ahead and to the port side. She checks her watch. This might be it.

She shrugs off the blanket, picks up the binoculars. It's hard to tell in the dark, the distance.

The crew is busy, ignoring her, as they'd mostly been since she boarded, handed the envelope of cash to Connor the captain, who opened it and counted it, no level of trust here. There were no introductions, no handshakes. This crew was apparently accustomed to the occasional unexplained passenger, undocumented cargo. Connor counted out bills, handed each man his bonus for seeing nothing.

Chloe opens the door, yells, "Hey!" Inclines her head toward this incoming boat, which it's now clear is moving pretty fast. Connor turns to look.

"That it?" she asks, and he shrugs.

If this isn't the boat that she's waiting for, it's a problem. And while problems are also something that this crew is prepared for, she really hopes it doesn't come to that, a sea battle here in the Wilkinson Basin.

She returns her eyes to the binoculars. Yes, this must be it, her ride out of the country without passing through an American airport, across the gulf to Nova Scotia, to the world beyond. Chloe zips her bag, hoists it onto her back. It has been fifteen years since she backpacked, since the relative innocence of traveling for the pure adventure of being a traveler. Like every type of innocence, impossible to recover.

HÚSAVÍK, ICELAND

There's nothing elegant about the weather-beaten boat, dingy white with faded blue trim, rigging and winches and thick ropes everywhere, a stolid sixty-foot workhorse, ramming against the choppy waves of the incoming current.

From the stern Will watches the mist-shrouded village recede, corrugated steel that's painted in bold solid hues, brick reds and royal blues and the minty green facets of the church roof, set off from the backdrop of the lumpy brown mountain called Húsavíkurfjall.

The boat turns starboard, headed north in the Skjálfandi Bay, out into the open water of the Norwegian Sea. Will continues to face south, watching the land shrink away while the boat chugs toward nothing, no landfall ahead until the polar icecap.

A couple dozen passengers are scattered around the decks, perched on high wooden benches or leaning against the hard metal gunwale, their gazes washing over the churning gray water, watching for whales. This is what the town is known for, tourist-wise. People come here to climb into bulky foul-weather gear, thick and rubberized and bright orange, the better to see you with if you fall overboard, not a terribly long time before hypothermia sets in. The Arctic Circle is fifty miles away.

There are three crew on this boat. The skipper is in the wheelhouse, younger than you'd expect a skipper to be, tall and fair-skinned and icy-blue-eyed. There's a middle-aged woman, broad-shouldered and beautiful in a hale, unadorned way, who helped everyone get into their inmate-like jumpsuits, and is now handing out hot chocolate in paper cups. And there's the man in the crow's nest, holding military-looking binoculars to his face, white stubble along a strong jaw, a dark tight watch cap. It's hard for Will to get a good look at him, standing fifteen feet above in the slate-gray sky.

Forty-five minutes out, it starts to rain, wind-blown and face-pelting and bone-chilling, the boat pitching and rolling. Will can no longer see any land in any direction.

"There!" the man cries from the crow's nest, his arm outstretched. Everyone looks up at him, then follows his pointing finger to the whale a couple hundred yards to port. The crowd oohs and aahs—these are the actual sounds—and the boat turns, accelerates, giving chase toward an animal that appears to be the same size as the boat. Jesus that thing is huge.

The whale breaches again and again while the man in the crow's nest recites cetaceous trivia, mating habits and pup rearing, flukes and baleen, lobtailing and spyhopping, a whole argot. Suddenly a handful of people start scuttling, and it takes Will a few seconds to realize that they're fleeing from a woman who's leaning overboard, throwing up, vomit spattering soundlessly into the sea, the mustard-colored sick washed quickly from the hull by a wave. Water crashes over the gunwale with regularity, sloshing around the deck before draining back into the big cold drink.

The whale breaches a dozen times while the boat keeps it company, but then after one dive it doesn't rematerialize. Five minutes later the skipper gives up, turns the boat back toward land, wherever that might be. There's no sun visible, no stars, no horizon, no nothing to indicate which direction is where.

PARIS

"Madame Fourier? My name is Inez d'Auvergne."

The old woman squints at Inez, but doesn't say anything.

"I work at *Travelers*."

"Ahh, *Travelers*. It is a busy day for you people."

"Yes, I am sorry to disturb you. My colleague who was here earlier—"

"The American?"

"Yes, the American. What did you two discuss?"

"Why do you not ask him?"

"Because I am asking you."

Mme. Fourier looks like she's about to slam the door in Inez's face. But she doesn't. "Not much. He did not know that my father was dead, so I told him."

"Is that all?"

"The American asked if I found anything unusual in my father's possessions. I told him there was a mobile phone that I did not know about."

"May I have a look at that phone?"

"No."

"May I ask why not?"

"Because I gave it to him."

"To the American?"

"Yes, of course." Mme. Fourier shrugs. "He wanted it. I do not."

HÚSAVÍK

The boat is bumping against the pier. The passengers shed their foul-weather gear, disembark, relieved to be on solid ground, hustling to find shelter from the rain, a toilet that doesn't lurch from side to side, a dry place for a hot lunch.

The expedition was a success. The whale was captured on thousands of frames of still images plus hours of video, blurry and out of focus, the horizon not horizontal, devices shaking and tilting with the boat's pitching and rolling, lenses spattered with spray and blocked by humans, the audio garbled and static-riddled.

Will loiters until he finds his opportunity, asks the grizzled guy if he has a few minutes to spare for a travel writer, and do you mind if I take some notes?

"Okay," the man says. "You can keep me company while I tidy up."

"So you're American? How'd you end up here?" Will's pen is poised, reporter pose.

"Got sick of it."

"Of what?"

"America." The man is coiling a big heavy rope, wrapping it around itself. Passengers continue to shuffle past, handing over coins as gratuities.

"What about America?"

"The whole thing. The consumerism, the capitalism, the politicians and their bullshit, the health-care system, the war on drugs, the mass incarceration, the permanent underclass . . . Need me to go on?"

Will shakes his head. "When did you leave?"

"Five years ago."

"Why Iceland?"

The man inclines his head toward his coworker, who's folding the jumpsuits, stacking them. "We met on a hiking trail. In Utah."

"And you followed her *here*?" Will puts his hands out, the dark gray, the rain, the workmanlike little harbor.

"Love is more important than weather, isn't it?"

Will takes notes for another five minutes, nothing much of interest, not from his current perspective.

"Listen," he says. "I'm looking for an American. About your age, maybe older. East Coast guy. Would have arrived about a year ago. You know of anyone like that? Hear of anyone?"

"In Húsavík?" The man laughs. "No. Americans don't just show up in Húsavík. Have you seen this place? There are like eight people here."

"I think that's exactly what this man might be looking for. A place to disappear."

"Well, there's nowhere and there's *nowhere*. Húsavík would *not* be a good place to disappear. Too many people would notice you. And too many tourists show up, hard to keep track of people who might have come here to find you."

"So where in Iceland would you go instead? To disappear?"

The man drops the giant coil of rope with a deep resounding thud. "Sorry," he says, "I really wouldn't know. And now if you'll excuse me, I have to get back to work."

NEW YORK CITY

"You all set?" Lucinda asks.

"Thanks again for this," Gabriella say. "I owe you."

"I appreciate that, but no, you really don't. This is a fair bargain: you do the sixty seconds on the cruises, then you can say whatever the hell you want as long as you don't break any FCC regulations." Lucinda smiles broadly. "Seriously."

Lucinda is a reasonable person. This doesn't necessarily look like a reasonable place to work, but who knows? Looking in from the outside, absolutely no one would suspect that *Travelers* is the sort of workplace it is. The sort where employees get killed.

Terrance's abduction hadn't come out of nowhere. It wasn't entirely unexpected, not a low-percentage scenario. In fact, the contrary: something they'd anticipated, discussed, planned for.

He was one of the staff photographers, as well as the magazine's African correspondent. It was a good job for him, and vice versa. But it was a dangerous position, everyone recognized that. And the thing they were most worried about—politically motivated kidnapping—is exactly what happened. It wasn't the first time in the magazine's history.

Travelers never got the chance to pay the ransom. Terrance was held in captivity for barely forty-eight hours before he was killed, gruesome footage that eventually made its way to the web via a fringe sect of Sudanese radicals. They denounced Terrance as an American spy who'd gotten what he deserved while trying to steal state secrets; the president of Sudan apologized for the regrettable incident. The magazine unwaveringly maintained that he was an innocent photojournalist. The State

Department condemned the terrorism, and issued a new travel advisory. The CIA denied any knowledge of the man.

And Terrance's widow, Gabriella Rivera, traumatized, asked her new boss for a new job, a desk job. She put away her various passports, picked up the editing pencil. She took over the long-standing TV-morning-show gig, the latest incarnation in a half-century's worth of coded electronic communications that were broadcast one way or another—radio-drama advertisements, network evening news, daytime talk radio—out to the *Travelers* network of operatives, alerting them to the location of the next mission, relaying instructions from someone Gabriella would never meet to an unknown number of assets in undisclosed locations.

Maybe her time at *Travelers* has come to a close. It has taken her youth, taken her husband. And what does she have to show for it? Nothing positive. Just a deep distrust of everyone.

She has been staying at *Travelers* till she can think of something better, but she isn't convinced she's ever going to think of something better. Maybe different will suffice.

Lucinda leads Gabriella to an upholstered chair. A PA rushes over, attaches a microphone to Gabriella's lapel, clips the transmitter to the waistline of her skirt, does a quick sound check, retreats.

Gabs perches on the edge of the seat, crosses her legs at the ankle, sits up straight, pulls down the back of her jacket. She turns to Lucinda. "Were you serious about me working here?"

"I was. Still am. You change your mind?"

"I don't know. But let's talk about it."

Lucinda smiles, and nods, and backs away just as the light on top of the camera goes on.

"Thanks Ted," Gabriella says, "it's *great* to be here. This fall, Ted, all bets are off when it comes to international travel."

And with that phrase, a few hundred clandestine operatives, scattered around the world, are ordered to go dark.

HÚSAVÍK

Will has a big bowl of the seafood stew that everyone else is having, fish and potatoes in saffron broth, the same thing he'll confront everywhere in Iceland. Without thinking, he takes out his notebook, an unbreakable habit, to write down the name of the town, the restaurant, the menu description, the price. But this is one foreign trip he won't be writing about. He closes his little book, and eats in relative peace.

The rain is driving, bitter, cold. He trudges to his rental car, turns the ignition.

The passenger door suddenly swings open, violently.

LONDON

"You're right."

"Of course I'm right." He turns away from the window.

"So what's my actual objective?" Elle asks.

"You have to realize it's for your own good that I haven't told you."

"Oh don't give me that bullshit. You don't do anything for anyone else's good."

He opens his mouth to object, but doesn't bother. At this point, who cares? Instead, he takes a seat. Crosses his legs. He's looking thoughtful, or trying to. Then finally he speaks. "For a long time, there's been a rumor of a supersecret CIA cadre that operates outside the normal chain of command."

"Meaning what?"

"Meaning that they can do whatever they want, wherever they want."

Elle fights the urge to roll her eyes. There are always rumors like this, conspiracy theories of shadow networks, plots to assassinate the president, to steal nuclear weapons, to frame foreign leaders, to take over the world, hand control to the extraterrestrials.

"Okay," she says. "And?"

"A few years ago, I learned on good authority that this cadre was real. That they were operating behind a completely legitimate front: an international media operation."

Elle's mouth falls open.

"A news-gathering outfit whose reporters are really spies; whose editor is the director."

"You are fucking with me."

"I am dead serious."

"You're telling me that *Travelers* is a top secret Agency division?"

"That, my dear, is what we're trying to find out. That's your objective."

Elle lets this sink in, tries to work it out. This seems so utterly implausible. But the CIA has a long, almost proud history of implausible-looking gambits. Is this one of them?

"At first I investigated the international wire services, but came up with nothing. Then a couple of news magazines. I was handicapped by my assumption that the serious business of espionage would be handled by equally serious reporters of world events."

"What made you change your mind?"

"At a cocktail party, I met Jonathan Mongeleach. His Africa correspondent, a guy named Terrance Sanders—"

"Gabriella Rivera's husband?"

"—had recently been kidnapped in Africa, held for ransom, killed. A gruesome scenario. He was just an innocent American civilian, doing his job."

"Unless he wasn't just an innocent American civilian."

"Exactly. Daniel Pearl was one thing, a *Wall Street Journal* bureau chief, a Jewish man working a Muslim beat. But Sanders?" He shakes his head. "I did a little research. Do you know how many articles *Travelers* runs per year, on average, about Africa?"

He holds up two fingers. "Why do you need an Africa correspondent for two articles per year? That's an odd misallocation of resources, I thought. So I looked deeper into *Travelers*—their staff, their advertisers, their history. And lo and behold, what happened?"

"Can you stop quizzing me, please? I'm not in sixth grade."

"Jonathan Mongeleach disappeared. It doesn't look like Mr. Mongeleach was murdered, or kidnapped. It looks like he *chose* to vanish. Why would he do that?"

"Seriously? I'm not participating in this quiz format anymore."

"Because he was caught. But at what? That's the question. Maybe he was caught light-fingered with the company coffers. Maybe he was caught with his pants down. Maybe he was caught trading media coverage for money, or cocaine, or blow jobs. Maybe he was caught with a gambling problem, a vodka problem, a sexual-harassment problem, a hostile-workplace problem. If any of that is true, I don't give a damn, and I don't want to buy *Travelers*, much less their parent company. I'm in *new* media. I don't want to own a bunch of antiquated magazines that'll be huge headaches, then slide dismally into inevitable bankruptcy."

Elle is no longer worried about getting killed by this man. Now she's worried about getting killed by everyone else involved.

"What I want to own," he says, "is my own private spy network."

38

Will doesn't even have time to panic before the man asks, "Do you know who I am?"

"You're the American from the boat."

"That's not what I mean."

The rain is pelting the car, loud splatters. Will stares at the guy, wondering whether or not to lie. "Your name is John Collins," he says. "You used to be a Navy pilot."

"Are you in Húsavík looking for me?"

"In a way. I came here because you're the only American in our Iceland files."

"Your files? What does that mean?"

"My magazine keeps files of all sorts of people, especially American expats. Some whom we might turn to when we're looking for advice, for information, for other people. For specific local information. I saw you in our Iceland file, and thought you might have some info about the American I'm looking for."

"And who's that?"

"My ex-boss."

"I don't know anything about your magazine, or your ex-boss. I'm just a guy who used to fly planes, and then I worked in military procurement, and now I don't. I have no idea why I'm in your files, and I don't appreciate your coming here and harassing me."

"I'm sorry. I don't mean to harass you. I'm just looking for a guy, that's all. Not for you. But you seemed like the type of person who might be able to help me."

The man stares at Will, then turns and looks out the window. He doesn't speak, but neither does he leave. They sit in silence.

The guy sighs. "Okay," he says. "If I came to Iceland to disappear, I'd move closer to Reykjavík. Somewhere within a couple hours' driving of the city, where there's a larger population that's more anonymous, more transient. Some hippies, some seasonal people, some foreigners. You know Bobby Fischer lived down there?"

Everyone here has told him this.

"Plus it's easier and cheaper to get food, supplies, closer to the capital, especially in winter. Half the year, this is a godforsaken place. The north coast of Iceland seems to have actually been forsaken by God. You have no idea."

Will doesn't find this hard to believe. "Do you know of anyplace in particular? Anyone?"

"Yeah. In spring, we went camping near Snæfellsjökull. You know where that is?"

"Sort of."

"We were talking to Emilíana's nephew who lives at a collective, something like a commune. We were discussing the recent changes on the Snæfellsnes Peninsula—new woman working at the gas station, that type of thing."

"Anyway."

"He told me he played cards with an American, sort of an old guy, on his own, living some of the time in a farmhouse but not farming, surrounded by sheep. That sound like who you're looking for?"

"Maybe."

The man nods, puts his hand on the handle, but doesn't open the door. "Why are you looking for people who don't want to be found?"

That's a good fucking question. "It's my job."

"You ought to find yourself a different job." The man pushes down on the handle, opens the door. "This one is very dangerous."

PARIS

It takes only ten minutes on the Vespa to get back to the office. Inez goes upstairs straightaway to the tech personnel who are engrossed in their cyberworlds, right hands resting on mice, headphones covering ears, listening to music while they scan silent surveillance footage of street corners and hotel lobbies, cash points and Metro stations, searching for signs of Will Rhodes.

The headphones come off as she enters, asks, "Anything?" All heads shake.

Inez heads downstairs, to the clutter of the main office, and plops down in her swivel chair. She slept only three hours last night.

She punches in the digits to unlock the desk. Pulls open the middle drawer, which contains the Western European contacts; Eastern Europe is below. The fattest of the hanging folders are for France, Germany, the U.K., all a couple of inches thick, filled with individual files for cities. She thumbs through France, pulls out the hefty Paris sheaf, a hundred pages, each representing a person, headshot and contact numbers, address and known associates. Will must be in Paris to talk to one of these people.

She slams the drawer shut, and her whole desk shakes. She opens the file.

But something is nagging at her, has intruded on her consciousness; something is wrong. Something where? Did she see something on her ride back from the Île St-Louis? Did something catch her eye as she accelerated through the Place de la Concorde, or up the Champs-Élysées?

No: it was more recent. It was something here. Upstairs?

No: something in her desk.

She reenters the code. She opens the heavy drawer again, rolling it forward on its tracked wheels till it comes to a fully extended shuddering halt. She stares into the bin for a few seconds before she realizes what's wrong: the file tabs are misaligned.

No: it's not that the tabs are misaligned. There's a file missing.

No: there are two files missing. Iceland and Sweden.

What Inez is about to do is contrary to protocol, the strictly adhered-to rules of secure communications, the first commandment of the overseas bureaus. But this is an extraordinary situation.

She dials the main switchboard in New York. She's transferred to the assistant, then put on hold. She waits.

Finally, she hears "Hello" and the implicit criticism in those two syllables, in his failure to state his name, to ask who's calling. He doesn't want to say or hear anything specific. He doesn't want this call to exist at all.

"I believe our mutual friend is on his way to either Iceland or Sweden," she says without preamble; better just come out with it. "Or already there."

"What makes you think this?"

"He took those files. In the middle of last night." She realizes that this type of description can be confusing, looks at her watch, clarifies: "Nine hours ago."

"You're positive?"

Inez has now seen video-surveillance proof that Will entered this building last night at 2:41 A.M. Security-card proof that his keycard was the one that opened the office door. Physical proof that the files are not in their drawer. "Yes."

"Anything else?"

"No."

Inez waits for him to say something further, ask something else, then realizes the line is dead. She holds the phone, gathering her strength to return upstairs, to redirect their search, ask if anyone needs food, or drink, or drugs, because they're going to be here awhile.

NEW YORK CITY

"Who's that?" Gabriella asks.

"Apparently Will was in Paris last night, stealing the files for Iceland and Sweden."

"That's odd. He must know something."

"Yes. And he's traveling under a different name. Must've procured himself a passport. You have any idea how Will would do that?"

"Not from me, if that's what you're asking."

"No, I'm not."

Gabriella crosses her legs. "If I were Will, I'd probably go to Dean Fowler for help. Dean dabbles, you know. And they've been friends for a long time."

"Yeah. Listen, Gabs, could I ask you to go have a little chat with Dean?"

"Sure. And what are you going to do?"

"I'm going to Iceland."

"Why Iceland?"

"It's a lot closer than Sweden."

AKUREYRI, ICELAND

Speeding through the traffic-free valleys alongside rushing rivers and craggy ridges and woolly sheep and more woolly sheep, racing to catch the plane to Reykjavík, Will is making good time, but still cutting it awfully close. He keeps glancing at the dashboard clock, then accelerating, driving faster than he should. Twice he needs to come to a complete stop to allow a herd of sheep to cross the road. There's no way to hurry along sheep.

He's just a few miles from Akureyri when he finds himself in an impenetrable bank of dense fog, forced to slow the car to the barest crawl, the road now treacherous with severe switchbacks and low visibility, descending toward the eastern shore of Eyjafjörður, the longest fjord in Iceland.

Will glances at the clock. He's running out of time. He increases pressure on the gas, feels the transmission switch gears. Leans forward in the seat, his face closer to the windshield, closer to whatever it is he won't be able to see coming through the—

Shit! He yanks the steering wheel to the right, swerving away from an oncoming car that's climbing the hill that Will is descending, its horn blaring, and then Will is pulling the wheel hard back to the left, to avoid flying off the road into a ditch, and now fishtailing on the wet surface, his heart hammering—

He brings the car under control, white-knuckling the wheel.

The road levels and straightens out beside the fjord that separates Will from the town, from the airport, from the small plane that'll take him where he needs to be. He turns the car onto the bridge and floors the gas, the speedometer climbing, the engine whining.

He can see the airport, nestled beside the water. The Akureyri airport is far from the tiniest commercial strip he's ever visited—it has both rental cars and food, while plenty of airports offer neither—but it's still pretty small, and from afar he can clearly see all the goings-on. He sees the plane he ought to be boarding, a short walk from the small terminal.

Will's car is halfway across the bridge when he sees the plane's door close. Then the rolling staircase roll away. He is just arriving at the end of the bridge when the plane begins to taxi.

He has missed the flight, the last one of the day.

LONDON

"Tell me." Elle pushes her hair away from her ear, adjusts the phone's angle.

"I'm at JFK, where fifteen minutes ago the editor passed through security. I called our main contact in Virginia, but he didn't answer any of his lines. So I called his boss."

Elle knows that their main contact in Virginia is never going to answer any phone, ever again. But she doesn't want to tell Roger about this, or he might start to worry about the longevity of his own ability to answer the phone.

"Good thinking," she says. "And?"

"The editor checked into a Saga-class seat bound for Keflavík. Due to arrive in seven hours. Me, I'll be in coach."

Elle is scanning the departure board, looking for the next Iceland-bound flight. She's been waiting in Heathrow for exactly this type of information since the end of her conversation in the hotel suite. She'd previously assumed that her employer is a supergreedy amoral capitalist. But now she understands him to be a stupendously devious megalomaniac. She can't quite decide if this represents an improvement in her predicament, or the opposite.

"Is *Travelers* the spy network I'm looking for?" he asked.

And as ludicrous as this whole thing sounded, it might be true. She admitted, "I really don't know."

"You know who does?"

She didn't answer.

"Before Rhodes deleted Malcom Somers's files from this drive, he copied them, right?"

Elle nodded, understanding where this was going.

"Rhodes found something, didn't he? And then he took that something, and he fled with it."

She was still nodding.

"Rhodes knows."

She was already standing.

"Go get him."

NEW YORK CITY

"Hello Dean."

"Gabriella Rivera! You're certainly a sight for sore eyes."

"Are your eyes sore? Maybe from all your ogling. You should rest them now and then."

"Har-har." Dean turns toward the man behind the bar. "Marlon?" The bartender looks over at his boss. "Yours is a Manhattan, right?" Dean asks.

Gabriella shakes her head. "Just a club soda, if you don't mind."

It's pretty obvious that Marlon does mind, but what's he going to do? He reaches into a refrigerator, removes a small bottle, unscrews the cap. No mold-filled soda gun here.

"Dean, I'm going to ask you a question, and I'm going to need the truth, okay?"

Dean smiles. "Sure, glad to tell you the truth." He leans toward her, whispers in her ear. "Yes, it really is as big as you've heard."

"You're a degenerate bastard, aren't you?"

He shrugs, but the smile remains.

"Will Rhodes is in trouble, Dean, and he has disappeared, traveling under a false passport. I need to find him. You know anything about this passport? And before you answer, let me tell you that I'm willing to trade information."

"Oh yeah? What's that?"

"I'm aware that Marlon dispenses more than just artisanal cocktails and cute little bottles of soda." She taps her nostril with her forefinger. "But I'm willing to keep this information to myself, Dean. Instead of, say, informing the NYPD."

The smile has disappeared. "What do you want?"

AKUREYRI

Will passes the entrance to the airport, now useless. He stops at a gas station, stretches his legs. He consults the map, traces his new route. He uses the bathroom. He buys some food, some caffeine. He finds a pay phone, and he calls his wife. Will is going to continue to call her, every day. There may be nothing else he can do, so that's what he's going to do.

He accelerates away from the wet gray dimness of one of the cloudiest places in the world, and after a few minutes finds himself alone on the road again, speeding on a straight narrow strip of asphalt through a valley lined on both sides by glaciers, by fields of black volcanic rock covered in soft green moss, and practically no trees, anywhere.

Also no nighttime. The sun drops below the horizon, but darkness never descends, the sky suspended in a state of permanent-looking dusk. Will continues through the non-night, passing just a handful of cars, no police. There are only a few hundred cops in the entire country, and almost none carries a gun. In a typical year, there's perhaps a single murder in Iceland; last year fifteen thousand homicides were committed in the United States.

This is one of the morsels that Will digested from Jonathan's Iceland article—the negligible rate of violent crime, the minuscule police presence. As well as the universality of English—everyone speaks it, which makes being an English speaker unremarkable. And the near irrelevancy of Iceland on the world stage, and the attendant unlikelihood that any intelligence operatives or international law enforcement would poke around here, for any reason. All the same reasons why Bobby Fischer chose to disappear in Iceland: all good reasons for Jonathan Mongeleach to disappear in Iceland.

Will has been driving for three hours when he realizes that he has just fallen asleep at the wheel, jolting awake in a panic, blinking his eyes violently. He's still two hours shy of his destination, without any sign of civilization in any direction other than the clothesline-straight road ripping through the lichen-blanched volcanic rock. He's not going to make it.

There's no hurry, he reminds himself. He wants to solve the puzzle, but there's no actual urgency to it. No one knows where he is, and no one can find him.

Will glances around at the unforgiving, unwelcoming landscape. He turns into a pullout, the car bumping over a rutted dirt path. There's nowhere to hide out here, no trees, no hills to lurk behind, no way to not be noticed, if anyone is looking. He heard a joke: What do you do if you find yourself lost in an Icelandic forest? Stand up.

He kicks off his shoes, reclines the seat. Turns onto his side, shuts his eyes.

Then he remembers to lock the door. There may be almost no murders in Iceland, but he's an American, and Americans tend to kill one another with very little provocation.

HALIFAX, NOVA SCOTIA

Chloe inserts the phone's battery. She waits for the cellular service to connect, expecting—hoping—to find a new message, a destination. She still doesn't know where she's going.

The bars appear. She receives a text message, alerting her to her new cellular provider, to the applicable fees for data, text, calls. She's roaming. She opens her email program, her eyes scanning down the list. Nothing she cares about, from no one important.

And there's no voice mail. Damn.

She closes the phone. She's about to power it off, to remove the battery again, when the device buzzes at her.

It took a minute to connect, but there are, after all, two new voice mails.

The first is from Larissa, whom Chloe pays to make sure the roses stay alive. The teenager has been coming by once a week to water, to prune, to add homemade fertilizer—coffee grounds mixed with vinegar—since early spring, when Chloe noticed that the plant looked like it was dying. Larissa is going to be away next week; her younger sister will fill in.

The second voice mail is from just a few hours ago, an unrecognized number, with the +354 international dialing code.

Where the hell is +354?

39

Elle is waiting curbside at a terminal that's exuding wave after wave of bleary red-eye passengers from the other side of the ocean, from Denver and Seattle, from Boston and Toronto, and finally from New York, clumps of people wheeling luggage, checking phones, carrying children, boarding buses and taxis, looking around for glaciers and geysers, for volcanoes and hot springs, for things you don't find in airport parking lots, even in Iceland.

Malcolm Somers emerges. He looks like any other luggage-free day-tripping businessman, suit and tie, chin up and shoulders back, impatient at some holdup or another, where's my car, my meeting, my whatever. He looks like exactly who he is, cocky overpaid son of a bitch. It's too bad that it's not this guy she's here to kill.

He strides toward the car rentals, which are right here across the street, no shuttle bus, no air-train, no transport between the transports.

Roger emerges. Elle flashes her headlights, and he marches over, climbs in.

"Hey," he says. "Do we know his alias yet?"

Elle turns the computer toward Roger, shows him a headshot, a name that's not Malcolm Somers, a passport number, driver's license.

She opens another browser window, data from the rental-car company, make and model and color, license plate number. She scans the lot, finds Somers's rental car before he does. The same model she's sitting in, different color. The rental lots are filled with them.

Elle turns to Roger, inclines her head across the street. "We'll have to switch off A and B cars. I'll start A, you'll take over on the highway. Your phone fully charged?"

"It is."

"Good." She hands him an adapter, a cord, the other rental's keys.

"Keep it that way. Let's stay one kilometer back for A, another kilometer for B."

"That's a lot of space."

"Somers knows what he's doing, and he's going to be on the lookout. We need to be extra careful."

"Weapons?" he asks.

She shakes her head. "Reykjavík isn't exactly Mogadishu."

Elle can see that Roger is uneasy. Although he's a big strong man, hand-to-hand combat has never been his forte. What Roger is good at is shooting people.

SNÆFELLSNES PENINSULA, ICELAND

"Sure," the chef says. "I think I know who you're talking about."

"Really?" Will has been driving and stopping and asking after an old American for the better part of the day, growing tired and frustrated, increasingly worried that John Collins of Húsavík lied to him, sent him off on a wild-goose chase, just to get Will out of his orbit. That's probably what Will would've done, in his shoes.

Will is standing in the parking lot of a roadside restaurant. The chef has come outside to collect a delivery, a burlap sack of red-skinned potatoes. "He is called Joe, this American. But I think he arrived two years ago, not one. And he does not live here all the time. He returned a few months ago from his other home."

"Where's that?"

"Munich. Or at least that is what he said."

"Could I ask you where his house is?"

"Sure, just up the road, perhaps forty minutes' drive. Do you have a map?"

Over the past few years, Will has stopped using paper maps entirely, in favor of the irrefutable superiority of GPS-powered mobile applications, the unassailable wisdom of the crowd's biofeedback mechanisms replacing the hard-earned expertise of the individual. Traffic apps are great. But he doesn't have a computer or a smartphone now, and the rental didn't come with a navigation system. So he'd bought an old-fashioned gas-station map.

The chef unfolds this map, lays the paper on the hood of the little car, dirty and spattered from its journey across the terrain and the weather of northern Iceland. "Somewhere in here"—finger tracing road. "You can see the house from the road as you approach. The house is orange. Way out near the edge of a cliff."

The landline is ringing. Only a handful of people know this number, all of them local residents, all native Icelanders except Stas, who lives way out on the far side of the peninsula, a crazy goddamned place to live, the German out there to prove something.

"Hello Joe? It's Einar."

"Einar! How are you?"

"I'm well, thank you. Listen, Joe, a man was just here asking after you."

"After me?"

"Eh, not by name. He was asking after someone of your description—an American man of about your age who lives here."

"And what did you tell him?"

Joe cranes his neck forward, looking out his kitchen window toward the road from the east, the road from the rest of the world, intruding upon him, as he knew it eventually would. But he's prepared. Always. "Did you tell him where to find me?"

"I did, yes. I'm sorry if that wasn't the right thing."

"No, no, don't apologize, Einar! It was completely the right thing. But I was about to go make a boat repair, and I wonder if I still have time. How long ago did he leave?"

"Just now."

"Okay, thanks. I'm curious about who this is. Maybe my estranged brother has finally hunted me down to apologize for being such a jerk."

Joe doesn't have a brother, estranged or otherwise.

Einar laughs. "No, I don't think so. He was my age, this man. Maybe your nephew?"

"Was he driving the biggest Mercedes you've ever seen?"

"No, this guy was driving a little white Chevrolet."

"Then probably not. My nephew is an obnoxious prick. He'll drive only luxury cars, even rentals." Joe now has a description of the man and his car, and didn't need to ask for either. "Okay, Einar, thanks for letting me know. I'll see you for poker on Sunday, I hope?"

"Definitely."

Joe returns the phone to its cradle, gazes out the window. This phone conversation will definitely make it difficult to get away with killing whoever's about to show up—difficult for Joe to claim he was taken by surprise, difficult to categorically deny any knowledge of any stranger who disappeared, difficult to pretend he doesn't have any idea who this was. Yes, it'll be more difficult. But it won't be impossible. And he probably won't ever need to explain himself anyway. He'll be gone.

He kneels. Opens the bottom cabinet drawer, which contains nothing except a couple of dish towels. He pulls the drawer completely out of its frame, and places it on the kitchen floor. Reaches far into the darkness of the cabinet's cavity, and extracts another dish towel, this one folded over and secured with twine, which he unties, unwraps, revealing a forest-green passport from the Republic of South Africa, and a rubber-banded roll of currency, and a big, long, ferocious-looking hunting knife.

From the road, Will can see the orange house perched near the end, where the land meets the sea and the sky, both dark and gray and forbidding. But from the top of the driveway the house isn't visible, lost behind an uneven rise covered in an undulating blanket of moss. Across the road, a waterfall tumbles from the crook of the elbow of a dark brooding mountain.

This spot is isolated and lonely, and also stunning and serene. This makes complete sense for someone who'd already lived a big noisy life. This is the opposite.

The driveway is carved crudely out of the lava field, narrow, bumpy, curvy. Will takes it slowly, worried about the undercarriage of the car. The drive takes longer than expected, just like all the drives on this island, with sheep and fog and unpassable trucks chugging along in low gear, no one except him in any rush to get anywhere. Apparently for months at a time the sheep roam freely, basically wherever the hell they want to go on the entire island, and then in autumn they all get sorted, hey, here's your sheep, yeah that one's mine, thanks.

Will arrives at the house, but there's no other car there; no one home. He looks around without getting out, without even shifting into park. What should he do?

He turns the car around in the small yard, pointing it back toward the driveway, ready to make an exit. But where is he going to go? He has nowhere to go, nothing to do except find the man who lives here. He'll take a look around.

It has started to rain again, lightly, a cool mist settling from the sky, as if from an aggressive humidifier. Will presses his face against a window, but can't see much inside. He moves to a different window, a view onto a spartan living room, a half-measured existence, like a rental cottage, the sort of place that's inhabited by its owner for just a week or two per year, the rest of the time rented out by a managing agent, occupied by tourists who arrive for Saturday-to-Saturday holidays, leafing through the three-ring binder that offers helpful hints about where to buy groceries, how to turn on the temperamental hot tub.

Will's hand hovers above the doorknob, wondering about what level of trespass he's willing to commit. If the person who lives here is not the man he's looking for, there's no sense committing any trespass whatso-ever; on the other hand, if it is the right house for the right man, trespass-ing might get Will killed.

"*Halló?*" he calls out, not expecting a response. Not getting one.

He walks around the perimeter, nothing notable, a small shed with tools and a bicycle, a woodpile covered in plastic tarp, a table with—

What's that? Will's eye catches movement to the right, a rustling in the low shrubs.

"*Hello?*"

And there—what's that?—someone moving, a flash of dark clothing, light hair.

"Hey, wait!" Will hurries to the footpath that leads through the dense shrubs, his feet squishing in puddles of mud, the wind and the rain pick-ing up. From afar, the terrain looks inviting, the moss a soft mohair blan-ket. Up close, though, the volcanic rocks are sharp, their crags stark, the ground uneven and punishing to the soles of his feet, to his battered legs, to his whole body, an assortment of intersecting aches, bruises, strains. It was only three days ago that Will was jumping off New York City rooftops, landing badly. Blood is still pooling beneath his skin, bruises settling, his legs and shoulder and rib cage deep mottled patches of purple and black, his swollen ankle stiff and painful.

He jogs up the path tentatively, careful of his footing, then comes around a rock protrusion and suddenly he's at the end of the earth, atop a high bluff, much higher than expected. He comes to a nervous stop.

"Jonathan?" he calls out, into the wind. "It's Will Rhodes!"

Far below, the beach is covered in rocks of every size, a base layer of pebbles topped with boulders. Will can see a set of wooden stairs a couple hundred yards east, a narrow cove with a short dock, a small motorboat. There aren't any other houses out here; that dock must belong to this property. That boat to this man, who's running from Will.

"I just want to talk!"

He senses movement up ahead, more ruffled foliage. He continues around another dramatic rock protrusion, something fashioned by a toddler's imagination, or Dr. Seuss. At the far end Will sucks in his breath, suddenly flush against the cliff's precipice. His shoe pushes a pebble from underfoot, out over the edge, landing sixty feet below, maybe seventy, the sound of its impact lost in the din of crashing waves.

Will is now distinctly aware of his feet, of his footwork, his precariousness, every step an opportunity to make a fatal mistake.

He spins around at a sound behind him, a snapping of twigs, a rustling of foliage, a bird maybe, or a bear—are there bears in Iceland?—or maybe another sheep, they're absolutely everywhere.

Another big piece of volcanic rock looms in front of him, with just a narrow band of dirt path between its vertical face and the cliff's edge.

"*Hey*," Will yells again. "Come on, just give me a minute."

No reply.

He glances over his shoulder, considers retreating, back to the house, to the car, to the relative safety of any other existence, of not being on a slippery path at the edge of a cliff, pursuing a fugitive.

The rain has picked up, and he feels his shoulders getting wet, drops falling from his hair onto his cheeks.

He's almost around this boulder, just another step until the dirt path heads inland, away from the precipice.

Here. Whew.

But it's only a brief instant of relief that Will feels. Because from the far side of the boulder a hand grabs Will by the shirt at the back of his neck, and yanks him away from safety, and thrusts him in the other direction, pitched forward, over the lip of the cliff.

40

A t a busy gas station, Malcolm unfolds himself from the little car, his joints creaking, his muscles aching. His right knee in particular feels wobbly.

He takes a minute to stretch before he walks across the pavement to the ubiquitous minimart—junk food and cheap beer, Saran-wrapped sandwiches and quarts of motor oil, a refreshingly clean restroom, a diversely stocked gift shop. This station is big, bigger than Malcolm would want, but he doesn't have a choice. In places like rural Iceland, there's usually not much choice: the hotel is the hotel, the gas station is the gas station, take it or leave it.

From the convenience store he buys a cup of coffee, a snack bar, an apple. From the gift shop he buys a folding knife with a four-inch blade.

After driving for two hours, he really needed that bathroom. Within a few years, he'll probably prefer urinating to orgasms. Maybe he'll divorce Allison, take up with a urinal.

He stands near the window, surveying the big wide tarmac beside the busy two-lane road, sipping his coffee, waiting to see who arrives. A couple of cars drive into the service station, another couple leave. Nothing familiar.

Malcolm returns to his vehicle, opens the fuel cap, starts to pump gas. That's when he notices the black Ford sitting on the far side of the lot, parked around back of the building. Same year and model as Malcolm's. Probably same rental company; maybe same pickup location. This car wasn't here when Malcolm arrived, nor did he see it pull in; it arrived while he was inside.

A woman gets out of the car. So she's been sitting there for at least a few minutes, waiting for something. What?

Waiting for Malcolm to exit the building, so she can enter.

The woman is half-turned away from him, and doesn't glance in his direction as she walks away, perhaps headed to the head. Malcolm doesn't get a good look at her, but he feels as if he has seen her before.

She disappears inside. Malcolm leaves the nozzle in his tank and walks across the paved plaza to the side of the woman's car that's shielded from view of the store. He makes sure he's not being observed, then kneels at the rear tire. He plunges the souvenir knife deep between the treads, twists the blade, yanks it out. Repeats this in another section of the rear tire, then again twice for the front tire.

There will be another one, he knows; there will be two vehicles. Malcolm has not completely shed his tails. But he has made it twice as hard for them to follow him.

He returns to his own little Ford, caps the tank, climbs into the driver's seat, and waits for the woman to emerge. He wants to get a good look at her.

He waits one minute . . . two . . .

Maybe there was a queue for the ladies' room.

Three minutes . . . four . . .

Malcolm doesn't want to risk being seen searching for her, doesn't want her to know that he's onto her. So he shouldn't go inside to check. And he can't just continue to wait here, because that wouldn't make sense to the other person who's watching him, whoever and wherever that is.

Seven minutes have gone by.

Malcolm walks back inside, establishes himself at a bank of refrigerated cases, squeaky-clean glass doors that he can use as serviceable mirrors. He pretends to browse the drinks, tilting his head this way, that—

There she is. Not waiting in a bathroom queue, not in the bathroom. She's doing the same thing as Malcolm: pretending to browse. Why? She must be waiting for him to leave, to pull out of the gas station. Which means that her partner, whoever's in the second car, is also nearby, watching Malcolm watching her, keeping her apprised of his whereabouts.

She definitely looks familiar. But from where? Not here in Iceland. Not on the plane either, nor at the airport. Not from his rearview mirror.

This is bugging the shit out of him.

Malcolm grabs a bottle, turns around, and that's when he gets a good look at a nonreflected version of her face, and now he's even more certain that he's seen her before, that he maybe even *knows* her, is that possible—?

No.

Is this forgetfulness a function of age? The steep slope into the abyss of dementia?

Malcolm unfolds a wad of bills, greens and purples, men in beards and women in hats, one of those currencies with a berserk valuation scheme, everything costs at least a hundred krónur, the everyday notes are in multiples of thousands, everyone is forced to do four- and five-digit math all the time. Malcolm recently learned from his eight-year-old that there are long-multiplication methods other than his, which is apparently called the U.S. Algorithm. This infuriated him.

He turns away from the cashier, and on the way to the door gets a good full-frontal. He *knows* he has seen this woman before—

But not, he suddenly realizes, in the flesh. Where he saw her was on a screen. It was a little screen.

It was on the tennis court, last spring. This woman who's following Malcolm is Will's Australian temptress.

"Who are you?" the man yells from behind Will. "What do you want?"

Will is suspended out over the edge of the cliff, his face pointed down toward the rocky beach. He doesn't know how to answer, doesn't know how to get to the point quickly and clearly and nonthreateningly enough to save himself.

He knows how this would end up appearing, just another overconfident unprepared American with the wrong footwear on a muddy path at cliff's edge, easy to slip and fall, no evidence to suggest otherwise, no one for miles around to offer an alternative scenario. He visualizes himself launched into space, flipping forward one and a half rotations, landing on his head, snapping his neck and spine, crushing his skull, his splintering ribs puncturing his lungs, being killed in many different ways all at once, right after he gives the wrong answer.

"My name is Will Rhodes," he yells into the wind. "I'm a travel writer. I'm looking for a guy who used to run my magazine, Jonathan Mongeleach."

"I'm not him."

"Okay!"

Will feels his right foot giving way. It would be so very tragic if he died here by mistake. He tries to adjust his weight, to shift the pressure from his arch to his heel, to make his foot more secure. But this movement only serves to pitch him farther forward, and the man's grip on his nape shifts, suddenly unsteady—

Will screams—

But he doesn't fall. He's still dangling.

"Why did you come here?" The man seems less angry now; he's not screaming.

"An American guy in Húsavík, he thought you might be who I'm looking for."

The man doesn't answer.

"Listen, can you pull me in? I'm scared to death out here."

Still no answer, no movement. Then another shift of weight, of position, and for the slimmest of time frames Will thinks he's being thrown over this cliff, but that's not what's happening, he's being yanked to the safety of the muddy path, onto which he collapses in desperate relief, practically hugging the thick moist soil, like coffee grounds at the bottom of a French press.

Will looks up at the man, grizzled and wrinkled, ropy-muscled and fully bearded. A mane of long gray hair, tending toward white, hangs from under a tight black watch cap. He bears a passing resemblance to the Gorton's Fisherman on his day off, but none to Jonathan Mongeleach.

"Don't misunderstand," the man says, "it's still possible that you're going to die today, in any one of a half-dozen ways that I can kill you. So get up, very slowly."

Will struggles to his feet.

"Don't even consider doing anything stupid."

Too late for that.

Malcolm's cell phone is connected to the car's Bluetooth, Gabriella's disembodied voice coming through the tinny speakers. "It's another thirty miles," she says. "The driveway will be on your left, narrow, looks like it's dirt, a quarter-mile long. The house is about eighty yards shy of the bluff, but there's some stuff in between, it's hard to tell what from the satellite image. Little hills maybe? It looks green, but not like trees or shrubs."

"It's probably moss, covering volcanic rock. This whole island is a lava field."

"Okay. So there's a path that winds through that stuff, from the house out to the bluff. The path continues east another few hundred yards, where a set of stairs goes down to a cove, a pier with a small motorboat."

"Do we have any hard evidence about the occupant?"

"Not really, no. The house is owned by a local farmer, whose family has had the property for eighty years; electricity bill is in the owner's account, which is shared with a few other properties nearby. No phone, no Internet, no cable."

"Jesus," Malcolm says, "how monastic. Get it?"

"Hilarious."

"Does someone definitely live there?"

"I don't know, Mal. Electricity is used. There's a car there that's not Will's. But if you're asking if I have access to twenty-four-hour surveillance of a secluded house in eastern Iceland for the past year?"

Malcolm looks around at the landscape he's hurtling through, the stark mountains, the fog draped over the bay, the sheep dotting the fields. His mind keeps articulating that there's nothing here, a completely empty place. But that's absolutely wrong, there's plenty here; what's missing is humanity. Iceland is filled with an absence of humanity.

This is disappearing done right. It's not surprising that this is what Jonathan Mongeleach would do, not at all. What's surprising is that Will is the one who found him. And what's unfortunate is that Malcolm has to kill him.

"Okay Gabs, thanks. So the satellite will be out of range when?"

"Already happened, two minutes ago. That's it for the next hour, Malcolm, you're blind. Do you think it's really Jonathan out there?"

"I do."

"Well, good luck. And Mal?"

"Yeah?"

"Let's be careful out there."

◆ ◆ ◆

The house is snug, tidy. There aren't many things, and what few things there are aren't particularly nice, but they're all clean things, neat and arranged just so, squared-off corners and perfectly aligned piles, folded blankets and stacked plates and a handful of matching mugs all hanging at the same angle from a handful of matching pegs.

The guy hands Will one of these mugs. "Why are you looking for this person?"

"It's a long story."

The man doesn't look surprised. "Tell me."

Will takes a sip of the hot black coffee. "Who *are* you?"

"That's not important. What we're discussing is who you are, and why you're here."

Will is exhausted. He's tired of running, and tired of lying, and tired of not trusting anyone. He's tired of keeping secrets. Fuck it, he thinks. It's time to tell someone.

So he does, starting from the very beginning, from Elle baiting the hook in Bordeaux to reeling in the line in Mendoza, scaling and gutting him in New York and in Virginia, filleting him into something they wanted, something easy to chew, to digest, along the way discarding the bits they didn't need—his marriage, his conscience, his good night's sleep.

The man interrupts with questions—very specific, very personal questions:

"And this was full-on sexual intercourse?"

"Did either of these people in the hotel room have a weapon?"

"Approximately how many miles north of the bridge-tunnel was the training camp?"

"Did you ever have sex with her again?"

"Did you attempt to contact the real Elle Hardwick in Australia?"

"For how long did your wife work at *Travelers*?"

"How many times did you practice these surveillance-detection routes?"

"What did the receipts look like for your monthly payments?"

He also asks questions about the magazine, the merger—when did Will first hear the rumors, who's the purchaser, what's the timeline supposed to be.

And then the man stops asking questions when Will relates the chase through the East Village, to Paris and Akureyri, to the long lonely drive through the uninhabited, unwavering twilight, to here, now.

Will feels as if a huge weight has been lifted, as if he's been trudging around with a lie-filled backpack for months, and has just slipped out of its straps, let the thing crash onto the floor, its contents spilling, being sorted through by this stranger.

The man sits in his straight-backed wooden chair, leaning forward, hands steepled, staring at the fire through the glass door of the iron stove. He closes his eyes, and Will thinks he may have fallen asleep. Then he says, "This situation is complicated."

Will guffaws.

"I don't think those people in Argentina worked for the CIA."

"Why not?"

"First, there's no female employee of the Agency whose job it is to have sexual intercourse with men. Flirting, cockteasing, *sure*. And if a kiss or two is going to open doors that would otherwise be tightly closed, then who knows, some case officers would do it, and their superiors wouldn't object. But intercourse?" He shakes his head.

"Not for a black op?"

"A *black op*? I don't want to be unnecessarily condescending, but I have to tell you that you don't know what you're talking about."

Will can't deny this.

"You know what it's called when people have sex for money, right?"

Will doesn't answer.

"The CIA may do many unsavory things, immoral things, illegal things. Especially in what you call *black ops*. But the Agency isn't a brothel, and its employees aren't prostitutes."

Will nods.

"No team would sit in Langley and rationally orchestrate an op that's entirely premised on, *one*, paying a case officer to have sex with a potential asset, and, *two*, surreptitiously videotaping that sexual act, and, *three*, using that evidence to extort the potential asset into cooperating."

Now that a dispassionate observer is saying it aloud, it does sound ludicrous.

"That breaks a half-dozen federal and state laws in one fell swoop. Plus it's an op on a *domestic* target, taking place *within* the borders of the United States, which in and of itself is illegal. *Highly* illegal. The type of thing that would *really* antagonize the FBI."

"Well, to be fair, those crimes took place in Argentina. Does that matter?"

"Plus—let's be honest here—for what? For *you*? It's not like you're the premier of China or the director of Russian intelligence services. No insult intended."

Will shrugs, physically and emotionally.

The man gets up, walks across the small room, past folded blankets, and a stack of books. "It's obvious that someone thinks you have access to something extremely valuable, something worth considerable effort and expense to acquire. But whoever this is, it isn't the CIA."

The man opens the stove's little door. He picks up a poker, rearranges the wood amid crackling and sparks and a wave of heat that rolls across the room, rippling the cool air. Behind the stove, cross-country skis lean against a wall, on which hang a big crossbow, a tube of arrows, a pair of snowshoes.

"Do you have any idea what that valuable thing might be?"

Will does have an idea. In fact, he knows for certain. Elle—whoever she is, whomever she's working for—is after the records of *Travelers'* employees. Not the employees of the New York magazine, nor the travel agents abroad. All those people would be easy enough to identify without any complicated extortion schemes.

What Elle must be looking for is the identity and location of the freelancers. Why? Only one explanation makes sense: because those people are spies. They must be.

Both men jump at a shrill beep that's suddenly emanating from the kitchen, like a fire alarm.

"What's that?" Will asks.

"Someone's coming." The man hustles to the window, peeks out. "Why do you think you weren't followed?"

"I drove here from Húsavík and slept in the car by the side of the road. I would've noticed anyone following me."

"You rented this car in Akureyri?" The man is talking quickly, moving quickly. "Under what name?"

"Fake name. Some Canadian's passport and driver's license."

"How'd you procure those?" The man pulls on his jacket, pats down his pockets.

"Bought from some guy in Brooklyn."

"A guy you know well?"

"A guy I don't know at all."

"That guy screwed you over." He grabs Will's jacket from where it has been drying, hanging from a hook by the stove, and tosses it to Will. He then walks over to the open closet, collects a backpack.

"When whoever is coming arrives, I'm going to run down the cliff path. I'll get chased, but I won't get caught before I get into my boat, and I will be unfollowable. I'll never return to this house again, and you'll never see me again. You understand?"

Will nods.

"You, leave this house and do not come back. This is very important. Got it? Do not return." He looks Will in the eye, awaiting confirmation. Will nods.

"Take my car." He hands Will a key. "Follow the path around the shed, you'll see a dirt driveway, the car is around a bend. Hide in the car until you see whoever this is follow me. Then count to fifty and get out of here as quickly as you can."

Will pulls on his jacket, follows this guy to the back door.

"Turn left onto the road, and take it all the way around the north side of the peninsula. Don't stop anywhere, for any reason. Drive straight to a tourist destination. You know where Geysir is?"

"Not exactly." They step out the back door, into the wind and the rain.

"What about Þingvellir?"

"Sort of."

"What kind of goddamned travel writer are you?"

Will smiles. He pulls up the waterproof zipper of his high-tech jacket, bought at the pier in Húsavík before getting on the whale-watching boat.

"Þingvellir is easy to find, there's a map in the glove box. Park the car in the lot with the tour buses. Find a bus that's reboarding. Explain to the driver that you got lost on a path, left behind, here's five hundred, can you take me back to Reykjavík? He'll say yes."

They're walking through the backyard, out of view from the driveway, but not necessarily of anyone who might be lurking somewhere else.

"You understand all this? *Don't* drive back to the city. There are choke points leading into Reykjavík that are easy to cover physically, to monitor electronically. They'll find you immediately. Take a bus, sit away from windows."

They've come to the shed, where the paths diverge, Will's wider one toward the hidden car, and the narrow footpath toward the cliff, the water, the boat. The man pats Will's arm, then turns away.

"Hey?" Will calls out.

The man turns back.

"Are you sure it wasn't the CIA in Argentina?"

"I'm positive."

The rain is now pounding down on Will's unprotected head, soaking his hair. He wipes water out of his eyes to get a good look at this man, for the last time. "How?"

"Because you were already working for the CIA, Will. You just didn't know it."

41

Malcolm kills the headlights. He lets the car roll up the driveway, his eyes darting between the rutted path in front of him and the distance beyond, scanning for signs of life, for danger.

He comes around a bend, and pulls to a clearing on the side. Gets out. He abandons the car, sets off on foot, away from the driveway, parallel to the shore and to the main road, tromping over uneven ground, the moss spongy and slippery, the sharp edges of the rocks discernible beneath the leather soles of his custom-made wingtips. Malcolm is really not dressed for this.

He scampers down the far side of a ridge, finds himself in a gully, a drainage swale of the lava field, hidden from view of the driveway. He starts walking toward the house along this path, picking his way around pools of rainwater. Up ahead he can see Will's car, lights on in the house, smoke rising from the chimney. There's no movement visible through the windows, nor outside, anywhere.

And then there is, but from the other direction, the road. It's another car, coming to a stop at the top of the driveway, in a position that's invisible from the house, and from Malcolm's abandoned rental car. But it's visible to Malcolm from his vantage in the lava field.

He can see the woman climb from the passenger seat, the man from the driver's. It had probably taken a few miles before her car started listing, pulling toward the shoulder, and then finally the tires started to thwump. Did she know immediately what had happened? Then her companion collected her in his own car, from which they both fan out now, taking a similar approach as Malcolm—advancing on the house obliquely, out of sight. But Malcolm's angle is more indirect; he's more out of sight. He ducks lower, pushing into the wet moss, the rock digging into his stomach.

If this were merely a woman who seduced Will in France, she wouldn't be here, acting like this. No. Something other than adultery is going on. Malcolm is pretty sure that this woman compromised Will with something compelling and undeniable.

When exactly was it that he started behaving oddly? Early spring? Four months ago, maybe five.

What has Will been doing on this woman's behalf for the past half-year? Or did she recruit him in spring but wait until now, until a few days ago, when she demanded that he steal the *Travelers* files? Why?

And why now? Why at the exact same time that this woman—it *must* have been this woman—hired a guy to seduce Malcolm's wife in order to steal the files from his home computer . . . ?

This woman is the one who's assailing Malcolm, attacking *Travelers*. Who is she?

Malcolm watches her move competently over the uneven terrain. He doesn't actually give a shit who she is. But whom is she working for?

One possibility is that she's working for the Central Intelligence Agency, for some rogue division with a secret agenda, some strategic mission that led her to investigate *Travelers*. Perhaps the magazine is suspected by someone of being a front for a foreign entity, or for an American nongovernmental outfit. Someone at Langley wants to find out what *Travelers* is up to, and this is how they're doing it: by stealing records, by following current employees, by looking for former ones.

Another possibility is that she's working for one of those external entities. Malcolm wouldn't put it past the Russians or Chinese, nor for that matter the North Koreans or practically anyone in the Middle East. Although it's a sophisticated play, it's not prohibitively expensive, nor does it risk much exposure.

This woman and her team are probably freelance, maybe disaffected ex-military, possibly even ex-Agency. They might be innocent mercenaries, if there is such a thing, with no idea for whom they're working.

And who does, really? Maybe the do-gooding NGO is funded by a Swiss account endowed with Nazi loot. Maybe the supposedly pure research lab is financed solely by big pharma that turns a blind eye to fatal side effects.

Maybe the magazine group is undergoing a corporate takeover orchestrated by a megalomaniacal sociopath. Someone who wants to know what he's buying before he buys it. And maybe it's this sociopath who hired a mercenary to infiltrate Malcolm's operation.

Maybe that sociopath already knows precisely what's he's buying. That's why he's buying it. And that's why this is happening now.

Yes. That must be it: this man who's staging a takeover of the American Periodical Group is doing it for one reason, and it has absolutely nothing to do with publishing. He wants to buy the *Travelers* intelligence network. He's spending two billion dollars of corporate leverage to purchase his own privately controlled international spy service.

Now it all makes sense.

Looking back, Malcolm can't believe how naïve he'd been, how oblivious to the way the world works.

It was four months after his knee surgery, the procedure that the doctors were hoping wouldn't be necessary. The possibility hadn't yet occurred to Malcolm that he'd never again suit up, never pull the shoulder gear over his head, tuck the pads into his pants, snap the chin guard onto his helmet. He was still doing a lot of physical therapy, but it was the off-season, and his academic load was heavy, and he was trying hard to be an assiduous student at an elite university.

Financial aid wasn't in the forefront of his consciousness when he met with his adviser, a month before the end of the school year. For five minutes they had a perfectly pleasant pro forma chat—grades were fine, handling pressure okay, nothing much wrong except this leg, and two big papers were due on the same day.

Then there was a rap on the door. "Come in!" the professor called out.

Standing in the door was an unfamiliar man wearing a business suit. Not one of the sorts of suits you're used to seeing on college campuses, the old rumpled suits that always need dry-cleaning, or the fastidious tweedy types. This was a low-lapeled two-button loose-fitting sack suit, the uniform of politicians and bureaucrats, of lawyers and lobbyists, a navy suit and white shirt and red tie, shined black shoes that match the black belt, a pin to prove your patriotism, or your fealty to people who require that you prove your patriotism by wearing a pin.

"Malcolm Somers, this is Gerard Hastings, an old friend who works for the government." The professor stood up. "Gerry, it's good to see you."

The grown-ups shook hands. Malcolm's adviser said, "I need to run to the men's room, back in a couple minutes." He left.

Malcolm thought it was strange that the professor shut the door behind him, and even stranger when Hastings took the seat behind the big desk, said, "I hear you had some tough luck on the field, Mr. Somers. You were starting varsity quarterback as a sophomore? That's impressive."

"Yes, I was having a decent season."

"But surgery hasn't been entirely successful, has it?"

"Oh, my recovery's coming along fine."

Malcolm had grown accustomed to saying things like this, things that weren't true but were simpler for him to say, and for other people to hear. He'd said these things so frequently that sometimes he mistook them for the truth.

"Your financial aid is year to year, isn't it?"

There was no such thing as an athletic scholarship in the Ivy League, but on occasion those schools were willing to construct aid packages that approximated the charity of more sports-minded institutions. Otherwise there would have been no way for Malcolm to afford Harvard. His parents had reverse-mortgaged their house for a family health crisis that wiped out their salaries, both of them tenured at neighboring universities; they themselves had been college sweethearts, classmates in the English department. Their wedding invitation specified the date as Bloomsday, and tough luck to you if you didn't know when that was. They were hoping that their son would become a writer of the intellectual sort, fellowships and residencies and prestigious prizes from little magazines. Look what they got instead.

"And your parents, do they have the, um, *wherewithal* to cover the expenses here?" This was an odd conversation to be having with some stranger. "Tuition? Room? Board? Textbooks? None of it's cheap, is it?"

This man was asking two different questions, and Malcolm wasn't sure which he was answering when he said "No sir." But the answer was the same to either.

"No." The man agreed with Malcolm agreeing with him. "Listen, Mr. Somers. I'm sorry for your bad luck. I truly am. But where one door closes, sometimes another opens."

"Yes sir."

"My suggestion is that you switch your concentration to Near Eastern languages and civilization."

"That's interesting. But I'm pre-law."

"Is there such a thing?"

"Not officially."

"Don't you think there are already enough lawyers in America?"

Malcolm didn't understand what that meant—there were enough everythings in America, that's America—but didn't ask. In general Malcolm was not intimidated by adults, but somehow this gray bureaucrat scared the crap out of him.

"There could be opportunities for you, Mr. Somers. For someone like you: an athlete, a leader, a scholar. A good-looking, well-spoken guy."

"Opportunities in what? What would I be doing in the Near East?"

"Perhaps as a journalist? I wouldn't be surprised if we had, um, *engagements* in the coming years. You'd do well. I'm sure of it."

Malcolm was starting quarterback at Harvard; he already believed that he could do well in almost any endeavor. He didn't need anyone to tell him so.

What he did need, though, was what Hastings said next: "There's a scholarship." From his breast pocket he removed a piece of paper, folded in thirds to fit in there. "It's generous. Covers everything." He placed the paper in front of Malcolm. "It's open only to undergraduates in a limited number of concentrations. You'll see them listed, at the top."

There was a knock on the door.

"One minute, please," Hastings called out, aiming his voice at the door, at a tenured professor knocking on his own door. That's when Malcolm realized that this really was happening, and his adviser knew what was going on here, because it went on all the time.

"The deadline is the end of the school year. Decisions announced midsummer." Hastings tapped the paper. "Think about it, Mr. Somers. It's a good place to make a career."

Malcolm was almost positive he knew what the guy was referring to, but this was one of those situations that called for absolute certainty. "What is, exactly?"

Hastings stood, extended his hand for a shake. For a second there, Malcolm thought he wasn't going to get an answer.

But then he did: "The Central Intelligence Agency, Mr. Somers. I'm talking about a career in the CIA."

Will runs up the dirt road, finds the man's car. He opens the driver's door and climbs inside, out of the rain, out of view. The car's exterior is dented and dirty, but inside it's neat and clean, the automotive version of the little orange house.

Through the windshield Will can see land's end, the cliff's edge. He sees the man hustle past, a blur of blue raincoat and white hair.

Will sinks lower, sliding down in the seat, trying to stay out of view. But still he feels too visible in here, too trapped, too killable.

He gets out of the car. His jacket is bright red, a stupid choice. He takes it off, turns it inside out to the gray lining. He sets off through the lava field in the direction of the clifftop path. Halfway there, he stops and drops to his knees, crouching, hiding. It would really be useful if there were some trees on this island.

Another man rushes by on the path. For a second Will doesn't register who it is, because last time he saw this guy it was in a windowless conference room in downtown Manhattan; this guy is unexpected here in Iceland. It's Elle's partner, Roger. Which means Elle can't be far behind.

Of course. Who else would be pursuing him?

Elle must be furious about the incomplete duplication of the *Travelers* files. Is she here to punish him? That punishment wouldn't be lenient.

Will creeps over the uneven ground, the treacherous volcanic mounds, back toward the house, no discernible movement anywhere in there. Where is she?

They arrived by car—there's no other way they arrived, is there?—but that car isn't visible. The trip-wire alarm must be at the top of the driveway. Which means they must have parked somewhere between there and here. It's a narrow makeshift driveway, barely wide enough for a single car to navigate without scraping against tire-puncturing rocks, or tumbling into ditches. If their car is parked in this driveway, there's no way for Will to maneuver around it. He's trapped.

What can he do? He can run; he has outrun danger before. He can run up the driveway, he can disable their car—how? spark plugs? fuel line? Will doesn't know shit about cars—and go for a breakneck jog on the isolated road, hope that a passing stranger picks up a desperate-looking hitchhiker before Elle repairs the car, hunts him down, and kills him.

No, that's definitely not a plan A.

And there she is, coming around the near side of the house. He ducks behind the shed, and finds himself on the path that leads to the cliff.

Will walks quickly, his mind's eye picturing the locations of the big rock outcroppings that he can crawl around, find a spot to hide, and wait out . . . what? Wait for what event to transpire? Why would they leave?

They wouldn't, would they? Only if they thought he was on the boat, which now that Will is at cliff's edge he can see is speeding away from the cove. It's fairly obvious that there's only one person on that boat, and it isn't Will.

Shit.

Will starts to jog. The first outcropping is a hundred yards ahead, fifteen seconds away, twenty. He can make it. His eyes dart along the path, searching for rocks and ruts, for pitfalls that could trip him, send him crashing to the ground, or tumbling off the side, hurtling to his death; there's not a lot of room for error. He visualizes two and three and four steps ahead, right foot left foot, right left.

He's a few steps from the outcropping when he starts to look over its facets, to figure out where he might hide, and realizes there's nowhere. Facing the sea, the rock face is sheer; facing land, it's a gentle slope, nothing steep or angled enough to hide him.

Will has to keep going. The next outcropping is another fifteen seconds.

He speeds up. He can already see that this giant hunk will offer hiding opportunities, a crazy-looking pillar formation, plus something like an alcove. It will be hairy to get around to that side, and he'll have to be extra careful not to sink into some unseen void; this moss hides all manner of ankle-breaking hollows.

Just another few seconds, then he'll dart off the path, onto the lava, around the—

Roger appears. He's blocking the path, coming around from the far side of the rock.

Both men come to a stop, ten feet apart. Both of them are just inches from the edge of the cliff.

Elle peeks in the window of the corrugated-steel shed, dark in there. It's possible that someone's hiding.

She creeps around to the door. Turns the handle gingerly, wary of the squeaks and groans of hardware that lives outside, exposed to the elements. But the mechanism is quiet, well maintained. The door opens without a sound.

A quick look around. There's no one in here, not unless there's a trap-door down to a secret compartment in the earth. Low-percentage, and she doesn't have the time to screw around. She turns to leave, but her eye is caught by something, and she takes two long strides across the small room, to the pegboard that's hung with tools and garden implements, nautical supplies and winter-sport gear.

She snatches the ice-climbing axe off the wall. She hefts it in her hand. Small, lightweight, rubber grip, nylon strap. This will be more gory than she'd normally choose. But it'll do.

Once the woman is out of sight, Malcolm can no longer see anyone, all of them disappeared in the direction of the sea. He creeps toward the house, trying to stay out of sight as much as possible, but there's really no way. The best he can hope for is to be lucky.

Of course, he could beat a retreat. Return to his car, turn around, drive away. He could let them have Will, whoever they are. Let them have whatever information Will thinks he stole, which is becoming less and less meaningful with each passing minute, as word spreads to the *Travelers* network that their numbered accounts may be compromised, as private bankers in Luxembourg and Liechtenstein and Grand Cayman are paid unexpected visits from rarely heard-from clients, shutting down accounts, wiring funds to banks in Hong Kong and Singapore, in New York and London, and then forwarded on to fresh numbered accounts in Andorra and the Isle of Man or simply back to the same exact financial institutions they departed, the trails gone cold in the greed-driven shroud of secrecy that facilitates money laundering and tax evasion all over the globe.

It's possible that some stragglers might not make it. Stray operatives who are off the grid, who missed Gabriella's coded message on TV this morning, won't catch up with it until it's too late, until their accounts are frozen. But even so, what's the worst that would happen? A few people would feel compelled to abandon some money.

But otherwise there's nothing to steal; there's no one to expose. Nothing particularly incriminating can be found in Malcolm's files. This is— this has always been—half the point of *Travelers:* no files.

And also no electronic communications, not for anything meaningful. Because if what you are is a CIA cadre that operates outside the purview of the CIA, with a specific mandate of keeping secrets from the mainstream CIA, then you know that there's no such thing as secure electronic communication. There is no level of encryption, no subterfuge, no misdirection, that cannot be hacked, no phone that cannot be tapped. The only way to ensure that your communications are not intercepted is to not communicate electronically. Hence the envelopes conveyed around the globe by ignorant couriers.

So whoever is trying to infiltrate *Travelers*, and whatever it is they think they're going to discover, they're not. Not unless they find someone who knows the entire truth, and somehow manage to get it out of him.

There are only a handful of such people. Malcolm and Gabriella are two of them. Two of the others occupy offices in Langley.

And the fifth?

Malcolm doesn't know for certain where the fifth is. It's possible that this is his orange house, and the fifth person is here, about to be abducted, tortured, sold off to the highest bidder. It's possible that after three-quarters of a century of uninterrupted operation, the whole thing is about to come crashing down around Malcolm, in its wake sucking under not only the livelihoods but maybe the lives of hundreds of operatives and assets all over the world; Malcolm might very well be one of them.

So no: retreat is not really an option.

He creeps forward.

"Come on, Will. It's finished, this little flight of yours." Roger is spreading out his considerable bulk, feet planted wide, arms spread, making it clear that Will has no way forward. "No reason for anyone to get hurt here. And by anyone, I mean you. And by get hurt, I mean killed."

Will considers turning on his heel. He knows Elle is back there, but maybe he can dodge her? Or outmuscle her? Maybe not. She's a trained CIA officer, with who knows what level of combat skills. She might be armed.

But Roger doesn't appear to be. He may be bigger and stronger, but Will has gotten the best of Roger before. Plus Will has been training, and what he has been training for is this, specifically: to take out a bigger man. In fact, to take out *this exact* bigger man.

Will lunges forward, rears back his right arm, aiming for a jab at Roger's jaw, which the big man deflects, replying with a jab of his own that glances off the side of Will's head, stinging his ear, ouch.

Will takes a step back, out of reach.

Roger takes a step forward.

Will tosses another noncommittal jab at Roger's face, but again his punch is deflected.

He tries again. Deflected again. As expected.

Will has now set the table. He prepares himself for Roger's inevitable counterpunch, and here it comes, a hook instead of a jab, more momentum, more force, more pain if it connects—

But it won't. This is a move Will was taught, has practiced, again and again and again. He drops to his left knee while sweeping his right leg around, catching Roger on one ankle and dislodging it quickly. Will forces the same leg to continue its sweeping arc through to Roger's other ankle, Will now braced against the ground by his left elbow, kicking out his right leg with all his might, because he's going to save his own life—or not—with the power of this kick. If he can take out Roger's other ankle, the big man will come tumbling down, pitching toward the precipice—

Roger is falling. Both his feet are in the air, his rear end headed down while his arms are up, no balance whatsoever, no way to regain it. He hits the ground. Will can see his body shudder with the impact. Much like when Will lost his own feet on that dewy lawn in Argentina, his skull hitting the earth, knocking him unconscious.

Roger isn't knocked out. But only half his body lands on the path, while the other half is unimpeded by anything solid, shifting Roger's momentum outward, dragging his earthbound half along, sliding toward the cliff's edge, the man's arms scrambling, his fingers clawing, his eyes wide with terror, his mouth open in a swallowed scream.

Will is on the ground, watching. He can save this man's life, or he can allow him die. Or, rather: he can continue killing him.

There's no time to think about it, no time to consider what will happen if he pursues either choice, to weigh his options in any rational fashion. Is this a kill-or-be-killed situation?

Instinct takes over: Will reaches out. He grabs Roger's wrist, holds tight, keeps this man from falling to certain death, at least for the moment.

"Pull him in."

Elle is standing on the path, ten feet away. She's wielding an axe.

"Pull him in, Will, or I swear to God, I'll kill you."

Although it's still raining, clouds have broken along the southwestern horizon, and the setting sun is skimming the ocean. Will squints into the glare to see the man's face, pleading, his body half-hanging off the cliff, struggling to regain some degree of control over his destiny. He shifts his weight in a way that turns out to be unfavorable, and his wrist begins to slip through Will's grasp.

"*Will!*" Elle screams.

He feels her footsteps coming, and the corner of his eye catches a flash of light glinting off the axe blade, and Will turns just in time to see another body flying into view, another man, leaping forward, arms extended—

Elle sidesteps this other man while backhanding the axe across her body, ripping into the man's leg as he crashes to the earth.

Roger uses the opportunity of Will's distraction to twist his torso, to fling his free arm in the direction of Will, seizing Will by the shirtsleeve, losing his balance even further, sinking lower, and even lower, and now his entire body is in the air, and he's falling, and he's pulling Will with him, off the edge of the cliff.

Will is powerless to stop this, the momentum of a 240-pound man falling, attached to a 170-pound man kneeling. It's just physics: irresistible, undefeatable.

42

alcolm hits solid earth with a jarring thud, skittering toward the edge of the cliff, blinding pain in his leg where the axe gouged his flesh.

He sees Will tumbling off the cliff. Malcolm reaches out, takes hold of Will's ankle with one hand. He brings his other hand around to grab Will's calf, a two-handed grip, but Will is still slipping away, being pulled over the edge by that other man, and Malcolm squeezes his hands tighter, presses his legs into the dirt, trying to anchor himself in place, but—

"Ahhhhhhhhh . . ."

The noise trails off, then ends abruptly.

His hands are empty. Will has slipped from his grasp.

Malcolm scampers forward on his hands and knees, cranes his neck over the precipice. On the beach far below, a body is sprawled, both legs bent at an impossible-looking angle. But it's only one dead body down there. And it's not Will.

Where's Will?

Will is hanging from the side of the cliff, both feet with toeholds on a narrow shelf of stone, one fist clenched around the root of a tenacious shrub that has managed to survive out here on the exposed face of the windswept, sea-battered bluff.

Will is still alive. But perhaps not for long.

The axe is lying in the dirt. Malcolm lunges for it, just inches beyond his reach. He slithers forward on his stomach, hyperextends his arm, almost there—

But Elle arrives first. She steps on Malcolm's hand.

"Sorry, guys," she says, picking up the weapon. She glances at Will, just a finger twitch away from free fall; he's not much of a threat. She turns to Malcolm, lying on the path, bleeding from a gash in his leg, also not a serious concern. She peers over the edge, down at Roger, a jumble of crushed limbs. She's the last man standing.

"What do you want?" Malcolm asks, hoping to open some sort of negotiation here.

"I want the names. All of them. And their locations."

"What names?"

"Really? At this moment, Malcolm Somers, you want to patronize me?"

She digs her heel into Malcolm's knuckles, and he screams.

"Please!" Will calls from below. "I'll give you the files!"

"Where are they?"

"A thumb drive. In my pocket."

Elle is pretty sure this is not true. She glances at Will, then over at Malcolm, who looks defeated, like a guy who realizes that he has just lost everything. But then again, this might be an act; she wouldn't put it past him. Malcolm Somers is no moron. She has to continue to be vigilant.

And not just vigilant right now, in this moment, but vigilant forever. Even if she kills these two men right here—*especially* if she kills them— this is never going to end, is it? It would've been one thing to kill Will, disposing of one disposable man, a pawn, nobody really gives a shit. But Somers is no pawn. Killing him would be serious business, with serious repercussions. She'd never be able to show her face again in the United States, nor anywhere with a CIA presence, which is basically everywhere, or might conceivably be everywhere, which is the same thing.

A million dollars isn't going to be enough, not nearly. But she has no doubt that she'll be able to extract more. *If* she finds what her employer is looking for. If she doesn't? That might be an unsolvable problem.

"Help him up, Somers. But you two?" She hefts the axe. "Don't make me kill you."

Malcolm uses both hands to pull Will's wrist, yanking his friend back from the abyss. Elle can hear Will groan as his body scrapes up the rocky lip of the cliff, tearing the skin along his chest and stomach, his groin and thighs, one long abrasion.

It looks like hard work, dragging up this sack of body. And Malcolm's leg probably hurts like hell. These are two damaged animals. More dangerous than ever.

Will follows ten feet behind the limping Malcolm, who's dragging his bloody leg. Will occasionally feels the point of the knife that Elle clutches in one hand, while the other wields the axe. She can do a lot of damage, very fast, with these two blades.

A quarter-mile up the driveway, the road is silent. During the day, there were smatterings of tourists, in vans and buses and rental cars and campers, clusters of adventure-seekers headed to the park, the volcano, the glacier. But now, even if it's not dark, it's nighttime. They're all alone.

Will was dangled over the edge of the same cliff twice in one day, and both times was yanked back to safety, and brought to this house.

Elle turns her head slowly around the room, taking in the furnishings, the sporting equipment, the front door, the open closet, dark in there. She peers inside, flips a light switch, and looks left, right. She grabs something, emerges. It's a spool of fishing line.

"Will, sit," she says. "Somers, tie him up."

"Oh come on," Will protests.

"Sit the fuck down," she says, brandishing her knife, "and shut the fuck up."

Malcolm starts to wrap Will's arms and torso to the back of the chair.

"Who lives here?"

"A guy who calls himself Joe. I think he used to be CIA."

"It's not Mongeleach?"

"No."

"Do you know where Mongeleach is?"

Will shakes his head.

"Okay," she says, when Will is bound up. "Now let's have a look at that thumb drive. Somers? Get it."

Will searches for Malcolm's eyes, but he doesn't look up.

"Malcolm," Will says. "*Mal.* Front right pocket."

Malcolm looks up, nods. He digs around in there, fishes out the device, hands it over to Elle. This thumb drive contains worthless files, all their relevant info adulterated. The other drive, in Will's back pocket, contains the untouched files.

"Now you sit down."

Malcolm staggers into a chair, clutching his bleeding leg.

"Where's the computer?"

"I doubt there is one," Will says. "It's not exactly the twenty-first century in here."

He can see Elle's eyes searching the surfaces, covering all the territory. "Why didn't you just give this to me in the first place? Why the fuck did I have to chase you to the ends of the earth?"

"Because I don't know what it is you're trying to steal. And I don't know who you work for. But I do know it isn't the CIA."

"Oh yeah? How do you think you know that?"

"That Mike guy, in the conference room? Mike in the cheap suit, civil-servant lifer?"

"What about him?"

"Mike wore a ten-thousand-dollar watch."

She digests this, and Will can see that he's right. Mike was an impostor of a working-class agent. "Okay smart guy, so tell me who I do work for."

"*I* don't know. Do *you*?"

She stares at Will, then turns to Malcolm. "Somers, give me your car keys. Then get his."

Malcolm struggles to extract his keys, groaning at the exacerbation of his injury. Then he collects Will's as well.

"Now, Somers, your phone."

"I don't have one."

Without any warning she punches him in the face, a powerful jab to the cheek.

"Fuck!" Malcolm rubs his face. "It's in the car."

She stares at him, then wraps the fishing line around one of his arms, one of his legs, binding him to the chair, but not torturing him.

"Now I'm going to my car. Where I'll get my computer, and verify this." She holds up the thumb drive: the bank-account files with no names, no locations, nothing to ID the accounts' owners besides country codes, which aren't going to satisfy anyone.

"First, is there anything you want to, um, *clarify* about this drive? Before I waste my time and effort, and exhaust my patience, and have to come back here disappointed, and slit your fucking throats?"

She turns to Malcolm. His pants are ripped open, blood streaming down his leg, across his shoe, dripping onto the painted-wood floor. "Somers?" Elle has put down the axe, but she's still holding the knife. "You want to tell me something?"

Will can see that Malcolm is sweating, pale.

Elle bends at the waist, leans toward Malcolm, knife in her right hand, just inches from his face. But it's her left that suddenly does the damage, pressing on his wound, and Malcolm screams, and screams, and she continues to press for five seconds, a painful perpetuity.

She removes her hand, stands up straight. Malcolm's screaming subsides, replaced by hyperventilating. He's in bad shape. This type of torture doesn't take long. "Somers?"

He stares at her.

"Somers, you look like a man who wants to unburden himself."

He doesn't say anything.

"I'm wrong?" She looks at his leg. "Okay, we'll try this again." She reaches down—

"*No!*" Will calls out from across the room. "*Stop!*"

She looks over her shoulder. "Why?"

"There are no names on that drive. No addresses. Nothing but account numbers."

"You lied to me? Will." Tsk-tsk. "I'm disappointed."

Will looks over at Malcolm, who seems to be staring at a window, eyes open wide.

"I guess the only question now is: Who should I kill first?"

Malcolm says something, but too softly.

"What's that?" Elle asks.

"I'll tell you. Everything. I know. But please. Can you do something. About. My leg?"

Malcolm takes a slug from the glass of scotch. Elle rips his pant leg all the way open, and splashes on some of the booze as disinfectant. Malcolm digs his top teeth into his lower lip so hard he draws blood, but he doesn't scream again. She wraps the wound in gauze, tape.

"It's a long story," he says.

"We have forever." She refills his glass.

"Okay." Malcolm nods. "Benjamin Donaldson signed up for the Army right after Pearl Harbor."

"You're fucking kidding me? World War II?"

"You want to know what's going on? Or not?"

She sighs. "Oh go ahead." She sits.

"In Europe, Benji was recruited by the Office of Strategic Services, and spent the war spying in France. He eventually discovered that no matter how good the intel, it was worse than useless if you couldn't trust the messenger. And you could *never* trust any messenger completely. This is a truth Benji discovered via a literal stab in the back.

"He survived—barely—and spent months lying in Walter Reed, wondering how he'd been betrayed, how it could've been avoided. He came to the conclusion that the only way to completely trust messengers was to make them unaware that they were messengers."

Will realizes that Elle had been right about all those PERSONAL AND CONFIDENTIAL envelopes.

"But the war was over. Truman was wary of a permanent spy institution, and he didn't like the guy who'd run the OSS, Bill Donovan. He fired Donovan, disbanded the OSS, shut down bureaus in Asia and Europe, gutted the service. There had been twelve thousand intelligence personnel, now there were two thousand. Even Allen Dulles went back to a law firm in New York; Benji Donaldson got a magazine job."

Malcolm shifts his injured leg, elevates it onto a chair, grimaces.

"Truman started a new service, but he put an amateur in charge, a supermarket tycoon. The postwar intel was bullshit—collected by amateurs, communicated insecurely, analyzed insufficiently. A fiasco."

Malcolm takes another drink. He's beginning to look less awful.

"One of the cofounders of the Agency, Frank Wisner, started having potlucks in Georgetown. Sundays, servants' night off. The food wasn't great, though I think Julia Child showed up, before she was much of a cook. There was a lot of liquor, a lot of far-fetched ideas. One floated by an ex-OSS guy who was now in the magazine business in New York."

"No way," Will says. He's been wondering where the hell this story was going, and now he sees.

"Surprisingly, Benji's harebrained scheme got traction."

Will can't believe it.

"*Travelers* was invented for two very different ops. One, propaganda: magazine articles for an American audience that glorified our allies, or that reinforced the narrative that America had saved the world from Hitler—and that the world was grateful. You know what I'm talking about, Will."

All those jingoist articles from the forties, fifties, sixties: state-sponsored propaganda.

"The other op was a courier program: creating cover that allowed Americans to come and go worldwide without arousing suspicion. This was in the days when intelligence was passed hand to hand, people compromised face-to-face. *Travelers* was the ultimate back channel, all the more secure because the couriers—journalists and photographers and editors—had no idea whatsoever that they were spies. Had no idea who they were working for. What they were doing."

Malcolm fixes his gaze on Elle. "Do you know who *you* work for?"

She doesn't say anything.

"Are you going to tell us?" Malcolm asks.

"Are you kidding? Of course not. Go on, keep explaining."

"The magazine was profitable, the clandestine courier service successful. So Benji started thinking about expansion, for the same reasons that all organizations undergo mission creep: to justify their own existence, to serve ambition. Benji was ambitious. And this was in the heyday of the corporation, the dominant idea that it wasn't sufficient to thrive—it was necessary to expand, always. A flat year was failure. So Benji proposed a third operation: the actual gathering of intelligence, in small cadres that would parallel CIA stations. This was a tough sell in Langley, but eventually he received permission to try a test case, in 1949."

"The Paris bureau," Will mutters, mostly to himself.

"The focus was to monitor the immense disbursements of the Marshall Plan in Europe. This became the primary objective of *Travelers*' bureaus for decades, in Hong Kong for Korea and Vietnam, in Beirut, in

420 | CHRIS PAVONE

Mexico City: keeping track of the U.S. foreign-aid money, and who was spending it, in the name of advancing American interests.

"*Travelers* recruited its own network of assets, and a team of agents to run them. A service that invented its own necessity, with a specialty in very local intel. A lot of this intel was gossip that could provide recruitment leverage: who was paying bribes to the police chief, and why; who seemed to have more money than his job paid; who was screwing whose wife."

Malcolm pauses, stares at Elle. "That was fucked-up."

She doesn't respond. Will doesn't understand.

"Also less personal info," Malcolm continues. "Where did the recent German immigrants resettle? Which metal-fabricating factory was doubling its workforce? This was all info best collected by locals whose publicly verifiable jobs were known to be collecting info."

All those bureau managers at their desks in Paris and London, Rome and Istanbul, all those people whose jobs it is to know everyone in town. All spies?

"The foreign bureaus are CIA substations?"

Malcolm nods.

So Inez is a spy? *Mumblemore?*

"After the Hoover-fueled FBI-CIA squabbles, the secrecy of *Travelers* became ever more crucial, and the editor started reporting to the director of Central Intelligence himself."

"Are you saying your boss is the DCI?" Elle asks.

"Yes. Yours?"

"I'm not the one answering questions here, Somers. What's your mandate?"

"There are operations that the CIA can't handle for itself because it's impossible to know who in the Agency is utterly trustworthy. Information too sensitive to entrust to normal channels—info about double agents, moles, interior investigations. That is, info about unreliable people. So *Travelers'* primary task was to find people—to find ex-agents and current assets, foreign operatives, fugitives, criminals—who don't want to be found."

"That's pretty ironic, isn't it? Jonathan Mongeleach created an op to find himself."

She's right, but Malcolm doesn't answer.

"How do you transmit your intel to Langley?"

"Dead drops. Men's rooms in restaurants."

"And how does the funding get to you?"

"A fake advertiser. A few of them, actually. Numbered accounts in Switzerland, most of which directly feed the bureaus, which are free-standing enterprises outside of the American system, with independent operational funds. The only money that comes back to New York is what we need to keep the magazine looking healthy."

Will can tell that Elle is impressed with the intricacies of the sham. She herself has been perpetuating a few labyrinthine hoaxes for a very long time.

"Who knows about this?" she asks.

"Practically no one. Most of the bureau personnel think they work for a travel agency."

"And the street network?" Elle asks.

Will's eye catches something, some movement, some shift of light or reflection in the window across the room. What was that?

"All those informers—and the assets in the foreign governments and embassies, the businesspeople, the media—they all think we're journalists. And that's what we really are: journalists, like Will; editors, like me."

Will continues to scan the room, careful not to move his head, not to draw Elle's attention. Everything seems to be as it was before. The fire has died down, just embers glowing in there. But is something missing?

"And you?" Elle asks. "You've been CIA since your first job as a reporter, straight out of college?"

"Sort of. Started with a year at the Farm and in Langley."

Elle looks over at Will. "What about him?"

Malcolm too turns his eyes to Will. "I don't know what he *suspects*. But until tonight, I don't think he could've *known* anything about any of this. Unless his wife told him."

Malcolm is asking a question, wants an answer. Will shakes his head. But he's distracted, having just realized that there's definitely something missing, something that had been hanging from the wall before. He doesn't remember Joe taking it. But it isn't there now. The crossbow.

◆ ◆ ◆

"There are no records of the network?" Elle asks, her spirits sinking. "Names, addresses, aliases?"

"No."

Elle stands in the middle of the room, halfway between her two captives, looking at neither, weighing her options, none of them hugely attractive.

"Why don't you tell me who you're looking for."

"I'm looking for *all* of them, Somers, that's the point. I'm looking for the whole network. And I'm especially looking for Mongeleach. So where is he?"

Both men shake their heads.

"You understand that if you don't tell me where Mongeleach is, you're no longer any use?"

Neither says anything.

She has no choice. She has to kill Will. And Somers is here, so she has to kill him too. Loose ends. Will may not understand this, he's still a novice. But Somers does.

There's no point in drawing this out. She turns to Will, looks him in the eye. She takes a step toward him, then another.

"I'm sorry," she says. And she pulls the knife out of her pocket.

Chloe throws the door open, bursts into the room, yells, "*No!*"

The woman called Elle turns, knife in her right hand. It has a long blade, a heavy-looking hilt, a sharp curved tip, good for slicing or stabbing. But it's no match for the crossbow that Chloe is aiming.

"Well," Elle says, "if it isn't the wife." The two women stare at each other from twenty feet apart, sizing up the competition. "I've heard a lot about you."

Chloe is not terribly confident with this weapon. She'd used a crossbow at summer camp, but that had been a much simpler contraption, twenty years ago. This one she dragged off the wall, along with the arrows, when the house was empty. She figured out how to load it, took a couple of silent practice shots out in the Icelandic gloaming. Her aim was not very good.

She was hoping she wouldn't have to use it; still is. What she wants is for this woman to just go away, leave them alone, let them pick up the pieces and get back to their lives. But it doesn't look like that's going to happen.

"Tell me, Will, who'd you prefer fucking?"

So that's it. That's what happened. That's how Will got sucked into this, that's how they all got here. Chloe turns her eyes to her husband, who looks absolutely devastated—pained and apologetic and deeply, unbearably sad.

Chloe suspected as much. And she managed to convince herself that it didn't really matter, that he'd been tricked by a wily professional, that he loved his wife and she loved her husband, that she'd get over it, maybe even had already. But now that it's 100 percent confirmed, it hurts so much more than it had at 95 percent.

Elle takes a sidestep toward Will. "Was it your wife?"

She's trying to rattle me, Chloe thinks. Don't let her.

"Or was it me?" Another step.

"Stop moving," Chloe says.

"Or what, wife? Are you going to—"

Chloe pulls the trigger. The arrow flies across the room, faster here in the enclosed space than it seemed in the wide-open dusk, a short whoosh and a wet-sounding sucking noise as it lands, followed instantaneously by a yelp.

The arrow has missed the target, which was the center of this woman's mass. But still the point has sunk into her side.

Elle doesn't fall. She looks at the arrow, long and straight, lodged in her flank. Then she looks back at Chloe.

Just then the phone rings, echoing through the wood-walled house.

Elle turns toward Will, and Chloe knows what's about to happen. Chloe isn't aware of dropping the crossbow but she does, and now her feet are flying across the floor, then she's launching herself through the air—

Two rings.

Chloe crashes into Elle's side just as the woman is thrusting her knife at Will, who's trying to squirm his tied-up torso away.

Three rings.

Chloe is atop Elle. She seizes the wrist that holds the knife, digs her knee into Elle's abdomen. The arrow is still jutting out of the woman's side.

The answering machine picks up. "*Hi, this is Joe.*"

Suddenly Will manages to topple his chair, falling sideways, his feet up in the air, his tied-up arm falling directly onto the arrow, the weight of his body pressing—

"*Please leave a message.*"

—the sharp arrowhead deeper into Elle's thorax, breaking through her ribs, up—

Beep.

—through her flesh, piercing her lungs.

The knife topples out of Elle's hand, clatters to the floor.

"*Didn't I tell you not to go back to the house?*" It's the American who lives here, speaking to his own answering machine. "*Listen: you have about ninety seconds. Then the house is going to explode.*"

Chloe uses Elle's fallen knife to slice through the line that binds Will to the chair, and he feels himself leaping up, running across the room, using the same knife to unbind Malcolm, dragging him out of the chair, the whiskey glass crashing to the floor, shattering, Malcolm moaning from the pain, his leg immobilized for the past half-hour, swollen and bruised, plus the gash ripped open again.

"Come on!"

Malcolm hobbles across the room, through the open front door, and Will and Chloe drag him across the yard, and the three of them stumble up the packed-dirt driveway, hearing nothing except the sound of their own ragged breaths and uneven footfalls, wondering how far they need to get, how much time is left, and Will sees the sky light up just the tiniest fraction of a second before the force of the blast propels him forward, and the sound bursts in his ears, and he's flung forward, hits the ground belly-down, chunks of wood and stone and steel crashing all around him, ripping through skin and piercing flesh, until it's suddenly over, just the crackling of fire, and he rolls onto his back, looks up at what passes for night in the Scandinavian summer, the sky suspended in permanent twilight, stars visible along the dark horizon to one side, a royal-blue sunset sky to the other, his boss and wife lying beside him, all three of them wounded, but still alive.

EPILOGUE

—————

KEFLAVÍK

The American ex-spy watched through binoculars as his house was incinerated by the carefully arranged sequence of explosives and accelerators. He was a quarter-mile out to sea, and the house was high up on the bluff, a pyre surrounded by darkness, so he couldn't tell if the people were alive; he didn't even know how many there were. He didn't especially care.

He sped across the bay, dropped anchor in the secluded cove. He reclined, but he didn't expect sleep. Sometimes rest is enough.

In the morning he ran the boat up onto the beach, ditched it, hiked up to the road. He caught a bus to the city, made his way to the dumpy rooming house off Hverfisgata Street that always has vacancies. He napped.

He'd lived his entire life as a clean-shaven, clean-cut man, suits and ties and white linen pocket squares, monthly haircuts, shined shoes, a steady sequence of interchangeable supervisors in Langley. Then a couple of years ago, on the long journey to Iceland, he grew a beard for the first time in his life; he let his hair grow long.

Now he had to cut off that beard, a small sink filled with kinky white hair, a dozen nicks and cuts from the disposable razor on the unaccustomed skin. He buzzed his hair down to a half-inch of white, like a wall-to-wall carpet in a warm-weather McMansion. He bought a plain tee shirt and khakis around the corner.

He's recognizable from his old life, perhaps. But he's unrecognizable from yesterday's.

He needs to run again—farther this time, and faster, and forever. Because it's not just anyone who has found him, not some random travel writer who got manipulated by a run-of-the-mill corporate raider who's looking for inside information on a media acquisition. No, that would have been a much easier problem to solve. That problem would already have been solved by escaping, by burning down the house.

His unsolved, intractable problem is that what the corporate raider is actually looking for is the *Travelers* clandestine network—for the agents and the assets, for the whole apparatus, for the infinitely valuable secrets of the spies and their lies, for an American intelligence network that operates outside the purview of the CIA's oversight. And he has found it.

What's even worse is that the corporate raider is also looking for Joe. The two have known each other for decades. The man's name is Charlie Wolfe, and he'll stop at nothing to kill his enemies. By disappearing, Joe became one of them.

Joe has already arranged for his next home, a furnished apartment in the *centre* of Luxembourg, which has always been known as a good place to hide yourself as well as your money. A small quiet city filled with expats, with bankers and lawyers and accountants, not to mention good doctors, which he's sure he'll be needing.

Unless he gets captured—or killed—first. Before he gets to Luxembourg, he needs to not get identified here. He isn't yet out of these particular woods.

So he catches a bus to the airport. He finds a round table in the far corner of the big café in the main terminal. He thumbs through magazines and newspapers, and he watches, and he waits.

Then these three people arrive, looking like they've been dragged in from the end of the earth.

Chloe's first instinct was to check on Will. He was a bloody mess, cuts and abrasions, but nothing gushing. He seemed to be moving his body okay, rolling onto his side, staring up at the sky. Malcolm also seemed fine, in a general sort of way.

She let out a sigh of relief, not only for these men, relatively unharmed, but also for herself, that her first concerns were for the welfare of other people. Chloe had been worrying about her loss of humanity. For a long time she'd lived with the discomfiting knowledge that she was a liar; that she'd been a covert intelligence operative since before she'd met Will; that she'd never told him, not even after they got married, not even after he started working at *Travelers*, not even after she'd departed.

Because she hadn't really quit. Yes, she'd left the office. She'd left behind the piddling salary and long hours of a staff writer whose other responsibility was to look for disappeared assets and agents. Instead, she took a new freelance position: analyzing leads, plotting contingencies, and then assassinating the disappeared operatives who were un-disappeared by people like her husband. By people who *are* her husband.

So in addition to being a liar, she was now a murderer, and this wasn't something she'd wanted to admit to her husband. She didn't think this was something she'd need to admit, because Malcolm had promised that he would never bring Will inside. And he hadn't. So this whole thing wasn't really Malcolm's fault.

Was it Will's fault? She didn't know what exactly happened between him and that woman. But Chloe was pretty sure that it wasn't a simple matter of cruel infidelity.

Did she want to know the particulars? She'd already decided to forgive Will. Maybe the details would only get in the way.

Chloe reached out to Will's face, palm against his bloody cheek, and they stared at each other, lying there on the rough ground, side by side.

She realized that she was crying, and she didn't know when she'd started.

On the same day last spring when Will first met Elle, he mounted an electronic box on the dashboard of the rental Fiat that he was about to drive around southwest France. As a driving aid, this box was nothing special: no wide choice of voices, no exhaustive menu of map options, not very responsive to changing traffic conditions.

But what the device did do that was very unusual was capture cellphone signals, and transmit them via satellite to the mainframe computer in the cool windowless room on the *deuxième étage* of the Paris bureau, where an algorithm instantly recognized that a disposable mobile in the French Pyrénées placed a call to a mobile in central Moscow, which then connected to a landline a few blocks away. This was the event that caught Omar's attention.

The French mobile's signal then disappeared. Two days later that same phone reappeared in Montpelier, where a bank's security camera photographed a couple dozen different people who could be the phone's operator. A highly effective facial-recognition program then matched one of those faces to a small, extremely secure database. After cross-referencing Will's notes, Omar added the name Taylor Lindhurst as a known alias to this database; thanks to the bank's records, the new name Sean Cullen too. These aliases filled out the file of a well-connected ex-*Travelers* asset who'd been suspected of selling secrets to the Russians, a suspicion that was confirmed when the man disappeared three years ago. Now, thanks to an unwitting Will, that traitor had been found.

Omar relayed all this intel to Inez, who encoded it, then sealed it within a PERSONAL AND CONFIDENTIAL envelope, which she left for Will at his hotel on his way back to New York, where he handed it to Malcolm.

For better or worse, there was no way to prosecute someone like this ex-asset within the law, not without exposing the entire *Travelers* operation, which itself was illegal. And not just marginally illegal, not on a technicality, but illegal in a way that could bring down the director of Central Intelligence; in a way that could result in life-sentence imprisonment, or worse, for the head of the operation: Malcolm Somers.

No, such a compromised *Travelers* operative couldn't be brought to justice in the legal system. Nor could he be allowed to roam the globe, continuing to trade on a valuable cache of secrets. There was only one solution to this sort of problem. And that solution was now Chloe's job.

Taylor Lindhurst in Capri was the first of these problems Chloe had ever solved.

Her second was this woman, this ex-Agency sociopath who called herself Elle Hardwick. Though Chloe isn't sure if Elle really qualifies as her second kill. Yes, Chloe was the one who fired the crossbow. But the arrow probably wouldn't have been lethal if Will hadn't driven it deeper into the woman's body. Did it pierce her heart? That would be something.

A joint effort, then. Like being credited with a half-sack of the quarterback. Or like the ad hoc surgery on Malcolm's leg that Chloe and Will performed together, with household thread, a needle sterilized in whiskey and a cigarette lighter, three boxes of gauze, a couple rolls of tape, and an irresponsible quantity of over-the-counter pain meds mixed with the booze. All this happened in the backseat of Malcolm's rental car, parked on the edge of a lava field.

Malcolm is clearly still woozy as they walk through the airport terminal, trying not to draw too much attention. Will is bringing up a distant rear, fifty yards behind. A woman with a staggering man, that might arouse suspicion; add an extra, nonstaggering man, and they'd definitely be detained immediately.

In the middle of the vast hall, Malcolm mutters, "I have to sit," grimacing, limping, sweating. They make their way into the big café, and he collapses onto a chair.

This seems like a mistake, trying to board a commercial flight. But Malcolm is going to do what Malcolm is going to do.

He spilled a lot of secrets to that woman, and to Will, and to Elle. Malcolm didn't do it because he was being tortured; he did it because he'd been beaten. Besides his fucked-up right knee, this is the main thing Malcolm took away from his years playing quarterback in competitive full-contact football: sometimes simply not losing your shit is half the battle. Malcolm never loses his shit.

He made a quick, reasoned calculation that the only way he was going to survive was to tell the truth. That calculation turned out to be wrong—it looked as if the woman really was going to kill them—but, hey, he tried. And in the end, he survived.

Is it possible that he survived unscathed professionally? The woman who knows the *Travelers* secrets is dead. Her colleague is dead. Does the man who hired her know anything? Have any evidence? No, probably not.

Maybe Malcolm isn't thinking clearly, but it seems to him that if he can continue to manage his own people from within, the threat from without might be neutralized.

He plugs his dead phone into an outlet, and waits for the device to revive itself, and to start transmitting new problems. He still has a business to run, on the other side of the ocean. This is the middle of the business week.

Malcolm's resuscitated phone starts to buzz at him, as if excited to be alive again. Who wouldn't be?

◆ ◆ ◆

Will walks across the vast hall, aware of gazes falling on him, examining, assessing. He wonders if he'll ever again feel completely unwatched.

Chloe's eyes tell him that it's okay to sit at the table she's sharing with Malcolm, who's turned away, his mouth to his phone, one hand covering his nonlistening ear.

"Is he all right?" Will asks.

Chloe looks at Malcolm. "Honestly, I don't know. Are you?"

In the past day Will has been subjected to an overwhelming shift in every one of his paradigms; he's not sure who anyone is anymore, including his wife. And he's not sure how to answer Chloe's question. But before he can figure it out, Malcolm turns to them, sets his phone down on the table. He looks at Will, then at Chloe.

"That was Paris. One of our stringers is nearly certain he saw Jonathan yesterday."

"My God. Where?"

"Helsinki. An international ferry terminal."

Will notices Chloe close her eyes, and roll her neck, like a boxer getting ready for the opening bell. His wife has apparently been a CIA operative for the entirety of her adult life, recruited while still in college, just like Malcolm, like Gabriella, like Jonathan before them, who knows how many others. Does that make Chloe a different person? Did Will himself become a different person when he became a spy? When he *thought* he became a spy?

"The possible destinations," Malcolm says, "were Mariehamn—"

Will notices Chloe open her eyes, and find the departure board.

"—St. Petersburg, and Tallinn."

She takes a deep breath, exhales, nods: okay, got it.

"Chlo, are you ready for this?"

"I am." She turns to her husband, leans forward, takes his hands in hers. "Listen, Will, I have to go. I don't know—"

"I'm coming," he cuts her off. "I'm coming with you."

Chloe turns to Malcolm, who asks, "Are you sure about this, Will?"

He's not. But his old life doesn't exist anymore, his old wife. This is

THE TRAVELERS | 433

what's next, he can accept it or reject it. Will always says yes to everything. He nods.

"Okay," Chloe says, "good." She stands, straps on her backpack. "I'll explain on the plane. Now, we have to hurry."

They start to walk away, but too fast, too conspicuous, so Will grabs Chloe's elbow, gently, says, "A little slower."

They make it only a couple of steps before Malcolm yells, "Hey!"

They freeze, look over their shoulders.

"Let's be careful out there."

They both attempt smiles, then resume walking.

Will realizes that without making the conscious decision, he is carefully scanning the terminal, an involuntary new habit in his involuntary new life, looking for people who are looking for him, his eyes playing across the same crowd that's always in airports, tourists in sensible walking shoes and businesspeople in wrinkled worsted wool, everyone resigned or restless or exhausted or excited, on vacation or on business or on the run, but not one of them seems to be searching for Will, they're a crowd of thousands occupying their own private worlds, deep inside their own plans and problems, thinking about their own destinations, all of us travelers, all on our way to someplace else.

ACKOWLEDGMENTS

The Travelers is a novel about work, about labor, and I'm typing these acknowledgments over Labor Day weekend, so I'd like to thank all the people whose labor has made my life easier or better during the two years I've been working on this book, and, in particular, those who educate my kids in one way or another:

At P.S. 41, fourth-grade teachers Chris Strouse, Katie Zarkin, and Kristian Blum; fifth-grade teachers Nancy Wahl, John Baird, and Emily Cacciapaglia; guidance counselor Bob Caputo; parent coordinator Michelle Farinet; and principal Kelly Shannon.

At Greenwich House Music School, Joseph Ries; at Gilsports for Kids, Gil Rubin; at Greenwich Village Little League, Todd Irwin, Rob Magill, Tom Mullarkey, Frank Saracino, and Carin Ehrenberg; and at Veritas, Alex Wenger and Lee Reitelman.

At OYC, Willa Cassidy-Gardner, Allison Ferraris, Cooper Nefsky, Sarah Morton, and Cindy McKinney.

And, in general, Vera Pavone, Harriet Rhine, Susan McIntosh, and DeCourcy McIntosh.

And, of course, thanks too to the people who helped make this book better, or at least less bad: Matt Bromberg, Angus Cargill, Terry Deal, David Gernert, Adam Goldberger, Hannah Griffiths, Pat Herbst, Jane Lauder, Nate Roberson, Adam Sachs, Lindsay Sagnette, Molly Stern, Zachary Wagman, and, as always, Madeline McIntosh.

And to those who helped launch the book into the world: Sarah Breivogel, David Drake, Kayleigh George, Maya Mavjee, Donna Passannante, and Rachel Rokicki.

Finally, thanks to my son Alex for coining the name Stonely Rodriguez, which he invented for an actual stone that he adopted from a beach in the summer of 2014, a stone that his brother Sam later dropped from the car window on Main Street in Belfast, Maine, where we hope Stonely is living a long happy life.

ABOUT THE AUTHOR

Chris Pavone is author of the *New York Times* bestsellers *The Accident* and *The Expats*, which won both the Edgar and Anthony awards for best first novel. Chris grew up in Brooklyn, graduated from Cornell, and was a book editor for nearly two decades before moving to Luxembourg, where he started writing *The Expats*. He now lives again in New York City with his wife and children.